The Money Demon

Chen Diexian in 1918

Fiction from Modern China

This series is intended to showcase new and exciting works by China's finest contemporary novelists in fresh, authoritative translations. It represents innovative recent fiction by some of the boldest new voices in China today as well as classic works of this century by internationally acclaimed novelists. Bringing together writers from several geographical areas and from a range of cultural and political milieus, the series opens new doors to twentieth-century China.

Howard Goldblatt

General Editor

General Editor, Howard Goldblatt

Chen Diexian

The Money Demon

An Autobiographical Romance

Translated from
the Chinese
by Patrick Hanan

University of Hawai'i Press
Honolulu

Originally published in Chinese in 1913

English translation © 1999 University of Hawai'i Press
Printed in the United States of America
99 00 01 02 03 04   5 4 3 2 1

Library of Congress Cataloging-in-Publication Data

T'ien-hsü-wo-sheng.
[Huang chin sui. English]
The money demon / Chen Diexian ; translated from the Chinese by
Patrick Hanan ; general editor, Howard Goldblatt.
p.   cm. — (Fiction from modern China)
ISBN 0–8248–2096–7 (alk. paper). —
ISBN 0–8248–2103–3 (pbk. : alk. paper)
I. Hanan, Patrick. II. Goldblatt, Howard, 1939–
III. Title IV. Series.
PL2812.I437.H813   1999
895.1'352—dc21   98–33911
CIP

University of Hawai'i Press books are printed on
acid-free paper and meet the guidelines for permanence
and durability of the Council on Library Resources.

Designed by Barbara Pope Book Design
based on the series design by Richard Hendel

Printed by Maple-Vail Book Manufacturing Group

Contents

Introduction

The Money Demon (Huangjin sui), written in 1913, is an auto-biography—and also a novel about a youth's amorous and erotic development during a period of hectic social and cultural change. I hope that this translation will serve to introduce an example of the best fiction of its time as well as a rare, and perhaps unprecedented, kind of Chinese autobiographical writing.

The author, Chen Diexian (1879–1940), was one of the most remarkable of the intellectuals whose working lives spanned the old China and the new. He had two passions that are seldom found together: a passion for the practice of literature, music, and art; and a passion for industrial invention and entrepreneurship. This unusual combination has given rise to the impression that, to put it crudely, he was an opportunist who made a living from churning out popular romances until, during a nationwide boycott of Japanese imports, he managed to seize control of the Chinese market for tooth powder (the precursor of toothpaste) and promptly gave up his literary career for the life of a tycoon. The reality is a good deal more complex—and far more interesting.

Chen, whose personal name was Xu and whose most common pen name was Tian Xu Wo Sheng (Heaven Bore Me in

Vain), came from a wealthy Hangzhou family.[1] His father, Chen Fuyuan, practiced medicine, while his uncle served as an official, and both families shared a single large compound in the city. Fuyuan's first wife had been killed in the chaos of the Taiping rebellion, and his second wife, née Wang, was of delicate health and bore him no children. At her suggestion, he took as concubine (secondary wife) a girl surnamed Dai, who had been found, lost and homeless, during the rebellion and brought into the household. Dai bore her husband four sons, in whose upbringing Wang, as principal wife, took a leading role. Diexian was the third son, and his preference for Wang over his birth mother is made quite plain in *The Money Demon* and is discernible also in the memoir he wrote about his father's wives.

Diexian's father died in 1885 and Wang in 1893, while Dai lived until 1906. *The Money Demon*'s narrative begins in 1885 and runs to 1901, but it is concerned mainly with events from 1894 to 1901, the period of the author's adolescence during which Dai was the head of the family.

In 1897 an inheritance dispute led to a decision to split the household. Dai and her three younger sons moved to a house beside Mount Ziyang in the south of the city. By this time Diexian was married to Zhu Shu, whom Wang had picked out for him years earlier. Pressed by Dai to earn a living, he reluctantly took himself off to Wukang, northwest of Hangzhou, to serve as secretary to the commissioner of customs. Later in 1898 he returned to Hangzhou to take the licentiate examination. The following year he gave up his customs position and bought a share in a dealership in tea and bamboo, the main products of the hill country around Wukang. (In the novel Wukang is referred to as Xiangxi, the name of a nearby river.) In 1900, following the collapse of the dealership, he and two friends founded a daily newspaper in Hangzhou, the *Daguanbao* (Grand view), their main purpose being to publish literature, chiefly their own. By this time, before his twenty-first birthday, Diexian had some twenty works to his credit, including two novels, a *tanci* (verse novel), a play, several volumes of poetry, plus treatises on a variety of subjects.[2] Both the *Daguanbao* and another paper he founded were closed down by the authorities because of the political views expressed in their editorials.

Although heavily in debt, Diexian managed in 1901 to start a shop in Hangzhou, the Cui Li (gather profit) Company, that sold books as well as imported scientific instruments and appliances. It was the first such "modern" shop in Hangzhou, and it brought him little but ridicule from his peers. In 1902 he set up a publishing company in association with the shop, and followed it in 1906 with a public library-cum-reading room, the Bao Mu She (read-to-your-heart's-content society). Early in 1907 he began publishing a journal, the *Zhuzuo lin* (Forest of writing), which lasted until the end of 1908. It differed from most other literary journals of the period in that it was concerned not with fiction but with poetry, drama, and criticism, a good deal of it by Chen himself.

From 1909 until 1913, he held a number of positions as staff adviser. It was from one of these, while in Zhenhai on the Zhejiang coast near Ningbo early in 1913, that he wrote *The Money Demon* and published it in daily installments on the literary page ("Free Talk") of one of the major Shanghai newspapers, the *Shen bao*. It was also in Zhenhai that he began experimenting with a cheaper source of one of the main ingredients of tooth powder.

In December 1913 he was appointed chief editor of a new Shanghai journal, *Youxi zazhi* (The pastime), and in December 1914 he was appointed chief editor of another new journal *Nüzi shijie* (Woman's world), which was largely devoted to poetry and fiction (most of the poetry and some of the fiction were written by women), but which also contained a variety of practical and aesthetic information. Some of the fiction was written by Chen, and he and his wife, Zhu Shu, were responsible for most of the regular features.

From sometime before 1913 until September 1918, in addition to his other responsibilities, he was one of the mainstays of "Free Talk," of which he served as editor from late 1916 until the end of September 1918. Often two of his works, perhaps a novel and a *tanci,* or an original novel and a translation, would be running concurrently. (The original fiction dwindled after 1915.) From the time he took over the page, a daily feature, "Household Knowledge," began to appear, filled with practical scientific information. His eldest son, Qu (later a prolific novelist in Taiwan under the name of Chen Dingshan), and his daughter, known as either Xiaocui or Cuinuo (later an artist and professor of art in Shanghai), were brought in as authors or translators of fiction, the son at age sixteen in 1913 and the daughter at age thirteen in 1915, much being made of her tender years. The family sometimes combined their efforts in translation, with Chen Diexian polishing the work of the others. They also collaborated with Li Changjue, a novelist who later became a partner in Chen's business enterprises.

These last activities were evidently designed, at least in part, to provide start-up funds for business. By the middle of 1917 Diexian had perfected his tooth-powder formula and begun production, and in May 1918 he floated his Jiating Gongyeshe (family industries) as a joint-stock company. Afterward he continued to write poetry and essays, but he wrote no more novels, no doubt because he lacked the time, but perhaps also because his primary creative interest in fiction had been his own amorous history, and he seems to have exhausted that topic by about 1915.

A novel about Chen Diexian's youth might well have focused on his development either as writer or as inventor and entrepreneur, but *The Money Demon* does neither; instead, by concentrating on his amorous history, it gives us an entirely different version of him. The caption to its title describes it as a *xie-qing xiaoshuo,* a novel of love or passion, and it deals with the narrator's feelings toward, and relations with, several girls and young women—a beautiful nanny or maid, a cousin who occasionally visited, his wife by an arranged marriage, and, especially, the girl next door known as Koto. His writings, in which he must have taken pride, are quoted only for the information they shed on his amours. His early business and publishing ventures are described in some detail, but his scientific interests are never mentioned.

I have said that his own amorous history was the great subject of his fiction and drama. He related that history in a variety of forms over almost twenty years, from the play *Taohua meng* (Peach-blossom dream), evidently written in 1896, and the novel *Leizhu yuan* (Destiny of tears), begun in 1898, to the novel *Ta zhi xiaoshi* (A short account of him), which was published in installments in *Woman's World* in 1914–1915. He also painted and wrote poems on the same subject. On several occasions he did a painting of some crisis or turning point in his relations with Koto or his cousin and showed it to his friends and acquaintances, who responded with their own poems. He then published his selection of their poems together with his own critical commentary. In 1905, when Koto returned after a two-year absence, he painted a picture of their reunion and wrote some poems as well as a short prose narrative to introduce the poems. He then published (in *Zhuzuo lin*) the poems that his friends and acquaintances wrote in response. The prose narrative, titled "Zhenglouji" (The Koto story), is translated as an appendix to this book.

He also wrote three first-person novels about his early amorous history, all in Literary Chinese: *Jiao Ying ji* (Jiao and Ying), *The Money Demon,* and *Ta zhi xiaoshi. Jiao Ying ji* and *Ta zhi xiaoshi* are attributed to his wife, the poet Zhu Shu;

Chen describes himself as merely "recording" or "polishing" her first-person narrative. *Ta zhi xiaoshi* depicts the agony of a new wife who realizes that her husband has been in love with someone else since childhood. Despite the attribution, it is likely that Chen himself was the author, no doubt with some help from his wife.

The Money Demon, told in Chen's own voice, is his most complete attempt to relate his amorous history. It appeared in installments from June through October 1913 and was then published in book form by the China Library in 1914 with a postface by Zhou Zhisheng, a longtime friend and the editor of Chen Diexian's collected works. Zhou claims that, unlike *Destiny of Tears,* which is half fiction, half fact, *The Money Demon* is entirely fact, indeed that it can serve as a reference work for the earlier novel. He tells us that its provisional title was "The True Destiny of Tears," but that Chen first changed it to "The Koto Story" and then, in a flash of insight into the novel's real theme, decided on *The Money Demon.* In that case he must have rewritten much of the novel to reinforce the money theme, which is omnipresent and could hardly have been overlooked. In light of Chen's later career in business, the irony of the title will not be lost on the present-day reader.

Is *The Money Demon* really as accurate as Zhou claims? A surprising amount of it can be verified from Chen's other works. His family and friends appear under their real names or in their correct relationships, and most of the events, even the minor ones, can be substantiated. However, certain reservations persist. If we accept the nonfictional writings, especially "The Koto Story," as more likely to be reliable, we can easily discern differences from the novel. In "The Koto Story," for example, Chen's wife discovers the telltale photographs of Koto while her husband is still at home; only after Koto has refused to become his concubine does he depart dejectedly for

Xiangxi. In the novel, by contrast, he does not discover the loss of the photographs until *after* his departure, and negotiations have to be carried on by letter.

Another major change concerns his first love, his cousin Gu Yinglian, called Zhongjie (Secunda) in the novel. In *The Money Demon* she drowns while traveling to Yangzhou to be married, but Chen's wife, in some notes on Gu Yinglian as a poet in *Woman's World* (vol. 1, December 1914), explains why Gu Yinglian and Chen were not allowed to marry—Yinglian belonged to a different generation (the same explanation as in the novel)—and then remarks that she "died of melancholy." If so, it would help explain Chen's suicide attempt, which seems insufficiently motivated in the novel. Several other changes, particularly in the ordering of events, seem to have been made for structural reasons.

Chen Diexian was an early member of what has been called the "romantic generation" of modern Chinese writers.[3] The term implies a preoccupation with states of feeling, particularly romantic love. The main subject matter of these writers consisted of their own amorous longings, experiences, and reflections, which they took a keen delight in revealing to the public. They saw themselves as that much admired figure, the "man of feeling"—someone of true literary gifts, sentimental, sensitive, sometimes morbidly so; given to contemplation rather than action; and possessing a passion for natural and feminine beauty.

Chen Diexian's own romanticism derived from the Chinese tradition. His first novel, *Destiny of Tears,* which was written before the earliest translation of a Western or Japanese romantic novel, was consciously modeled on the eighteenth-century *Story of the Stone* (also known as *The Dream of the Red Chamber*); indeed he saw himself in his youth as a latter-day Baoyu, the hero of that novel, and his "extensive love," denoting his sympathetic attraction to a number of women, is clearly related to Baoyu's universality of affection. While the copious analyses of love in novels like *The Money Demon* surely owe their presence to the example of Western fiction, the terms in which love is cast are still largely traditional. For example, love is primarily a *transaction* between lovers; childhood love possesses a particular psychological force and enjoys a special sanction; and the power of karma, the legacy of a former life, may determine one's amorous experience. However, in addition to these notions, there is also a virtual worship of love and the beloved that, while not absent from the Chinese tradition, evidently owes something to Western literature.

The Money Demon is generally associated with the tragic romances of the so-called Mandarin Duck and Butterfly type, among the earliest of which are He Zou's *Suiqinlou* (The hall of the broken zither) and Xu Zhenya's *Yu li hun* (Jade pear spirit).[4] Chen's novels, however, are somewhat removed from others of the type. *The Money Demon*'s narrator, for example, has not one but several loves, and his novel ends in stalemate rather than tragedy. He cannot give us a proper ending, either happy or tragic, he explains, because he has to abide by the facts. His autobiographical stance has freed him from the necessity of a tragic outcome.

The same stance allows him other freedoms, too, notably the freedom to be discursive, to move from one subject to another with an associative, rather than a narrative, logic. The most obvious example is the narration of his attempted suicide, during which, after describing how he threw himself into the water, he pauses and then tells of an earlier, largely comic, incident.

Another major difference is the money theme. Money is a factor in certain other romances, notably *The Hall of the Broken Zither,* but it is nowhere articulated as strongly as in *The Money Demon,* where it is almost a refrain. It was certainly an appropriate theme for the times; the civil service examination system was not abolished until 1905, but it was already under threat, and in *The Money Demon* we find official careers being abandoned for business. Money has an ambiguous value in this novel, that much is clear. Part of the narrator's growing up is a gradually increasing perception of the power of money, while for Koto, who is forced to become the mistress of a succession of rich men, money is the essential condition of her independence.

A further difference, and one that greatly strengthens this novel, is the fact that the narrator does not present himself in an ideal light. Sympathetic though he is, he is also disingenuous, even deceptive, as well as sententious, prudish (although with a sensuous eye), effete, timid, feckless, and naive. (Of course we must take into account the fact that the narrator is a mature man writing about his youth.) So self-absorbed is the narrator that other matters, from world events to the death of his parents, are simply glossed over, while a mere report of Secunda's death is enough to send him into a suicidal depression. He is much given to adolescent anguish, perceptive or jejune, partly about the nature of love and partly about the motivation of the girls to whom he is attracted. (Despite numerous attempts, he never does manage to make much sense of Koto, who exhibits a surprising modernity.) His rapid swings of mood are presumably intended to suggest the nature of adolescence.

Like the Mandarin Duck and Butterfly romances, *The Money Demon* is written in Literary Chinese. There is a great irony in the fact that the flowering of the Literary Chinese novel (as distinct from the vernacular novel) took place only a few years before the literary language itself was eliminated for almost all purposes. What produced this late flowering? The example of the great translator Lin Shu, who wrote a clear, expressive Literary Chinese, must have been one factor. Newspapers, written almost exclusively in an expansive Literary Chinese, were surely a second factor. (Most of the novels first appeared in newspapers.) A third may have been the perceived suitability of Literary Chinese for the theme of romantic love. (Humorous and satirical fiction were more likely to be written in the vernacular.) For novels about well-educated young men and women of feeling whose natural mode of expression was poetry, the literary language, with its connotative richness, held definite advantages, particularly in the exploration of subjectivity. A large enough readership existed to appreciate such language and even enjoy a degree of stylistic virtuosity.

The Literary Chinese novels evolved a narrative method distinct from both earlier Literary fiction and the traditional vernacular novel (and also from the vernacular "new novel" of the first decade of the century). For example, the chapters tend to be more self-contained than those of the vernacular novel, and the narrator frequently addresses his readers directly, using expressions such as "Readers of my book" or "Ladies and Gentlemen." (*The Hall of the Broken Zither* is an exception). The addresses may be discursive or reflexive, and they are often introduced by questions asked of the reader, a common feature in vernacular fiction but one that is never found in traditional Literary narrative.

When *The Money Demon* was published as a book, it was divided into three parts corresponding roughly to stages of the author's youth. A more significant division, found in both the *Shen bao* and the book, is into some eighty untitled sections of varying length, some narrative, some discursive, many both narrative and discursive, but all of them more or less self-contained. The first and last sections consist of disputes between the author and two critics. In the first section, a visitor questions the propriety of bringing the subject of money into a romantic novel at all: "How can you even speak of it in the same breath as love?" The author defends his choice of subject by pointing to the power of money and declaring that it has bedeviled him at every turn; his purpose in writing the novel is to show how the bedevilment works. That is the *Shen bao* version. The book version inserts a few extra sentences; the visitor professes to be convinced by the author's arguments and then offers to tell *his* story. I have chosen to translate the *Shen bao* opening. In the concluding section the dispute is between the author and a reader who objects that the love story has been left up in the air. The author's explanation as to why he cannot continue—writer's block brought on by a nightmare about losing Koto—can be seen as a playful acknowledgment of the arbitrary nature of his ending.

The Money Demon

Part 1

I was working on a romantic novel entitled *The Money Demon* when someone heard about it and scoffed at the idea.[1] "The authors of romantic novels all *despise* money!" he exclaimed. "How can you even *speak* of it in the same breath as love?"

"It's such a pity!" I replied. "I, too, used to think of money and love as entirely separate things. What I failed to realize was that while money cannot be the mediator of love, it can indeed be its nemesis. When a man and a woman fall in love, they see marriage as their ultimate goal. But even if they are willing to endure poverty together, unless they have a little money behind them, they will lack even the means of preserving their health. Squalor and misery will be their lot, not to mention even worse conditions. Thus this deepest and most perfect form of love is the one that is particularly bedeviled by money. But I have also observed that the money demon stalks those who have a great deal of money just as it stalks those who fret about having too little. If my argument is taken to its logical conclusion, we will see that our every action, word, and smile is governed by money, and that where the joys and tribulations of love are concerned, its influence is particularly strong— such joys and tribulations have nothing whatever to do with heaven's supposed stinginess with good fortune. For these reasons I consider money the evil demon of mankind.

"Here I shall speak not of the money-grubbers of this world, but of my own life, in which money has bedeviled me at every turn. I propose to describe my experience in my own words in this book, to show you the nature of the bedevilment."[2]

The house next door to ours was a small but elegant villa that overlooked the water on two sides. Its green-framed windows were fitted with glass panes on which the rays of the setting sun glinted as if on burnished mirrors. It was the tenth month, and a single hibiscus rising above the corner wall was merrily in bloom. Beyond it stood the corner of our neighbor's house, and there, in her upstairs chamber a pigtailed young girl could sometimes be faintly glimpsed through a gap in the curtains. The scent from her dress would drift downward, and the clear, lingering notes of a koto could be heard.

I was six years old at the time. There were two people who used to take me out in the street to play, a nanny named Lu and a maid named Little Tan, who was twelve years older than I. Little Tan tended to giggle a lot, and I felt strongly drawn to her. Nanny Lu, on the other hand, was disagreeably negative about everything, forcing me to dress up warmly when it wasn't cold and to eat up my food when I wasn't hungry—she was fully as detestable as my teacher. And so it was that I always chose Little Tan rather than Nanny Lu to take me out, and on those occasions I would often stop in front of the house that the koto music came from, while Little Tan would be urging me to hurry on home. But whenever I asked her what kind of people lived there, she refused to say.

I had heard the music but never seen the girl who played it. Then one day my mother had a toothache and needed some hibiscus flowers as part of the remedy, and there were none available. When I reminded her of our neighbor's hibiscus, she sent Nanny Lu over to ask for some, and I went along, too, and met the lady of the house. She was a woman in her early thirties with a delicate kind of charm, whom Nanny Lu addressed as Cousin Mei.

Cousin Mei and her family appeared to be enjoying their leisure, playing a card game with several young men, one of whom happened to be the secretary from our house. At sight of me he blushed furiously and began making excuses for himself, seeming agitated and highly uncomfortable. Cousin Mei also blushed, but at the time I thought nothing of it. When Nanny Lu explained what we had come for, Cousin Mei laughed. "Such a trivial thing! You didn't need to come and ask. Those flowers have been out in all the wind and sun, and they'll soon wither, anyway. Take as many as you like."

As she spoke, she caught hold of my hand and went on and on fondling it. She asked me my name, and when I told her it was Shan, she called me Cousin Shan and, losing interest in the game she was playing, began asking me endless questions about how old I was and what I was studying. But I had noticed Nanny Lu heading for the corner of the wall, and I said good-bye to Cousin Mei and ran after her.

As I raised my hand to pick the flowers, I heard a sudden cry from behind me, "Who's that little boy stealing our flowers?" It was a girl's voice, clear and lilting. Abashed, I withdrew my hand, but when I turned my head to see who it was, I burst out laughing. It was my cousin Secunda! I was about to call out to her, when I remembered that Secunda lived in Suzhou and couldn't possibly be here. Then on looking more closely at the girl's face, I noticed a smile accompanying her frown and an angry glare in her beautiful eyes. In terms of their fragile, delicate grace, she and Secunda were much alike, but where

Secunda was exquisite, this girl was sheer enchantment. Impulsively I had blurted out, "Cousin!" At first she didn't know who I was, but then she looked at me, did a double take, and quickly exchanged her abrasive tone for a pleasant one.

"Oh, I didn't realize it was you, Cousin Shan," she said, flushing with embarrassment. Then she turned to Nanny Lu. "Those ones you've picked are starting to wither. Why don't you get some from the top?"

"How do you know my name?" I asked in surprise. "I wouldn't dare ask you yours, but if you are kind enough to tell me, I shall never forget it."

"You may not know me, but I've often seen you passing by beneath my window," she said with a smile. "You always look up and listen to me as I play the koto. Actually, my name is Koto. You hear my music well enough, so how is it you don't see me? Oh, I know! It's those dratted curtains. They may seem coarse, but actually they're very fine. From inside you can see out perfectly well, but from outside looking in you might just as well be in the middle of a thick fog. It's not your fault at all." She parted her lips in a smile, and the dimples in her cheeks were so deep you could have tucked the tip of her nose in one of them.

I didn't realize at the time that such a thing as love existed, only that her smile and frown appealed to me and gave me a deep sense of satisfaction. But by now that confounded Nanny Lu, her arms filled with hibiscus flowers, had got all she wanted and was urging me home.

I smiled at Koto. "See how quick on her feet she is, that old woman of ours! She grabs other people's things and then wants to rush off without a word of thanks!"

Koto laughed. "But why is she taking so *few?* The branches over here on the south side are simply laden. Look how vivid they are, as thick as the flowers in brocade! Why not break off a branch and keep it in your study window?"

"No, no, you mustn't harm such splendid flowers," I protested. "If you break them off, they'll be withered by morning. I'd far rather you left them where they are and let me come over and admire them from time to time."

She nodded and was about to say something when Nanny Lu pulled me away, thanked the girl, and set off for home. I was so furious with her for not letting Koto finish that I turned back and asked what it was she was going to say.

"Oh, I've forgotten," she said with a smile. "It'll come to me later. I'll tell you tomorrow."

Without a word I followed Nanny Lu. When I looked back at Koto, she was still standing beneath the flowers, gazing out over the water as if lost in thought. At the gate I called out to her, "Cousin Koto, I'll be back to see you tomorrow!" By now there was too great a distance between us, and I am not sure that she heard, but I did see her turn her head in my direction, and I know that she followed me with her eyes.

I had numerous girl cousins, four on my father's side and countless more on my mother's, but I considered Secunda the best of them all and used to liken her to a beauty in a painting. The only drawback was that she lived in Suzhou and I was unable to spend all my time with her. She and Koto may have had different names, but in looks and manner they were so alike that I regarded them as one person. At that age I had no intentions with regard to either, but a sense of appreciation arose spontaneously in me like a love of nature or moonlight or flowers—things a person finds worthy of his love no matter how dull his mind is. My love for Koto was of that order— I had never heard of so-called love between the sexes—and so I loved her openly and unashamedly. Every day, on getting out of school, I would head for her house. We felt a childlike affection for each other, and no one who observed it was inclined to criticize.

When my mother heard of Koto's uncanny resemblance to Secunda, she asked me to bring her to our house, where the whole family clucked over her in admiration.

"She might almost be Secunda's double," exclaimed my mother. "She could make up for that disappointment the Old Man[3] left us with." At first I didn't understand what she meant by this, but later I realized that Secunda, whom we called *jie*[4] because she was a little older than we were, actually belonged to the younger generation. My mother loved her like a daughter and privately regretted that she could not invite her to be my wife, which was why she made this remark on first seeing her. The following year my mother let Koto take lessons with my cousin, and we became even closer. My one regret was that Koto wasn't studying with me.

Koto was three years older than I, but she followed my cousin's example in addressing me as elder brother.[5] In quickness and intelligence she was far superior to me. In our free time she taught me the delicate art of origami. She would cut off a square piece of paper and fold it with miraculous skill until it came to resemble something or other. She would also loop a white string over her delicate fingers and make it into fantastic shapes. Hooking into it with one finger, she would suddenly transform it into something quite different. Trick would follow trick, all of this kind, far too many for me to describe here. She had a superb memory, too. She had only to read or hear something to remember it, and she could recite the texts I was studying just as well as I could. Because I was often in her company, I learned to do all the things she could do. She even taught me how to read music for the koto. As I inhaled her sweet breath and touched her white hands, a tender affection fused our bodies into one. Food lost its taste unless we ate from the same bowl. We felt uncomfortable unless we sat side by side, and upset unless we held hands as we walked together. Everything my mother gave me I shared with her. If it was one of a kind, I always offered it to her.

Over time our closeness aroused a certain jealousy in some quarters. When people heard that my mother favored Koto as my wife, they brought up the difference in social standing between our two families. Whatever did *that* mean? It was the bedevilment of money, nothing less. Let me explain. My family belonged to the upper bourgeoisie, and we considered ourselves to be of superior social standing. But if Koto's family had had a little money and put it to good use in the capital, wouldn't they have ended up as high officials?

However, I was a mere child in those days and gave no thought to marriage. If anyone spoke of our getting engaged, I would be filled with embarrassment and ridicule the idea as pure invention.

Time slipped by as in a dream. Soon it was the sixth month, and for some reason that I couldn't fathom Cousin Mei took it into her head to move house. Right up until the day of the move, Koto knew nothing whatever about it. In fact we were holding a banquet at the time to celebrate Lotus Birthday,[6] and the decorated lanterns had been strung up and the finest mats rolled out, when suddenly she was called away. Her family departed like the Prince of Huainan,[7] ascending to heaven accompanied by his whole household, including his dogs and chickens. It was so totally unexpected! To make matters worse, I didn't even know where she had gone. We hadn't even said good-bye.

My mother was just as astonished as I at the stealth of their departure. According to rumor, the move was a clever dodge designed to avoid the law, but my mother, who despised

Cousin Mei for her behavior, chose to ignore the whole affair. How tragic it all was! If I had had a little money of my own, I could have sent servants to the ends of the earth, if necessary, to find her. Why did I have to wait ten long years for a heaven-sent reunion? But that was out of the question, and so my book will be unable to give a direct account of her for the next ten years.

After Koto had left, I was like a baby nursing at the breast who is suddenly deprived of its wet nurse. I sobbed and sobbed, pestering my mother for help. At first she was sympathetic and promised to find Koto for me, but as time went by and I continued to pester, she began scolding me. And so I went and sobbed in front of Little Tan, who touched her cheek in a gesture intended to shame me. This made me so furious that I jabbed at her cheek with my fingers and, as bad luck would have it, my nails were sharp enough to break the skin. Wrenching herself away from me, she rushed off to examine herself in the mirror. Then, overcome with self-pity, she threw the mirror down on the floor and began sobbing. I had never meant things to come to this state and felt deeply ashamed of my wildness. With every ounce of persuasiveness that I could muster, I begged her not to be angry, but by the time she had stopped being angry with me, I was angry with her again.

One day she was helping me on with my jacket, standing beside me slim and graceful, half again as tall as I. I was holding up my head for her to button my collar when she happened to sneeze, sending a fine spray all over my face. I was so revolted by the thought that I shut my eyes and burst into tears. Giggling helplessly, she took a handkerchief from her sleeve and wiped my face. But I kept crying without pause, demanding that my face be washed. When Nanny Lu began washing me, Little Tan flung down her handkerchief and rushed off to her room and burst into tears.

Another time we were eating chestnuts, which were very big and hard, and I asked her to crack one for me. She looked at the chestnut and wrinkled her brow, not knowing what to do. No hammer could be found, so she tried cracking it with her teeth. At first she found it too big for her rosebud mouth, and even when she succeeded in forcing it in, it made her look foolish. A loud cracking sound followed, and the chestnut actually broke into pieces. Her frown changing to a smile, she handed it to me, but I was revolted by the thought that it was covered in her saliva. She picked off the shell and tried to feed me the meat, but I pushed her away and, throwing the chestnut on the floor, stamped on it until I had ground it into powder. Then I called the cat in to eat it, but that animal merely sniffed and wouldn't eat, so I threw my head down on the table and began sobbing uncontrollably. Bizarre!

At first all I knew of Little Tan was her pride; I didn't know the source of her suffering. Later I discovered it. She had an affectionate nature and giggled a lot, but she also carried about with her a secret frustration. She had been married the year before. Her husband had no assets of his own, but they loved each other dearly and had married anyway. Afterward he found himself unable to support them both, so she came to work for us at a monthly wage. Because she was about the same age as our own bondmaids, she was treated the same way they were. She gave her wages to her husband, who had enough to support himself and to whom her wages came as a bonus. He promptly overestimated the money available and felt he needed his wife with him, so he recalled her. But in less than three months their money had run out again, and she returned to us. This toing and froing had been going on for a couple of years now, and it had come to seem quite normal.

As for her beauty, no one with eyes in his head could have failed to appreciate it. But I was too far apart from her in age, and I felt that she treated me with undue severity and was most unhappy with her. Moreover, I was seething with grief and frustration over Koto's departure. But if I so much as mentioned Koto's name, Little Tan would get furious with me, as if she were determined to pluck the girl's image from my mind and wash my heart clean of her until no trace remained. Inevitably I saw her as Koto's enemy, and so I often behaved perversely. In retrospect I feel dreadfully ashamed of myself. Little Tan was prevented from sharing a bed with that wretched husband of hers whom she loved and who loved her, and had to spend her nights instead with a stupid, moody, boring child—the very last thing she wanted. She was the victim of money.

At first Koto was never out of my thoughts for so much as a day; I felt as if her image were engraved on my brain. It was constantly appearing on the page of the book I was reading or on the screen wall of our house. I could even conjure it up in the sky—Koto in all her moods, joyful as well as sad. I thought of her so intensely that heaven took pity on my morbid state. Suddenly the evil influence that gripped me was shattered by the greatest conceivable tragedy—my father's death.

Scenes of grief were everywhere—all one heard or saw was sobbing and weeping—but at length the three years of mourning passed, and my eldest brother was able to marry. His wife was a beautiful, virtuous girl whom people likened to Wang Xifeng in *The Story of the Stone* because she had the knack of cheering up my mother. My cousins on my mother's side also began to visit us more frequently. Among them was Secunda, who came to study needlework with my mother. Once more I began to see her as Koto and confided to her at great length all that had happened between us, but on the strength of a piece of malicious gossip she concluded that I was demeaning her by the comparison with Koto and became very cross with me. I tried to explain, but the more I tried, the more cross she became. From then on I never dared mention Koto in Secunda's presence, even though in my mind's eye I continued to see them now as one person, now as two.

During all this time my pleasures increased in keeping with the temperature, as winter gave way to spring. The one thing that distressed me a little was that the time I had to spend on my studies exceeded the time available for play. Fortunately I never needed to work very hard. The text that I toiled over one day I could generally recite from memory the next, so the teacher relaxed his rules in my case.

Secunda was four years older than I and could write poetry already. I heard my mother constantly praising her poems, and I began to study with her, which is how I learned to distinguish the tones. When occasionally I wrote something, I would submit it to her for comment rather than to my teacher. I had no interest in hearing what *he* had to say, whereas when she gave me her comments, whether they were pleasing to me or not, she so captivated me with her voice and charm that I never forgot them. And so I pleaded with my mother to let me withdraw from school and study with my cousin instead. But she accused me of wanting to play truant, not realizing that our school was by no means as quiet a place to study in as Secunda's room. For my brothers and my cousin the school was little more than a social club.

My eldest brother, who was eighteen at the time, was treated by the teacher more as a friend than as a pupil, and after his marriage he came and went as he pleased. Except when there were written exercises that had to be done, his seat remained empty. My cousin[8] was sixteen at the time. His father, my uncle, was living in the capital, and my aunt doted on the boy because he was their only son. He had a pet canary, and one day when the teacher was busy elsewhere, he brought the canary to school and hung it up in its cage opposite a mirror in the passageway. At the sight of its own reflection, the canary started feeling sorry for itself and began to sing. Then, just as we were applauding its performance, the teacher came back again, and my cousin slipped out of the room. The teacher ordered the page to remove the bird, but he refused. Then the teacher found out that the canary belonged to my cousin and said no more about it.

The moment the ban on canaries was lifted, my brothers followed my cousin's example, and more and more cages appeared along the passageway, until our recitations were regularly accompanied by birdsong. However, although there was an occasional break in the recitations, the birdsong, with the birds calling back and forth to each other, continued all day without pause. The teacher heaved a sigh. "Is this what is meant by the saying, 'Men are no match for birds'?"[9] Even now, when I think of that remark, I can't help laughing. But why would a teacher, given all the authority and dignity of his position, yield to the desires of mere boys? I was originally inclined to believe that he took a harsh line only with me—as if he and I were enemies from some previous life—and that he went easy on my brothers, fearing the strong and bullying the weak, as it were. But now I know better. All he cared about was his salary, and he knew that my brothers and my cousin had the power to terminate his appointment, whereas I, a mere child, could do nothing to him. His ingratiating behavior did not come from the heart; it was adopted solely for the sake of money. However, money did bedevil him in the end. If my brothers and cousin had not paid out money for the birds, or if the ban had not been lifted because of the teacher's concern for money, why would this man, who had been with us for three years already, have found it necessary to look elsewhere for the following year? He resigned his job.

Next year, *jichou* (1889), our school was moved to South Study Hall, which was airy and quiet. There were pavilions and terraces nearby; the one thing it lacked was a pond. Since ours was a large household, we were sometimes in danger of running short of drinking water, so extra water casks had been placed around each building, particularly this one, where they were lined up along the passageway that encircled the hall. We children each took possession of a cask and used it to keep goldfish in. The size of the fish varied in direct proportion to our ages, not because there was any regulation to that effect, but because the older children had more savings and could afford the size they wanted. The others, lacking the same opportunity, grew envious, and those in whom the envy ran deepest were tempted by thoughts of larceny. From time to time the fish in one cask would suddenly move to another, while the fish in the second cask would disappear to goodness knows where. Quarrels became a daily occurrence, and when they failed to stop, fights broke out. The losers started bawling, as did the victors, after which both sides went and complained to their progenitors, and thus the children's animosity spread to the grown-ups. The latter became so exasperated that they took all the goldfish, large and small, cheap and expensive, and threw them down a well. The more timid children broke into tears at sight of the well, but the bolder, more resourceful ones asked their servants to retrieve their fish, which they did, nearly falling in in the process. Then as a last resort the grown-ups gave orders to fill in the well, which was lost to us forever. From that time on a great rift opened within the family, and deadly animosities developed. Because of differences in the children's money, this trivial pastime had led to family strife and the loss of a well. What a shame! Even in the hands of children money had bedeviled the whole family.

The administrative head of the family was my uncle, my father's younger brother, who was an expert at accounting. While my father was still alive, my uncle had instituted a system of monthly disbursements, rather like a government budget. In addition to the cost of the central kitchen and the servants' wages, which were paid from the general account, the older generation received twenty taels a month each; married sons and their wives received ten; and the younger children, girls as well as boys, received five. People were constantly worrying about not having enough money, all except my mother, who always had plenty to spare. Well on in years herself, she had grown particularly fond of the younger children, favoring the girls over the boys, and for that reason she was constantly surrounded by children, like the North Star ringed by its satellites. In spring she would sometimes arrange to have music played in the garden, and in autumn she would see that melons and fruit were set out on the terraces and in the pavilions. If anything brought her pleasure, she would spare neither her precious time nor her money in offering it to others. Anyone who came to our house, even someone as detached from worldly concerns as a Taoist nun or as inconsolable as a widow, would soon be smiling and laughing with pleasure. It was not the site that produced the change, but my mother's love for all and her delight in giving. People saw her in a joyous mood, responding to all their requests, and they couldn't have felt unhappy even if they had wanted to. But since her income never went up, how is it that she was so well off? While others behaved like misers and hoarded their money, my mother realized that she was in the evening of her life with not very much time left. Thanks to the blessings conferred on us by our ancestors, her children and grandchildren would never lack the necessities of life. She once told people, "Be content with your lot; that's what brings lasting joy. Women often go to their graves clutching their money to their bosoms. They slave away the whole of their lives for the sake of their children and grandchildren, but all they are really doing is allowing them to live in idle luxury and never know the meaning of hard work. What's easily come by in this world is never highly valued. Extravagance and dissipation result not from any innate predisposition on our part but simply from the bedevilment of money. Personally, I'm afraid of bringing grief to later generations. I prefer to sow the seeds of future blessings rather than hoard money that can only spell disaster." People said that this rule of hers could hardly be applied universally, but I say that later generations have their own fortunes, just as the proverb says. It was no accident that a farsighted person like my mother enjoyed her long life, whereas my birth mother suffered a lifetime of misery. Their situations were the same, but the difference between them in terms of their enjoyment of life was like night and day.

There were four boys in our family, but after his marriage my eldest brother gave up his close attendance on my mother. My other brothers and I lived in West Court, on the east side of which stood Little Peach Blossom House. Whenever I went to South Main Hall to pay my respects to my mother, I would stop at Little Peach Blossom and collect Secunda. My mother loved Secunda as if she were her own daughter, and because she loved her so much, she extended her love to me. Secunda and I were always together in trying to please her. My mother loved to read fiction, but she had contracted an eye disease from excessive weeping at the time of my father's death, and since her vision was often impaired, she would get Secunda or me to read to her. After Secunda returned to Suzhou, I continued the practice on my own by lamplight. My mother would be propped up on a pillow listening to me, while two or three young maids stood by my side. I was always forgetting myself and addressing one or other of them as "cousin," which prompted my mother to laugh at me and say it was a case of calf love. I was ten years old at the time and hadn't begun to admire pretty girls, but I was completely candid by nature and didn't realize that there are things one just doesn't say.

I had heard Secunda claiming that her family's private garden was superior to all others in Suzhou. I had grown used to hearing about this or that rock or pond, and after we had been parted for a long time I missed her so much that I began having hallucinations about her. I often saw her in my dreams and we would recite poetry together, and sometimes on awakening I would still remember the odd line or two. As a result I liked nothing better than to sleep, and people suspected I was sick and forced me to take medicine, which made me really sick, even delirious. I wasn't aware of the delirium at the time, but after I got better Little Tan told me about it; apparently I was constantly babbling the names of Secunda and Koto.

My illness lasted over a month and then, soon after I recovered, my uncle suddenly passed away, plunging the whole family into such a frenzy of grief as defies description—it was as if a nation had lost its ruler. At my tender age I was still under the influence of others when it came to expressing emotion—my heart hadn't yet gained its independence—and so I purged myself of my longing for Secunda and began mourning my uncle instead. I felt that my cousins, his daughters, clad all in white and dabbing at their eyes with their handkerchiefs, were the most piteous creatures on earth.

I had no words of comfort I could offer them, so I simply joined them in their weeping. The second daughter was weak and vulnerable and about the same age as I, so I pitied her all the more. When I formed my close friendship with Secunda, this girl had blamed Secunda for coming between us and had extended her animosity to me as well. Now in this time of loss and confusion she simply took to her bed. The house was full of mourners as my uncle's body was laid in its coffin, and the family was fully occupied in attending to them, with no time to spare for a frightened girl turning and twisting in her bed. A faint lamp glowed in her room, which was filled with medicinal vapor. Apart from the maids, I was the only one to keep the lonely girl company, and she was touched and became no less affectionate toward me than Secunda had been. For my part I gave to her the affection I had once given to Secunda.

The following year this cousin became engaged, and my mother arranged my engagement, too, to a girl from Ziyang. Since I was still too young to know what an engagement implied, I took the news calmly and put it out of my mind. Then I heard that Secunda was engaged, and I assumed that being engaged meant just that and nothing more. My eldest cousin had been engaged for years, yet she was still living with us as if nothing had changed. With her example in mind, I was quite unconcerned about my own engagement, my sole objection being that it was all so unnecessary.

In an idle moment I brought up the subject with Little Tan. "Marriage is something you can't avoid," she told me. "The girls who are engaged now will have to leave the house one day and become wives to other people. Your eldest brother's wife, who married into our family, is a case in point."

Thinking this over, I realized that one day we would all have to part—none of my cousins would be my companion for life—and I couldn't help feeling dejected.

"But you will have *someone* as your lifelong companion," Little Tan went on, with a laugh. "You must have heard that her ladyship has arranged a marriage for you?"

Yes, I thought, but I don't know the girl. I've heard my mother say she's as beautiful as Secunda, but I've never seen her myself, and I don't feel anything for her. What joy would I take in her?

"I don't understand what Mother was thinking of," I said. "If she wanted to find me a fiancée, why didn't she choose Secunda? She's engaged, so why couldn't she be engaged to me?"

Little Tan spluttered with laughter. "Oh, why do you have to be so young and yet belong to the older generation?" she said, after a moment's pause. "Her ladyship did think of Secunda, but uncles aren't allowed to marry their nieces! There was nothing she could do."

"Well, what about my cousin, then?"

Little Tan was convulsed. "It would be even more unnatural for a boy to marry a close cousin," she said, when I pressed her for an answer.

"But why *should* it be unnatural? Who made up these rules, anyway? Some most unreasonable person, I'm sure."

She had no answer and merely replied, "You ought to go and ask your teacher or your mother about it."

"Never mind that for a moment. Look, Koto isn't *either* my niece *or* my cousin, so what's the excuse in her case?"

Again she was at a loss. "Koto? Her ladyship did think of Koto," she said at last, "but she put the idea aside because of the difference in social standing."

"What do you mean, social standing?"

"A difference in wealth and position."

"What are you *saying?* That I'm rich? I don't have a penny to my name. Or that I'm someone important? I've never held an official post. By your reasoning, a king would have to find a princess to be his queen, but since there can be only one king to a kingdom, there wouldn't be any princesses apart from his own sisters. He'd *never* be able to marry!"

Little Tan was stumped, so I went on to attack the argument about social standing. It couldn't possibly have originated with my mother, I insisted. Little Tan couldn't explain, so she took refuge in a non sequitur. "Look, Koto's been gone for all of six years, and she may very well be engaged herself by now. And if she isn't, well, there's no law in China against taking a concubine. Her ladyship has always been fond of Koto, and she might well accept her as your concubine. My only fear is that Koto might not be willing."

Dejected though I was, my longing for Koto revived, no doubt because I now realized that my cousins would have to leave me one day whereas she could be with me for life. My only regret was that we hadn't planned for this before. Instead we had let a slavish adherence to old ideas lead to this mistake about social standing. However, according to Little Tan, Koto's background would qualify her only to be a concubine, not a principal wife. Before my engagement, I couldn't by rights have taken a concubine, but if Koto reappeared now, I could count on my mother to agree. I still wasn't clear as to what distinguished a wife from a concubine; if there was a big difference in status, this was the first I had heard of it. I thought of the fiancée my mother had chosen for me as more or less like my teacher in school—someone to whom I had to go for my lessons but to whom I felt no attachment—while Koto would be like Secunda in her room. In the old days, when I used to study with Secunda, the teacher never forbade it, and for her part Secunda never declined to teach me on the grounds that I already had a teacher; whether I had one or not was of no concern to her. With this thought in the back of my mind, I wasn't in the least worried when Little Tan said that Koto might not be willing to be my concubine.

The first step in my plan was to find out where she was. Every day on getting out of school I would pester my companion to take me around the neighborhood in the secret hope of meeting her. Whenever I saw a pigtailed young girl, I would wonder if she were Koto, forgetting that Koto was three years older than I, and since I was now eleven, she would be all of fourteen and look quite different from the little girl she once was. But the image I retained in my mind's eye was a vivid one of a thin, pigtailed slip of a girl, barely three feet tall, and so I concentrated on looking for someone of that description. Some hope!

Time flew by, and soon another year had passed. My eldest cousin married and left us, and her brother and my second brother also married. I had lost one cousin but gained two sisters-in-law, and the general level of merriment in the family increased.

The head of the family at that time was my second cousin

(he and I had the same great-grandfather). He had been adopted by my uncle, my father's elder brother, and upon the death of my father's younger brother, as the eldest male in his generation, he had been entrusted with the management of the household.

In the past year or two, what with the various weddings he had had to see to, he had been weighed down with domestic duties. His wife, a beautiful woman and an accomplished musician, had not borne him any sons, but their marriage was such a happy one that my cousin had chosen not to take a concubine. They had one daughter, a regular tomboy of a girl who could do anything a boy could do, whom they named Sai'er ("rivaling a son"). She used to study with my brothers and cousins. I was too young to join them, but I looked up to her as to an immortal.

While my uncle was still alive, my second cousin was as free spirited as an immortal himself. On moonlit nights in his upstairs rooms he and his wife would play the flute, and Sai'er, who could sing classical arias, would sing all night long in a soft, lingering voice. When his wife was home visiting her family, my cousin would fairly waste away in her absence. Although he had plenty of pretty girls at his side, he would insist that he felt miserable without his wife. Nothing, not even the deepest of chasms, could begin to represent the depth of his attachment to her. He was constantly to be found with a clapper or a flute in his hand, his eyes glued to a musical score or else fixed on his wife's face. On one occasion he remarked jokingly to his maids, "Your mistress must have found the secret of eternal youth. We've been married almost twenty years, and she doesn't look a day older; in fact she's prettier than ever." And, my word! That was no idle flattery on his part. The doddering old nanny who had nursed Sai'er at her breast was still sighing over the mother's beauty, even when Sai'er herself had grown into a lovely young woman.

"My Sai'er's looks draw compliments from everybody, but to these old eyes of mine I'm afraid she'll never equal her mother." It was no wonder my cousin took such pleasure in his wife.

People used to claim that my cousin used his position as head of the household to heighten his pleasure. He had money enough, if he so desired, they said, to build a boudoir out of solid gold for his paramour, something the ancients could only dream of. I, too, used to echo these criticisms, but I now realize that what troubled him most was precisely his work as head of the household.

There is nothing in the world so difficult as running a household. In the case of a middle-class family of a husband and wife who possess the basic necessities and have no extra requirements, a household is easy enough to run, but our family numbered sixty or more, all of us in the one compound, and my cousin was the sole person in charge. At first I didn't realize how hard it was for him, but when I went up to his apartment, I found that the music scores he once pored over had been put away. His eyes were now glued to the ledgers, and in his hand he held an abacus rather than a musical instrument. His wife had charge of all the keys, and an endless procession of maids trooped back and forth on household business, a thoroughly vulgar sight that made me reluctant to visit.

However, Sai'er did come over from time to time to see my mother, who treated her exactly as she treated me, and so Sai'er and I became as close as a couple of brothers. After my brothers and my male cousin married, they had their wives for company and no longer spent time with me. Although I did visit them from time to time, they always seemed inhibited by my presence as to what they said and did. Outwardly they appeared affectionate enough, but in their hearts they disliked me, and so to avoid incurring their dislike, I rarely visited them. The only ones close to me were the girl cousin of about my age and Sai'er. As far as my younger brother and younger cousin were concerned, it was I who disliked them.

Sai'er was five years older than I. At first she thought me too young and spent her time with my brothers and my male cousin rather than with me. But now that they were paired off in inseparable couples, they looked on others as distinctly de trop, and Sai'er was left out in the cold. Her friendship with my girl cousin and me was the natural result.

Since Sai'er was fond of music, I studied the subject with her, learning all she could teach me and then going beyond it, until I could play all the instruments quite well. My mother liked to listen to us playing, so practically every evening South Court would be filled with music and song. In time the other members of the family came under our influence, and almost everyone learned to play an instrument. At the Mid-Autumn Festival we held a banquet for the entire family. My mother, my birth mother, my aunt, my second cousin and his wife, my cousin and his wife, my elder brothers and their wives, plus three girl cousins, my younger brother, my niece Sai'er, and I attended—eighteen in all, including the cousin who had married but was now back home visiting her family. The courtyard was suffused with the breath of conversation and the scent of flowers. Joy in the bonds of family seemed to have taken possession of all mankind. Little did I realize that the affairs of mankind wax and wane like the moon in the heavens. Tragically, by the same time next year my mother and my second cousin and his wife would all have departed this life.

Before I recovered from my grief, Sai'er was sent away to be married, and I was left all alone with nowhere to turn. After my mother's death, my birth mother[10] treated me even more harshly than my teacher, drilling me in my lessons by lamp-light after I returned home from school. My recitations seemed to drag on interminably. Luckily, Little Tan took pity on my grueling schedule and would occasionally make out that I was ill and so win me a brief respite.

One day Little Tan came home in a joyous mood, a gleeful expression on her face, and looked me in the eye and smiled. Intrigued, I asked her why. "You remember Koto?" she blurted out.

I leaped to the conclusion that she had seen Koto and begged her to tell me where.

"No, I haven't seen her," she replied, shaking her head.

"I could never tell *you* a lie," I protested. "If you've seen her somewhere, you've simply *got* to tell me. I miss her terribly."

"Ah, but you haven't seen Susu yet, and that's why you can't think of anyone but Koto. Wait till I tell you what Susu looks like."

I had no idea what she was talking about. "Who's this Susu?" I asked.

"Listen and I'll tell you. From time to time, since I started work in your household, I've gone with her ladyship to various functions, and I've seen practically every pretty girl in the city. My standards went up steadily until, when I saw Koto, I thought they had reached the top and could go no higher. I felt sorry for her, and even more sorry for you, of course. The reason I wouldn't tell you whether she was alive or not was that there was simply no way she could become your wife. If I had told you, you'd have been caught up in the snares of passion, with terrible consequences for your career.

"After she left I met your cousin Secunda and felt ashamed of my naïveté, for she belonged in a higher class still. But there was no way she could become your wife, either, because of the way in which she was related to you. I felt sorry for you and kept my eyes open for another girl like those two, someone who might conceivably satisfy you. Then when her ladyship arranged your engagement, I gave up, although privately I still hankered after Koto and kept hoping she might come back as your concubine. But today, quite unexpectedly, I met Susu, and I can't tell you how surprised and delighted I am."

"Well, what *is* she like?"

"Her complexion seemed to give off a sort of unearthly radiance that dazzled me. Luckily she was standing against a gray screen wall, and by screwing up my eyes I managed to get a close look at her. She's an absolute picture. Her face is like a slice cut from some immense pearl, except that a pearl would be too round. Her eyebrows, her eyes, her mouth, her nose—I cannot imagine what materials went into creating her or what model could ever have produced such incomparable beauty. Oh, dear! I have such a vivid impression of her in my mind, and yet I cannot find the words to describe it. All I can say is that, if you compare her to Koto, she is a white rose to Koto's red, and while all the white flowers of the world may be useful for comparison, I cannot conceive of one that could equal her."

I watched her as she said this. If she had gone on any longer, she might have had a fit, so I seized her hands and shook her.

"Look, are you out of your mind? What's the point of telling me all this?"

She laughed. "Hold on to something, will you? When you hear what I have to say, I'm afraid you'll collapse from sheer delight. *Susu is the girl you're engaged to!*"

At this point I concluded that she was pulling my leg and gave a snort of disgust.

"You had me believing there really was such a person, but you were just putting me on," I said. I shot out both arms, made a hissing sound, and darted forward and caught hold of her. She was ticklish and curled up at once, like a hedgehog, still happily protesting, "If you don't believe me, why don't you go and see for yourself?"

Taking no notice, I tickled her vigorously under the arms and backed her into a corner of the room. She joined her palms in supplication and begged for forgiveness, but I insisted that she let me nuzzle her on both cheeks before I let her go.[11] This was no mere childhood prank on my part. In those days women were always insisting on doing that to me. Whenever I took a fancy to a thing and asked someone for it, she would pretend to begrudge it and demand this favor of me first. There were times when I was most reluctant and preferred doing without whatever it was, but when my mother or Little Tan wished to do it, I never refused them. And so now, when I wanted to nuzzle Little Tan's cheeks, she did not think that I was being too terrible.

However, just at this moment our abominable old servant Turtle, his head sunk low between his shoulders, sidled up from behind me. "What's she taste like, eh?" he cackled. "Better than an apple?"

At once Little Tan's expression changed—rouge splashed on snow—and she turned on him. "Turtle!"

"Turtle! Turtle!" I echoed, punctuating my cries by thumping him on the back with my fists. He limped away yelping, the very image of a turtle.

To understand how he acquired this honorific, you would have to go back a dozen years. At that time we had a young bondmaid only seven years old—a sly little minx if ever there was one. Turtle was always tormenting her by telling her that the master had taken pity on him as an old bachelor and was saving her for him until she grew up, when she would become his wife, and so the little girl would often amuse herself by pulling a whisker or two out of his luxuriant beard. Because Turtle tolerated having his whiskers pulled out, people made fun of him and called him the little maid's husband. Then when she grew up and married someone else, they changed his name to Turtle.[12]

He had served our family for three generations, and everybody treated him with the utmost deference, with the result that he behaved as outrageously as a clown in a play. When I think of all the anecdotes told about him, I can't help laughing even now, but as they have nothing to do with my narrative, there is no need to relate them here.

I was fifteen that year, but because the rules of our household were extremely strict, I was as innocent as a child. I still kept company with Little Tan day and night. Accustomed to seeing her all the time, I was like someone who lived in a room full of orchids and so never noticed their scent. Her treatment of me, however, had undergone a change. Before, if our cheeks had brushed together, she would not have turned a hair, but now she would flush crimson, and I had no idea why. As we lay together in bed, she would turn away to avoid me.[13] I didn't dare snuggle up to her, because if I did, I would only be met with an angry outburst.

During this period our house was haunted by ghosts. I was terrified of them and became so upset every night that I couldn't sleep, and since Little Tan refused to take me in her arms, I grew even more scared. I would see tremors among the shadows cast by the lamp or movements among the curtains. When I stared hard at the curtains, I would see ghostly forms materializing among their folds, and the longer I stared, the clearer the forms became. Then as soon as the household was asleep, the mice would start scampering about. A sudden thump would be followed by a lot of squeaking under the bed, and with the hair rising along the nape of my neck, I would pull the coverlet up over my head. But on this particular night I continued to hear things, so I dived under the bedclothes and threw myself into Little Tan's arms. She was fast asleep and didn't push me away as she usually did. I wondered vaguely why she did so on other occasions but couldn't think of a reason.

All that night I was so scared I didn't sleep, suffering greatly from the stuffy air. Not until I heard a bird singing outside the window and then the other birds chiming in did I realize that it was dawn and cautiously poke my head out from under the

coverlet. The lamp on the table still flickered. In the bed opposite us Nanny Lu's snoring rose and fell like the lowing of an
ox. When I turned and looked back at Little Tan, I saw her
eyes closed in sleep and felt her gentle breath on my cheek.
Then she parted her lips as if in a smile. I thought she was wak-
ing up and called out to her, but got no answer. I called again,
and she awoke with a start. For a time she lay there drowsily,
then turned over and went back to sleep.

I refused to let her sleep, but kept pestering her to turn over
again and face me. She wouldn't, and so I resorted to an old
trick of mine, tickling the nape of her neck with one hand and
nipping at her waist with the other. She began giggling helplessly, then turned over and clasped me to her so tightly that I
couldn't move. I insisted she explain why she always kept me
at arm's length, and she mumbled something incoherent. I
placed my cheek against hers—it was burning hot. Her eyes
seemed about to water, and her breathing became agitated. My
hand was over her heart, and I felt a fluttering beneath it and
grew alarmed.

"Is something the matter?"

She shook her head.

I asked again, and this time she suddenly sat up and flung
my hand aside, as if she were too furious even to speak. I grew
even more alarmed, but by this time she had thrown on her
gown and got out of bed.

From then on she paid no attention to me at all, even doing
her best to avoid my eye. If I went near her, she would turn on
me. "If you don't stop harassing me, I'll tell your mother!"

I had no idea what she was going to tell my mother, but evidently she did tell her *something,* because Mother decreed that
from then on I was to sleep in Nanny Lu's bed. There was no
way I would accept that arrangement, and so a further decree
was issued; henceforth I would sleep in Mother's room.

Little Tan continued to give me the cold shoulder, as if she
never wanted to see me again, behavior that left me bewil-

dered. Mother, however, sang Little Tan's praises and seemed to respect her all the more.

Now, of course, I understand. Little Tan was flesh and blood, after all. I may have been ignorant of sexual love, but I had a genuine innocence and naïveté about me, and the sentiment of love always springs from perfect sincerity. How could Little Tan, as a grass widow, bear to receive such tender affection? Had she not taken forceful measures to correct her feelings, she and I would both have inevitably been drawn into the maelstrom of desire. She knew perfectly well that there are times when passion cannot be denied, and she banished me from her bed in order to preserve her good name. Such was her strength of character—truly admirable.

Personally I shall always be grateful to her for molding my own character. Just as the buds of my desire were joyously anticipating the gentle breezes and warm showers of spring, they were nipped by a sudden frost, and so all my life I have looked on women's bodies as sacred and inviolable. I owe it to Little Tan that I am known as a second Liuxia Hui.[14]

Just at this time Koto returned as our next-door neighbor, although at first I was unaware of it. Our teacher at the time prided himself on the level of his scholarship and disdained to teach the younger children, so while my elder brothers and cousin studied at home, my younger brother and I were sent to the neighborhood school, leaving in the morning and returning in the evening. Nanny Lu was our escort, and she hurried us straight there and back, never allowing us to dawdle on the way.

One day we were on our way home from school when we met a sedan chair turning out of our lane. I glanced inside and was astonished at what I saw.

"Isn't that Cousin Koto?" I asked, then laughed to myself. No, she couldn't possibly be as tall as that! But then I started comparing her height with mine and became convinced that it was her. I said as much to Nanny Lu, but she insisted I was wrong. In fact she was most reluctant to hear any more on the subject, so I said nothing, just trudged disconsolately home. But thoughts of Koto still gripped my mind. It occurred to me that since the sedan chair had come out of our lane it would have to return the same way, so I decided I would wait beside the gate in hopes of seeing her. After hovering about for some time, I managed to give Nanny Lu the slip. Then, just as I reached the gate, I saw the sedan chair passing by. The bearers shouted—and turned in to the house opposite!

I was ecstatic. Who *could* it be but Koto, I asked myself. I must go and see her. But then I realized that, if I had failed to recognize her at first glance, I could hardly expect her to recognize me. After the lapse of ten years, would she still think of me as a cousin? I would have to get someone to contact her first, lest I be met with a rebuff. Girls being so unpredictable in their moods, if I were too abrupt, she might break up with me, just as Little Tan had done, and leave me frustrated.

With this thought in mind, I took to awaiting my chance in front of the gate. As I returned from school, I would dawdle along in hopes of seeing her, my eyes glued to the upstairs room from which the koto music had once come. But several days passed and I neither saw her nor heard any music, and I began to wonder if I hadn't been mistaken after all. If so, someone must be playing a trick on me, a thought that made me burst out laughing.

Just then a candy vendor came by blowing his flute, and two children from the house opposite ran out, yelling at the top of their lungs. Soon they were joined by five or six other children from the houses on either side of us, all of whom surrounded the vendor. By the time the man had gone on his way, one of the children had a flute, which she strolled about blowing, as proud as punch. A few other children then tried to snatch it from her. At first it was just a minor squabble, but soon voices were raised, and one child started bawling. Then suddenly, above the bawling, there came a creaking sound as the window of the koto room opened and a vision of beauty appeared. If I hadn't been leaning against the gatepost, I would surely have fainted, because the joy I felt surged up and threatened to overwhelm me.

At first Koto didn't see me, but merely shouted at the children in the street below, "Who made Orchid cry? Go home at once, all of you!" Like so many little animals, they scampered back to their lairs. One child was running right by me when she fell flat on her face. I pulled her to her feet, which drew Koto's eyes to me—I could feel them at the back of my head. Then when I turned, our eyes met and locked together, but she acted as if she didn't know me and neither smiled nor spoke. At that point someone must have called her from inside, because in a flash the vision was gone.

I was full of regrets. Why not call out to her? But a moment's thought was sufficient to remind me that if I did and she failed to respond, I would die of embarrassment. And it would be worse still if she failed to recognize me, for she would surely not let me down lightly. I abandoned any thought of calling to her.

However, from then on the candy vendor took to coming along our street at the same time each day. As soon as Koto heard the sound of his flute, she would open her window and look down, and when she did so, I was sure to be waiting below. Before her appearance my eyes would be trained on her window, but as soon as I saw her I would start feeling embarrassed. I would avert my gaze, afraid to look directly at her, but I never really noticed whatever I was staring at. When I stole a glance at her, she would sedulously avert *her* gaze. Her feelings were identical to mine.

At first I wasn't sure just what those feelings were. If we really didn't want to meet, why did we face each other like this?

And since we faced each other, why did we avoid each other's gaze? I now realize that there are many cases of precisely this kind. When a well-brought-up little boy attends a banquet and finds bowls of delicious fruit set out in front of him, he will be sorely tempted, but for fear that people will laugh at him, he won't stare too hard at the fruit. Instead he will just happen to glance at it, and he will be highly nervous and ill at ease as long as the banquet lasts. To give another example, when a youth is walking with his parents past a photographer's salon and sees the photographs displayed on the wall, mostly of pretty girls, his parents will look straight at the girls' photographs as if it were the most natural thing in the world, but the youth will look first at the photographs of natural scenery and only later turn his gaze to the girls, and even then he will blush and avert his eyes and not dare look directly at them. The reason is that when we crave something too intensely, we can't help watering at the mouth, and so we try to dissemble and hide our craving, lest we be observed.

But people of genuine feeling cannot cover it up forever. Inevitably, the more they try to hide their cravings, the more those cravings will be revealed. Before long everyone in our household knew that I was lying in wait for Koto. My brothers and cousins heaped scorn on me, which prompted my mother to scold me severely, but I still couldn't imagine why it would be wrong for me to meet Koto. My mother used to be fond of her. Why had she changed all of a sudden? I pressed Little Tan again and again for an answer, but by now she had reversed her opinion of Koto, and she pouted and began to belittle her, flatly contradicting all she had said before. She told me that if I continued to dote on her, I could expect a lifetime of frustration.

Still more mystified, I tried asking Nanny Lu. "Oh, why did you have to grow up?" she replied, and at that point I finally understood that all of these things—Little Tan's cold-shouldering me, Koto's failure to acknowledge me, my mother's refusal to let me see Koto—were the result of my growing up, and I was furious.

However, growing up did bring with it a few freedoms. In the first place, I could now go out without a maid in attendance. And second, I had acquired a modest ability in poetry. Anything I wanted to say but couldn't, I could entrust to a poem. And so I made plans to write to Koto.

The next day the vendor came by at his regular time and the children swarmed about him as usual. Among them I recognized one girl with braids—Orchid, Koto's sister. I bought a flute from the vendor and played it, only to find that it was out of tune. I tried several more before finding a good one, then played the tune "Niao qing si" on it. All this time Orchid was watching my every move, consumed with desire for the flute, so I gave it to her.

"Don't you remember me?" I asked. "When you lived here before, you were only four years old, but now you're all grown up. I don't suppose you remember that time?"

"No, I don't," she said with a smile, "but my sister told me about it. I know your name, too. Aren't you the one they call Cousin Shan?"

I was so overjoyed to learn that Koto had not forgotten me that for the moment I couldn't think what to say. Meanwhile Orchid prattled away. "You grew your fingernails so long that she couldn't keep up with you." [15]

"Ten years ago when your sister and my cousin were studying together, they made a pact to let their nails grow. One of my cousin's nails has broken off. Are your sister's still all right?"

"Yes."

"Does your mother ever say she misses me?"

Orchid slowly shook her head, dashing cold water upon my growing excitement.

After a pause I went on. "Your sister used to be a regular visitor at our house. Why doesn't she come over one day when she has some free time?"

Orchid made a wry face. "I'm sure she's afraid Mother would tell her off." As she spoke, she seemed frightened herself and glanced back inside her house. "Mother will be wondering where I am," she said, and went off, clutching her flute.

That evening I was thinking of writing to Koto, but Little Tan's eyes were like rays of lightning flashing before me, and I didn't dare start. The following day I was all set to write my letter at school, but the teacher kept pacing back and forth beside me. Readers, let me explain to you why so many people were checking up on me when I was merely trying to write a letter. Without exception they were bought and paid for by my mother's money, although I was the real victim of that money. However, I did manage to put a trifling sum to good use with a little magic of my own. One day I moved my writing instruments to Spring Bark, a room in our compound in the shape of a boat. The person in charge was a page who could read and write, that is to say, someone fully capable of frustrating my plans. I showed him a few hundred sheets of fine notepaper and said rather grandly, "If you can find me a better paper than this, I'll give you a prize."

He brightened up at once. "You just give me the money, sir, and I'll go and find you some." I handed him several hundred copper cash and sent him off to the shops.

As a youth I took the keenest pleasure in hunting out fine papers, which I treasured as works of art in their own right. As soon as the boy had gone, I chose a sheet of my favorite notepaper and began writing.

Dear Cousin Koto,

I am not sure whether the one who opens this letter will really be Cousin Koto or not. I have been able to see your face for several days now, and if you really are Cousin Koto, you cannot have forgotten me, which is why I am in two minds as to whether you really are. You and my cousin were fellow students, and she cares deeply for you and has often urged me to ask after you, but I haven't dared do anything so presumptuous. If you really are the Cousin Koto I was so fond of ten years ago, I hope you will reply. If not, please disregard this letter.

Respectfully,

Shan

Readers, you must understand that there were certain things I found impossible to say in a letter and that I wrote in this diffident way only to spare myself from ridicule. I assumed that if Koto had not forgotten me, I would soon receive a letter resolving any doubts I had. With several years of schooling behind her, she could certainly write a letter, so I expected to hear from her at any moment.

But three days passed without a reply. I cannot begin to describe the state I was in. Then on the fourth day a parcel arrived, very soft and thick, which gave off a sweet fragrance as I opened it. It turned out to be not a letter, but a silk handkerchief embroidered with a Buddhist cross. There was nothing written on it. I examined and reexamined the wrapping paper but found nothing written there, either. Then I spread out the handkerchief and looked at it closely. It was immaculate and gave off a strong scent. Except for the creases in the embroidery, one would never have guessed that the handkerchief wasn't new.

I was musing over what this meant, when Little Tan advanced on me, eyes glaring, like a cat stalking a mouse. Hastily I stuffed the handkerchief into one of my sleeves, blushing furiously as I did so. In fact she hadn't been paying attention to me at all, but when she noticed my change of expression, she commented, "Sitting here all by yourself in the daytime—memorizing your texts, I suppose?" I made some casual reply but blushed worse than ever, fidgeting with my hands in acute embarrassment.

She knew I had something hidden inside my sleeve. I don't know what went through her mind, but she began blushing furiously herself. "The books you choose should be ones that are fit to read," she said, "books you would read in front of your teacher. If they can't be read in front of him, they're not fit to read. What was that book you hid in your sleeve just now? Kindly show it to me, please." As she said this, her face took on a stern expression and turned an even brighter shade of red.

I realized her mistake and was about to exploit it, having thought up a suitable reply, but I began to stammer and couldn't get the words out. Luckily she didn't press her inquiries, just swept from the room. At once I fell prey to a thousand worries. Where could I hide it? I had no private chest of my own, only a book bag, but when I tucked the handkerchief inside one of my books, the article proved to be too thick; instead of hiding the handkerchief for me, the book swelled up, revealing its presence for all to see. I was in a worse funk than ever.

Then I hit on an excellent idea. Removing a few of the books from my bag, I hid the handkerchief behind the others, so that it was no longer visible. The telltale scent was still there, but I came up with a way of masking it. Borrowing a bottle of perfume from my sister-in-law's apartment, I secreted it in my book bag and declared that I had found some silverfish among my books.

"Why don't you fumigate them with rue?" Mother asked.

"Rue has such an unpleasant smell to it," I said. "It's strictly for new brides and dead bodies. I've borrowed some perfume from Sister-in-law, and that should be just as good."

"Very well," said Mother.

"No wonder there's such an aroma clinging to your clothes," put in Little Tan. "But to go sprinkling the sages' classics with toiletries from a lady's chamber—that hardly seems suitable."

I was deeply embarrassed by this remark, and she suspected me all the more of harboring pornography. Awaiting her chance, she did indeed search my book bag. I wasn't aware of it at the time, and in my spare moments I often examined the handkerchief, devoting far more time to it than the texts I was committing to memory. The object of Little Tan's search was a book, and after taking out a number of books of about the same size and examining them chapter by chapter without discovering anything untoward, she gave up. In this way the article in question was safely preserved and has been in my possession ever since.

I fretted that I had nothing to send Koto in return. My own handkerchiefs were all inferior and wouldn't do as tokens of love, and so while returning home from school one day, I slipped off to the shops and picked out a real beauty. It was bordered with flowers and had a blank space in the middle for a message. Unaware of the dreadful quality of my handwriting, I strung together a few lines, only two of which come to mind:

> *The naiad's kindness gives me pause.*
> *How to repay her gift of tears?*[16]

It was intended as nothing more than a sentimental conceit. Little did I realize that it would prove all too prophetic.

I didn't know at first what reaction Koto had to my present. After receiving it, she no longer watched me from her upstairs window, and I rather suspected that she was upset with me. Orchid was the one who had carried our presents back and forth, so I asked her, "What did your sister say when she received my poem?"

Orchid shook her head. "She didn't say anything."

"But even if she didn't *say* anything, her expression must have told you something."

"She couldn't smile, because Mother's so strict with her."

"Then you mustn't let your mother know about the presents, must you?"

"No, but she already knows."

"You didn't *tell* her?" I cried in alarm.

"No, but the night before last, Sister had just spread out your poem in front of her and was thinking how to set it to music for the koto. She was trying out a tune, when Mother overheard her and asked who wrote the words. Sister didn't try to hide a thing. Then Mother asked her, 'Don't you know he's engaged to be married?' and Sister answered in an offhand way, continuing to tune her koto, 'Yes, but I don't see what that has to do with me.' Mother sighed. 'If you fall for this boy, you stupid girl, it will mean disaster for our whole family.' Then Sister got furious, flung her koto on the couch, and flounced out of the room, shouting, 'How many of those men *you* fell for in our house were unmarried, I'd like to know! Just because Cousin Shan's engaged, why does *he* have to be kept away?'"

I felt the sweat trickling down my back. "And did your mother get angry?"

"She has a very funny way about her," said Orchid with a laugh. "When Sister is soft, Mother is hard, as hard as steel, but when Sister flares up, Mother becomes as soft as putty. She gave a self-satisfied little smile and said, 'But who's stopping Cousin Shan from visiting us? He simply doesn't choose to come, that's all. I gather his mother is extremely strict with him, and I wouldn't dare invite him over myself. Besides, it wouldn't mean anything to me. But if it would mean something to you, I'm prepared to let him call on us all the time, if only to bring a smile to my girl's face.' Then, with a mocking grin, she left the room.

"Sister's face was streaked with tears, which dripped onto the table. I watched her as she slowly joined up the teardrops with one finger and traced out a pattern of interlocking rings, not saying a word the whole time. I had no idea what she was thinking. But Shan, you have legs, why don't you simply go over there? I don't suppose Mother will be able to do anything about it."

There was nothing I could say; I was too busy trying to work out what her mother had really meant. And Koto's angry retort—that was even harder for me to understand. By that point I was in such a daze that I seemed to see nothing in front of my eyes. I was so confused I even forgot where I was.

Then someone tapped me on the shoulder, and I snapped out of my reverie. Orchid had vanished, and the person standing in front of me was none other than the abominable Turtle.

"Have you heard the latest, sir?" he mumbled.

"No," I replied without interest.

"The cook bought a small fish for the cat and hung it up outside one of the upstairs windows on the shady side of the house and then forgot about it. The cat meowed underneath, but the cook didn't realize why. So now the cat's all skin and bones, while the fish is rotten. What do you make of that?"

At first I took him seriously, assuming that the incident had really occurred, but a couple of sharp-witted servants standing nearby gave me a knowing grin and tried to stir me up. "Go on, hit him! Hit him!"

Turtle was complacently stroking his beard. To vent my frustration, I launched a surprise attack on him and pulled out one of his whiskers. With a yelp he took to his heels.

I trudged gloomily back to my room, where I pondered my dilemma. Well, shall I go over? asked my heart, playing the role of interlocutor.

Don't do that, my mind told me. You'll only earn her mother's dislike.

But how can I avoid it? asked my heart.

To which my mind had no reply. Then my anxiety affected my other organs as well, causing me unbearable distress. No doubt my readers will have little trouble in guessing the answer. All her mother loved was money. Had I given her some of that, there'd have been no question of any dislike. But in those days I had no money whatsoever at my disposal, and even if I had had some, I would never have suspected that her mother would set such a high value on it. We generally impute our own attitudes to other people, and in those days I never had to worry about where the necessities of life were coming from; they were simply there when I needed them. I never had to pay for anything I wanted; I could get it from my mother simply by asking for it. I really had no idea of the function of money in the world. I even thought of it as filthy, and I would never have dreamed of making anyone a present of something filthy. If I gave people anything like that, they would conclude that I thought they were filthy, too, and break off relations with me. That is why, when my heart posed that question, this answer never occurred to me. Hadn't my poem asked "how to repay her gift of tears"? I felt that the ancient ballad in which the lover asks if he can repay his beloved in the finest gold was simply disgusting.[17] The finest gold was of no value, whereas tears were the most precious commodity in the world. Putting gold in front of a great beauty or a famous poet and saying, "This is yours because of all the tears you've shed for love"— I ask you, who would be capable of such a thing? I now know, of course, that any number of people would be capable of it. But let me put that aside for the moment, while I tell you about Koto.

She was eighteen at the time and as innocent in the ways of the world as I was. The visitors to her house were mostly of her father's generation, and at first she didn't try to avoid them. All of her clothes and jewelry came to her as gifts from such men, and she thought that quite natural and accepted the gifts without question. But sometimes the visitors would banter with her, and occasionally their talk would verge on the indecent, and then she would get angry, feeling she had been insulted, and burst into tears.

On these occasions her mother would complain to her, "What you don't understand is that as a family we have no assets. My only asset is my face, and now that I am getting on, heaven has taken pity on me for my self-denial and blessed me with a beautiful daughter. *Of course* I'm concerned about your virtue! If I couldn't bear to see you as a rich man's concubine, you surely don't imagine I would stand for anything less? As for your future, my husband never managed to distinguish himself, so you will never get a good husband on the strength of our position in society. We need to put together a lot more money than we have now. When your cousin is grown up, if he takes a great deal of money with him to the capital, he'll have no trouble finding you a high official for a husband, and then you'll receive a title, and the whole family will enjoy a higher standing. For the sake of your future, a title is absolutely essential.

"However, I can't turn base metal into gold or summon the Five Genies[18] to bring us a fortune. But I do have some experience of the world, and I know this much, that the one thing in this world that attracts money like a magnet is a beautiful face. 'One smile is worth a thousand taels'—that's no lie. A laugh or a smile may be of no great value in itself, but if it brings in a thousand taels, why not try it? If everyone could get a thousand taels per laugh, the world would rock with laughter. But that's beyond the capacity of the average person, which is why, if someone *is* capable of it, she becomes such a precious commodity. But when such a person defies heaven and man by crying and getting angry and petulant instead of laughing and smiling, I find it very hard to imagine what her motives can be. Even so, petulance and tears are *possible* alternatives to smiles and laughter; anger is the only one that's totally unacceptable. My dear child, if you are really going to get angry with people, I shall be bankrupt in no time. Could you bear to let that happen?"

Vulgar as this harangue was, it could only have been delivered by a most perceptive person. Koto, however, completely ignored it. Since she couldn't break away from her mother and assert her independence, she was condemned to decades of misery. Had she accepted her mother's prescriptions and faithfully practiced them, I would naturally have been excluded from her company, and once that had happened, I would have seen through the illusion of life and become a buddha. Unfortunately, she was unable to break away from her mother.

By the next year Cousin Mei's savings had grown somewhat, and the money god appeared to her and began to bedevil her. Suddenly she found her quarters too cramped and planned a move to Pingan No. 2 Bridge. Koto sent Orchid over with the news. She wanted me to seize my chance before the move to make a few visits to the new place and try to get on good terms with her mother.

I did as she suggested, taking a circuitous route home from school one day. Cousin Mei was standing by the lakeshore, directing the workmen as they carried in the furniture.

"Hard work, Aunt?" I asked.

She had never borne me any personal grudge. "What brings you here all on your own?" she asked, then pointed to the gate. "We'll soon be moving in over there."

"I suppose your new house has the best of everything—flowers, trees, pavilions, terraces?"

"Flowers and trees, yes, but pavilions and terraces, they're strictly for immortals, and I'm not quite so lucky, I'm afraid. But I expect you're just saying that to flatter us."

I looked at the gate, which was quite imposing. There was also a tall building half hidden among the willow trees as in a painting.

"Is that yours, too?"

"Yes. If you have nothing better to do, why not come inside and sit down? I'll go home with you shortly. All right?"

I responded with alacrity, as to an imperial decree.

She led the way into the house, where I was astonished to find our old servant bustling about hard at work.

"Turtle, how do *you* come to be here?" I asked.

He was just as astonished to see me. "Oh, I predicted you'd be along, sir, and was just tidying up in readiness. Look at this house, now—isn't it splendid! Let's go upstairs. From up there you can see half the city, as clear as in a picture. Here, let me show you." He opened the door of the anteroom and, gripping my elbow, steered me upstairs, then threw open the windows all around, offering me a choice of views. I saw Mount Wu, a towering mass of emerald green, like some great beauty with a tall coiffure smiling at me through the window. The people on the summit looked tiny as they crawled about.

"With a telescope this should be spectacular," I said. "If you took a telescope up Mount Wu and pointed it at this house, I wonder if you could see the people in here?"

"When you have a free day, I'll take you up there and we'll find out." He pointed below. "The water's lovely, too." I looked down and saw beneath the window a few weeping willows and, through the tips of their branches, a stretch of clear lake. A couple of small boats were ferrying people across, just as in a painting. As before, I wondered if the people in the boats could see inside the house. What set me wondering in both cases was the thought that, even if I couldn't get upstairs myself, I might at least be able see Koto from Mount Wu or a boat.

As these idle fancies passed through my mind, I heard a bell toll, and a couple of crows flew by, cawing as they went.

"It's getting late," I said gloomily. "I'd better be going back."

"So long as you're with me, sir," said Turtle, "it won't matter if you're out late. I'll just tell her ladyship I took you down to Plum Blossom House, and you won't be in any trouble."

I realized that he was right and that his coming was a great boon to me. "My dear, adorable Turtle," I said, "I shall have to present you with a bottle of the very finest wine."

Retracting his neck still further, Turtle laughed. "Finest wine, eh? When I hear those two little words, I get the most terrible thirst on me." He mimed a man with a desperate thirst.

Cousin Mei saw him and laughed. "The more you imitate a turtle, the closer the resemblance gets."

He laughed, too. "If you make me into a turtle, what else can I do?"

She looked me in the eye and smiled. "Well, Shan," she said after a pause, "and what do you think of our house?"

I was quick to praise it, adding, "Aunt, this room would be ideal for you."

"No such luck," she said, pointing to the room on the left. "We'll put your elder cousin in here and your younger cousin over there. I shall be downstairs."

It occurred to me that if she was not living upstairs I would have no chance to go up there myself. I was bitterly disappointed, but she didn't seem to notice and busied herself giving directions to two or three men who were bringing in an armoire. Once it was installed, the workmen left and she brought a low table up to the window and sat down, raising her elbows to let the southerly breeze cool her under the arms.

"The Dragon Boat Festival will soon be upon us," she said to me. "I forgot to bring a fan with me today. But of course you scholars lead such quiet lives, you never work up a sweat."

"If you need a fan, Aunt," I said, realizing that I, too, had forgotten to bring one, "tomorrow I'll do a fan painting of this scene for you."

"You're a painter, too?" she asked.

"The young master does extremely fine landscapes," Turtle affirmed. "If he's going to do a painting for you, I hope I can persuade him to do one for me, too."

"I'll do a turtle as a portrait of you," I said. Cousin Mei started laughing, while Turtle muttered something that I couldn't quite catch.

In the distance one could see smoke rising from the chimneys. We returned together, and my mother accepted Turtle's version of events without question. I felt extremely grateful to him, and from then on I frequently accompanied him to the house.

Turtle was nearly seventy but still quite active. Since he was fond of a good joke, people enjoyed his company. Originally he had no connection with Cousin Mei, but when she became our neighbor, a couple of our young servants went over to her place and caused a ruckus. Turtle put a stop to it and so earned her gratitude. In addition, she often held gambling parties in her house, and people from the yamen would sometimes show up and start sounding off, but Turtle knew them all and never gave them a chance to try any of their tricks. That was why he was always welcome at her house.

At this stage I was only too eager to please Cousin Mei and would do anything for her that lay within my powers. I memorized where each household item had been put so that I could lay my hands on it easily. She herself was quite vague about such matters. If she needed something, I would anticipate her need and have it in front of her before she had even opened her mouth to ask. She was always saying to Turtle, "What a memory the young master has! No wonder he's at the top of his class. My Orchid now, she'll put something away and then forget where she's put it the moment her back is turned."

Turtle would then marvel over this observation and go on to brag about my superhuman cleverness. On one occasion

Orchid brought her twelve-year-old sister, Jade, along and, after looking about, complimented her mother on how neatly everything was arranged. Cousin Mei gave the girl a piece of her mind. "All you can do is wag your tongue, lazy little pig. Without Cousin Shan here to help me, I'd be worn out!"

At her mother's praise, Orchid gave me a sidelong glance and a smile that slyly mocked my complacency. Then, after looking all around her, she asked, "Isn't there a staircase somewhere? How do we get upstairs?"

Jade ran off behind the chamber and found the stairs. I opened the door to the east wing and showed them the way. By visiting so often I had become quite familiar with the layout, and I actually thought of myself as the owner and of Orchid as my first visitor.

She felt thirsty but didn't know where the tea was, so I found it for her. Holding the teacup, she sipped the tea, her eyes fixed on me as if there were something she hesitated to say.

I asked what she had on her mind. "Sister's a deep one, all right, and you may well be the cleverest man in the world, but Mother's a fool," she said.

I hushed her before she could say any more. She set the teacup down on the table and laughed out loud. "But Mother really *is* a fool," she repeated, while I squirmed with embarrassment, a sight that only added to her amusement. She began laughing helplessly, until Cousin Mei came in, having overheard the last remark.

"Why are you calling me a fool?" she demanded, as I squirmed even worse than before.

Orchid answered calmly, "It's so glorious up here, and yet you choose to sleep downstairs. Now, isn't *that* foolish?"

Cousin Mei laughed. "But you're no fool, which is why I've put you up here. Isn't that so, Shan?" I made some noncommittal reply, and she left the room.

"Amazing!" said Orchid. "I never thought it would be so

easy to turn someone's feelings around. Well, in that case, I'm the one who deserves all the credit. I wonder what reward I'm going to get?"

"Reward? Anything your heart desires!"

I don't know what she was thinking of, but she blushed furiously and began checking off the days on her fingers. "The day after tomorrow is the Dragon Boat, and five days after that it'll be Sister's birthday, which happens to be our moving day. You *must* come and see her then. I can't imagine how you two will act toward each other, but I'm sure it'll be a sight worth seeing."

I, too, wondered what I would say to Koto. Orchid would surely laugh at me, as would the other people present. "I really don't want to see her that day," I said. "If I am allowed to meet her, why does it have to be *then?*"

"In that case you simply don't understand her at all. She really does want to see you. It won't be her fault if you don't come."

"But if she doesn't invite me and your mother won't let me in, I'd never have the gall to just show up!"

"As you say, without a summons from Mother you two would never be able to meet as long as you live. But I'll work on Mother and see she sends you an invitation. If you don't come, you'll be like someone on a ship bound for paradise who veers off in another direction when he's almost there." I had no reply to that; I just felt acutely depressed.

The next day Cousin Mei spoke to me, "Tomorrow's the Dragon Boat. Why don't you come over and share a little calamus wine with us?"

I accepted but then began worrying that she would think me a little too eager to gratify my desires, so I made some polite excuse instead.

On the day itself I joined my family for a celebration in the Cedar Room. My sister-in-law had a daughter who was three years old, and my cousins wrote the character for "king" on her forehead in red orpiment and dressed her up in an embroidered tiger outfit that came down below her elbows, utterly captivating my mother. Each cousin braided a longevity cord[19] from threads of multicolored silk, which made me think of Secunda, whose skill at such crafts was far superior to anyone else's. Had she been there, I would have been assured of a real work of art. Then I remembered that she was far away in Suzhou and that I couldn't see her. From Secunda my thoughts swirled around and finally came to rest on Koto, and I was in the middle of a daydream about her when my mother called on me to drink a toast. At first I didn't hear her.

"Silly boy! What silly things are you dreaming about now?" I didn't know what to say.

At that moment the smell of burning artemisia[20] from the courtyard was carried in on the breeze, and the smoke blew just where I was sitting, giving me an excuse to leave the gathering and wander over to the gate, where I lingered about. The corner of the koto room was swathed in bands of mist, like some abode of the immortals wreathed in multicolored clouds.

Then I noticed someone leaning over the upstairs balcony and beckoning to me. It was Orchid, using sign language. She stuck up her thumb and shook her head, turned and pointed inside, then opened her hand and beckoned to me.

I was itching to go, but I also had my doubts. If I went, I would be involving myself in an awkward encounter with nothing to commend it. Why was it necessary to wait until Cousin Mei was absent before going to see Koto? It would only heighten suspicion. So I shook my head, rejecting the invitation. Orchid waved her handkerchief vigorously and darted a furious look at me. Next I saw Koto come up behind her and seize her hand in apparent anger, then shake her head at me with an earnest expression on her face, as if about to say something. I listened intently, but all I heard was the window creaking shut.

Readers of this book should understand that I loved Koto as one loves a flower in some famous garden. All I asked was to be allowed to feast my eyes on its beauty; I never had the slightest intention of plucking it, although that was precisely what the garden's owner feared. If I now took advantage of her absence to sneak into the garden, even if I didn't pluck the flower, she would suspect me of meaning to, and how would I ever clear myself? Moreover the owner was just getting to know me and gradually relaxing her suspicions. If I aroused them again, she would bar the door and put a stop to my visits forever. That was why I placed restrictions on myself that were more severe than any Koto's mother placed on me. As for Koto, she likened her mother to a little man with a great treasure for which he wanted to get the best possible price, while I was just a poor Parsee, but a Parsee with the magical art of attracting the treasure with a magnet. That was why her mother took such stringent precautions against me. If the treasure showed any signs of restlessness in its chest, she would hide it away in some inaccessible place and never let the Parsee set eyes on it. However, if he did see it and did not take much interest in it, or if he tried out his magnet and the treasure did not respond, she would dismiss her precautions as unnecessary. That was why the closer Koto and I came in terms of our love, the more distant we were in expressing it.

On the fifth day after the Dragon Boat Festival, Cousin Mei waited for me and then, surprised that I had not shown up, sent Turtle over to fetch me. It was toward evening when I arrived. The lanterns shone like a galaxy of stars, and music played in the reception room. There was hardly anyone in the throng of guests whom I knew, but Orchid beckoned me into the back room, where Koto, glistening in white finery like a heron, leaped to the eye. I bowed first to Cousin Mei, and then to her.

"You two haven't met in almost ten years, yet you still recognize each other," remarked Cousin Mei with a smile.

"We spent so much time together as children," I said, "that I'd know her by her voice, let alone by her looks."

I turned to Koto. "My cousin has the fondest memories of you, and scarcely a day goes by that she doesn't think of you. Do you miss her at all? Oh, and one other thing—you and she let your nails grow, and hers are now as long as mine. In fact, whenever she looks at mine, she thinks of you. Are yours as long, too, I wonder?"

I held out my left hand to show her, and without thinking she stretched out her own slender fingers. "They can't compare with yours," she said with a smile. The friends standing beside her gathered around to look and coo in admiration. One pretty girl got so carried away that she grasped my hand and drew Koto's alongside to compare our nails.

Koto pulled her hand away. "I can't possibly compare with Cousin Shan," she said with a smile. "Perhaps it's because he has a calmer nature than I do. But how *is* your cousin? I miss her just as much as she misses me. When it's convenient, I hope you will bring her over." I promised to do so.

As I vainly searched my memory for what I wanted to say, Cousin Mei offered me a seat. It happened to be next to Koto's, which made me very uneasy. My mind was focused on her, but I could hardly turn and look at her, so I kept my eyes straight ahead.

I noticed the pretty girl who had compared our nails whispering to Orchid but glancing at me and smiling. She had a free, uninhibited manner about her. Then I noticed Orchid gesturing with her fan to invite me to join them. As soon as I did so, this girl grasped my hand. "If Orchid hadn't reminded me, I might have forgotten you, Cousin Shan. Do you remember me?"

My mind was a blank.

"This is Alcyon," said Orchid. "She used to live with us. Have you forgotten her?"

I conjured up a vague memory of her. "Weren't you the girl who snatched away the hibiscus blossoms I had picked, then rubbed them together and scattered the little pieces over the pond to feed the fish?"

"If you can remember that, there's nothing wrong with your memory," she said. "You got all upset and started crying. I remember someone wiping away your tears and picking you some more flowers to make up for the others. Who could it have been, I wonder?"

"I know. It was Cousin Aimee."

Alcyon pointed to a girl some way off. "How is it you don't recognize her when she's right there in front of you?"

I followed the direction in which she was pointing and saw a beautiful girl in a filmy dress, her hair swept up like a bank of clouds, a girl with melting eyes and the faint trace of a smile. She was whispering something to Koto, but her eyes were focused on me as if I were the subject of discussion. I left Orchid and hurried over, but by the time I arrived Aimee had turned away and was ignoring me.

"Oh, Aimee!" I whispered. "You don't remember me!"

She snorted. "The only one *you* remember is Koto; you've forgotten everyone else. Even if I did remember you, what would be the use?"

I flushed a deep red. "Just listen to her," I said to Koto. "She's never outgrown her childhood snippiness. And she knows you and I are meeting tonight for the first time in ten years."

"It's ten years for me, too," said Aimee with a laugh, "but Koto's the only one you haven't forgotten. Either you feel something different for her, or else her face has some special quality to it. Here, let me take a look at you."

She held Koto in a sitting position while she stood up and examined her face. Koto couldn't help giggling, and as she turned her head toward me, she was like a rose in full sunlight with a faint breeze stirring it—sheer enchantment. I felt there was nothing in this world that could represent more than a fraction of her beauty.

By now I felt so affected by Alcyon's and Aimee's example that I livened up and lost my habitual reserve. Besides, none of the girls there thought of me as belonging to the opposite sex; as we held hands and chatted, as we smiled at each other, their scent assailed me until I felt as if I were immersed in a sea of flowers. But people who are used to a particular situation are no longer surprised by it; after time spent in a room full of orchids, they no longer notice the scent; and after living in a great city, they no longer find anything to marvel at. Such people represent my state of mind that day. My every word and gesture brought the girls' eyes on me, and I was secretly elated. It's all due to my fingernails, I thought. Because they love my nails, they extend their love to me, so these nails of mine really are precious. I imagine that these girls tacitly deduce my true nature from the fact that I have been able to cherish these inanimate objects for so long. They are convinced that I would show an even greater love for a human being, and they would like to be transformed into my nails and receive my loving care. Still, I have ten nails, and only these two have received it. I *could* have let all ten grow, but in practice that would have been almost impossible. I assumed that it *was* impossible and felt I had to cut the others from time to time, rather than let them grow long and find myself reluctant to trim them later. This notion is one that I have cherished to this day, and the couple of people who have received my loving care have responded to it with a deeper love of their own. In those days I used to imagine one nail as representing Secunda and the other as Koto. Later, when someone tried to snatch my love away, it was this notion that made me label her the evil demon of love. But enough of that for the moment.

I was put off by the large number of guests and the loudness of the music. Moreover I was placed at a table with a group of men, none of whom I knew, which was even less to my liking. But it would have been unsociable to leave, so I had to go glumly in to dinner. There the food and drink disagreed with me, and I began to feel queasy, so I took my leave before the party was over and made my way home.

It was about one in the morning when I arrived, and the fish in the lake were leaping again. I had my mother's permission to attend a fellow student's birthday party—that was the excuse I had concocted—but I came home too late and received a good scolding for it. By now I deeply regretted my visit, which had proven completely useless. But the thought struck me that I had at least managed to see Koto, and although I hadn't been able to unburden myself to her, from now on I would be able to go over there quite often. My visit had not been so useless after all.

The following day, on the excuse that I had a written exercise to complete, I arose particularly early. Little Tan helped me get ready, praising my devotion to study, while I smiled to myself. When I got to school, none of the other students had arrived, so I pretended I had forgotten something I needed and, telling my brother to wait there for me, I slipped around to Koto's.

I arrived to find Cousin Mei combing Jade's hair. Apparently Koto and Orchid were still in bed. Cousin Mei's room was in the east wing, and I sat down there for a moment. The stairs were off to one side, but I hadn't the nerve to go straight up. I was used to a regime in which one never entered the women's quarters without an express summons—a notion that over the years has caused me to respond to opportunity in some highly inconvenient ways. Later I did go boldly upstairs without any excuse. Had I done so on this occasion, the chances are that Cousin Mei would not have stopped me and, once the precedent had been set, I would have been freed of any such inhibitions. But at the time, misled as I was by Confucian morality, I didn't even consider it.

I sat there a long time, until the clock on the wall showed half past nine, when I had to take my leave and return to school. I left with my hopes dashed, gloomy beyond words. I hated Cousin Mei for her insensitivity to my feelings, and I saw her indifference as evidence of positive dislike. If I made frequent visits there, how could I be sure that at some point I wouldn't be met with a cold stare and feel utterly humiliated?

But my yearnings were not to be denied. After leaving school that day, I slipped over again. This time Koto was out, but Orchid and Jade were still there, and we held a meaningless conversation. I had never felt any awkwardness with the girls before, but for some reason that I can't explain, I was distant with them on this occasion. For their part they were exceptionally warm and affectionate, as if they had been my own sisters, but I concluded that Koto was deliberately avoiding me and felt dejected nonetheless. After three unsuccessful visits, I feared I was making a fool of myself in the eyes of her family. I began to interpret their every action, word, and smile as mockery, even when it had nothing to do with me. I became convinced that my visits were utterly pointless. If Koto missed me, I kept thinking, she would write me a letter inviting me to call. Every day I waited for such a letter, but none came, and I began to feel a deep remorse. In the small hours of the morning I was sure that Koto had no love for me and that my longing for her merely added to my humiliation.

One day I was lingering beside our gate, looking up at the room from which the koto music had once come. I was lost in reverie, and my gloom must have shown on my face.

Our servant Turtle shuffled up to me, looked me in the eye, and smiled. "Brings back memories, does it, sir?" he asked.

Hearing this in my present mood, I almost broke down.

"Well, the place is the same, but I'm none too sure about the feelings of the person who used to live there."

"That's right," said Turtle. "You've been altogether too naive about this, sir. You have to understand that Cousin Mei's house is like a public park. The flowers and birds in the park are all very delightful, but we can't claim them as our own. Our love for them springs from our natural feelings, but simply because we love them, that doesn't mean that their owner is going to hand them over to us. Unless we who love them are prepared to sacrifice our time and money, we will not be able to get close to them very often. And in the end, even if we do sacrifice our time and money, the flowers and birds may not welcome us for long. You must realize they have no feelings of their own—that is merely an assumption made by men of feeling. The truth is that flowers and birds have *nothing* in common with their admirers."

"But that's ridiculous!" I exclaimed. "You can't go likening people to flowers and birds!"

"Likening Koto to a flower or bird is absolutely right, in my opinion. She's someone you can enjoy but not get too close to. A rose can stab you with its thorns, a parrot can tear you with its beak—that's the kind of thing I mean. Get too close, and you'll be sorry."

"I must say I find that even more incomprehensible."

"Look, sir, you know the kind of person Cousin Mei is; the only thing she cares about is money. You consider love the most precious thing in the world, but she thinks there's nothing so precious as money. Aren't you always reading poetry? Have you never come across the lines

> *In choosing friends, money is all;*
> *Otherwise friendship won't be deep.*

That goes for Cousin Mei and even more for her daughter Koto. And I'll tell you another thing. Have you ever heard of a Mr. Sheng? He has enough money to build a boudoir out of solid gold. In fact, Cousin Mei's place is an example of such a boudoir, and Koto is the one who is living in it."

I was startled by this news. "Is that true?"

"Forget whether it's true or not, just think where Cousin Mei got up the nerve to move house. She's certainly never had to worry about having too much money, and yet she took on this move. To repeat what I said, if you treat Cousin Mei's house as a public park, it's perfectly all right. Visitors to parks don't need lots of money in order to get in. But if you try to compete with someone who does have lots of money, you'll only bring misery and frustration upon yourself. It's not because I hold any grudge against Cousin Mei that I'm trying to shock you with these words of warning; it's just that you're the third generation I've served in this family, and I feel bound to give you my frank advice. So *please* take note of what I'm saying."

Now, there *was* a Mr. Sheng attached to Koto's family. When I first heard of him from Turtle, I wasn't entirely convinced, but afterward I realized that he was speaking the truth. At the time I condemned Koto in my heart without making any allowances for her. Later I learned the facts, and she became the object of my deepest sympathy. Let me explain.

Mr. Sheng was a northerner who served as an official in our county. When Koto and I were neighbors, he often visited Cousin Mei's house. He was about thirty, with a round, plump face, and a paunch—you could tell at a glance that he was a rich man. He was married, but his wife had remained in the north, and while serving in our county Mr. Sheng lived on his own. Nominally he was an official, but actually he was an aide to His Honor ————. Whatever money he made he kept in a cabinet in Cousin Mei's house, as if she were his banker. She accepted the responsibility for looking after his money, but in reality she was hoping to get her hands on it.

Then Sheng lost his wife, and he wept and wailed in front

of Cousin Mei, who praised him to Koto as a man of feeling. "My dear," she said, "do you happen to know who all that lovely silver in my cabinet belongs to?"

"Yes, it's Sheng's savings," said Koto.

"No, it's not. You, my dear, have it in your power to get hold of that money and pass it along to me."

Koto was aghast.

Cousin Mei expanded on what she had said. "Mr. Sheng's a widower. If you were to become his second wife, all that silver would come to you."

At this suggestion Koto flushed crimson. At first she was too shocked to reply, but then she became angry. "Mother, you must have had too much to drink, saying such crazy things."

"You young people are so quick to show anger! Really, it's your worst fault. You're still not old enough to know how things work in this world, so I'm going to tell you. You need to take stock of yourself. You come from a poor family, and your looks are all you have to boast about. It's also your looks that are your main attraction for other people. However, your looks aren't going to stay the same for ages, like those of a lady in a painting. If even the lady in the painting eventually gets corroded by dust and loses her luster, think how much worse off we are! For an example you need look no farther than your own mother. When I was your age, I was every bit as attractive as you are, and if I hadn't made a few clever moves to acquire a little money and save it up, you children would have starved to death long ago. There wouldn't even *be* a Koto for you to place such a high value on! The greatest value for us is our personal freedom. But to obtain it, money is essential, which is precisely why you are not yet able to enjoy any freedom. All I want is money, and if you can satisfy my desire for that, I shall let you have anything you desire. The one thing you must never do is oppose my desire for money or thwart me in my attempts to get it. If there are times when there's something you don't want to do or someone you don't want to meet, that's perfectly all right with me, but although you may *feel* like that, you must never let your feelings show. Do as I say, and you'll have mastered the essential art of acquiring money."

Readers, Cousin Mei's advice was nothing if not perceptive, and if it were to be used as a textbook in brothels, it would soon acquire canonical status. As advice from a mother, however, it was both perverse and misguided. It was Koto's misfortune to be born into such a depraved family, one that allowed her virtually no ray of hope except in death. And at this point she did indeed resolve to die. But it wasn't yet necessary, and she merely voiced the intention, often declaring that if she weren't permitted to exist properly, she would have to end her life. Cousin Mei grew so used to hearing the threat that she ceased to take any notice of it. And one day, after she had obtained Mr. Sheng's approval, the money in the cabinet did revert to her, along with a quantity of gold and jewels that served as an engagement present. All this time she had eyes only for the money; she wasn't worried about any other developments. She also received a great deal of help from Sheng with the moving expenses. But then she began to worry that her own person was hardly a sufficient reward for Mr. Sheng, so she stifled her conscience and got Koto drunk, and in that manner the girl's purity was defiled. Poor Koto! After suffering such an appalling disgrace, how could she *fail* to end her life? Following this incident she did indeed try to kill herself, by taking poison.

Had she succeeded, my book would have come to an end at this point. But heaven feared that I would be so heartbroken over her death that I would die, too, and it dispatched the money god with the medicines needed to ensure her survival. As to Koto's state of mind at the time, I had no chance even to ask, for she wouldn't let me see her. Whenever I called, she would withdraw, from which I concluded that she was too embarrassed to see me. Then when I heard about the incident with Sheng, I came to a conclusion about her. I assumed that she had been a willing participant and decided I would no longer concern myself with her. I felt that the pleasures of family life would prove to be more enduring.

It was the beginning of summer, and my mother had excused me from school because of the oppressive heat. Only my second brother and the other boys his age continued their studies in the Cedar Room. Compared to them, I was as free as a bird in the sky, and when I looked at those other birds in their cage, I felt as happy as an immortal.

My companions were the cousin next to me in age and Little Tan. I used to love Little Tan's nature, but I now thought I knew all of her secrets and had adopted a certain contemptible attitude toward her that I couldn't quite shake off. My cousin had fallen out with me over some trifle, and she was constantly snubbing me. When I came upon her in the passageway, she would turn away rather than face me, leaving me standing there dumbfounded beside the railing, gazing after her retreating form. On one such occasion I nodded and gave a sigh. "Well, there's the power of money for you!"

Little Tan was just behind me and overheard. "And just what is *that* supposed to mean?" she asked with a smile.

"You must know why my cousin's cross with me," I said gloomily.

She laughed. "It wouldn't have anything to do with a trivial little matter of a jasmine rosette, would it?"

"You're perfectly right, a rosette is a trivial little thing, not worth very much. I had only a little money on me when I went out that day, and I used up every penny on three rosettes. I meant to give one to my mother, one to you, and the other to her. Unfortunately my younger cousin snatched the lot and ran off with them. If I'd tried to take them back from her, she would only have started squalling. As I see it, the rosettes don't have any value, but Cousin insists that I favored her younger sister over her. Can you imagine what motive I could possibly have for doing such a thing? If I'd never bought the rosettes, I couldn't have been blamed at all. I now know what a burden money can be. This is all due to the power of money."

Little Tan gave a wry smile. "What's so difficult about going back to the shop and getting her another one?"

"I offered to do that, of course, but she thought I was just trying to make her look small-minded and became even more upset. I really don't have any talent for making my motives clear to people. In fact there's no one in the whole world who understands me. And as far as other people's motives are concerned, I can only infer them from mine."

Little Tan smiled. "And are you able to infer *my* motives, then?"

I looked her in the eye and smiled. There was something on the tip of my tongue, but I was afraid it would embarrass her too much, so I suppressed it and passed her question off with a smile.

Curious as to what I might say, she had fixed her eyes on me and tilted her head to one side. When she saw that I was going to suppress my opinion and was merely grinning at her, she suspected that I was thinking certain thoughts and her cheeks flushed. Then she turned and walked off.

My readers, perceptive as ever, will understand that what I was about to say was simply this: She had the word *money* engraved upon her heart. In fact that wasn't the case with her at all. It is characteristic of the young to seize on one small insight and apply it across the board, without making any allowances whatever. This is a general human failing, of course, but it was one to which I was especially prone in my youth.

Now that my cousin was so upset with me, I felt entirely alone in the world, with no one to turn to, and so I began thinking back over the past and concluded that Secunda's treatment of me was not remotely like my cousin's. The trouble was that in those days I was a mere child and didn't know enough to respond to the love she offered me. Instead I gave my response to Koto, on the assumption that, since she and Secunda looked alike, their hearts would be alike, too. How wrong I was! And now Secunda was engaged and lived far away from me. If one day we happened to meet, our behavior would be circumscribed by convention; the old intimacy could never be restored in this life. And Koto, too, belonged to someone else. If I went to see her, I could well imagine the distant manner in which I would be received.

I did search my conscience, however. I had never had any improper intentions with regard to Koto; I looked upon her merely as a sister. The trouble was that Cousin Mei suspected me of having designs of some kind on her. But now that both of us were either married or engaged, we were on equal terms. If I continued to treat her as a sister, it stood to reason that I wouldn't be turned away. Moreover, if I never went over there, wouldn't she be entitled to accuse me of disloyalty? I considered the matter again and again from that point of view. I really had no grounds for blaming her. Girls are expected to marry, after all, and since she wasn't going to be *my* wife, what right had I to ask her to remain single? If one compared her to Secunda, well, Secunda was engaged, so why shouldn't Koto be married? By this point I was quite clear as to what I should do.

The next day I made some excuse and went out, taking Turtle with me. When we were halfway there, I told him what I had in mind. He smiled.

"You're a man of feeling and no mistake, sir. I hesitate to pour cold water on such a splendid idea, but I do hope that while you're indulging in your wine, women, and song, you'll remember what I'm about to say: A horse on the edge of a cliff can still be reined in." I laughed and nodded.

When we arrived at Koto's, Turtle knocked and went in. Cousin Mei came out to greet us, and seeing me with Turtle, smiled. "Cousin Shan, what brings you here?" I made some casual reply.

At the sound of my voice, Orchid and Jade parted the curtains and came rushing up to me, seizing my hands and asking breathlessly why I hadn't visited them in such a long time.

"Oh, I've been ill," I said by way of an excuse.

By now Turtle had drifted over toward the east wing. "Why isn't Koto here?" he asked, turning back to Cousin Mei. A moment later he answered his own question, "Oh, of course. I expect she's still on her honeymoon."

"Hold your tongue!" snapped Cousin Mei. "It's remarks like that that make her ashamed to see anyone."

"But bashfulness in a young girl only makes her more appealing," persisted Turtle. "Why won't she see us? If she won't come down, the young master and I will just have to go up there. An old fossil like me doesn't need to worry about appearances, and the young master's still too innocent. Moreover, he's a cousin of hers and should really be treated as a member of the family." He took my hand and started upstairs.

By this time Cousin Mei was shouting for Koto and also telling Jade to go up and urge her to come down. I knew she objected to our going upstairs, and reluctant as I was to incur her dislike, I found an excuse to turn aside and chat with Orchid, asking if she had seen anything of Alcyon and Aimee recently.

"Alcyon misses you and would like you to go and see her," said Orchid, giving me her address and assuring me that a visit would be greatly to my advantage. She even offered to take me there herself, at which point Cousin Mei snapped at her,

"Cousin Shan's too young! If you take him over to Alcyon's and the two of them become friends, his family will blame *us* if they hear of it!" She turned to face Turtle. "Now, you just listen to me, old fellow. I'm dead against Shan's visiting Alcyon."

"On the other hand," said Turtle, "all she cares about is money, and although the young master comes from a wealthy family, he still doesn't have any money at his disposal. I'm sure she won't fall for him."

"The way she carries on, you'd think she was a fox-spirit in human form," said Cousin Mei. "That's why I'm so concerned."

As she spoke, Jade's voice could be heard calling out, "Sister wants Cousin Shan to come up here!"

"Why doesn't she come down?" asked Cousin Mei.

"She insists on his coming up to see her."

I watched Cousin Mei's reaction. "Very well then, we'll have to trouble Cousin Shan to go up," she said. "The airs she gives herself, the little minx!"

Her words struck my ears like an imperial command. I stood up, took Orchid's hand, and urged her to come with me, hoping by that means to allay Cousin Mei's suspicions.

"I'm going to have a nice long talk with Cousin Mei," said Turtle. "You might as well do the same with Koto, sir." I smiled and said nothing, just went upstairs with Orchid.

Jade was waiting for us on the landing. As soon as she saw me, she began tugging at my lapel. "She's in a terrible state. Quick, go in and comfort her."

I left Orchid and went in to see Koto. She was leaning over the dressing table sobbing, her slip of a body as thin as a sliver of jade. I put a hand on her shoulder. "Why are you so sad?" She didn't reply, merely sobbed all the harder. I recalled the dignified demeanor she had always maintained and thought how rash it was of me to put my hand on her shoulder. I removed it and tried gentle persuasion instead.

"The fact that you won't turn and face me—I suppose that means you blame me too much. Still, although you may not understand *my* feelings, I do understand yours, I assure you."

At these words she raised her head and looked at me. Her tears glistened, dazzling the eye, and a warm flush suffused her cheeks, which were lovelier than peach blossoms after rain.

"Cousin Shan," she sobbed, choking on the words. "I really didn't want to see you today. I'm afraid I can't tell you what's troubling me."

At such a pathetic sight I felt a chill in my heart, and a peculiar ache shot through my brain and dissolved into a stream of tears down my cheeks. I tried to find words of comfort but could think of none, so I simply hid my face in my sleeve and wept. Then I remembered that Orchid and Jade were present and would surely be laughing at me, so I jerked my head around to see, but they had already gone.

Plucking up my courage, I went close to Koto and took her hand in mine. "My only wish is that you and I can be brother and sister forever and never be at odds again. In that case all my desires in this life will be fulfilled. If you care for me, you will grant me that."

"We've been like brother and sister for almost ten years, so it's not a matter of my granting you anything. But I now think of myself as already dead. What survives is only a cast-off shell, which I no longer consider part of myself. My only wish is that you will think of me as dead, too, and not pity me or miss me. That would only affect your hopes and ambitions in life."

These words ran like ice water down my spine, and my limbs froze. "That means you're thinking of me as a stranger already," I said.

She could not reply, but the tears rolled down her cheeks like beads from a broken necklace, wetting the front of her dress. Her expression suggested that she had much more to say but could not express it.

My own imagination was too feeble to comprehend even a fraction of what she felt. I reminded myself that Koto now belonged to someone else, and the hopes that she and I had cherished were naturally consigned to oblivion. Once more I searched my conscience. If I found I could not give her up and somehow contrived to make her fall in love with me, on receiving her love I might not be able to restrain myself, in which case I would be guilty of ruining her good name. With this thought uppermost in my mind, I curbed my tears and spoke gravely to her, "From now on I wish *you* would forget *me*. I can't bear the thought that the sight of me might cause you further misery. I only hope you will take good care of yourself."

She gripped my hand. "I don't suppose you will be calling on me again," she said through her tears. "And as long as I'm alive I know that I shall be too ashamed to face you. My only hope is that after I die you will shed a tear for me so that I can rest in peace."

"It breaks my heart to hear you say such things! There's nothing I can say to comfort you, except that everything that happens to us is decreed by fate, and if you insist on taking your own life, you'll be confined in the other world to the City of Wrongful Death and denied any chance of rebirth. The next existence is our only hope, and if you take your own life and cannot be reborn, we will be deprived even of that. Oh, Koto! That's all I wanted to say. If it's the same as what you wanted to tell me, then please remember what I've said and keep our pledge for the next life."

She let go of my hand and flung herself, weeping, on the bed. I couldn't bear to leave her at such a time, but there was nothing more I could say. Hesitantly I approached the bed and urged her not to grieve.

"There's nothing I can say to comfort you, either," she said. "The only reason I'm grieving is because of my own unlucky fate. 'A single slip, regret forevermore'—those words might have been written for me. I'm now my enemy's wife, and I shall have to stifle my conscience and suppress my true nature in order to avenge myself. That pure, innocent Koto whom you loved—you should consider her as dead of a draft of poison. The Koto of the future will be her wronged soul bent on violence. All my actions will be directed toward avenging myself on my enemy and will have nothing whatever to do with you. Should we meet during my last days, please remember what I am saying; it will help explain what would otherwise be impossible to understand." As she said this, her face set in harsh, cruel lines. Not knowing what she meant to do, I found myself unable to respond.

At that moment the evening bells began to toll, and a large flock of crows returned to the willows beside the house. I had to force myself to say good-bye and leave her.

As I thought over what she had told me, it seemed to me she must already have some plan in mind. But would she really take violent action against Mr. Sheng? Later, in my dream, I saw them fighting a duel with swords. As the weaker of the two, Koto suffered a wound, at which I cried out and awoke, my heart still pounding. When I had collected my thoughts, I concluded that her fury might well lead to a tragic denouement, and I couldn't rid myself of a secret feeling of dread.

A few days later I received a letter from her that began, "Dear Shan, you should know that I have today received a great deliverance . . . " I went pale with shock, assuming that the letter was a suicide note. Hastily I read on:

> In the depths of my despair the thought came to me that the only reason for my lack of freedom was, as my mother had said, the pressure of poverty. Had she had plenty of money, she would never have forced her own daughter to give up her virtue in exchange for a fortune. Had you had plenty of money, you could surely have found favor with my mother, just as Mr. Sheng did. In the light of these

facts, the ill fortune in my destiny is due to money and money alone. But "the past is gone forever, the future is ours to mold." From now on I shall devote my talents to attracting money and saving it up so that we can regain our freedom, yours as well as mine. I fully expect this decision to meet with your contempt. However, you are also a very wise person, and when you think the matter through, you will realize the truth. Bear in mind that the reputation I once had was destroyed by my mother, and that any reputation I have since acquired belongs to Mr. Sheng, for I have none of my own. Therefore I prefer to sacrifice that reputation in order to attain my final objective. Once I had made this decision, my pain and sorrow vanished. But I was afraid that you might still be feeling pain and sorrow on my account, and that is why I am writing this hasty note to reassure you. I hope that you will call on me as soon as you have some free time. You and I must sweep our grief and anguish clean away and find occasion for romantic pleasure. If we do that, we may ourselves become the gods of freedom.

For a long time after finishing this letter, I was flabbergasted. I read it aloud to myself again and again, and ended by sighing with admiration. What a tragic figure you are, Koto! But how wise, too. I don't see you for three days, and then when I do, you've turned into a heroine! My knowledge of the world is not comparable to yours, but although a bold spirit of adventure may be mandated by the law of nature, I still could not bear to ruin your good name.

I wrote the following in reply:

Your letter sheds a beam of light on the whole situation. You are the wise one, not I. Recently I, too, have come to an understanding of money. The misery that the people of the world bring upon themselves is due solely to the bedev-

*ilment of money. The fact that you have succeeded in
transforming yourself* into *the money demon is a matter
for rejoicing. I only hope that from now on you will indeed
regain your freedom and become sacred and inviolable in
your chastity. With that hope in mind, I prefer to remain
forever on brother-and-sister terms with you. I pledge not
to let you lose your reputation on my account. Should I
break this pledge, may heaven and man forsake me! Please
tell your mother what I have said, so that when I visit she
will not need to take any precautions against me, in which
case I shall gain a small measure of freedom myself.*

Koto did tell Cousin Mei of my pledge, and she laughed. "As
I told you before, so long as you do as *I* wish, I shall let you do
whatever *you* wish. There's no reason for me to keep a close eye
on him." She took the occasion of Lotus Birthday to give a
dinner and invite me over. At the dinner I found that her previous dislike for me had completely changed; she was now a
warm and gracious hostess. I was so astonished to find myself
in favor that I felt uneasy and asked Koto about it.

She laughed. "Didn't you tell me I had turned into the
money demon? Mother's likes and dislikes are in direct proportion to the money a person has. She actually worships me
as the money god, so in her eyes whatever mood I am in is inti-
mately related to money. Have you never seen poor people
praying to the money god? They think he likes the heads of
suckling pigs, so they collect and prepare the heads to get into
his good graces. These days Mother sees you as a suckling pig,
that's all. It's perfectly natural." And she gave way to a fit of
the giggles.

Cousin Mei, unaware of what Koto was thinking, continued to be solicitous of her and also of me. When I thought over
what Koto had said, I felt like laughing to myself. Cousin Mei's
behavior did seem both pathetic and ridiculous. Unbeknownst
to her, she had become a mere plaything in Koto's hands.

Koto had now purged herself of all her sorrows and vexations. She offered one toast after another, as if she were ecstatically happy. In the past, while we were in love, she was afraid of ridicule in all she did, but now, because she thought of us only as brother and sister, she was entirely at her ease. For my part I had never felt awkward in front of her family, so I thought it quite normal to be sitting down with Cousin Mei and Koto, Orchid and Jade. Only when Koto's eyes inadvertently met mine and lingered there a moment, did I feel at all embarrassed.

Cousin Mei had a generous capacity for drink and assumed that everyone else had, too, so in pouring wine for Koto and me, she filled our cups to the brim. My own capacity was nothing marvelous, but on this occasion I enjoyed the wine more and more. Koto thought her mother had given her too much and merely sipped at hers, scarcely reducing it at all, then noticed that I had drunk over half of mine and switched cups with me. "Shan's quite a drinker," she said to her mother. "Fill his up again."

Cousin Mei smiled at me. "Your cousin is trying to get you drunk. Your face is redder than hers as it is. If you're drunk when you get home, won't you get a telling off from your mother?"

I was already nervous, and when I heard her say this, I felt alarmed. I knew I wouldn't escape a thorough grilling from my mother, and I began to sweat with fear. But this cup of wine came to me as a gift from Koto, so how could I possibly refuse it? I longed to gulp it down and set off for home, but I couldn't bring myself to do so.

"This is plenty," I said. "Please don't fill it up again." When I raised the cup to my lips, I pretended that it had an unusual bouquet and a distinctive sweetness.

"Isn't this rose dew?" I asked. "Why does it taste different from what I had before?"

Koto laughed. "It's all rose dew. How could it taste any different?" She took my cup and drank from it. "Yes, yours does seem sweeter than mine."

"That bottle was empty," said Cousin Mei, "so we opened another one. I suppose it might taste a little different." She poured herself another cup and rolled the wine on her tongue. "You're perfectly right," she said.

I burst into laughter. My remark was designed solely to get Koto to taste the wine in my cup. Her mother had fallen for my ploy, too, and concluded through the power of suggestion that the wine really was different. Ridiculous!

When at last I finished my wine, Koto still had a third of hers left, but she pushed her cup away and refused to drink any more. Instead she turned to Cousin Mei and demanded some supper.

As soon as her mother left the room, I took the chance to speak to Koto. "May I change cups with you?"

"I suppose you have nothing left."

"If you let me drink yours, I'll really enjoy it." I downed it in a single gulp.

Cousin Mei offered me supper, but I was too drunk to eat. I strolled out to the central courtyard, where the moon glowed with a silvery light and the ground was covered with the shadows of flowers—a supremely romantic scene. I felt a blissful sensation pervading my entire body, and I thought back to this same day and hour ten years before, when I had held hands with Koto in the passageway as we went in to dinner at our house. I recalled, too, how she had left abruptly before the first toasts had been drunk. How strange that ten years later we should be enjoying this magnificent reunion! Clearly, so long as we remain alive, no limits can be set on our happiness. I began to wonder when Secunda and I would ever see each other again. I felt a pang of regret and, looking up at the moon, wondered how Secunda was at that very moment. If she knew

I was celebrating with Koto on such a beautiful night, would it make her happy or sad? As I mused on these matters, the servant who trimmed the lamps knocked at the door, and Turtle came in, too, and urged me to go home. I couldn't bear to part from Koto, but I was so nervous about the stern reception awaiting me that I had to leave.

When I arrived in the east courtyard, I found Little Tan leaning against the passageway railing and gazing up at the moon. She didn't see me at first. The flower shadows formed a complex pattern over her entire body. Her graceful bearing was in no way inferior to Koto's. I tiptoed up behind her and surprised her with a shout, "Ho!" Snapping out of her reverie, she turned around and saw it was me.

"Oh, it's you, sir! You gave me quite a start. I thought it was someone else."

I laughed. "You were homesick, I suppose? You thought it was that fellow of yours."

"You're crazy," she said crossly. "That sort of remark is most uncalled for! Who gave you too much to drink, anyway? How can you go in and see her ladyship with such a red face?"

I felt my cheeks—they were burning hot. I stood stock still, not knowing what to do.

"My dear Little Tan," I pleaded, "if you care for me, please think of some way for me to sober up. Otherwise I'll be nagged to death."

She ignored my request. "You'd better go and ask the person who got you drunk to sober you up," she said slowly, then went in to join my mother. I felt sure she would tell her, and equally sure that when I went to bed in my mother's room, I would be subjected to bitter recriminations that would go on all night. I regretted what I had done, but there was no way to redeem myself. I walked back and forth in the passageway, trying vainly to think of a solution.

Peeping into the room, I saw the lamp flickering and the bamboo blinds rolled down. My mother was sitting beside the window talking to Little Tan, but I was too far away to catch what they were saying. I hated Little Tan, who was no doubt at that very moment blabbing away, getting me deeper and deeper into trouble. If I went in, the tirade would start up at once, but even if I didn't, I would still have to confront my mother eventually. I turned this dilemma over and over in my mind. In the long run there was no hope of escape, so I decided to face the music now. Straightening my clothes, I walked in.

I was astonished to find my mother sitting there with a calm expression on her face. I didn't dare say a word.

"It's not wise to drink too much in hot weather," she said. "Your teacher considers you a promising boy and gives you special privileges by way of encouraging you, but you act as if it were some great honor and start drinking like a fish. That's not right for a young boy. What you have to understand is that if you get drunk and misbehave, it reflects on your mother for not bringing you up properly."

"I know," I said, not daring to add another word. I realized that Little Tan had covered up for me, but I could hardly express my gratitude at that moment. As she helped me off with my coat, my mother wasn't looking, and I pressed my palms together in a gesture of thanks. Little Tan took no notice whatsoever, merely telling me to go to bed. I then hid inside the bed curtains and bowed low before her, which made her chuckle. "Hurry up and go to sleep," she whispered. "Don't say any more, or you'll be sorry." I grasped her hand to show my gratitude, but she shook me off and walked out.

The next morning, before my mother was up, I dashed across to Little Tan's room, where I found her at the wash-basin. "Why are you up so early?" she asked.

"Thanks to you, I escaped a telling off last night. If I hadn't gotten up early this morning, I might have been unlucky enough to receive a makeup session."

She laughed. "Well, who *were* you drinking with last night?"

"Only Turtle."

She made a wry face. "Turtle would never dare get you drunk. In any case, you'd think it beneath you to go drinking with him. I know that can't be true. Very well, if you won't tell me the truth, I'll go and confess to her ladyship that what I said last night was wrong."

"No, don't do that," I said in some agitation. "Tell me, what good would it do you to see me told off?"

"I couldn't bear to see you looking so pathetic last night, so I told a lie for your sake. But now you're lying to *me*, and that's something I cannot abide."

"Then let it be whoever you want it to be."

She was drying her face at the time, and she paused with the towel at her cheek, turned to look at the expression on my face, and then said in a slow, sweet voice, "I very much doubt that there's anyone you'd allow to get you drunk. If there were, it could only be your beloved Koto."

I blushed furiously and, concluding that I could no longer deny it, I threw myself at her and tried to pinch her mouth, while she protected herself as best she could with the towel.

"Why is it that when a single word hits home, you go berserk?" she said, laughing. "Stop your fooling around! I'm not Koto, you know."

"There you go again! I shall have to pinch you."

She pushed me away from her and got up, flinging the towel down beside the dressing table and speaking in a stern voice, "You mustn't treat me the way you did when you were a child. It will only make people talk."

"Who would talk? And what would they say?"

An exasperated look passed over her face, and she hastily finished combing her hair, pushed away the mirror, and left

the room. I sat down where she had been sitting and looked at my reflection in the mirror. I hadn't changed my ways since childhood. As a child, whenever I looked in a mirror, I had to have people beside me; I would never look on my own. I didn't like mirrors, but if others were there with me, I was only too happy to sit beside them. A few years before, if I'd been looking in a mirror, Secunda, Koto, or Little Tan would have been sitting beside me, cheek to cheek, with no qualms whatsoever. But now, no matter who it was, she would be giving me a wide berth, as if I had thorns growing out of my face or as if my hands and feet were as deadly as snakes or scorpions. Had I turned into some fearsome, detestable, poisonous *reptile?* How had it happened? It was my age that was the cause of the trouble, and—dreadful thought!—I was still only sixteen! A few more years, and how would they treat me then? I pondered this problem more and more deeply, until I felt there was no more detestable creature in the world than a man. If I had been born female, the situation would have been just the reverse. Look at Little Tan. She was half as old again as I, yet I had never found her detestable. And I wasn't the only one; *nobody* found her detestable. And take the case of my mother. Wasn't she half as old again as Little Tan? And yet no one had ever found her detestable, either. I was the only one that my mother disliked, that Little Tan disliked, that even some of my cousins of about my own age often disliked, to say nothing of my sisters-in-law. Did I have some special talent for arousing dislike? I had no idea.

Just then Little Tan came by and saw me looking into the mirror and talking to myself in a ridiculous fashion, and she burst out laughing. "Who are you talking to?"

"I was just asking myself a question that I find I cannot answer. Perhaps you can help me. Why is it all of you dislike me so? Tell me frankly, and I'll do my best to change."

She chuckled. "Your knowledge hasn't kept pace with your

age, that's all it is. Recently you've become sillier than ever, and your behavior is more irresponsible now than when you were a child. Of *course* you make people dislike you!"

"All right, from now on I'm going to be responsible. If I'm not, you must do your best to correct me. If you love me, you won't let me become an object of dislike."

She laughed. "There you go again! You can't do as you did when you were a child and make demands on the basis of so-called love."

"What an odd thing to say! Is my mother being irresponsible when she says she loves me?"

At a loss for an answer, Little Tan busied herself combing my hair. I watched her in the mirror and realized that she was holding something back, so I pressed her harder. "Is what *you* mean by love something different then?"

She laughed. "I never saw such an idiot in all my born days."

"I really am an idiot, but if you're so smart, why don't you use your brains to enlighten me?"

She giggled and rapped my neck with the back of the comb. I watched her in the mirror and saw her smile. Around the eyes she reminded me strongly of Koto, to whom my thoughts now turned, my heart pounding. I wanted to visit her as soon as breakfast was over but was deterred by the thought of my mother. I waited several days and then, on the pretext of going out to do some shopping, paid Koto a visit.

Mr Sheng happened to be there. He was rather amiable, and showed not the slightest resentment when he learned that Koto and I had been childhood friends. He mentioned that he used to play the zither with my second cousin, but that after my cousin's marriage they had drifted apart.

His zither playing matched my own interests, and we held a lively discussion of technique and got along rather well. Koto gave us a look and a smile, then interjected, "Are you only talk-

ing about the zither because you don't know how to play the koto?" She evidently meant to imply that Sheng was a cultural poseur. He didn't answer her directly, just took a koto down from the wall, tuned it, and gave a rendering of "Wild Geese along the Shore" with a rhythm that neither Koto nor I could equal. Because of her dislike for the man, Koto suppressed her own talent—a patently disingenuous act. From then on, whenever Sheng and I met, we would compete at playing the zither, but Koto, who had a good voice, would never agree to sing while he was present. Only when she and I were drinking on our own and I began fingering the koto, would she sing, and then she would do so without waiting to be asked.

There were many buildings and courtyards in our compound, and I had no fixed routine to keep to. Except at mealtimes, my mother never sent for me, so I had plenty of time to visit Koto in the afternoons. Little Tan and the others were unaware of my visits, until one day something came up and I couldn't be found. The servants were questioned, but none of them had gone out with me. Turtle was the only one absent, and they all assumed that he and I had gone off together. When he returned, he realized I must be at Koto's. He felt obliged to keep my secret, but he hurried me home and issued a stern warning that he would tell my mother if ever I transgressed again. He also urged the gatekeepers to place tight restrictions on my movements. And so I languished as a prisoner in the City of Despond, while the fiery-hot days dragged on, each one as long as a year. Everything before my eyes was calculated to upset me. Even if I had tried to avoid an illness, I could not have done so.

By the time I recovered, it was the beginning of autumn, but during this whole period there was nothing of particular interest to record. As for my occasional visits to Koto, they went as might be expected, and I mention them here only in passing.

The following year my second cousin died of an illness, throwing the family administration into chaos. When my cousin and my eldest brother came to examine the books, they found them in a state of utter confusion and could make neither head nor tail of them. On checking our reserves, they found a deficit of over ten thousand taels, and everyone accused Sai'er of embezzling the money. My second cousin had no son, and Sai'er claimed that his share of the estate should go to her as his daughter, but my cousin insisted that we nominate a male heir for the deceased. At that time my eldest brother had no son, either, while my cousin did, and some of our relatives held that if the eldest had no son of his own, the eldest son of the next in line should inherit. My brother then asked how they could be sure that he wouldn't father a son himself one day.

And so a great contretemps arose, of which the ultimate solution was that *both* should inherit. It was also recommended that the property be divided. The first division was into three parts, of which each branch of the family got one. The part that my brothers and I shared was subdivided into seven sections, one to maintain the sacrifices of our branch of the family, one for my mother, one for my eldest brother, and another to be held in trust for the eldest grandson. As for the part of the property that my second cousin would have received, it was divided between my cousin and my eldest brother.

Sai'er was furious and brought suit against them both. A single change in the family had resulted in vicious conflict! The division of the property also caused bad blood between my mother and my aunt. The subdivision of our share into seven sections was not my mother's wish, either, but she was pressured into accepting it by the weight of opinion. "All four of them are my own sons," she sighed, "so why are they so generous to this one and so stingy with the others?" But we younger sons had next to no power, certainly not enough to

take on our eldest brother. My second brother did put up a bit of a fight, but he carried little weight and ended up no better off. As for me, I was utterly ignorant of such matters and paid them scant attention, as did my younger brother.

In her resentment, my mother began treating my eldest brother as if he were no longer a member of the family, and open hostility developed between them.

It was fortunate that each branch of the family had its own quarters, so no actual strife ever took place. But we had split into rival kingdoms, each of which simply removed the objects it wanted from the central hall, claiming them as its own property. Little by little all the family antiques disappeared, and nobody dared call for an explanation.

Then one or two of the shiftier characters among the servants caused trouble, and no action was taken against them, either.

There was a good deal of unrest in the neighborhood at the time, and our relatives' houses were among those targeted by thieves. Rumors circulated on the street that cat burglars were responsible. Then our next-door neighbor's house was burgled, and although a heavy loss of property resulted, no arrests were made. Any number of suggestions were put forward in our compound, and we were all on edge. But the more edgy people are, the wilder the rumors become. When cats were heard on the roof and rats in the rafters, our simpleminded young maids screamed in fright, and panic set in. Then some of the bolder servants volunteered to climb up on the roof and conduct a search, in the course of which they damaged the roof tiles, and as no reserve fund had been set aside for repairs, the roof was left to leak. If the leaks made some rooms uninhabitable, there were plenty of others, and so people simply selected their own quarters and moved in.

My eldest brother and my cousin were not socially active, so they had no need of a central reception room in which to entertain guests. Anywhere outside their doors might as well have been open country so far as they were concerned. The servants all had their own responsibilities, but nobody had been put in charge of the central rooms, not even of cleaning them. The people living upstairs took the opportunity to move down to the first floor, after which the magnificent upstairs rooms were used for storage only; if you needed something, you took a candle and went up there and looked for it. Apart from that, the rooms were given over to the fox-spirits and ghosts that seized on this evidence of family decline to make their appearance. Maids spread rumors, which they swore were true beyond the shadow of a doubt, and none of our precious family ventured upstairs, while our precious possessions disappeared one after the other. When a loss was discovered, it was impossible to determine when the theft had occurred, so the day of its discovery was reported instead. Once the authorities had carried out an on-the-spot investigation, they considered they had done everything humanly possible, so no case was ever solved. Among the servants, however, certain charges were sometimes leveled in secret. The victims of burglary in one house would say that the people in another house were the prime suspects, and when that house suffered a loss, they would say the same about the first one. Each accused the other, without regard for evidence, and animosities developed even on that level.

In the past the one who exercised power in the household was Old Cai, otherwise known as Turtle, but my mother had put him in charge of my younger brother and me, and with the exception of the school pages, none of the other servants reported to him. His authority had vanished, and the other servants got even for past slights by making fun of him. Turtle sighed. "I never thought money would bedevil us to this extent," he said, and retired on the grounds of ill health.

The family school had been closed down, but my mother

engaged a tutor to give lessons to her three younger sons in Spring Bark.

Before long, discussions began on how to divide up the estate. The compound couldn't be arbitrarily assigned to any one person, so it was sold at auction and the proceeds allocated as before: My cousin got half; my eldest brother a third; and my mother, my two other brothers, and I the remaining sixth. My mother was bitterly upset and sobbed aloud, but her hopes were pinned firmly on the future, and she dinned it into us that we should work hard at our studies.

She arranged my wedding for the ninth month. My wife, Susu, was a year older than I and every bit as naive as I was. Her interests were mainly literary, a severe disappointment to my mother, who remarked to Little Tan, "I never expected Shan's wife to be such a beauty, but her looks are the *only* thing to be said for her. She could never take charge of the household." As a result of the marriage I, too, gradually lost favor with my mother.

Each month Mother allowed me a stipend of only ten taels, from which I had to pay the wages of a maid and a serving woman. Fortunately my wife had no extravagant tastes, and we were never short of funds for our daily needs. And the pleasures of the bedchamber were enjoyable as always. But our situation was immeasurably inferior to my eldest brother's. He and my cousin had each brought a courtesan home from Shanghai, and peals of merry laughter were often to be heard issuing from these charming creatures. But the sound of quarreling was also to be heard, and I was reminded of Turtle's prophetic remarks: Money was up to its usual mischief.

By the beginning of winter my cousin had bought a new house, and my eldest brother had rented a spare property belonging to his wife's family. My second brother and I found a place called One Grain Garden at the foot of Mount Ziyang that offered magnificent views of the hills and woods, and we asked Mother to put up a mortgage of five thousand taels. There were five courtyards, and the only residents were my mother, my second brother and his wife, my wife and I, and my younger brother—no more than a dozen people in all, including servants and maids.

It was a refreshing change of scene. The courtyard that faced south had a hill as a backdrop. The ancient trees on top of the hill were a good two arm spans in circumference and afforded dense shade in spring and summer. Gnarled plum trees surrounded the base, and when they were in bloom, their interlacing branches almost thrust their way inside our windows. On the right side, facing a pond, was a pavilion, from which a small passageway led behind the courtyard. To the left was a spur of the lake hills, in which steps had been cut for climbers, and from the top of the spur the sails of the boats on the Qiantang River were clearly visible. In the other direction you could see Mount Wu's soaring emerald mass, against which the magnificent towers and temples were arrayed as if on a screen. I named the spur One Chamber Hill and set up my study there, my sole companions being my parrot and my wife. I thought of it as a private retreat in which I could live in seclusion from the world's affairs. How wrong I was!

The next year my mother decreed that it was a mistake for us not to work for a living; we should all resolve to make ourselves financially independent. She packed my second brother off to Haining as staff adviser to the subprefect and told me to go along, too, as a trainee. I was most reluctant to go, and by feigning an illness managed to get off. My younger brother, who had married a girl from Pingyang, joined the firm her family had set up and learned the business. And my second brother's wife, who had a daughter, was always taking the child home to please her mother.

That left only three of us—my mother, my wife, and I—

and with no one but ourselves for company, we soon became bored. My mother's melancholy cast of thought now took on a frightening aspect. She found everything offensive, no matter what it was. Our talk, our laughter, the slightest thing we did, would set her trembling. Her looks were those of an elderly woman, but she was actually more nervous than a child on its first day at school.

Little Tan was the only one who enjoyed her confidence, increasingly so, and it was to her that all our financial dealings were entrusted. My second brother hardly qualified as a financial adviser, to say nothing of my younger brother and me. Since we had more rooms than we needed, Little Tan began renting them out to tenants. And so the studio I had named One Chamber Hill ceased to be mine. I was left with the pavilion facing the pond.

The family with whom we shared our compound were the Lings. Mrs. Ling was a gifted poet, who became close friends with my wife. Their two sons were much the same age as I, and we wrote poetry and drank wine together and got along rather well.

The following year Mr. Ling was about to set off for Xiangxi[21] as commissioner of customs, when he invited me to join him as his secretary. I was extremely reluctant to leave my wife for any length of time, but under orders from my mother I couldn't refuse. So on the first of the second month I hastily packed up and set off. I had never in all my life spent so much as a day away from home, and my misery on this occasion was more than can be put into words; I was in the depths of despair. No longer could I spend my days and nights with my wife. I even ceased to daydream about Koto.

In fact the family income at the time was still over three thousand taels a year. Even if we had chosen not to work, we would never have had to worry about going short. But my mother believed that if you didn't worry about the long term, you'd be forced to worry in the short term, and she kept on at us untiringly, fearful that one day we would come to the end of the road. My second brother had a name for her: a latter-day Man of Qi.[22] But at that time I paid little or no attention to the family finances. My mother had given the order, and who was I to disobey?

From Xiangxi I sent my first wages back to her, a gesture that only made her laugh. "I don't need *this* to keep myself in goodies! My only wish was that the boy should pick up a little experience." She handed the money to my wife, who had no need of it, either, but kept it for me, as she explained in a letter:

> Since you managed to earn a little money, your mother has reduced the volume of her criticism, and now because of this gift, she has even shown me some affection. I owe it all to you. But I cannot bear to use your hard-earned wages to keep myself in idleness. You have all the hardship of being away from home, and you must see that you take good care of yourself. Since your mother doesn't need the money, and I have nothing to spend it on, please don't send us any more; it will only remind me of how much I miss you and make me feel even more depressed. With what you sent, I have bought some food for you. Do see that you get more to eat. This has upset me for days and turned my gratitude into grief.

In Xiangxi I was well treated by my superior. The house I lived in, although only a cottage with a thatched roof, was delightfully secluded. Outside my window were five or six weeping willows. A river wound its way past the cottage, and boats went back and forth, the plash of their oars continuing all day long. The other side of the river was ringed with pleasant hills, and the cottages along the shore looked as if they belonged in a painting.

I replaced the paper window panes with glass, laid mats down on the floor, put up curtains to keep out the draft, and placed a low table near the window. At times the shimmering light reflected off the water would strike me as I sat there, and I would feel that everything in front of my eyes was the stuff of poetry. I did write many poems, but all of them were full of nostalgia for home and loved ones; none had any reference to the scene before my eyes. Each day I would copy out the poems I had composed and send them to my wife, who often replied with matching poems. It was a way of passing the time while away from home.

Corresponding with Koto was extremely difficult. My letters were bound to fall into Sheng's hands, so there was virtually nothing I could say. I would pick up my brush, only to find that I couldn't express my feelings. All I could do was repeat the usual banalities and try to convey my message between the lines. As her replies were generally of the same kind, there is nothing for me to relate.

I didn't need my monthly salary to support my family, and there was nothing else to spend it on, although I did send some food home to my family and to Koto. Sometimes Koto also sent me gifts, the ones I treasured most being a pillow slip embroidered with butterflies and some recent snapshots. To receive such gifts while away from home was enough to inspire thoughts of love, and so whenever I was sitting alone, my thoughts would be occupied by Koto or my wife, and in my dreams my soul would be haunting either Koto House or One Grain Garden. I had never much cared for a siesta, but now, if I had no business in the middle of the day, I would drink to get a little high and then look forward to a pleasant dream.

Unfortunately, the men in the agency took advantage of my lack of supervision to get into a great deal of mischief. Boats passing through the checkpoint would be inspected but not required to pay a toll; after a little money had changed hands, they would simply be waved through. This policy met with the approval of the merchants, of course, but it worried my superior no end.

"I know that you come from a wealthy family and think such petty sums beneath your notice," he told me, "but those petty sums just happen to be my main reason for coming here. If we go on like this, I'll never be able to recoup the money I paid out to get this job." To my embarrassment and chagrin he went on to list the various corrupt practices my colleagues were engaged in.

"I never realized that what you call corruption existed," I said. "I'm not personally capable of it, so I couldn't detect others doing it. I would like to point out that I'm only able to infer other people's feelings from my own, and since I've never felt that particular desire myself, I could never have suspected anyone else of it. Besides, sir, if you knew they were so corrupt, why didn't you fire them?"

He heaved a sigh. "A customs checkpoint is always a hotbed of corruption. Get rid of these men, and their replacements will be just as bad. You can't root it out. Only with close supervision will the system work—after a fashion."

I smiled. "Since it can't be rooted out, even close supervision won't help. However, since those are your orders, sir, I'll do my duty as a loyal member of your staff. From now on I shall give up my siesta."

"I'm greatly obliged."

From then on I devoted all my energies to my supervisory duties—and the men in the agency found themselves in trouble. The next month's audit showed that the tolls we had collected were indeed up over the previous month, which brought a smile to my superior's face. "How did you do it?" he asked, as he awarded me 20 percent of the increase as a bonus.

Toward the men, however, I felt terribly apologetic. In a sense all I had done was take money out of their pockets and award it to myself. Although my superior gave out differential bonuses to all of them, mine still seemed excessive to me. That was why, whenever I went out drinking with them, I would insist on playing the host, until gradually it became the accepted thing. If I wasn't planning to go drinking, they would cajole me into doing so. I may have received more than my share of the money, but I was never stingy with it.

There was only one decent place to eat in town, the Fragrance of Virtue. The cooking was poor at first, but I taught them how to prepare some of my favorite dishes, and gradually the food became quite palatable. I went there every evening with my colleagues. Most of the patrons knew me. They knew, too, how free I was with my money and nicknamed me Lord Mengchang the Younger,[23] which is exactly how I thought of myself. I always bought drinks for anyone who greeted me—the waiters wouldn't have dreamed of taking anyone else's money. In this manner, conscientious though I was in carrying out my duties, I never became the focus of the men's resentment.

Xiangxi was a tea-growing center. It was now the third month, and the girl tea pickers were at work in all the villages. Whenever I visited a village, everybody knew me. At the time I favored rather outré clothing and fancied myself as a dandy —a rare bird in those parts.

Just as the tea market was about to open, someone asked my superior to change to the promissory method of paying taxes, which he declined to do. This fellow then incited the other dealers not to open for business on the regular date. On the first of the fourth month the villagers, following their traditional practice, started bringing their loads of tea to market —only to find it closed for business. The firms then issued a statement: "This year we had an agreement to switch to a promissory method for the payment of taxes, but the new superintendent refuses to honor it. For that reason we decline to do business here. Those of you who wish to barter your tea for rice should take it over to the customs officials."

A great commotion then arose among the crowd, who swarmed over to my superior's quarters and almost erupted into violence. At this point my modest expenditure of money came into play and revealed its magical powers. As a wining and dining companion of most of the dealers, I played the role of Lu Zhonglian[24] and held repeated discussions with them. Fortunately we managed to settle the dispute, and the boycott was lifted. If credit were to be given where credit was due, it would go to cold cash and hard liquor.

This episode brought me even closer to the buyers. From time to time I visited them at their work and acted just as they did. Sometimes I even bought tea directly from the girl tea pickers, among whom I found one genuine beauty.

There was a girl named Alian who looked the image of Secunda about the eyes. Every day she would come to market with her elderly mother, carrying a basket of tea to be weighed. The buyers' usual practice was to wait until the arm of the scales rose to a forty-five degree angle, but in her case they accepted a horizontal arm, no doubt as a way of showing their appreciation. Her demeanor, however, was always quite dignified, and she simply ignored the buyers who tried to engage her in a little decorous banter. I imagine she could have retorted in kind had she wanted to. The fact that she didn't was presumably because she knew that the frivolous young men responsible, having once gotten a rise out of her, would only have roared with laughter, and the exchange would have gone on forever. I knew the way her mind worked and wouldn't have dreamed of speaking to her without some good reason. Not that I didn't have things I wanted to ask her; I did, but I feared the embarrassment of asking and getting no reply, so I confined myself to greeting her with a glance as she approached and gazing after her as she departed.

Then for three days she failed to appear, and the buyers asked her mother why. "She's sick," said her mother. The buyers asked about the treatment. "Oh, I just pray in General Fan's Temple and then do whatever the magical prescription says."

I couldn't help interjecting, "But you can't rely on magical prescriptions!"

I was fully prepared to volunteer my own services, because my wife was in delicate health and I had studied some medicine myself, but the old woman completely misunderstood me. Calling on Buddha's name, she muttered, "A mortal sin! A mortal sin! The general's magic works *wonders!* Those who take his name in vain will be struck with an instant bellyache. You'd better rush over to his temple this minute and pray for forgiveness, and perhaps he'll let you off."

As I doubled up with laughter, she took herself off, but a few days later I was surprised to find her back at the market soliciting contributions, a tragic look on her face. As soon as the buyers caught sight of me, they began to reassure her, "Here comes Lord Mengchang. He'll help."

I asked what the trouble was, and the old woman, with tears in her eyes, answered in a quavering voice, "Alian's dead!" Although I hadn't the slightest attachment to the girl, I went pale with grief.

"Poor old thing," said the buyers. "She doesn't have the money for a coffin, so she's asking for contributions."

"What a pity my poor girl's wretched life should end like this!" she said. "Sixteen years I raised her, and now she's gone. She was engaged, too, but the man's father won't recognize her anymore as his daughter-in-law, so I'm begging for a coffin to lay her in. They say that people you beg coffins for have to turn into dogs or horses in the next life to repay those who helped them. Oh, my poor girl! I don't know how many dogs and horses you'll have to turn into to repay all these people. When I think of that, I don't want to beg, but I can't bear to give her a pauper's burial, so I really have no choice."

Tears came into my eyes as I listened. I asked how much she needed. "We've contributed one tael each," said the buyers, "and the dealers have given two. She has eight taels already. If you give half that amount, she should have enough."

"But that's such a piffling sum! It'll never be enough for a funeral," I said. "What you've given her should cover the paper money. If I give her all the cash I have on hand, it'll come to about fifty taels. Would that do for a coffin and a shroud?"

One of the buyers tugged at my sleeve and drew me into the inner room. "You certainly do things in style," he said with a grin. "But you don't need to give *that* much. Give her ten taels—that's plenty."

"But I've already given her my word! I can't go back on it! If you trust me, lend me the sum I mentioned. Otherwise I'll take her over to the house and get it for her."

The buyers shook their heads, grinning derisively, but they opened their chests and counted out the money, at the same time reiterating their advice about reducing my contribution. I took no notice of them.

When I gave the money to the old woman, she kowtowed before me, tears of gratitude running down her cheeks, and assured me that if Alian knew of my generosity she would certainly turn into a dog or a horse to repay me. That made me feel even more embarrassed, and I stammered so badly that I couldn't reply. It wasn't any kind of quixotic gallantry that inspired me, just the thought that in my family a coffin would cost several hundred taels. Even for the meanest, cheapest sort of funeral a dozen taels would not be sufficient to lay someone to rest, let alone someone as charming as Alian. How could one bear to send her off in a flimsy coffin and coarse winding sheet to seethe with resentment in the other world? To me, my salary was nothing more than a windfall, something for which I had no real need, and I was quite content to offer it to her.

Oddly enough, however, because of this gift rumors began to circulate, and some people claimed that Alian was my mistress. Poor Alian! It wasn't that I didn't love her, but she was dead, that pure, innocent young girl, and because of my paltry sum of money she had been burdened in death with a calumny she could never clear herself of. My own reputation was none the worse for it, but I had long seen myself as a sort of Liuxia Hui, and how could I explain to myself the deep uneasiness that I felt? It was the bedevilment of money, nothing more.

I lapsed into a depression in which I felt an infinite remorse before Alian's spirit in heaven. I often saw her in my dreams, frowning and glowering as if she had a deep hatred for me—although she was always beautifully dressed and looked more elegant and graceful than ever. In the confusion of one of my dreams she was suddenly transformed into Secunda, but when I went up to her and took her hand, she was transformed again, this time into Koto. The balance of my mind became disturbed, and inevitably I fell ill. A letter arrived from my wife, which I failed to answer for five days, because whenever I took up my brush I had a dizzy spell and couldn't write. After a few more days someone came to see me—Little Tan's husband. He had arrived in Hangzhou to persuade Little Tan to go back with him, and my mother had sent him here to check on me. As a child I used to call him Toad. I suppose I must have been imitating Little Tan in giving him that particular honorific, but his looks did indeed suggest a toad. Now, however, when he suddenly showed up to see me, I was too embarrassed to use the word in front of all the others and merely welcomed him with a smile and a nod.

When Toad saw I really was sick, his eyes opened wide and he croaked, "Oh, but you're so thin!"

Hearing that voice and looking at his face, I was reminded of his nickname and burst out laughing. "Who sent you?" I asked. "What really brings you here?"

He told me at inordinate length. My second brother, who had just returned home, had asked my mother if I could go with him to take the examinations. I had already been twice, without success, and had no desire to repeat the experience, but I was quite prepared to use this as an excuse to get home. My superior agreed to give me leave.

Small boats were all they had for hire in Xiangxi; otherwise you took the packet. I was hoping to find a boat like the one I came on, but none was available, probably because the river was too narrow and the bridges too low. That boat had had to lower its mast, and even so it had barely squeaked under the bridges, giving the locals their only glimpse of a Wuxi pleasure boat. How could I hope to find another one like it?

I detested the rolling and pitching of the little boats—enough to make one dizzy at the best of times, and in my present state of health even harder to bear. But there was nothing else I could do, so I packed my clothes and went aboard. The cabin was low and cramped, sufficient to sour anyone's temper right off, but fortunately I had Toad there with me. He had an engaging personality, he loved telling jokes, and he liked his wine, much like Turtle, except that his experience was no match for Turtle's. Along the way he regaled me with hilarious anecdotes about Xu Wei,[25] and my health improved a little. When drunk, he would launch into fascinating accounts of his life. As children he and Little Tan had been neighbors in the same village, and at first they had mixed freely without any inhibitions whatever. Little Tan was an only child, and her mother was in poor health, so Toad did the chores for them, and he and Little Tan became like two brothers. She wasn't put off by his looks, either. In any case, to hear Toad tell it, he was quite dashing in his youth, and it was only in his thirties that he suddenly developed a pot belly and bulging eyes—a story I didn't believe for a moment. At night he snored like a lowing ox. I tried to imagine what life was like for Little Tan, and I couldn't understand how she put up with it. I came to the conclusion that when love is deep and perfect enough, it doesn't concern itself with externals. At the outset their situation was much like Koto's and mine, but they had managed to become a happily married couple, so they must have been blessed with a good portion of plain luck. They may have forged some kind of karmic bond in a previous life—like Alian and me, perhaps?

From this thought I moved on into dream. I had a confused vision of Alian, transformed now into a fairy creature, whispering endless endearments in my ear, telling me that she was about to be reborn and live out the destiny of a Jade Flute.[26] It was dawn, the sails had been unfurled to the wind, and the waves were lapping at the bow. I felt adrift in clouds and mist—until I heard a sudden grating sound beneath the boat and my rapturous soul was startled from its dream by the fish weir we had just scraped over. When I had focused my thoughts, I couldn't help laughing at my sentimental folly. Now that Koto clearly belonged to someone else, was I pinning my hopes on Alian in the world of shades? Then I saw Toad squatting in the bow and scooping up water to wash his face in, and my thoughts turned to Little Tan, who was about to return home with him. Of all the girls I knew, only Susu could stay with me forever, just as Little Tan had predicted. But my love for Susu was by no means exclusive; it extended to other girls as well. Although Susu didn't consider me unfaithful, I felt I could not absolve myself of such a charge. My heart seemed to revolve in a perpetual cycle, with Secunda, Koto, and Little Tan also turning and turning within it, and each of them, Secunda, Koto, Little Tan, and Susu, was, I felt, entitled to regard me as unfaithful. Sadly, the fact that they didn't meant only that I had deceived them with my affection. All those in this world who receive the deepest affection feel the desire to respond to it. These girls' desire to respond had increased their affection, which they had then applied to me, and I in turn now felt the desire to respond to their response. My feelings were growing ever more intense and the karmic consequences were becoming ever more severe—a process that would go on, life after life, without end. Because of that extensive love of mine, I had acquired a boundless sense of unfulfilled desire, a desire that I attributed to karma from my previous life. In that case, how could I possibly justify sowing even more karmic seed in this life? As I pursued these thoughts, I felt my mind becoming devoid of feeling, unclouded by desire. Another moment, however, and I would be plunged once more into the river of love, the sea of passion.

Part 2

It was toward evening when we joined the Canal at Gua-shan,[1] which not long before had been opened up to foreign trade. There was music and singing along both banks, and a forest of lanterns cast their light on the dark waters, which seemed alive with thousands of writhing golden serpents. Many young men and women from the city had hired boats to come out and enjoy the revelry. There were rows upon rows of their boats, wedged tightly along both banks, and the gentle breath of conversation mingled with the scent of flowers to drift up and form a light haze overhead, dulling the brilliance of the moon.

Toad took one glance and was enthralled. "Why not step ashore, sir, and have a look around?" he urged. Having no feeling one way or the other, I went with him. As we passed the gates of the silk factory, we heard the roar of the looms and I thought of all the girls inside who faced such hardship and wondered how depressed they must be. The roar was like a rumble of thunder out of a lowering sky.

In those days the First Spring Restaurant, serving Western food, was still situated on the west bank, and it was there that Toad took me. It was packed with gaily dressed and elaborately coiffed women, and scarcely a seat was to be had, but it turned out that one of the waiters had been a servant of ours, and he spotted me and went out of his way to help, leading me to a private dining room with a table big enough to seat a dozen people. Two guests, neither of whom I knew, occupied one corner of it. I had always disliked sharing a table with strangers, but at this point I had no choice, so I took the corner farthest away from them and ordered for myself, sending Toad off to drink in the anteroom. I hadn't intended to drink alone, but again I had no choice. I ordered a couple of dishes and a glass of brandy. To put myself in the mood for drinking, I strained to catch the singing from the next room. However, the other two guests had their heads together and were staring at me in such a ridiculous fashion that I was quite put off. I was about to push my glass away, when I heard a burst of shouting and laughter from behind me, and the two men began a prolonged clapping to welcome some new arrivals. A bevy of maids appeared escorting three or four beauties. From a distance they looked like goddesses, but when they passed directly in front of me, my eyes functioned like an exorcist's mirror, for the women's ugliness could no longer be concealed. In fact the makeup they wore served only to accentuate it.

The two guests, however, were in raptures. Every time they cracked a joke with the women, they glanced triumphantly at me, prompting me to give a disdainful sneer in return. By this time I had lost any interest in food and drink, and I called Toad in to clear away the dishes.

He was aghast. "Such a glorious spread, and you haven't even touched it!" he exclaimed.

"I'll only throw up if I try to eat it," I said with a laugh. "If you want to take my place and finish it up at your leisure, you're welcome. I'll wait for you back at the boat."

Toad took in the scene with ravenous eyes, first the food and drink and then the women. "This must be what they mean by a feast fit for the gods!" he said with a sly smile. I chuckled, but the other guests and their women roared with laughter, at which point I swept out of the room.

On my way back to the boat, I tried to imagine Toad's situation and couldn't help laughing to myself. He was just like a clown in a play, reveling in his newfound glory, toasting everyone in sight, and revealing a whole array of comical pretensions.

When I returned, I found the boat covered in moonlight as white as snow. It was a quiet, lonely scene. The boatman brought me in some tea, and as I leaned out of the cabin window and looked up at the moon, I felt perfectly at ease with myself. Then I noticed someone on the boat next to ours opening the window and also leaning out. I could see that it was a girl of extremely attractive appearance with a gleaming black swirl of hair, but unfortunately she had the moon behind her and I didn't get a clear view. To my astonishment I heard her call out, "Isn't that Cousin Shan?"

I was overcome with surprise and joy. "You must be Cousin Koto!"

She gurgled with laughter—and her laugh was quite different from Koto's. I felt like sinking into the ground. By the time I had turned and found a lantern to shine on her, she had vanished. I was still searching for her outside the window, when I felt a tap on my shoulder and heard someone say with a laugh, "I always knew there was no place in your heart for anyone but Koto!"

I turned and found it was Alcyon, whom I hadn't seen in three years. "I never expected to meet you here," I said with a smile, setting the lantern down on the table. "Who did you come with?"

"None of your business," she said. "What I want to know is whether you're going to let me join you for a little tête-à-tête?"

"Marvelous! Just what I was going to suggest. Of course

you may! I was merely wondering if there was someone outside who might not approve."

She smiled. "I'm not Koto, you know. I don't have anyone
in charge of me. Oh, Shan, when I heard that she had actually
married Sheng, I felt she had been *so* unfair to you."

"Isn't that a case of 'If the spring breeze ruffles the water /
It's no concern of yours'?"[2]

"Let me sit down and I'll tell you. Koto is undoubtedly
smarter than the rest of us, but she's also more foolish. She
took Aimee's experience to heart, and that's why she gave up
any thought of marriage to you."

I was mystified. "Why, what happened to Aimee?"

"You mean you don't *know*?" She paused for a moment,
then went on. "Oh, I suppose it's not so surprising. In the last
ten years you've met her only once, rather briefly, at Koto's
place, and unless Koto told you herself, you could hardly be
expected to know. Still, it's something you ought to know
about. But if you want me to tell you, you'll have to offer me
a drink first."

"Ask me for a drink, by all means," I said with a laugh, "but
you don't have to give me this rigmarole in order to get it."

"Does that mean you're not going to offer me one?"

"I was just feeling like a drink myself. This moon and your
company—why, it's the perfect occasion!" I sent the boatman
off for some wine.

Alcyon leaned out of the window and looked at the moon's
reflection in the water, maintaining a deliberate silence.
"What's that swimming over there?" she suddenly called out.

I went and stood beside her and looked, but saw nothing.
We were leaning out of the window together when she turned
her face toward me and gave me an enchanting smile. Her
perfume stole into my heart, and at the sight of her, with her
melting eyes and cheeks suffused with color, my heart began

to pound. But then I recalled what Cousin Mei had said about her and I told myself, She's nothing but a fox-spirit in human form, and the memory helped me to see her behavior as contemptible.

"You're just putting me on, I know that," I said with a smile.

"I must tell you what really happened with Aimee," she replied. "Five years ago she married a Mr. Du as his concubine. At first she thought everything was perfect, but after a few months Mr. Du fell in love with his wife all over again and began regarding Aimee as de trop. Put yourself in her place and you can easily imagine what she went through. If he hadn't died, she'd have spent the rest of her life trapped in that dreadful situation. How could she ever have regained her freedom? So Koto took Aimee's experience to heart and declined to become *anyone's* concubine. That's the sole reason why, despite her love for you, she wasn't willing to marry you. However, Mr. Sheng isn't unattached himself, any more than you are. When he told people he had lost his wife, it was just a trick on his part. I warned Koto about him ages ago, but she wouldn't listen, and now, of course, it's too late."

"But she had no *choice* where he was concerned!"

She made a face. "People can be forced into anything at all except that," she said. "Unless both parties are willing, they definitely can't be forced to do *that*."

"Look here, Alcyon," I protested, "you don't see Koto very often, so it's hardly surprising you don't know how she feels."

"Excuse *me!* Unless they loved each other, they could hardly have had a baby together, could they?"

"How do you know that?"

"It's just arrived. You're the only one who's been kept in the dark."

"When was this?"

"You're still in time for the Third Day celebration,[3] if you want to go. But there's one thing I have to impress on you. Whatever you do, don't let on that I told you. She's desperately ashamed of herself and doesn't want anyone to know, especially you."

Only half convinced, I replied, "Even if it's true, it's all perfectly proper, you know. Why does it have to be hushed up? Anyway, you can hardly keep a baby out of sight! Is it a boy or a girl? Does it look as pretty as its mother?"

Alcyon grinned. "You're taking it all so calmly! I know! Perhaps the little girl's your love child!"

I flew into a rage. "What kind of person do you take me for! That's an insult! What's more, it could lead to Koto's death!"

"What an extraordinary thing to say! She's not *really* married, and so nobody's in a position to put her to death. So far as I can see, the only thing that could possibly lead to her death would be condemnation coming from you."

"What right would *I* have to condemn her? We're only cousins, after all."

"Oh, yes, indeed! And you and I are also cousins of a sort. How do I differ from her?"

"I don't make any distinction between you, I assure you."

Alcyon gave a cynical smile, and her eyes gazed directly into mine and remained there without wavering. Still at a loss for a reply, I heard a thump from the bow of the boat—the boatman was back with the wine and refreshments. I wiped the table clean and brought out cups and chopsticks, then invited Alcyon to join me.

"I think I'll send a boat for Koto, so that she can come and join you," she said in a sarcastic tone, and walked slowly out of the cabin.

I ought to have begged her to stay, but I was deeply offended by her rudeness, and in my resentment I simply let her go and poured myself a drink, calling after her, "I can drink by myself, you know! If you're so upset, kindly ignore me the next time you see me. You'll save me a lot of pointless anxiety, and we'll both be better off."

There was no reply. By that time she must have reached her own boat.

When I consulted my conscience, however, I couldn't help hating myself for what I had just said. In fairness to Alcyon, every word she had uttered was meant for my own good. Her love for me could equally well be described as deep and sincere, but because of my love and respect for Koto, I hadn't hesitated to quarrel with her, and from now on there would be one more person who thought of me as heartless. Oh, Alcyon, it isn't that I have no feeling for you. It's just that I am caught up in the snares of love and trying vainly to extricate myself. How could I bear to shackle you with the same bonds that shackle me?

In the midst of these thoughts, I noticed that the wine jug was empty. I was just thinking of getting some more when Toad returned, royally drunk. The way he staggered on board was hilarious, and when he gave me an account of the goings-on in the restaurant, he gesticulated so violently that the whole boat shook. He never could hold his liquor, and now he forcefully disgorged it overboard to the accompaniment of a series of truly revolting noises. I myself was full of frustration and anxiety, which welled up inside me together with the wine I had drunk and then were churned by the motion of the boat until I, too, had to lean out of the cabin window and vomit. Once rid of my nausea, I flopped face down on the bunk and lost consciousness.

When I came to my senses, the boat had already made its way unsteadily into the city. I had a vague memory of someone covering me with a quilt during the night while I was drunk and also giving me some cardamom to take, an act of tender concern that suggested Susu, although my visitor had borne a closer resemblance to Koto. Was it all a dream, I wondered. But a cardamom shell lay beside my pillow, clear evidence to the contrary. The only possible conclusion, one that the boatman confirmed, was that Alcyon had come back during the night.

This led me to reflect on how touching her affection really was. In an attempt to deduce her motives, I asked myself what feeling existed between us. Her love for me sprang from her fascination with the love that I had for Koto, which she wanted to snatch away for herself. But if I *were* to love you, Alcyon, what conceivable good would it do you? I wrestled with that question but couldn't for the life of me imagine what it was she was after. Surely she didn't want to bestow on me her own most precious gift of love in exchange for something from me? All over the world a girl's virtue is considered her most precious possession, and the girl herself regards it as the most valuable gift she can bestow in return for something given to her. When you've reached the top, you can go no higher. In that case, what matching gift *could* she be hoping for? Generally speaking, a man's virtue is of little or no value, and as far as his love is concerned, every woman gets that from the most ordinary of admirers and comes to think of it as commonplace. The objects that would make appropriate return gifts must be things that we men have but women lack.

Only by offering a woman something she needs are you able to bring her pleasure. But generally speaking, the one thing she needs above all else in this world is money. Ah, Money! Are *you*, then, the price of love? And Love! Money may not be your motive, but in practice you will never escape its control. Let me put other people aside for the moment and take the case of my own Susu. What she hoped for from marriage was nothing less than money. If she and I were beggars in the marketplace, helpless victims of hunger and cold, sleeping in abandoned shacks and old tombs, our hair matted with sweat and our faces caked with grime, peering at each other through a veil of tears, could one still say that any sort of love existed between us? On the other hand, if we did sink into such a state, even if we died of hunger and cold in each other's arms, one could hardly deny that it was love. The only difference is that love accompanied by money is blissful, while love deprived of money is tragic. In Aimee's case, she left the marriage after Mr. Du's death and transferred the love she had felt for him to some other man. If you seek her motivation, it has to be attributed to money. Since Alcyon and Koto were in the same situation as Aimee, it was also possible to infer from this instance the way *their* minds worked. My relationship with Koto had lasted a dozen years, and although money had never been involved, it could in the end deprive me of her love. All of which emboldens me to offer a word of advice to people all over the world: True love can exist only in the *absence* of money. Only if we lived in an age with no use for money would we know true love. Taking this argument a step further, we can see that money may bedevil love just as love may bedevil money.

I was squatting on my bunk like a Buddhist priest in meditation, when all of a sudden a shaft of love's magic split the heavens and entered the cabin. Through the window I glimpsed several clusters of willows and the corner of a tall house whose glass windowpanes reflected the morning sun in a riot of colors. A girl was emptying a washbasin out of an upstairs window, and the water cascaded downward in a silvery stream that transformed itself into a curtain of crystal. I was more than familiar with that house, but this was the first time I had seen it from the water. My long-cherished dream was at last to be realized, for this was what I knew as Koto House.

Gradually the boat drew nearer, until I could make out who the girl was—Jade. At first she didn't see me, although her eyes were focused on our little boat bobbing in the waves, probably because it was the only one out on the lake at the time. When I waved to attract her attention, she seemed surprised and excited. After taking the basin inside, she emerged a moment later with a telescope, which she leveled at me. I made an ugly face to scare her, and suddenly she went in again and did not reappear. As the boat approached the shore and tied up near the willows, a faint breeze from the east filtered through the window. I told Toad to pack up our bags and take them home, explaining that I had some shopping to do and would be along later. Off he went, suspecting nothing.

I stepped ashore and made my way through the willows. Jade had been waiting for some time by the shore, and she threw herself into my arms, seizing my lapels and grasping my hands. "I just knew I was right and that it was you!"

I, too, felt an unexpected joy as I grasped her hand and patted her shoulder. "You really must love me—you didn't even take the time to do your hair! Your sister's still in bed, I suppose?"

"Yes. She's not well."

"Who isn't?"

"Koto. She's been sick a long time."

As she told me this, we arrived at the entrance. The gate was unlocked and, holding hands with Jade, I went in. Cousin Mei was busy at her ablutions in the east wing. When she saw me come in, she smiled. "So you *are* back, Shan! I thought it was more of Jade's nonsense. It's really sweltering today. Do take your coat off. Jade, go and get your cousin some tea."

"It doesn't look as if he's done his hair this morning," she went on. "Tell Orchid to come and do it for him."

Orchid had already come in, doubled up with laughter. She grasped my hands but was still giggling too hard to speak.

"Stupid girl!" said Cousin Mei sharply. "To get so carried away."

116   The Money Demon

"Jade said she saw someone in a boat who looked the image of Shan," said Orchid. "She fetched the telescope, but got such a fright she started screaming that it was some monster baring his fangs at her as if he were going to gobble her up. I was sure it was Shan. Well, Shan, so you learned to do imitations on this trip, did you? Come on, give us another demonstration!"

Cousin Mei gave an involuntary chuckle. Jade was bringing in the tea, and she began laughing, too, and spilt the tea all over the floor. Had I not reached out and caught her, she would have fallen down herself. Orchid then pushed me into a seat next to Cousin Mei, placed a cloth around my shoulders, and began undoing my hair.

"Doing his hair without washing it first—oh, you're too stupid for words!" said Cousin Mei in an exasperated tone. With a rueful grin Orchid went off to fetch the basin. I glanced at the cloth, which was dingy and frayed, and was rather put off by it. Guessing my reaction, Orchid showed me one corner, which made me blush, for there were a pair of butterflies embroidered on it—it was Koto's. The year before, when the cloth was new, I had drawn the design for her to embroider, so that she could tell it was hers. She had a passion for cleanliness and would never use even her sisters' cloths—or let anyone else use hers, for that matter. I was the only one with that privilege; if I was eating with her, she would always let me share her cloth.

I asked after Koto, and Cousin Mei mumbled, "Oh, she's all right. A touch of malaria, that's all."

"Is she awake? If she is, I'd like to see her before having my hair washed."

Cousin Mei hesitated. "Why the rush?" she asked.

Without a word I hurried over to the basin and let Orchid do my hair. Inwardly I was urging her on, but she deliberately dawdled. When eventually she finished, I looked over toward the staircase as if intending to go up. When Cousin Mei seemed to raise no objection, I gathered my gown about me and set off up the stairs. Jade followed me into the room, where I found Koto still in bed, hugging the quilt about her. At the sound of my footsteps, she parted the bed curtain and called out, "Is that you, Shan?"

"Yes," I said, and went up to her and looked at her closely. Her face was pathetically drawn. Her knitted brows seemed blacker than ever and her parched lips a more vivid red. I felt her forehead, which was scorching hot, and asked what the trouble was. She shook her head. "I feel a lot brighter now. Pull up the curtain, would you? I want to sit up."

"Aren't you afraid of a draft?" I asked.

"Oh, that's all right."

Jade, who was standing beside me, hooked up one side of the curtain and helped me raise Koto to a sitting position. I placed a padded jacket around her shoulders, while Jade brought in a low bamboo table and set it on the bed in front of her. Koto leaned over the table for some time, her chin cupped in her hands, then looked up at me.

"Shan, why are you so thin?"

"I've been ill, too, but I'm better now, I'm glad to say. I hear you've been sick for almost a month. I expect you feel better than you did, but you're still so peaky! Who's your doctor, I wonder?"

She hung her head and said nothing. I looked into her face; it was flushed with embarrassment, as if she preferred not to be asked such questions. Recalling what Alcyon had told me, I felt acutely disappointed. I regretted even asking, and quickly changed the subject.

"Will you join me in some breakfast?"

"I really don't care for anything. You haven't had any yourself yet, I suppose?"

"That's right, he hasn't, but Mother's heating him up some sago," Jade put in. "It should be ready by now. Let me go and get it, and then you can have some, too."

Koto thought this over and finally said, "I'll try." Jade went off to get the sago.

Koto looked at me and was about to say something when she stopped herself. Instead she asked about the scenery in Xiangxi. I described it in some detail, supplementing my account with the story of Alian, whom I portrayed as the innocent victim of injustice. At first Koto rather enjoyed my story, but when I came to the rumors that had swirled around about Alian and me, she gave me a knowing look accompanied by a sweet smile.

I was covered in confusion. "Don't *you* believe me, either?" I asked.

"Why shouldn't I? I was only thinking of things from her point of view. Her death is absolutely the right time for it, in my opinion. I believe you ought to write something in her memory."

"If I write anything more, I can't *imagine* what people are going to say! Besides, there's nothing I can write."

Koto smiled. "And so when I die, are you going to write nothing in my memory?"

I laughed. "'The greatest sorrow knows no words.' I'm afraid I may not be able to."

"Then you ought to tell that to Alian's spirit."

This remark made me feel even worse, and I had nothing to say. I reflected privately that all women probably had a suspicious streak in them. It was my good luck that Susu had never shown any signs of it. But even so, although she didn't *show* any signs, how could one be sure that she didn't *feel* the way Koto did? Now, if Koto were suspicious of Alian, Susu had every right to be suspicious of *her*, in which case Koto would consider herself the innocent victim of injustice, a notion that brought a smile to my face. She noticed the smile, then evidently thought of something, and flushed.

"Forgive me for being so thoughtless, Shan," she said after a pause. "But I couldn't help being impressed by the purity and nobility of your sympathy for Alian. I was deeply moved on her behalf."

I smiled and said nothing.

Jade and Orchid brought our breakfast in on a tray, and I squatted on the edge of the bed and ate it together with Koto. She took one or two sips, then put her bowl aside. I finished mine, but Jade kept pressing me to eat more. I could hardly refuse and, handing her my bowl, asked for just a little extra. Orchid took the bowl away and at the same time handed me the one Koto had started. "It's a shame to let this go to waste. Do her a favor and finish it up."

I chuckled, but Koto gave her an angry glare. "A sick person's leftovers shouldn't be given to other people. Aren't you afraid he might catch something?"

"It would be marvelous if I could catch your illness instead of you," I said. I picked up the bowl to drink from it, but Koto covered it with her hand, and I gave up.

Orchid offered me a cloth, the same one I had used before. "This one's frayed," I said. "Couldn't you find me another?"

"If you had a new one," said Koto, turning to look at me, "this one would be discarded." Apparently some sarcasm was implied, but I had no idea what it might be and passed off her remark with a jest.

"I'm going to buy a whole lot and give them all to you," I said. She smiled and nodded, then told Orchid and Jade to clear away the dishes and bring her a teacup and a spittoon. After rinsing out her mouth, she stared into space with the teacup still in her hand, then suddenly remarked in a serious tone, "I hear your servant Turtle has become a monk. Is that true?"

"Who told you that?"

"Mother saw him."

I sighed. "If Turtle has become a monk, he'll be a buddha before long. He's no ordinary person. Everything he comes out with is like scripture—memorable things of lasting value."

"Such as?"

I realized the slip I had made as soon as she asked the question. Turtle on the subject of money was hardly something I could repeat to her, so I changed the topic and spoke instead of his loyalty to our family and the protection he offered me, which led me to give a detailed account of my mother's strictness.

Koto was silent for a long time. "In that case," she said at last, "won't you get into trouble for stopping off here on your way home?"

I glanced at the clock on the wall—it was ten already. "You're right," I said. "If you care for me, let me take my leave of you for awhile."

"When you have time, I hope you'll come and see me. But don't bother if it's at all inconvenient. Don't go getting yourself into any trouble, now." She smiled as she said this, and I realized that she was referring to Susu, but I saw no point in contradicting her and merely smiled. After saying good-bye, I went downstairs, took leave of Cousin Mei, and returned home.

My mother seemed calm enough as she asked me detailed questions about my time away from home. Meanwhile my wife was standing by her side. Unable to express our feelings for each other, we confined ourselves to exchanging fond glances. I felt an intense desire to speak to her, as if I had a million words on the tip of my tongue, but in my mother's presence we were never allowed to interrupt. Until we received permission to withdraw, we had to stay where we were indefinitely. Then, just as my mother neared the end of her questions, my second brother came in. Normally when brothers are reunited after a year's absence, they go on talking forever, but on this occasion I restricted myself to whatever he asked me. In the first place, it was the custom in our household to let a person ask all of his questions before you asked any of yours. And second, I had been unable to talk to my wife yet and was hoping to get away as soon as possible. So I merely asked how he was and when he planned to go back. After he left the room, I glanced over at my mother, but her expression gave no indication that I was permitted to withdraw. Looking about me, I noticed that both my second brother's wife and my younger brother were absent, and I asked after them. My mother responded with an icy smile. "Your sister-in-law has gone home and I *imagine* she's all right, but whether she's *really* all right, I have no means of knowing. As for your brother, he became so worried that he went off to fetch you, and I expect him back at any moment."

At this point in the conversation Little Tan came gracefully into the room. "It must have been quite an ordeal being away from home," she said. "You look so thin." I glanced at her face, which was radiant with joy. I realized the joy was due to Toad's return and couldn't resist giving her a knowing smile.

"I wasn't seriously ill. It was just a minor complaint, and I'm feeling better now."

"I see. Well, in that case you ought to get plenty of rest. You've only just arrived after a long journey and won't have had your hair done yet. Here, let me do it for you quickly." After a pause she went on, "My, it's so shiny I can see my face in it! Who did this for you?"

How I loathed that woman! "It was badly matted," I replied hastily, "and Toad hasn't had any experience with that sort of thing. I happened to be at a teahouse, so I called a barber in to do it for me."

My mother now looked at my hair and commented to Little Tan, "No wonder it's so loose, just the way those young hooligans downtown wear their hair. Hurry up and redo it for him."

At last I was free to make a relieved exit. Back in my room, I found my wife's maid, Ajin, putting my clothes away. She greeted me with a smile. "You must be worn out, standing there all this time. But why hasn't the mistress come back with you?"

I was so disappointed that Susu hadn't come back with me that I snapped at Ajin, "Why don't you bring me some tea instead of asking all these stupid questions?" Seeing how upset I was, she didn't dare say a word, just hurried off to fetch the tea.

I looked about the room. Everything in it projected a sense of loneliness, which made me wonder how depressed Susu must have felt, sitting in here on her own. And now I was here, and still she wasn't with me, and the thought distressed me beyond words. From my brief experience with loneliness, a great deal could be inferred about her much longer one.

Absorbed in these thoughts, I heard the patter of feet outside the door. It must be her, I thought, and parting the curtain went out to greet her, but it turned out to be Little Tan. "The mistress is still discussing various domestic matters with her ladyship," she told me.

"Who asked *you?*"

"I thought I'd just mention it for what it's worth."

"Little Tan, are you here to do my hair?"

"Yes."

I sat down at my wife's dressing table. As she undid my hair, Little Tan gasped in surprise, "Was a barber responsible for this?"

"Yes."

"You may be able to deceive her ladyship, but just look at this knot! If a barber had tied it, the ends would have been pulled out from the inside. This looks to me like the handiwork of some young girl. You're not being honest with me."

Greatly embarrassed, I had to acknowledge her shrewdness. I felt I could hardly deny the truth, so I threw myself on her mercy. "Please don't do anything hasty, or you'll get me into trouble with my mother!"

She smiled. "And that's not the only thing. When a barber

does your hair, the braids are round and tight, because of the strength he has in his hands. Yours are all slack and shiny."

I pleaded with her in great agitation, "Stop it, will you! Spare me the commentary, please. I'm totally convinced. You're a bodhisattva in human form."

She laughed. "Her ladyship doesn't have the best of hearing. She'll never hear us through the wall. Why are you such a timid little mouse, anyway? On second thought, I don't think I *will* do your hair. I'll leave it as it is and let the mistress draw her own conclusions."

At precisely this point someone parted the door curtain and came in. I thought that this time it must be Susu and turned to look, but it proved to be Ajin. I took the cup of tea from her and sipped it, motioning in the mirror to Little Tan to hurry up with my hair. She smiled and nodded, but her hands began making all the wrong movements and, when I turned my head to look, I found that she had tied my hair up again. Worse still, she now turned and left the room. I called after her to come back.

"People have put *such* a lot of effort into doing your hair," she said. "If I come along and undo it, I'll be ignoring all their hard work." She slipped out of the room, still chuckling to herself.

I told Ajin to redo my hair, but although she didn't dare refuse, she was full of excuses. "It's so shiny and smooth. If Little Tan's work isn't good enough for you, mine certainly won't be."

I told a fib. "Look, there's a strand of hair on the crown of my head that has been pulled too tight and is giving me fits. Hurry up and undo it."

Taking my word for it, she quickly undid my hair up to the crown and gave it a careful combing. As I watched her image in the mirror, I noticed a distinct resemblance to Alian. Then my thoughts drifted to other matters. "Did your mistress ever miss me while I was away?" I asked.

She gave a scornful little laugh. "The mistress and I don't share the same heart, so how would I know whether she missed you or not?"

"If she did, she would have mentioned it."

"Then she didn't miss you."

"I find that very hard to believe. If you won't tell me, I'll appeal to your mistress, and she'll have reason to beat you."

Ajin smiled. "That's all very well, but I doubt she has the strength in her wrists."

I smiled, too. "Then I'll do it for her. Come on, hold out your hand!"

I seized her hand and flicked her on the wrist with two of my fingers. She flew giggling into my arms—and at that precise moment Susu arrived. She came timidly around the edge of the curtain, then stepped briskly into the room.

"Silly girl!" she said to Ajin with a smile. "Are you out of your mind?"

"The master was beating me, that's all," protested Ajin, scrambling to her feet and patting her hair into place.

I let go of her and stood up, then went over to Susu and grasped her hands. "My dear, you kept me waiting here such a long time on my own! I was just asking Ajin whether you missed me at all."

Susu looked at Ajin. "And what did she say?"

"She said you spoke about me all the time," I said. Susu colored, while Ajin tried to explain. Susu shooed her out of the room.

"And so you didn't miss me?" I asked softly, gazing into her eyes. "Oh, Susu, *your* image was engraved on my heart the whole time I was away."

She stared back at me and blushed, unable to reply, but her eyes revealed an infinite tenderness, and I couldn't resist the temptation to bring my face close to hers and try to steal a kiss. Now, my readers should be apprised of the fact that in China at that time kissing was something that could be done only in private. Susu herself always maintained a dignified reserve; normally, even in the privacy of our bedroom, she would never indulge in any frivolous banter, and this was the only occasion during our marriage in which, while standing side by side, we engaged in the Western practice of kissing. Even now, if she were to read this out loud, I am sure she would blush to the roots of her hair, fling the book aside, and say what utter nonsense it all was. In Western fiction kissing is referred to all the time, but our Chinese women persist in regarding it as something shameful—an attitude that we men simply have to put up with. The other events that occurred on this occasion cannot even be referred to, so let me pass on to another subject.

As examination time drew near, my brother and I made ready to set off. My mother prepared the finest and most elaborate food for us—her fond hopes had transformed both of us into pearls of great price. I often think back on that episode, and I am convinced that her love for us was never greater than it was then. I myself was lucky enough to pass, coming in fifth, but my brother was once again rejected. Humiliated and resentful, he packed up and left for Haining. But because of that same examination, I found myself out of favor with my mother again. Not that she wasn't happy about my success—she was —but because our expenses and gifts had cost a lot more than expected, she began worrying about our financial problems and came to regret the whole affair.

The person in charge of our finances was really Little Tan, but she was at home on leave at the time, and my mother had to entrust me to make the withdrawals from the bank. I found from the passbook that our account at the close of the *bing-shen* year (1896) held a balance of over seventeen thousand taels, but that in the year prior to the present one, *dingyou* (1897), it had shrunk by a third, and that it now stood at under four thousand. As far as our expenditures during that period were concerned, the only one I knew of was the five thousand-tael mortgage. However, I was used to hearing my mother complain about the low rate of interest paid by the banks, so I assumed that she had used the money to make other loans, too. But the treasurer in all those transactions was Little Tan, and I had no idea what kind of collateral she had secured to gain my mother's approval. Since I didn't dare question my mother about the loans, I simply ignored them. However, it was precisely those loans that caused her such anguish all year long.

She had always liked accumulating money and in the past had used the Huiyuan Bank as her safe-deposit box, but the bank collapsed, costing her 40 percent of the money in her account, after which she regarded all banks as too dangerous. Little Tan was a frequent visitor at our relatives' houses, and whenever an aunt or a cousin asked for a loan against her jewelry, my mother would approve it. Then last year during a rash of burglaries, we were among the victims. When the borrowers tried to redeem their jewelry, they had to be compensated in cash. After that experience my mother and Little Tan gradually reformed their lending practices and accepted nothing but real estate deeds as collateral. However, mistakes were constantly being made over the monthly interest payments, and occasionally, when we needed the money and tried to recall it, it was not forthcoming. And even after my mother and Little Tan had retrieved the money, they had the additional worry of what to do with it; they needed to find someone to lend it to before they could rest easy again. For these reasons the two women spent their time agonizing and never enjoyed a single day of peace—another example of the bedevilment of money.

Self-interest played no part in Little Tan's calculations; she acted solely out of loyalty to my mother. Her trouble was that she simply wasn't cut out to be a bookkeeper. How much knowledge would you expect from a village girl, anyway? She had never experienced one iota of the chicanery that is routinely practiced in the world at large, being in that respect every bit as naive as my mother. As for my second brother and me, we not only had no right at the time to intervene, even if we had had such a right, we would have been equally innocent in the ways of the world, not to mention the fact that we were by no means as conscientious as Little Tan. And so my book will set such matters aside and pass on to another subject.

I had won myself a scholar's gown and also managed by some fluke to place near the top among over a hundred candidates, and in the spirit of youth I was not above taking a certain pride in these achievements. Now that I had a government stipend, I felt I no longer needed to work as an aide to some official. When a letter arrived from my superior congratulating me on my success and urging me to return as soon as possible, I actually wrote back declining the invitation—and received a frightful tongue-lashing from my mother. She told my wife to write to Mrs. Ling explaining the situation and at the same time pressed me to pack up my things.

It was the height of summer and the weather was oppressively hot. Miserable though my wife was, she didn't dare disobey my mother, so we had no choice but to part. She was seven months pregnant at the time and in increasingly delicate health, and I was far more reluctant to leave her than I had been before. On previous trips I had always had a boy accompanying me, but this time I explained that I was traveling with a friend. My mother believed me implicitly, but in fact there was no friend. I had arranged with Koto to take this opportunity to hire a pleasure boat and visit the sights of Guashan.

Our boat was too large to sail right up to Koto's gate, so we moored at Cross River. Having seen my bags that far, the servants said good-bye and returned home. Before long two sedan chairs arrived to the accompaniment of the bearers' shouts. With their jeweled tassels flashing in the sunlight and their white silk curtains in a snowflake design, they differed from the usual style; even from a distance you could tell that they were Koto's. I stood in the bow of the boat and motioned them forward. Then the passengers emerged—Orchid and Cousin Mei. My hopes dashed, I asked why Koto hadn't come, too.

"She's sick," said Orchid, plunging me further into despair.

"Stop maligning your sister," snapped Cousin Mei. "Don't listen to her, Shan. Koto had nothing to give you as a farewell present, so she decided to part with her pride and joy, those jasmine plants from her room. She's arranging to have them brought over."

Just then some men arrived with the plants swinging from their carrying poles. The earthenware pots in the bamboo baskets were each over two feet high, and the vivid blossoms were like flecks of snow amid the green. The bearers arranged all four pots in the bow, from where their scent alone was enough to lift one's spirits.

"Aren't these the ones she has on display in her room?" I exclaimed with pleasure. "Won't she be depriving herself, if she gives them to me?"

"She *wants* you to have them," said Cousin Mei with a laugh, adding "*I'm* not allowed to pick so much as a bud." I blushed.

Soon I saw the chair returning. I felt awkward about leaving the boat to welcome her, but Orchid had already gone to do so, while Cousin Mei had parted the curtains and stood waiting for her. Koto's arrival was heralded by a whiff of scent from her clothes. In the mirror screen I saw her moving slowly and gracefully toward me, and I turned and greeted her. She was wearing a jacket of moiré silk and a Hunan crepe-silk skirt, and with her lustrous hair swept up like a bank of clouds, she looked more elegant than ever. In pale, soft fingers that glowed like rich jade she held a tiny, round fan, and as she walked one heard the tinkling of her bracelets, the yellow gold and the green jade vying proudly with one another.

I showed her into the middle cabin, where I served tea to her and Cousin Mei. Orchid had to go without; the boat provided us with only two cups. Cousin Mei gave hers back to me and opened the hamper she had brought, which was stacked full of cups and dishes. She put some of the finest tea in the pot and went to the stern to fetch some water, then brought out a basin for people to wash their hands in and offered them towels. I apologized profusely.

"You're not taking a boy with you this time," said Cousin Mei. "Won't you find that rather inconvenient?"

"Oh, I expect I shall be all right," I replied offhandedly.

"If Mother hadn't mentioned it, I might have forgotten," said Koto. "Our Pearlie's quite sharp. Why not take him with you?"

I laughed. "Pearlie? I'd be the one attending on *him*—or something pretty close to it."

"In my opinion," said Orchid, "we should *all* go with Shan to Xiangxi and come back again on the same boat. It would be a lot more fun than touring the West Lake."

Cousin Mei was still laughing at her when the boatman cast off. To the gentle plash of the sweep oar we moved slowly away from land, but the people along the shoreline still strained their eyes to keep us in view. The sunlight reflected on Koto's complexion, which looked almost transparent, like melting tallow. From Koto my thoughts traveled to Susu. If Susu's looks were compared with Koto's, I didn't know who would come out ahead. From there my thoughts ran on to Secunda, and I began to see Koto as a fusion of all three women.

There was nothing else of note to report, except that in those days I always took my musical instruments with me, packed in a case—lute and viol, flutes, castanets, and so forth. Of course, I couldn't play them all at once, but I felt uneasy if I left any behind. I had two additional cases, one each for my koto and my zither. At home I kept them hidden away in a separate room, and when I was packing up to leave, I could never afford to let my mother know that I was taking them with me. The one exception was my zither, the only instrument I carried openly to the sedan chair. She didn't forbid me to take that because I had inherited it from my father. In fact my passion for music was also something I had inherited from him. It wasn't that my mother disliked music, but in recent years she had descended into a world of religious compassion in which she found that music grated on her nerves.

With nothing else to do on board, I brought out my instruments and handed them to the girls to play for Cousin Mei's enjoyment. Orchid knew how to keep time, but she frequently made mistakes, prompting Koto to laugh, and eventually the castanets changed hands. Now, of all the things in the world that are calculated to move our emotions, music is the most powerful; anyone with the slightest aptitude for it will find his spirits uplifted. And so the four-foot long koto was placed on Koto's lap, while I accompanied her on the panpipe, and although a fierce sun beat down on our cabin window, we were almost oblivious to its heat. Perfect bliss, I thought. My sole regret, one that I still feel to this day, was that on board the boat it wasn't convenient to ask Koto to sing.

It was past noon when we arrived at Guashan and made our way to First Spring Restaurant for lunch. At that time the highway had just been opened. The Yangchun Theater was not yet finished, however, and performances were held in a large shed erected on some open ground nearby, but only during daylight hours. The sole evening performances were given by an all-girl troupe known as the Gao family. While my mother, my father's principal wife, was alive, whenever any of us children had a birthday, it was always this troupe that she called in. Familiarity had bred contempt so far as I was concerned, and I didn't think it worth watching, so that afternoon I took Koto and the others to see the Yangchun Opera. There were many townspeople there who seemed to recognize me, and the whole audience, seeing me with Koto, trained their eyes on her. I was the only one enjoying the martial piece being performed on stage.

Driven to distraction by the scrutiny of the audience, Koto felt acutely uncomfortable and soon wanted to go back. I was more than ready to go with her, but Orchid wouldn't hear of it and pestered me to stay. In the end it was Cousin Mei who accompanied Koto back to the boat; all I could do was follow her with my eyes. Then I began to find the mood of the audience unbearably irritating. The play now being performed was *The Gift of the Green Hairpin*,[4] and the depiction of hero and heroine was simply revolting, although the audience gave both actors thunderous applause. That was the last straw so far as I was concerned, and I urged Orchid to go back. By this time she herself was so embarrassed by the play's bawdiness that she agreed.

When we arrived back at the boat, Cousin Mei announced, "I just this minute sent the boatman to find you. Didn't you run into him on the way? We've had a message from town to say that Jade has been taken ill, and I shall be going back. Orchid, you can stay here with your sister, but see you don't upset her. You are both to come back tomorrow morning. I'll send some chairs for you."

Privately I was astonished at Cousin Mei's action. Why was she suddenly so unconcerned about her daughters? Then it occurred to me that Koto must have braved a confrontation with her mother in order to be allowed to stay.

Once Cousin Mei had gone, Orchid was like a child let out of school, a gleeful expression on her face, but Koto remained as serious as ever. In the evening, because she didn't wish to risk further annoyance by going to a restaurant, I ordered supper brought to the boat. As we ate and drank beside the picture window, I felt wonderfully at ease. The moon's light shone through the chinks in the curtain and, when the evening mist closed in, the moon itself, like a freshly ground mirror, bathed our faces in a pearly glow. At the same time the jasmine flowers in the bow began to give off their mild fragrance, vying with the blossoms that Koto wore at her temples. We considered whether to go and see the Gao Family Troupe, but in the face of Koto's vehement opposition the idea was dropped. Then, as we continued to drink, we began playing hide-the-hook with melon seeds. Time after time I guessed which hand Koto and Orchid held the seed in, and they ended up drinking a great deal, until both of them were quite drunk.

Afterward Orchid went up to the bow to enjoy the cool night air, while Koto lay down to take a nap. I was at even more of a loss, but I feared that Orchid might get careless and fall overboard, so I went up to keep her company. I found her leaning against the cabin wall gazing up at the moon, her body imprinted with the shadows of the flowers and a faraway look on her face. As soon as she saw me, she took my hands in hers. "Are you drunk, Shan?" she said. Her breath gave off a strong smell of cardamom.

"You have some cardamom?" I asked.

"Yes."

"Give me one."

She nodded and made a motion with her lips as if to give me the one she was sucking. My heart began to pound.

"It's not for me. It's for Koto."

"She has her own. She doesn't need you to do a Weisheng⁵ for her and cadge one from somebody else."

I was about to reply when I heard Koto calling me. Leaving Orchid, I went back inside. "I'm too drunk to get up," she said. "Please bring me some tea and help me drink it. And if you could also peel me a handful of lotus seeds, I'd be ever so grateful."

I brought the tea, but it was still too hot, and I had to blow on it for some time before holding the cup for her as she drank. When she had finished, I went over to the window and began peeling lotus seeds. As soon as I had done two or three, she would demand them and I would have to rush over and give them to her. Then, before I had done many more, she would demand those, too. I was reduced to sitting on the edge of the bunk and handing them to her as fast as I could peel them. Closing her eyes, she tried to sleep, but she continued holding out her hand for the seeds, often finding my wrist or nails instead, which made her giggle. She was so exhausted that I felt sorry for her and began holding the seeds to her lips.

Observing her as she slept, I felt that the cherry-apple blossom, for all its beauty, could not compare with her. However, I had never harbored any improper desires with regard to Koto, only an intense feeling of love. Soon she was sound asleep. When I popped a seed into her mouth, she would hold it there for a moment, then let it roll onto the pillow. Placing a silk coverlet over her, I drove the mosquitoes away with a fan, let down the netting, and went out.

Orchid had been peeping at us through a chink in the door curtain. Now she touched a finger to her cheek as if to say "shame on you," so I tiptoed out of the cabin. The moonlight struck the side of the boat and lit up Orchid's face so that she looked gorgeous, as if her cheeks had been freshly rouged.

"Why 'shame on me'?"

At first she said nothing. "I was just thinking that, since you're so much in love with Koto, it's such a pity she's made of stone," she said at last.

"If you were in her place, how would you behave?"

She shot me an angry glance, then pinched my arm. It hurt like a bee sting, and I flared up.

"Cruel little beast! I'll get you for that!"

She threw herself into my arms, looked up at me, and begged me for forgiveness, a pose that I found absolutely enchanting. But I had never felt any interest in Orchid, and my thoughts swung back to Koto. Why were the two sisters so different in nature? Even so, if Koto *had* been exactly like Orchid, I would long since have come to look down on her; I would never have continued to cherish and respect her as I did. I began to see Orchid's behavior as thoroughly odious.

"Stop it!" I insisted. "Your hair's all mussed."

She stood up and patted her hair into place, pouting in her characteristic way. "Oh, hurry up and see to Sister's needs!" she fumed. "We mustn't make Sister angry, now, must we?"

I was about to go and see how Koto was, but after this outburst I could scarcely do so. Instead I went up to the bow and lingered there among the flowers and the moonlight. The lights were thinning out along the shore. The music and singing had almost died away, but from somewhere far off there came the notes of a viol ascending alone to the heavens, plaintive, wistful for some lost love, evoking in me an infinite sadness. My thoughts turned to Susu on her lonely pillow, thinking of me as far away. *She* wouldn't be wistful over some lost love. Then suddenly I thought of another evening once before, in a situation just like this, when Alcyon and I were enjoying the moonlight here, and I began to see Koto as Alcyon. Once more I was in a boat with a girl. Was it not a crime to waste such a glorious night in lonely contemplation? I was hesitating as to whether to go in when I heard Orchid's voice, "Sister's calling you." At first I thought it was a trick, but then I heard a cough and realized that Koto was awake, so I hurried into the cabin.

She was sitting cross-legged on the bed, pressing her silken lapels to her eyes. When I came closer, I saw that her eyes had a dull look and that her cheeks were still flushed. She had a delicate charm about her that was calculated to melt the heart. "What time is it?" she asked.

"Late. Well past midnight."

"Is Orchid asleep?"

"No."

"Why don't you go to bed?"

"It's so stuffy in here, I'd rather stay up."

"Let's change places. It won't do you any good to be up all night." She pushed back the coverlet and began to get out of bed, but at once I stopped her. I glanced at her slender feet in their silk stockings, each one so small that it could be cupped in the hand, and my eyes were inevitably drawn back to them. She seemed to be aware of my fascination, for she pulled the silk hem of her dress down over her feet, and a faint flush spread from her cheeks to the corners of her eyes. As I observed her, my heart raced almost out of control, until a certain thought occurred to me and caused it to subside: The reason Koto loved me was that she respected me, and if I held myself so cheap, how could I be sure that she wouldn't take offense?

By now the moonlight was shining directly on the bed. Koto was looking up at the moon, and for a long time she seemed lost in thought. "It's so chilly," she said, her voice soft and delicate. "Won't you catch cold without anything on but that thin silk gown?" She pointed to the wall on the left. "Would you mind handing me down that bundle with the white brocade cover?"

I handed it to her, and she undid it and took out a vest. "Here, try this on underneath," she said.

"You ought to dress up more warmly yourself," I said. She nodded and took out a sleeveless silk jacket, which I helped her into and then buttoned up for her. When I reached the button at her neck, her face was directly opposite mine and I was acutely aware of the scent of her rouge and the moist red of her lips. Had it been Susu there in front of me, I could not have resisted the temptation to kiss her, but with Koto I didn't dare. The reason was far from clear to me, but in essence I was genuinely afraid that she might be offended and break up with me. In fact she would have done no such thing, but in those days women's bodies were sacrosanct to me, and I didn't dare violate them. If Susu often complained prettily about the ardor of my lovemaking, think how others might react! Although I wasn't cold, I could hardly refuse her thoughtful gesture. I went into the other cabin to change.

When I returned, she laughed at me. "Why, Shan—how very modest!"

I merely smiled. It was a habit ingrained in me since childhood. No one went about half-naked in our house. Even my wife would withdraw from my presence in order to change her clothes, and I would have thought it demeaning to appear undressed in front of women or children. I have retained this attitude to the present day without the slightest change. After all, if you put someone on a pedestal, you cannot help feeling inferior yourself.

Koto's vest fitted me well enough in the body—I was very thin in those days—but it left something to be desired in other respects, being too small in the neck and too short in the sleeves, so I put on a jacket over it. Koto lifted up my sleeve and peeped inside. The vest was over two inches too short, and she gave way to a fit of the giggles. Then she noticed that my nails were longer than ever and her fancy turned to them. After comparing them with her own and finding that hers were only half as long, she asked me what my secret was, and then went on to ask after the cousin with whom she used to study. "Oh, her!" I sighed. "We haven't seen each other in nearly two years."

"But how could you grow so far apart?" asked Koto in surprise.

"It's not that I dropped her," I said. "But my mother and

aunt fell out over the division of the property, so after we moved into our separate houses my cousin never came to visit us, nor would my mother let any of us go over there."

"Oh dear, family quarrels arise far too often over property. If we had no property at all, we might be able to live in peace."

"*Exactly!* That's why I see everything in the world as bedeviled by money."

Koto couldn't suppress a chuckle at this, then went on, "Except that the bedevilment is worse in the case of the older generation."

"There I disagree with you. I imagine that the older generation may not be trying to take their money to the grave with them. They may be thinking of the long term, planning ahead for their children and grandchildren, and feel they have no choice but to save their money. Who knows, one day you and I may do the same."

She laughed. "Shan, your ideas are far ahead of mine, but I simply *do not approve* of the way the older generation hoards its money."

It was my turn to laugh. "Then why do you hoard yours?"

"My aims are *quite* different. What concerns me is that I have no one I can rely on—not, I hasten to say, that I would ever want to rely on anyone else. My ambition is to live free without a care in the world. I shall build myself a retreat in some beautiful natural spot and live there entirely on my own. All I shall need will be a host of lovely flowers and a few fine bamboos, plus a censer and a koto."

I laughed. "But what will you do for company?"

"Perhaps you'll drop by sometimes when you're not too busy painting your wife's eyebrows.[6] And even if you don't drop by, I'll still be thinking you *might.* I'll have the flowers and the bamboos, and I'll gaze up at the moon and feel the breeze in my face—these things I shall enjoy more than ever. So long as I have enough money for the necessities of life, I shall devote anything I have over to buying a burial plot on Lone Hill or below Xiling Bridge, where I shall build a tomb like Su Xiaoxiao's[7] and get you to inscribe the tablet as follows: 'Here Lies the Lady Koto, Free Woman.' Once that is done, my lifelong desire will be fulfilled."

I laughed. "In that case, where will you put Mr. Sheng?"

Her face took on a stern expression. "Since you bring that up, you ought to know that Mr. Sheng is my enemy. In my opinion, he should be seen for what he is—a rapist. I may have had the bad luck to be born into Cousin Mei's family, but I'm Koto, not Cousin Mei. He who touches pitch isn't always blackened by it, you know. As a child attending school at your house, I was influenced by what I saw and heard, and took your family as my model; I feel I have parted company with my own. If I happen to forget myself and betray my hereditary nature, I suffer from a guilty conscience. As I see it, my innate self was dark and coarse, but after frequent contact with you, some of your qualities have rubbed off on me. But the road ahead is even longer, and since my innate wickedness has not been eradicated, how can I be sure that at some time in the future I may not regress until I am just like my mother? Oh, Shan, if you think of me as Cousin Mei's daughter, I am really fit only to be Sheng's wife. But if you think of me as what I aspire to be, I could never be the wife of such a flunky! I have never dared express my innermost thoughts to you before, but now that we are here together in the middle of the night, there's no reason not to open our hearts to each other. I have loved and admired you now for thirteen years, but I have always thought that—born in the mire as I was, even if I might boast of being a lotus rising from it—I could never compare with the finest flower of womanhood. I kept hearing how strict your mother was, and I assumed she would never accept me as your concubine. Moreover your wife is deeply in love with you—how could I bear to snatch your love away from her? In any case, my own virtue has been tainted and can never be restored. I have no need to consider Sheng's reputation; the fact that you value me even more highly because of what I have been through brings tears of gratitude to my eyes. That is why in my heart of hearts I will never give up all hope of you. Who knows, heaven may one day take pity on me and allow me to regain my freedom. Even if I cannot be described over the entrance to my tomb as married to you in some fashion, provided my soul is fit to receive your elegy as a wife mourned by her husband, my lifelong desire will have been in some small way fulfilled."

As she said this, she was on the verge of tears. I, too, was more moved than I can say. "My dear Koto, you really do know and love me. I, too, have never dared express myself to you before, but now, after hearing what you have just said, if I fail in any way to do as you ask, I shall stand condemned as the greatest villain of all time. If my heart could be cut open and placed before you, only the word 'love' would be found engraved upon it. I have never dared entertain the slightest dishonorable thought with regard to you."

"Oh, I know your heart well. If you were not like that, I should have dismissed you long ago as just another rich playboy. Oh, Shan, the things you love and respect in me are the very things that make me love and respect you."

She took my hand, placed it in her delicate palm, and began stroking it vigorously. At the time, however, I was quite untouched by sexual desire, and the stroking did not excite me in the least. I continued in a serious tone, "What you have told me tonight means that my thirteen years of loving you have not been in vain." She sighed.

By now it was almost daybreak, and Orchid could be heard talking in her sleep. "Shan!" she cried out. "So you hate me, do you?"

Koto snickered. "Now *there's* someone who has the family

characteristics in their purest form!" I couldn't help feeling a moment of embarrassment for Orchid's sake.

Before long the sky brightened, and the birds on the shoreline trees began their clamor. "It's getting light," said Koto with a start. "You have a long journey ahead of you and need to get some sleep. I insist on changing places with you." She drew back the quilt and sat up, then hunted for her slippers, which I found for her. She did not put them on at once, but instead dropped her eyes and stared at the floor and only after a long pause put on her slippers and stood up fastening her skirt, almost too slender and graceful to stand alone. It was a scene I had observed on countless occasions with Susu, but this was my first time with Koto. From contemplating her beauty, my mind raced on to Susu.

"Why don't you take a nap?" Koto asked. I couldn't say no, so I buried my head in the pillow and pretended to sleep, while she sat on the edge of the bed tending her nails, the very picture of boredom. Often she glanced over at me, and seeing my eyes still open, tenderly urged me to get some sleep, which was something I felt less and less inclined to do. I lay there deep in thought, my eyes closed to conjure up her beauty and compare it first with Secunda's, then with Susu's, then with Little Tan's. . . . Under the impression that I was sound asleep, Koto drew the quilt up around my shoulders, then turned and smoothed it. I pretended not to know what was going on, fearing that if she realized I was awake it would only add to her anxiety. I had to pretend to be asleep, and after a while I did indeed drift off.

When I awoke, the sunlight was dancing upon the waves and beating on the windowsill. Koto had already finished her toilette. Orchid was threading jasmine buds on a silver wire, making a rosette to wear on her lapel. I rubbed my eyes and smiled. "No wonder I sensed a certain fragrance in my dream," I said to Orchid. "Is that a present for me?"

"You'd expect to find some fragrance on a warm, soft pillow,"[8] she replied offhandedly, picking up a bud and flinging it in my face.

I smiled to myself. Koto and I had actually sat fondly facing one another all night long, I reflected. No one else in the world would have been capable of such restraint. With Orchid one would certainly have ended up on a "warm, soft pillow." The comparison made me realize how precious Koto's dignity and refinement were. And so my eyes turned to Koto, who was watching me in the mirror. She nodded, then asked into the mirror, "Did you get enough sleep?"

"I had a wonderful sleep," I replied into the mirror. "I almost forgot where I was."[9]

Orchid snorted with laughter, which brought her a glare from Koto. I had gotten out of bed and, feeling the heat more intense than ever, I took off my jacket. When Orchid noticed the vest I was wearing, she started giggling again.

"*Most* becoming, Shan," she said when she had recovered her poise. "All you need is a bracelet or two on your wrists and you'd pass for a girl without even powdering your face."

I meant to take off the vest and return it, but Koto stopped me with a glance. There was a basin of fresh water on the table, so I went over and began washing myself.

"That's Koto's," said Orchid. "We shall have to get some more for you." I took no notice of her.

When I had finished, Koto offered me her seat. I looked at her in the mirror and silently compared her to Little Tan. In terms of a certain vivacious charm, I felt that Little Tan had to yield to Koto.

Readers of my book should understand that although Koto and I had known each other for thirteen years, we had never before had the fortune to spend a night together, to talk to our hearts' content, to share the same mirror in the morning, or to express our tender affection in an unhurried way.

People often feel anticipation before some event and nostalgia after it, but during the event itself they merely go through the motions and even take it for granted. Well then, how *should* we act during an event so as to feel completely satisfied later on that we have made the most of our time? You may solicit opinions from men of feeling all over the world, but you will not receive a satisfactory answer.

By this time that *un*feeling sun, as if fearing that my body and heart were about to melt with love, had vaulted high into the heavens. On shore the sedan chairs from town were lined up waiting for us. Then Pearlie came in, stooping low to get in the door. He was about forty years old, towering over us like some monster but stupid as an ox. In Koto's household he worked in the kitchen and hobnobbed with dung beetles, bedbugs, and the like, as a result of which his mind and speech were too vulgar even to be represented in this book. Anyone just hearing his name would have imagined him a marvel of sophisticated urbanity, but he was exactly the opposite. Looking at him, I couldn't help smiling. "What brings *you* here?" I asked. "What was wrong with Jade, anyway?"

"The mistress was worried about your setting off alone on a long journey, so she sent me along to escort you. Cousin Jade had a touch of summer sickness, that's all, and after the medicine man came and said his magic words, she got better." He gesticulated in imitation of the spirit possessing the medium. Disgusted by the sight, I asked him no further questions, merely motioned him from the room.

"I feel sick to my stomach if I so much as look at Pearlie," I said to Koto after he had gone. "I don't know how you people stand him."

She laughed. "Who judges him by his looks? But if you don't take him with you, you'll make us all very uneasy."

"If I have to take him with me, I'll only get sick. Please thank your mother for the kind offer."

"I think you should ask your own family to send a page along," said Orchid. "You can just say that your friend got sick and couldn't go."

"Great idea!" said Koto. "What about it, Shan?"

I reflected that I had never taken a journey on my own and that Orchid's suggestion made excellent sense. I took out a sheet of paper and wrote a note, then handed it to one of the bearers and asked him to go and fetch the page Huanong.

Meanwhile Pearlie was busily gathering up the teacups, mirror, washbasin, and so forth. Orchid glared at him. "Afraid they'll be stolen, are you?" she asked.

"The mistress told me to," said Pearlie. "She expects us back as soon as possible."

"Don't be in such a hurry," said Orchid. "Master Shan has sent for one of his servants, who won't be here until this afternoon. You can go home and tell Mother that we'll return after lunch. The bearers might as well wait here for us." Koto added her voice to Orchid's, and when Pearlie heard Koto speak, he didn't dare disobey. After a moment's hesitation he took himself off.

Inevitably I began to feel sad over our parting. Koto was packing up my things when she noticed that my underclothes were damp with sweat. She told Orchid to fetch some water and began washing them. However, she had no experience in such work, and her efforts drew hoots of laughter from Orchid, who finally snatched the garments away and washed them herself.

I offered Koto a towel to dry her hands on, and afterward she let it soak in the basin of water with her own. Orchid laughed. "When I dry my hands, I wonder who'll wash out *my* towel for me?"

"Perhaps *I* will," I said.

Dipping her hand in the basin, she flicked water all over my face. There were no lapels on the clothes I was wearing, so I had nothing to dry myself on, but Koto, who was standing beside me, dried my face with the lapels of her dress. I thought it a shame, but she seemed quite unruffled, no doubt because she really did care more for me than for her dress. I am still moved by that incident—I can't forget it. Whenever I notice a beautiful woman's lapels, I am struck by this sudden fancy: Have those lapels ever been used to dry her lover's face? I'm positive they have not.

All these things went by in a flash. As I set them down now, they extend for several hundred words, but at the time they took only a few moments.

Soon the factory whistle sounded—otherwise we might have forgotten to have lunch. But none of us could drink anything, nor did we have much to say. Knowing that after this meal we would go our separate ways, we couldn't face any food or drink. I once wrote the line "May neither farewell feast nor sunset ever end," which gives some idea of my feelings on this occasion. I had the foolish notion that if the meal never ended and the sun never set, the moment of parting would never arrive. Such things don't happen in reality, but we all have our fantasies. Even Orchid, who wasn't personally involved, seemed dejected.

We were interrupted in our grief by a face at the cabin window—our servant Awen. He was Nanny Lu's son and an inveterate tattletale in his own right. A piece of gossip would travel from his mother to mine with a speed rivaling that of the telegraph, which is why I was alarmed to see him here.

He came aboard and greeted me respectfully. "Her ladyship thought that Huanong had too little experience, so she sent me in his place," he said, staring goggle-eyed at Koto and Orchid.

"Don't you know these ladies?" I asked.

"It's years since I've seen them," he said with a smile. "I barely recognized them."

Koto did not remember him at all, so I told her who he was. She still didn't quite understand, but on hearing that he was Nanny Lu's son, she greeted him warmly and even asked after his mother. I told her that Nanny Lu had been asked for by my eldest brother's wife and was now serving as my nephew's nanny. I then asked Awen, "And what instructions does my mother have for me?"

"Her ladyship asked me to give you this message, sir," said Awen. "She wants you to know that Guashan is no place to be visiting and you're not to spend any more time here. She has given me just three days to report back to her. If I miss the deadline, I'm to get a beating. The way I figure it, if we get to Wulintou tonight, we ought to be able to make Linxi by noon tomorrow and Yubu by the afternoon. Then if I take the boat straight back, I'll be able to report in before the deadline. Otherwise, I'll be a day late." I made no comment.

"In that case we mustn't hold Master Shan up," said Koto. "Shan, do eat something. I'm afraid I can't."

"I can't, either. Awen, you won't have had any lunch yet. Clear this away, and you can finish it up yourself." He took the food off with him.

I hesitated a moment, then went to the back cabin; Koto followed me. As I turned and looked at her, I felt so miserable that I was on the verge of tears. I grasped her hands but choked on the words I was about to say. "I hope we can write to each other," I said at last. "I'll be down by the shore every morning waiting for your letters, to see they don't fall into someone else's hands."

She promised to write, then added, "If there's anything you want to say in your letters, don't hesitate to say it. Mr. Sheng knows that I belong to you, body and soul. He's guilty of abduction, and if he should leave me, I shall have my freedom all the sooner. For you, Shan, there's practically nothing I'm not willing to sacrifice, but that's for you to consider. And now it's getting late. I don't dare linger here, lest I get you into trouble with your mother. See you take good care of yourself on the way."

"I'm overwhelmed by what you've just said. Are you really going to leave me in such a hurry?"

"Oh, Shan! Every feast must come to an end. Where there's life, there's hope, as the proverb says, and perhaps we may meet again. Why wrangle over these last few minutes? Take good care of yourself. You needn't see me off. You may not be aware of it, but your eyes are full of tears, and it wouldn't do to let people see you looking like that. If we break down on deck as we say good-bye, they'll only laugh at us."

"They wouldn't dare! Anyway, let them!"

"In that case, you leave me no other choice. If you're going to insist, you need never come and see me again."

When I saw how upset she was, I didn't dare refuse. I turned and, sitting at the table, buried my head in my arms and wept. Koto came up, put her hand on my shoulder, and tried to calm me, but I motioned her away. "Off you go, then! You'll have to leave sooner or later, so there's no point in staying."

"Well, I'll be going, then," she said with a catch in her voice. I ignored her.

All I heard was the patter of feet and the tinkling of bracelets. It sounded as if she were helping Orchid gather up the dishes. Then I heard Orchid calling out, "Shan, I'm off now!" Apparently Koto stopped her, because she never came to say good-bye. Next I heard the bearers' voices and realized that Koto was already ashore. For some reason I felt so miserable that my tears streamed down, and I could do nothing to hold them back.

From the cabin window, I peeped at Koto as she got into her chair and saw that her eyes were still fixed on the boat, although she didn't see me at the window. Even after she and Orchid had stepped inside and the bearers had hoisted the chairs onto their shoulders, Koto was still staring out of the window of her chair, and our eyes unmistakably met. But soon the bearers' sturdy legs had borne her swiftly away. I followed her in spirit into the dark woods until her chair looked no bigger than a tightly folded billet-doux. I watched the bearers' legs undulating over the ground until finally I could make out nothing at all and gave up.

After some time, when I had still not emerged from the cabin, Awen felt obliged to come and see me. I felt as if I were awakening from a dream.

"It's getting late, sir," he said. "Shall I tell the boatman to weigh anchor?" I nodded, and he left again. Then I felt the boat rolling from side to side and saw the sandy shoreline giving way to woods. A breeze sprang up, rippling the water, but I felt that the scene and the feeling it evoked were only calculated to depress the spirit, and I was so overcome by dizziness that I had to lie down. In my dream my rapturous soul followed the sedan chairs as they raced along, until we came to a world where nothing at all existed, at which point I lost consciousness, sheer exhaustion having plunged me into a grateful oblivion. When I awoke, I could hear the drum beating the hour. The boat was moored for the night. From the window I saw a pale yellow moon obscured by the steam from the lake until it was practically dark. So broad was the lake that one could make out the other side only as a thin line where the water met the sky.

In the middle cabin I found a solitary lamp miraculously sporting a green corona. I glanced around at the chairs, pillows, mats—all places where Koto had sat or lain—and now they appeared forlorn, with no recognizable trace of her. The jasmine flowers in the bow looked dismal, devoid of scent. Only my underclothes and the towel she had washed for me were still there, flapping in the evening breeze as if proud of the fact that they had been touched by her fair hands. I felt them and, finding that they were dry, called Awen in to fold them up.

"These things must have been washed in perfumed water,"

he remarked as he took them down from the line. "Otherwise they wouldn't smell so fresh." Then he continued, "Why don't you change into this, sir? You must feel hot in those tight-fitting clothes." I was amused at his assumption that my vest was the sort of clinging undergarment one wears in winter.

"In the summer," he went on, "there's nothing to beat Canton gauze for coolness and fit. I used to have a shirt made of that stuff, but I had to hock it. Every time I start sweating, I miss that shirt. I wonder if it ever misses me as it sits quietly there in its box."

I couldn't help laughing. "What did you need so badly that you had to pawn your shirt for it?"

He sighed. "Oh, that wasn't the only thing I pawned. I always used to redeem my things after I'd pawned them, but no sooner had I done so than I'd pawn them again. I didn't want to, but I couldn't help myself."

"I suppose you pawned it for something your mother needed?"

"Oh, no!"

"Then who made you do it?"

"I simply couldn't help it. This is something I've never dared tell anybody else, because if I did, it would get back to my mother, and as soon as she heard, I'd get a beating right then and there. But in front of you, sir, I don't have to pretend. Last New Year's Eve, her ladyship gave me a whole lot of money. I was at a loose end on New Year's Day, but the money in my purse kept jangling in protest, as if to say, 'We don't belong in here.'"

"You always like to wander off the subject like this and then go on and on without ever coming to the point," I said, amused but also exasperated. "I'd be greatly obliged if you'd spare me these digressions of yours."

With a rueful grin he continued, "There was nothing to do to pass the time, so I went over to a friend's house and started gambling."

"You *gambled?* How could you help losing?"

"While I was gambling, the gods were on my side, and the money in my purse was able to get all its friends and relatives to come and join it there. Within a couple of days it had multiplied so fast you couldn't even count it anymore. But just as I was rejoicing in my good luck, what do you know, the money in my purse started dancing about again and wouldn't settle down. The next day it gathered up all its friends and relatives and left me. I lost heavily, and my mother's money went the same way."

"That was the end of it, then? You can't rely on gambling, you know."

"Ah, but there's a proverb that goes 'The only way to get it back is to win it back.' So I decided to pawn something and try again. And that proverb is right, too, except that you lose more than you win, and when you stake everything, you always lose. I was cleaned out; I hadn't enough money left to redeem the things I had pawned. I pride myself on being a man of my word, so I've had to go on pawning my things and then redeeming them. That's why all the clothes my mother made for me have gone to the pawnshop, which at least keeps them safe and sound, so that they don't vanish altogether."

"But you're utterly *irresponsible!* Haven't you ever had any regrets?"

"Not at first I didn't, no. But now with my mother questioning me and checking up on me all the time, I find myself spending a great deal of effort just making up excuses, so naturally I do feel a bit sorry. That's why I have this dream about winning a prize in the Manila lottery.[10] If I win, I'll be able to redeem all of my possessions. But heaven has not been kind to me—I'm always off by one or two numbers. Nowadays I pawn things not to gamble, but to invest in the lottery."

"But how does that differ from gambling? You need to come to your senses right now. If you go on like this much longer, the chances are you'll end up as a beggar."

"But, sir, the lottery's my only hope!"

"Apparently you've never heard what Turtle used to say. Your troubles are all the work of the money demon."

He laughed. "That's right! I've seen that demon in my dreams, with a round face, square eyes, and a booming voice."

"Stop it, will you? You're starting that nonsense of yours all over again! It's enough to make anyone throw up. Go and see to the wine—I could do with a drink." He jumped to his feet and went out.

I began wondering about him. If he became any poorer, he would end up either as a beggar or a thief. He had smarts enough, but not a lick of sense. He'd been sent to escort me and had seen me all too clearly in the girls' company; it was only reasonable to assume that his tongue would start wagging as soon as he got home. Unless I won him over by doing him some favor, he'd be beyond my control. My best plan would be to offer him enough money to redeem the things he had pawned. That way I could prevent him from getting any improper ideas and secure his allegiance for the future. Since several advantages would flow from that one gift, why not make it willingly?

Awen returned, and, as I drank, I gradually led up to the subject. "How much are they worth altogether, those things you pawned?"

"The original sum was only ten or twelve thousand cash, but with the interest it's almost double that now."

"So if you had twenty taels, you'd be able to redeem everything?"

"Yes. I once worked it out that if I could get the last two numbers of the winning ticket right, I'd have enough."

I couldn't resist a smile. Slowly and deliberately I put my next question to him, "But if you got your wish, I suppose you'd be able to start pawning and gambling all over again?"

His expression changed. "If I received a direct order from either my mother or the emperor, I daresay I'd be confident enough. But short of that, even if someone threatened me with a sword and said, 'Unless you agree to gamble, I'm going to chop off your finger,' I'd offer him both hands rather than start gambling again."

I laughed. "Whenever you start saying anything, you always launch into this sort of nonsense. If you do as I say, I'll see that you win a prize as good as the one you'd get if you had the last two numbers right."

It was his turn to laugh. "You're no god, sir! But supposing you *could* do that for me, I'd certainly do anything you say."

"Very well, then. Stay right where you are. Don't move and don't say a word."

I went into the passenger cabin and took twenty taels from my case.

Awen had remained silent and motionless as ordered. "If you can really do as you say, there's hope for you yet," I said, taking the money out of my pocket and handing it to him. "I'm giving you this for the sole purpose of redeeming your things from the pawnshop."

His suspicion yielding to amusement, Awen looked at the money and smiled, but didn't dare take it. "You're pulling my leg, aren't you, sir?" he said after a time.

"I've never in all my life pulled anyone's leg, let alone yours," I said sternly. "But you are to do only as I say, not get any improper ideas or start treating this money as if it were some kind of windfall. If you fail to redeem your things, and start gambling again, I'll tell your mother and drive you away without mercy."

Finally he realized that I meant what I said and, prostrating himself before me, began to kowtow, overwhelmed with shame. Through his tears he addressed the money I had given him, "O, Money, you're the earthly embodiment of a god. I shall bow down my stubborn head before you and attain the fruits of enlightenment."

"Oh, come on!" I said. "I told you just now not to say such preposterous things, but you've forgotten already. You'd better take the money off with you and go and face the wall and start meditating on your sins. Don't disturb me unless I call you."

"Yes, yes, of course, sir," he said over and over again as he left the cabin.

As I watched him go, I couldn't help grinning to myself. Such was the magical power of money that I, as the money god, held Awen in the palm of my hand. What a pity I didn't have *more* money! If I had, I'd be able to control practically everything in the world. Then I began thinking of what Koto had told me the previous night. If I had a great deal of money and could build her the most exquisite and beautiful retreat as well as the most secluded and elegant tomb, I'd take her by the hand and point out all their features, and every plant, tree, mound, and rock would be exactly to her taste, and whatever delight she took in them I would take, too. Unfortunately, both retreat and tomb were beyond my means. Koto insisted on having them, so she was willing to accept disgrace and degradation in hopes of acquiring the necessary money. What an appalling thing money was! If I had charge of the economy, I'd overthrow the rule of money and substitute gravel instead, causing the people of the world to prospect for gravel instead of gold, in which case China, being such a large country, would be in a splendid position. If the gravel were exported, it would be useless, while if it were left by the side of the road, there would be too much of it for anyone to pick up, and so nobody would bother. The resulting social harmony would recapture the spirit of the Three Dynasties![11]

The readers of my book should understand that as a youth I was much given to fantasizing. But for the intrusion of external events into my life, I should long since have gone out of my mind. So lively was my imagination that some stimulus would set it off, some sight would stir up my emotions, and I would find myself starting down the path of the most tender, romantic passion. And so on this occasion, as I drank alone in the cabin with the breeze in my face, I was overcome by yesterday's emotions, which returned with feverish intensity and extended themselves to Koto. However, this book has not been written merely to speak of passion, and I need not go into any detail. Let me pass on to another subject.

Awen accompanied me as far as Xiangxi, then took the same boat back. I found room for several pots of jasmine under the willow trees shading my thatched cottage, and in the evening I used to sit by my window and look out at them. They held all the unexpected charm of a beautiful girl encountered in the wilderness, and in my dreams I felt as if I were back on the boat at Guashan.

Finding myself with time on my hands the following day, I was looking through my cases when I received a fearful shock. The photographs Koto had sent me were missing—every last one of them! And that wasn't all. The poems I had written expressing my longing for her—poems I had gathered up and bound into a slim volume—were also missing. They must have been stolen by Susu, no question about that. Not once since our marriage had she or I ever mentioned Koto. She knew perfectly well of the relationship, of course, but she chose not to speak of it. As to what view she held of Koto, I had no idea. But now that she possessed all this evidence, what could her silence possibly mean? Her love for me was, in my estimation, as great as any love could be—she could never bring herself to make me suffer and then tell my mother—but there was no way I could face her, nonetheless. My reason for not mentioning Koto to her in the beginning was my fear that if I did, it might affect the love that she and I had for each other—the same reason, no doubt, for her failure to mention Koto to me. However, at this point she would surely become suspicious—suspicious that I harbored some ulterior motive. Very well, then, I would just have to write her a letter dispelling her suspicions. But what should I write? I spread out the sheet of paper in front of me, dipped my brush in ink, and thought long and hard—but failed to write a single word.

Still at a loss as to what to do, I heard a buzzing of voices down at the ferry. Craning my neck, I saw that the overnight packet from Guashan had arrived. The boatman called at my office and drew a letter from his pocket. A glance at the envelope told me it was from Susu. I wanted to open it then and there, but the boatman began complaining about something that had happened to him on the way. During the night he had run into some bandits at Douwei in Fengshan and been robbed of twelve hundred taels in cash; he wanted me to notify the authorities. He bared his left arm and showed it to me—covered in gashes. The people in the agency crowded around to look, filling the room to overflowing.

With no time to read my letter, I rushed off to inform my superior, then sent the boatman over to the county offices to file his report, after which I applied for a warrant of arrest. These matters kept me busy until lunchtime.

As I ate my lunch, I began wondering whether the twelve hundred taels were to blame for the boatman's injuries as well as the shock the passengers had suffered. If so, Turtle's warnings about the bedevilment of money were pearls of wisdom.

After lunch my superior came back and spoke very freely to me about the current state of affairs. He said that the Imperial Court had accepted Kang Youwei's and Liang Qichao's proposals and decided on sweeping reforms;[12] it was almost impossible to predict the changes that might occur. However, at the time I hadn't the slightest control over the events in my own family—I couldn't even think how to secure my own happiness—let alone over national or international affairs, so I made only an offhand response.

Not until evening did I have a chance to open Susu's letter, which filled me with shame. It ran:

My dear Shan,

I have long known the story of your relationship with Koto. I myself am the reason why you and she were unable to fulfill your desires, and I feel guilty about it and reproach myself. Life holds no greater frustration than the one you and she have had to bear. But you have always been so tight-lipped, as if you feared I might be jealous of her, which goes to show how little you know me. I often think of the fact that you and she have been together since childhood. Under such circumstances, who wouldn't have felt affection, particularly a girl and a boy? When I left my sisters to marry you, I regretted having to part from them, so your distress over Koto is easy for me to imagine. But in the three years in which I have received your love, I have been especially favored, for which I am deeply grateful. It seemed to me that you must have forgotten her, and in my mind I even took her part and resented your lack of constancy—until I came upon these lines in one of your lyrics:

My love I left in two different places;
Borrow the scales, you'll see it weighs the same.[13]

I also found these lines in one of your art songs:

At the green gauze window there was once a beauty,
Whom I saw as double;
She must be you.[14]

From these and other similar references too numerous to mention, I came to realize that you truly are a man of feeling and that the reason you love me is simply that you see me as Koto. At first I didn't know what she was like, and I imagined her as I wished to imagine her. I thought that if you could transfer to me the love you felt for her, I must be superior to her. But now that I have seen a photograph of her, I cannot help blushing with embarrassment. I have come to feel a greater sympathy for her, to say nothing of you. Under these circumstances the fact that you transferred your love to me makes me even more grateful for your favor. Ah, Koto! To me she is the lucky star in the constellation of my birth, the source of all my blessings, which is why I have hung up her photograph in my room. On festival days I shall do homage before it and pray that it may always bring me luck and you even more luck. But Shan, I know how you are suffering. You and Koto must be allowed to marry! The reason you cannot is that you are afraid of your mother's severity and of my jealousy. But I do have some responsibility in both of those matters.

I have appealed to your mother with all the persuasiveness at my command and have succeeded in winning her consent. As for my own feelings, I have considered them from every possible angle. My attitude toward Koto is genuinely free of any trace of resentment. Provided she does not dislike me, I shall enjoy the benefit of her protection. And even if she does dislike me, so long as you do not—or if you do, and I find I can live with that—I shall do nothing whatever to earn anyone's dislike.

Your mother suggested that we wait until Little Tan returns and then get her to serve as matchmaker, but in my opinion this is an opportunity we cannot afford to miss. The bright mirror of your mother's judgment has shed a beam of light on the whole situation, but if we fail to take up this solution, I'm afraid that the mirror may soon be obscured once more. Write to Koto as soon as possible and get her mother's consent, then write back to us. We shall need to send Ajin over with the betrothal gifts.

Appended to the letter was a note.

Your mother has dictated the following:

I have approved your wife's request and consented to Koto's becoming your concubine. I was influenced in the past by the fact that your eldest brother and your cousin both took concubines who brought misfortune to our family, an outcome I would certainly not wish to see repeated. However, I am impressed by the fact that your wife is different from the others, and in order that you and she may enjoy a long and happy marriage, it is important that there be no ill will between you. Koto's conduct as a child was most gratifying; she is by no means unworthy to be your concubine. If the proposal is accepted, act on it immediately. You should have your wife prepare some rooms as an apartment for her.

Readers, just look at these letters and you will see the dreadful dilemma I was faced with. Was Susu sincere in writing her letter? Lest I suspect her of insincerity, she had added the dictated note to convince me of her good faith. I knew perfectly well that my mother's instructions could not have been forged, but it boggled the mind, nevertheless, that she had actually agreed to a request from Susu. As I pondered these questions over and over again, I still could not resolve all of my doubts. I certainly couldn't know in advance that Koto would *not* be willing to be a concubine. I had heard that only from Alcyon; Koto had never told me so herself. But what made my mother think she *would* be willing? Perhaps I was simply being overanxious. Then another thought struck me. Koto was now married to Mr. Sheng, a fact of which my mother was no doubt unaware. Oh, if she *was* going to let me marry Koto, why did she have to wait until now before giving her blessing? By now Koto was another man's wife, so how could I even put the suggestion to her? At this point I felt two impulses, one reflecting my moral sense, the other my passionate desire, and both were at war inside me, a war from which I could scarcely detach myself. After a long battle, passion declared itself the victor, and I decided not to write anything in favor of the proposal, merely to send Susu's letter to Koto together with my mother's note. I also wrote a separate note to Orchid asking her to observe Koto's reaction and report back to me. I anticipated that Koto would have trouble framing her reply, and it made sense to enlist Orchid's help in giving me an outsider's impression.

I was on tenterhooks after the letters were dispatched— every day I waited down by the shore for a reply—but one or two days turned into five or six, and still no letter came. I had nothing I could pass on to Susu, but even so I didn't dare press Koto for a reply. Eventually after ten days or more I received a letter from Orchid, which ran as follows:

> *Dear Cousin Shan,*
>
> *When your letter arrived, my sister had nothing whatever to say. Over the past few days her behavior has departed from its normal pattern, but I don't know what it is she is contemplating. She had no reaction to any of my indirect inquiries. However, her expression, if one studies it closely, seems to indicate a state of extreme despair, and in the last couple of days she has succumbed to a mysterious ailment. She has intense pains in her chest, and when she retches, tiny silverfish-like organisms appear in her vomit. The doctor says her condition is caused by a depression of the liver, but lately she has rejected all treatment and resolved on a speedy death. At least that is her intention, although it is not something an outsider can judge. Shan, you have known my sister a long time. I expect you will be able to deduce what she has in mind. . . .*

I was utterly perplexed by this letter. Time and again I tried to deduce Koto's intentions, but I could find no clue. Then I tried putting myself in her place and realized that at this point she had a fearful dilemma of her own. It was not that she *couldn't* leave Mr. Sheng, but that such an action would be improper, as she had no doubt calculated, in which case my sending her Susu's letter had only spurred her on into carrying out her promise to join me in the next life. I would have to write to her at once and set her mind at rest, I decided, but then it occurred to me that that letter would be even harder to write than the other. Twice I picked up my brush, only to lay it down again. In the end I flung it down, screwed up the sheet of paper, and heaved a great sigh of despair. I began to reproach myself, bitterly regretting all the time I had wasted. Had I known what an effective advocate Susu would be with my mother, I would have planned this ages ago. What good did it do to pursue the quarry after it was safely locked in the barn?[15] Then I remembered that Koto had already been taken by Mr. Sheng before Susu even came on the scene, so the crucial blunder had been made years before. As I see it now, it all happened because I was too hesitant to speak my mind. I now know that nothing is impossible in this world, provided we have the will to act. But at that point I was like a condemned man who receives a pardon after his execution has been carried out. What possible good does it do him? And so I blamed myself, quite unable to think of anything that would absolve my guilt.

In the evenings I sat alone by my window and drank to forget my sorrows. But the scent from the flowers would stir them up again, and I found it impossible to gain relief. Instead I caught a chill from the autumn winds off the river.

At first I forced myself to keep going, but before many days had passed I could no longer get out of bed. I was suffering from undulant fever with overheated blood, which became agitated and had to be brought up. My illness had developed into consumption.

The doctor furrowed his brow and declared there was nothing that medicine could do for me. I was convinced I would not recover and, ill as I was, dashed off farewell letters to my mother and Susu. I also wrote Koto a note reiterating my vow to join her in the next life. After the letters had gone off, I felt a great emptiness in my heart. Of all the things in this world, none belonged to me. Only Susu might follow me to the grave. As for my mother's grief, I had no idea what form it might take. I began fantasizing about many things, happy as well as sad, all of which flashed before my mind at once. Such was my mental confusion that I almost lost track of time.

One morning at dawn I was told that someone had come by boat to fetch me, someone who said he had been sent by my mother. When I called him in, however, I thought my addled brain must be deceiving me.

I must inform my readers that my visitor was none other than Pearlie, the servant I had always detested. However, on this occasion seeing Pearlie was tantamount to seeing Koto herself—he was her surrogate. I was so grateful for her concern that I forced myself to sit up, sent the servants out of the room, and, calling him up close, questioned him about Koto's health. He stammered as if he couldn't speak but showed me a letter he had brought. It was a personal note from Koto herself, part of which ran:

> *The other day, when your letter arrived, I was unable to reply at once. It has been my lifelong desire to serve you, but I kept thinking about her ladyship's severity. How could I be sure that her feelings for me might not change? I suffer from family despotism as it is and am doing my best to escape it, but if I escape it here only to fall into a terrible trap elsewhere, my death will not be long delayed.*

*In itself my death may be of little consequence, but what
would it do to Shan, who loves me? I have thought about
this over and over again. If I were to become your wife,
you and I might sink into depths of misery from which we
could never escape. Your love for me is not concerned with
the physical side, and if I desire to respond to it, it is not
necessary that I do so as your wife or concubine. In that
case the marriage that is being proposed is really unnecessary, and while it would bring us no benefit, it would
destroy your wife's love for you. I am hoping to repent my
sins so that I may be blessed by good fortune in the life to
come. How could I allow myself to become the enemy of
love in this life, something that would only compound my
sins? Perhaps by leaving our love incomplete, by cherishing
our unfulfilled hopes, you and I may, in this life or the
next, arrive at a perfect union. Surely you know how I feel?
Today I received your letter of farewell. As I read it and
reread it, I sensed that your language expressed regret.
Oh, Shan! So long as I was with you, I wouldn't mind
if I were burned to ashes. The one thought I cannot abide
is that you should be plunged into pain and despair on my
account. Sadness and joy are inescapable in our lives, but
if we fail to enjoy ourselves while we can, if we lead those
whom we love into despair, are we not, as the saying goes,
conspiring in our own misfortune? Shan, you are an intelligent person. Settle your doubts and pack up your things
and come and visit me, and we'll enjoy ourselves and laugh
together. I also have a piece of news that will cheer you up.
That Sheng fellow has been driven away by the money
demon. (Whether he has gone for good remains to be seen.)
    I have more things to say than can be said in a letter,
and they will have to wait until we meet. I am sending
Pearlie by boat to fetch you. Take good care of yourself
on the way. I shall give you a warm welcome and nurse
you through your illness. Do come back!*

On finishing the letter, I felt as if I had sipped the nectar of perfect understanding, a taste I can no longer describe. After telling Pearlie to pack my bags, I took leave of my superior and boarded the boat. All along the way I was plagued by the demons of illness. To make matters worse, I had always had a hearty dislike for Pearlie and didn't care to converse with him. Instead I languished in my bunk, where from time to time I took out Koto's letter and reread it over and over. Her love for me was deeper than the deepest chasm, I concluded. My original plan was no different from the one she now proposed, which was why I had never seriously entertained the thought of marriage. The reason wasn't necessarily any concern I might have over Susu's jealousy, but the thought of the impossible position I would have been in, between the two women.

Although my love drew no distinction between them, from the point of view of the one left out at any given moment, such a distinction would often seem to exist. If that was the case even with my cousins when we were children, think how much worse it would be with wives! There was no prior bond of feeling between Susu and Koto. It was only because I loved Koto that Susu, out of her love for me, had extended her love to Koto. And Koto's relationship to Susu was of exactly the same kind; it was *my* love that they both prized. Now, supposing they were standing in front of me, unless I could somehow split my gaze and look directly at both, one was bound to think I was favoring the other. Unless my every word and smile were directed to both at the same time, one would inevitably feel left out. Suppose I were returning from a journey and they came out together to greet me. I could grasp their hands in mine, all right, and there was no reason why I couldn't greet both of them with the same words. But as soon as we took a step anywhere, one would have to go in front and the other behind. Even if I held hands with both and we walked abreast, we couldn't be together during *all* of the day's activities, and one of them was bound to feel dissatisfied. In the eyes of that one, the other's talk and behavior would always convey a certain smugness. And next day, when they changed places, the reverse would apply. A rapid alternation of contentment and discontent was unavoidable. Eventually, without their even being aware of it, jealousy and frustration would develop. When that time came, if I could split myself in two, or if all three of us could fuse into a single being, well and good. Otherwise, I would find myself in trouble no matter what I did.

Pursuing these thoughts, I imagined a situation and put myself in it, then let every conceivable fantasy, every conceivable problem—evoking happiness, anger, laughter, tears— flash one after the other before my eyes, while with all the wisdom and intelligence I possessed I tried to find a solution. I failed.

Then the truth dawned on me, and I gave a rueful smile, realizing that Koto's judgment was far better than mine.

Toward evening the following day our boat arrived at the gate, several hundred yards from Koto's house, and tied up. I wondered where we were, and was told at Wan'an Bridge. Why didn't we go farther in, I asked.

"We've moved here," Pearlie told me in some surprise. "Surely you knew that, sir?"

"You're so tight-lipped about everything," I burst out. "How *would* I know?"

He smiled. "But didn't the letter say anything about it?"

"Why did they move here?" I asked, ignoring the question. "I suppose this is better than the other place?"

"Yes," he replied, his eyes searching in the distance. Then he pointed up ahead. "That's it over there, where those tall trees are tossing in the wind. The mistress bought it for two thousand taels. It's as cool and refreshing as Purple Cloud Cave."

I looked where he was pointing. I could see the tall trees, but nothing more.

Pearlie went ashore and hired a sedan chair for me. It was

the height of summer, and the heat inside the chair was stifling, but we had gone no more than a few hundred yards before we suddenly entered a dense wood, where the trees formed a canopy overhead and our ears rang with the trilling of cicadas. It was like stepping into a world of coolness. Although I am a native of Hangzhou, I had never set foot here before.

I asked one of the bearers where we were. "This is the Chen Garden," he said. The name took me by surprise. Had Koto approved it when she decided to live here? As I wondered, the stone path that we were following veered slightly to the east and brought us to a parapet wall plastered in green with a coping of fine tiles arranged in a pattern of Buddhist crosses. A group of tall willows, driven by the wind, leaned over the wall, their delicate fronds reaching almost to the ground. Skirting the wall, we turned west and came to the main entrance to the compound. A pair of red gates, tightly shut, with a large brass knocker, proclaimed that some great beauty lived there. The bearers hammered furiously on the gate so that the sound would carry into the house. Had no one opened it, the gate might have been damaged, so I shouted at them to stop, then stepped from my chair.

By this time the gate had been opened by a pigtailed young girl who didn't recognize me and whom I didn't recognize, either. We've made a mistake, I thought. "Isn't this Cousin Mei's house?" I asked the girl.

"Who's Cousin Mei?" she said in a surprised tone.

Embarrassed, I turned back to the bearers. "This is the wrong place," I said. "Why have you brought me here?"

"Pearlie told us to," they replied.

At the sound of Pearlie's name the girl gave a broad smile. "Pearlie? He went to Xiangxi. Is he back already?"

"Is Pearlie one of your servants?"

"Yes."

I couldn't help laughing. "In that case we haven't come to

the wrong place, after all. Go and tell them Cousin Shan is here."

At mention of my name the girl gave another broad smile and was about to say something when she caught herself. Turning on her heel, she went back into the house with me following. Inside the second gate it was all dark green shade. At the end of a winding passageway was a moon gate and beyond it thousands of lush bamboos, none over ten feet tall, above which stretched a green canopy of foliage that reflected the light onto our clothes, turning them a shade of turquoise. From behind an ornamental rock, the path wound its way east, until it brought us to a south-facing building, tall and imposing. A roll-up screen covered the doorway, and bamboo curtains brushed the ground. The girl led me inside the room, which was deserted. It was furnished in the grand style with pieces I had never seen before, except for the painting by Wang Hui,[16] which I recognized as Koto's.

Not knowing which was her room, I wasn't sure where to go next, so I asked the girl to announce my arrival. Then I heard laughter that sounded like Orchid's, but when someone came out from behind the screen, it wasn't Orchid, but a youth wearing a padded white gown. He was no one I knew, and I was perplexed. He asked me something or other, and I replied. He looked about fifteen or sixteen, and I had the impression I had met him before but couldn't think where. When I asked him his family name, Orchid came out from behind the screen laughing uproariously and clapping her hands. "I was *positive* you two wouldn't recognize one another!" Cousin Mei and Jade followed her out.

"Orchid's up to her tricks again," Cousin Mei said to me. Then, pointing to the youth, she went on, "This is your cousin, whom you haven't seen in more than ten years. I'm not surprised you didn't recognize him."

It dawned on me that the youth must be Koto's cousin. He had been adopted in infancy by his maternal grandparents in Nanjing and had never returned to Hangzhou, which was why I hadn't recognized him. He behaved toward me in a distinctly awkward manner, and as I could find nothing to say to him, either, I confined myself to the usual pleasantries.

Cousin Mei noticed that my clothes were damp with sweat and told Orchid to help me out of them, then had the youth take them inside.

Jade clung to me, gripping my hand. "Shan, you're standing here like a perfect stranger! Why not come on inside?"

"It's his first visit here," said Cousin Mei. "Why don't you show him the way?"

Jade took my hand and led me inside and, with Cousin Mei and Orchid following us, we went around the screen. The rear court, facing north, was festooned with beaded lanterns, tinkling in the breeze. Windows and tables gleamed; not a speck of dust was to be seen anywhere. Jade pointed to the room on the left. "This is Mother's room." And then she pointed to the one on the right. "This is my cousin's." I nodded but did not go into either. Then we descended some steps and turned west. She pointed to a side room. "This one's mine. Orchid's is opposite."

The two rooms faced one another, their glass windows both done in the "ice plum" style. In the center court was a paved terrace for peonies, with banana plants and a few ornamental rocks at each side to complete the picture. Overhead was a greenish blue awning to screen out the fierce sun.

The path took us behind the side rooms, and I realized that this wing of the house had windows on opposite sides, rather like the pleasure boats on the lake. To the north the path led to a small studio with six ornately decorated windows. It was screened off by a bamboo curtain, through which a cloud of medicinal vapor curled upward. Below the steps were several asparagus ferns interspersed with pots of chloranthus and jasmine. There was also a stone bench, shiny and inviting.

"I suppose this is Koto's room?"

"Yes."

Cousin Mei, who had already parted the curtains and gone in, looked back at me. "She's been sick a long time. I don't even know if she's awake."

"Please don't startle her," I said, following Cousin Mei in. Facing us was a mirror some six feet wide, beneath which was a couch, a small table, and some bamboo chairs covered with cool summer mats. To the left was a door leading to Cousin Mei's room. If you went around the mirror you came at last to Koto's bedroom with its bed facing south. The room was quite spacious. The windows in front looked out on the roll-up screens in the south courtyard. On the west side were two huge windows, both done in the "hundred leaves" style. In the middle of the room was a tent of silk gauze, equipped with a small table and a couch, on which Koto was resting. Seen through the gauze she looked like a hanging peony in a faint mist.

Cousin Mei was the first to enter. I was still beside the bed when Koto called to me from the couch. Letting go of Jade's hand, I went in to greet her. Her face was terribly drawn. She was about to sit up when Cousin Mei stopped her.

"You're very thin, Shan," said Koto. "Bringing up blood is a dangerous thing, you know. What brought it on?"

"Shan's been bringing up blood?" cried Cousin Mei in alarm.

Embarrassed, I tried to deny it. "Oh, I just drank a bit too much and found a few flecks of blood in my vomit. I'm quite all right, though, just awfully tired."

"Then you ought to take a nap," said Cousin Mei, pointing to the bed. "It's quite cool in here. Let me drive the mosquitoes away. Take a quiet nap now, and then you can have a nice long talk with Koto later."

"I really don't feel like a nap just yet," I said, but she had already gone over to drive away the mosquitoes. I was about to protest, when Koto silenced me with a glance.

"I've been sick for ten days or more," said Koto. "Only today have I begun to feel a little better. The trouble is that I get nauseous as soon as I try to sit up."

"You're still vomiting?" I asked.

"No, that's stopped, but I can't take much food or drink. And I really can't stand any fuss and bother. Luckily I have this room all to myself, with just the vaporizer for company, so it works out well enough."

She called to Cousin Mei. "Mother, take a look at the medicine for me, would you? Don't let it run dry again and burn, or it will taste too bitter."

Cousin Mei called Jade in to see to it.

"I tend to get ill, and when I do, Mother finds it just *impossible* to cope," commented Koto in an icy tone.

I knew this was a jab at Cousin Mei, who got the point and left the room. Koto watched her go, remarking with a smile, "I simply don't understand why older people are so insensitive to others' feelings. As you can well imagine, Shan, there's a multitude of things I want to say to you. It's as if I had the whole *Twenty-four Histories* in front of me and didn't know where to begin! In a word, though, you must know what I've been through, so there's no need for me to go into all that. What I really wanted to say to you was summed up in that letter I wrote. What did you think of it, by the way?"

I flushed with embarrassment, and it was some time before I replied. "Your judgment is far better than mine. My wife made that appeal out of her love for me, but so far as you were concerned I couldn't help feeling ashamed. Please forget the whole idea. Just write it off as so much nonsense."

Koto's eyes searched my face, and for a long time she said nothing. It crossed my mind that when I spoke that last sentence I might have had an odd expression on my face. I felt a mixture of embarrassment, shame, and regret, and these emotions must have registered on my face and produced a similar reaction in her. She and I were almost like mirror images of one another, sad when the other was sad, glad when the other was glad, as the saying goes.

As I sat there silently, with nothing I could add, Orchid came in with the medicine, and Koto told her to put it on the table. "Is Pearlie back yet?" she asked. "If he is, Shan's bags can be brought in here."

"He's not back yet," said Orchid.

Just then his voice could be heard in the front courtyard. "There he is," said Orchid, bustling out.

It was evening, and outside the tent the whine of the massed mosquitoes filled the air like a woodwind orchestra. The pigtailed young girl brought in a lamp and placed it in a holder hanging from the ceiling. I was reminded of the incident at the gate. "When I first arrived, I thought I'd come to the wrong place," I said to Koto. "Who's the little girl with the pigtails?"

"She's a first cousin of mine on my mother's side. My uncle died young and she and her brother were raised by her grandparents. Now that they have passed away, the children have come here to live with us. Her name's Brightie, but she's incredibly dim, no match for her brother. Have you met him, by the way? As gauche as a new concubine. He's been with us a good ten days but knows nobody here except my mother. He has a book in his hand all day long, and he shuts himself up in his little cubbyhole, quite oblivious to the heat. He's seen me just twice, and exchanged only a couple of words each time. I compared him to a new concubine, and that's more or less how he looks and thinks."

I laughed. "A new concubine would have her own maid as well as the wife to talk to. He seems to be even more isolated."

Brightie was standing by the door and peering inside, hesitant to leave. Koto laughed. "There's your maid for you." To Brightie she added, "What are you waiting for?"

"Mother told me to collect the medicine cup."

"Oh, I almost forgot. Shan, see whether it's cool enough, would you?"

I touched the cup, which was still rather warm, and then raised it to my lips and blew on it.

"You mustn't blow on medicine," said Brightie, "or it won't do any good——" Koto turned on her and, breaking off in midsentence, the girl fled.

On tasting the medicine, I found it extremely bitter.

"Whoever gave you this prescription?" I asked. "He can't have been a women's specialist."

"It was Wu Jiuxiang, who's a well-known women's specialist."

"Then he doesn't deserve his reputation. He has no understanding of the female psychology. With women you always need to add some licorice to take away the taste, no matter what kind of medicine it is. This is harsh as well as bitter. How do you manage to get it down?"

She laughed. "You can't consider *taste* when you're taking medicine. In any case, I believe that a bitter taste may do you more good than a sweet one. But it would be a waste of time getting *you* to try anything bitter."

I laughed and said nothing, just offered her the medicine. She lay on her stomach and sipped from the cup as I held it. As soon as she had drunk it, I handed her another cup to rinse her mouth out with. I was left with a harsh, bitter taste myself, and I also rinsed out my own mouth.

"I'm feeling a bit brighter," she said. "Help me up, would you?" I put the medicine down on the bed table and helped her sit up. She straightened her dress and got down from the bed, then sat at the table, her chin cupped in her hands. The lamplight filtering through the silken gauze lit up her face, which looked like cherry-apple blossom in autumn, with an incomparably delicate beauty. Touchingly, her cheeks still bore the faint imprint of the bed mat.

She told me to open the window and let in some fresh air. Although I feared the night air might be bad for her, she insisted it would do her no harm. I noticed a small garden outside, about half a *mu*[17] in size, filled with lush bamboo. A cold, silvery moon shone through the bamboo onto the corner of the west wall, and I recalled that it was the seventeenth of the month.

"With moonlight like this, the West Lake ought to be spectacular tomorrow night," I said. "What a pity we're too ill to take a boat out!"

"Come over here," she said. "There's something I want to tell you. I now feel quite capable of being up and about. How about you?"

"Oh, almost back to normal."

"Then we *will* go and enjoy the moonlight tomorrow night."

"You're *crazy,* you know that?" I said with a laugh. "How can you even think of it in your condition?"

"I shall be all right. Let me see if I can walk." I took her arm. "I don't need any help," she said. Then, holding herself erect, she made her way by tiny steps over to the window, where she stood gazing at the new moon.

She looked as graceful as a willow swaying in the breeze. The line in *The West Chamber* "Her every step bestirs one's pity and love"[18] might have been written for her. Standing by her side, I praised the quiet beauty of her house. "My first thought in buying it," she said, "was to live here on my own. As it turned out, I was joined by two other people. Still, it was because of this house that I got rid of one odious character, which does give me a certain satisfaction."

I knew that the odious character was Mr. Sheng. "Where is he now?" I asked.

She laughed. "Oh, it's a long story. Let me sit down, and I'll tell you."

She went to the bed and, supporting herself on the rail, sat down, while I took a seat beside her.

"The owner of the place we used to live in," she said, "wanted to sell and put a price of three thousand taels on the house. I asked Mother to demand the purchase price from Sheng, but he thought it too high and wanted it reduced by one thousand taels, which the owner wouldn't agree to. At that point we started looking about and found this place. It's a better house, and the price was more reasonable, too, so we bought it. The furnishings cost over a thousand more. However, it turned out that the purchase money from Sheng had been borrowed from someone else, and the very first week we were in the house the creditor called half a dozen times asking for his money. Sheng didn't have it, and a week ago he packed up and took off for the capital, telling us that he was going home to get the money for the loan. But when he left, he took every scrap of his belongings with him. He even took a photograph of himself that I had tossed into a drawer. All of which leads me to believe that he has no intention of returning. As he was about to leave, he had a word with me. 'Eventually someone should repay that three thousand taels I borrowed from my friend,' he said, 'but if it isn't repaid, it won't matter.' Then an even stranger thing happened. When his friend came back again, he said nothing about any debt. At the time I didn't understand his motives, although I did suspect that if Sheng was really leaving me for good, I would have to repay the loan myself. He must have introduced his friend to our house so that the man could call on us, the pair of them being as close as two brothers. The friend looked as if he had some nasty little scheme in mind; he was constantly making eyes at me. The fact was that he had only agreed to the loan because he had designs on me. Shan, just think how colossally stupid the man was! He mistook me for a different kind of person altogether. In short he and Sheng were both bedeviled by money, and so they had only themselves to blame when I bedeviled *them*."

She spoke these words with an air of satisfaction, but I took a very different view of the matter. Koto saw only that the two men were bedeviled by money. What she failed to see was that she herself had *become* the money demon. In her relationship with me, however, she was the love demon and had nothing whatever to do with money, a fact for which I was more grateful than ever.

Before long Orchid arrived with a hamper. When she saw the two of us sitting side by side on the edge of the bed, she stopped and was about to withdraw, when Koto called her in. As she deposited the hamper on a table near the window, Orchid slipped me a sidelong glance and a smile. I guessed the reason for the smile and couldn't help blushing, but Koto was sublimely unconcerned and merely told her to move the table closer to the bed.

Jade now came in and helped Orchid with the table. Koto also had them bring a porcelain stool over by the table and told me to sit down. She then opened the hamper and looked inside. It contained cups and delicacies arranged in the form of a tangram, all fresh and inviting. Then she called for some wine to share with me. Orchid moved a chair up to the table and, dropping down on one knee beside the chair, poured me some wine from the ice jug in her hand. My glass was huge, but Orchid filled it to the brim and urged me to drink up. Jade was amused at my obvious reluctance. "Don't you feel guilty, refusing to drink your wine after Sister has gone down on her knees to you?" Orchid made a face at her.

Next Jade poured some wine for Koto, but when she had filled only a fraction of the glass, Koto stopped her. Orchid then poured herself a full cup and pulled Jade over to sit beside her. Giggling, she raised the glass and in one draft drank more than half of it, after which she began pressing Jade and me to drink up.

"What makes *you* so happy?" Koto asked Orchid.

"Ever since we moved here, you've been looking like Guan-yin, with your head cast down and a sorrowful look in your eyes, sitting there all day long inside your silk tent, but today for the first time you're smiling and up and about. Now, isn't that enough to make anybody happy?"

Koto flushed and gave Orchid an angry glare, which only sent her into an even worse fit of the giggles. At the sound of her laughter, Cousin Mei came in and, seeing all four of us at the same table, wanted to join us, but a look of loathing crossed Koto's face, and she pushed her cup away and declined to eat or drink anymore. Instead she lay down on the bed, pleading fatigue.

"Your cousin can't stand any fuss and bother," said Cousin Mei. "Why don't we take everything out to the center court and enjoy the evening breeze?"

"Mother is *ever* so sensitive to my feelings," murmured Koto.

"Shan, let's have a drink together," Cousin Mei said to me.

Koto intervened before I could reply. "Shan's unwell, too, and shouldn't have any more to drink. A breath of fresh air in the courtyard would do him far more good." I had intended to stay with Koto, but I couldn't bear to contradict her.

I accompanied Cousin Mei through her room to the center court, while Orchid and Jade brought along the hamper and lantern. A table was set up under the banana palms, and there we continued our meal, at which we were joined by Koto's cousin and Brightie.

My thoughts were still with Koto, however, and I took no pleasure in the drinking. I declined any more wine and asked for something to eat, but after a few mouthfuls I found that I couldn't swallow. I left the table but could hardly go straight back to Koto, so I lay down on a rattan couch in front of the steps and gazed up at the moon.

"Tired, Shan?" asked Cousin Mei. "I've made up the couch for you in the east chamber. You'd better go to bed."

"The east chamber?" I said casually. "I'll be sharing with your nephew, I suppose?"

"Oh, no. His room's next to yours. You'll be on your own, but you won't be lonely."

"It's decorated exactly like the west chamber," said Orchid with a chuckle. "At first I wanted it for myself, but Mother wouldn't let me have it. The fact that she puts you in there shows how much she loves you. But I also think I was rather lucky *not* to get that room. Mine is close by, and sometimes I hear footsteps in there—awfully scary."

"Oh, rubbish!" said Cousin Mei. "You're only trying to frighten him. Those footsteps are just the grandfather clock ticking away. Don't be taken in, Shan."

"I'm not used to being all alone in an empty room. I'd be perfectly content to enjoy a cool night out here on the couch."

Jade laughed. "Shan, you may be a boy, but you're just as scared as Koto. Ever since she got ill, I've been keeping her company. Every night, just when I'm falling asleep, she calls out and wakes me up. We ought to get you to take over for me." Just then Koto's voice could be heard calling her, and Jade rushed off.

Before long she was back again. "Sister wants me to stay with her."

Cousin Mei laughed. "She's so scared she can't be on her own in that room for a second. Go on with your supper, Jade. Shan, would you mind keeping Koto company for a while?"

Responding as to an imperial amnesty, I hurried off to her room, where I found her still lying inside the silk tent. "I'm tired and I want to sleep," she said. "Please don't disturb me."

"Why don't you sleep in the bed?"

"I've been using the couch for some time now. I've left the bed to Jade, who's been keeping me company. You're welcome to take a nap there yourself, if you want to."

If I take a nap and fall sound asleep, I thought, I don't suppose Cousin Mei will be able to do very much about it. I went up to Koto and took her hand. "Look, would you do me a favor? If I fall asleep and your mother starts calling me, please tell her to stop."

She gave a slight nod. I don't know what she was thinking, but a pink flush suffused her cheeks and she motioned me away from her. "Off you go. Don't disturb me while I'm trying to sleep."

I knew she had tacitly agreed to my staying, and I took leave of her and went over to the bed, where I chased away the mosquitoes, lowered the net, and lay down. I sensed a different kind of fragrance on the pillow, not orchid or musk, but something I couldn't quite put a name to. At home, when Susu was away at her parents' and I was left alone in the empty bedroom tossing and turning beneath the quilt, I often sensed a similar odd fragrance, which served only to intensify my loneliness. But the fragrance from this pillow had something different about it; it was warm, not cool like the other. The cool kind of fragrance was calculated to bring sorrow and anguish, so that you couldn't sleep all night, but this warm fragrance was like a sleeping draft, stealing into the heart and stirring the soul, so that imperceptibly, as if drinking nectar, you drifted into oblivion.

My readers should understand that my illness had lasted some ten days, during which I had been really unwell, but that now I felt wonderfully content—content without any reservation. How shall I describe my feelings? Generally speaking, when people arrive at such a state, their hearts are free of all impediments and they have a constant sense of well-being. But I couldn't help thinking of Susu, and of how she didn't know I was here, but thought I was still on my sickbed in that cottage in Xiangxi. She would be constantly worrying about me. Beneath her thin quilt, on her lonely pillow, who knows how she might be longing for me? And so I forgot about Koto in front of me and let my thoughts drift back to Susu, alone in her room. In my dream we shared the same pillow and talked on and on, in a scene of the most tender, romantic passion. Even if I had a pair of brushes writing together and thousands upon thousands of words at my disposal, I could not describe more than a fraction of what we said and did.

Susu seemed to sympathize with me in my illness, patting me on the shoulder with her delicate hand. I awoke, focused my eyes, and there she was, unmistakably, right in front of me. I stretched out my hand to grasp hers and kissed it. "My dear . . . ," I began.

To my astonishment I heard a strange voice reply, "You're talking in your sleep! Quick, wake up! You mustn't let Mother hear you."

Startled, I sat upright. It was Koto who had touched me. I looked at her in her white gown of raw silk, as slender and delicate as Flying Swallow,[19] and wondered what I might have said in my sleep. "I'm afraid I may have forgotten myself. It's this illness . . . ," I began.

She motioned to me. "Not another word!" Pointing behind the bed, she went on, "Mother's asleep behind that screen. I heard you talking in your sleep, so I woke you up."

I took her hand in a firm grip. "You've been so kind, I really can't find words to tell you how grateful I am. But my dream was so scary, I don't think I'll be able to sleep anymore. Let me get up, and we'll talk the rest of the night away, to help me over my nightmare."

"You can't do that! You don't understand. Just now you had something that looked very like rouge in your spittle, which means your illness is far from over. If you don't get any more sleep than this, you'll be in even worse shape tomorrow."

"If I could cough up my heart's blood at your feet, I should not have died in vain!"

She said nothing, but her manner was one of the most tender concern. Supporting herself with one hand on the bed, she turned and stood up. Her eyes remained fixed on mine, as if there were an infinite number of things she would like to say if only she could.

"There are thousands of things I want to tell you, but you won't let me," I said with a sigh. "If only you would, we could lie down together now that everyone's asleep and have a real heart-to-heart talk. I could express all the feelings I have been storing up inside me for so long."

Still she said nothing. I took her by the shoulders. "Look, perhaps you don't *want* to hear what I have to say?"

"Oh, Shan," she said, "you do pester so! You'll be lucky if you escape a telling off from Mother." As she said this, she moved the pillow out a little and then, with one hand supporting her coiffure, drew her knees up and lay down beside me. "Well, what is it you want to tell me?" she asked.

I whispered in her ear. "All I want to know is whether you really have any love for me."

She turned away and wouldn't answer. Fearing she might leave, I held her. She was ticklish, so she turned to face me again, her head tucked low on her breast. I was conscious only of the scent of her hair as it dissolved the last remnants of my will. Those lines from *The West Chamber*, "A tender jade, a fragrance mild, I clasp her to my breast,"[20] might have been written just for me that night.

My readers should understand that originally I had no such intention with regard to Koto. But the predicament I now found myself in was worse than the one faced by Liuxia Hui, who had a woman sitting on his lap. At normal times, with other people, I have been able gradually to get control of myself in a situation like this. Only with Susu was I unable to restrain myself, because in her case it was entirely proper not to do so. With Koto I had not previously thought it proper, but my illness had been given to me by her, and it seemed entirely proper to ask her to cure it for me.

Thirteen years had gone by, and it was only now that we fulfilled our long-cherished desire. But at the time we didn't think of it as entering the realm of bliss. Only the expression "We couldn't help it" would do justice to the situation. My book cannot describe more than an infinitesimal part of all that happened, but on another occasion I wrote a set of eight narrative poems that will serve as a general account. Let me include them here as my "Encounter with an Immortal."[21]

"I am sick, and the wine has gone to my head,
So please don't scold if my speech sounds inane.
Just cure me of my lover's malady,
And of your frail form I'll not complain."

Scared to sleep alone, we were allowed to lie
In adjacent beds and talk the night away.
Even then her heart wouldn't melt with love,
For beyond the double curtains her mother lay.

Now clearly midnight by the water clock,
And still I could not sleep, my thoughts aflame.
I begged her to join me on my pillow,
And silently in stockinged feet she came.

"Haggard with love, I'm ashamed to face you,
But what's the harm in lying here in secret?
With sweat my silken gown's already damp;
Surely we can do without this coverlet?"

Before she would let me undo her sash,
Like an armful of flowers, her fragrance clung.
I knew one part of her mind was willing—
Her love conveyed on the tip of her tongue.

"Your ten years of love are this night repaid.
I pitied you. You wished to talk, you said.
Lest Mother awake beyond the curtains,
I'll take the rest of my love back to my bed."

Nervous, I awoke from a moment's sleep.
"Such a night is worth a golden dower.
And still there's much on my mind I want to do.
Don't say you're too tired and so waste the hour!"

Lovingly back to my pillow she came,
Revealing an even more tender heart.
"Damned be that cock with his ceaseless crowing!
With such a noise we cannot help but part."

I hope my readers will forgive me, but they should understand that this book was not written as an encouragement to license. That is why, like the "precious mirror of love,"[22] it has no text on its obverse side.

As I arose the following morning, I felt that the entire contents of the room were smiling sentimentally at me, as if they knew our secrets of the previous night. Apparently the one person still unaware of them was Cousin Mei. Orchid, supremely astute as always, had long fancied herself in the role of Reddie,[23] but on this occasion, wary of Koto's temper, she thought it better to avoid any flippant remarks and limit herself to a covert smile or two in my direction. In the past I would have been embarrassed, but on this occasion I thought of the affair as something to be proud of and couldn't help beaming with delight. For her part Koto showered me with loving attention. She was washing as I came up to her, and she handed me her towel to dry my face. Noticing that the collar of my shirt was undone, she buttoned it for me, then straightened the front of my jacket. All the while Orchid stood off to one side, a sly half-smile on her face, but Koto paid not the slightest attention to her.

Before long Orchid took herself off, and I placed my cheek against Koto's. "My dear, you're so loving!" She said nothing, just looked into my eyes with infinite love and tenderness. Her crimson lips were moist, deliquescent almost, and more luscious than cherries. I was just about to kiss her, when that confounded Cousin Mei came hesitantly into the room.

"I'm taking Orchid and Jade to visit the bodhisattva,"[24] she said to Koto. "You two ought to get some rest."

"Do you feel up to going?" Koto asked me.

"If you go, I'll certainly go with you."

"Cooped up in a little room—that's how one gets ill in the first place," Koto said to Cousin Mei. "We're both feeling a little better now, and we'd like to join you and get some fresh air."

"Are you two out of your minds? You're so weak, you'll find the traveling far too much for you."

Privately I wasn't at all sure I wanted to go, but Koto had set her heart on it, so I backed her up. Cousin Mei felt she couldn't disappoint us and sent Pearlie off to hire two more sedan chairs.

After breakfast Cousin Mei told Brightie and her brother to mind the house, then led the rest of us to our sedan chairs. Koto's happened to be just in front of mine, and I was entranced by the glint of her jewels against her dark hair. From time to time she would turn her head and look back, presumably worried lest the effort be too much for me, and I felt the same concern for her. As I thought more about this excursion, I asked myself why on earth she and I were not sitting side by side in the silk tent baring our hearts to one another. Why had we chosen to put ourselves through this ordeal in tiny, cramped chairs swaying along under a fierce sun? Then it dawned on me that this was just another exercise in wasting money, in which case we, too, were to be numbered among money's victims.

Only when we had left the city behind did my spirits begin

to lift a little. But sunlight flooded the lake and, reflected off the waves, seemed to pour like molten gold over the land, scorching the eyeballs of all who gazed on it. Wherever the warm wind reached, it was sultry and humid. The bearers' backs fairly ran with sweat—revolting sight! We circled the embankment for a few hundred yards before reaching the shade of some willows. I had always loved the lake for its tranquil beauty, but on this occasion I felt it was no match for Koto's bedroom.

Fortunately, before we had gone much farther, we arrived at Qixia Ridge and stopped to rest at Xiangshan Cave. The monastery, which was packed with monks and worshipers, held nothing of interest, but the hill face that formed a sort of backdrop was covered in lichens and mosses, and it seemed a little cooler there, so we sat down. Cousin Mei, noticing how I was suffering from the heat, began fanning me. Although Koto showed no sign of perspiration and seemed perfectly at ease, her eyebrows looked darker than ever, and I knew that inwardly she was suffering, too. After we had settled ourselves, the abbot came out to greet us. A man of about fifty with a pious, otherworldly look, he seemed familiar, and I was trying to place him when he smiled and spoke to me, "It must be nearly ten years since I last saw you, sir. I wonder if you still remember me?"

Surprised, Cousin Mei asked how we had met.

"I used to be in charge of visitor reception at Fenglin Temple, and the young gentleman's family had ordered a water-and-land service for his late father. In those days the young gentleman loved to play, and once I took him out boating. I can still see that sight to this very day."

He turned to Koto. "And you, miss, you gathered rose petals with the young gentleman, then put them in a pot at Lakeview House and brewed up some flower dew. I asked you for a cup of it, and it was better than sweet dew. I can still taste it now."

Koto burst into laughter, which brought the event back to my mind. "The girl who brewed up the flower dew with me was my cousin Secunda," I explained to her. "You two look so alike it's no wonder the abbot mistook you for her."

"Holy name!" muttered the abbot. "That any two girls should look so alike! Perhaps you're reincarnations of the Dragon King's daughters beside Guanyin's throne." [25]

I smiled to myself. If that were so, I must be the reincarnation of Sudhana,[26] a thought that brought me back to Secunda. At first my relationship with her was no different from that with Koto, but after we parted, all news between us was cut off, even about family matters like weddings and funerals. I couldn't write to her in a personal capacity, and after my mother's—her aunt's—death she had no excuse to write to me. As my thoughts ranged back over the past, it seemed like another world to me. We might have many long years ahead of us, she and I, but we could never be sure of meeting again. And even if we did meet, could she ever love me the way she did when we were children? In those days I used to liken Koto to Secunda, but now Koto's love for me was incomparably deeper. I concluded that Koto was more deserving of my love than anyone except Susu, and so I fastened my gaze on her.

She was chatting with Orchid when her glance turned in my direction. Our eyes locked, and we couldn't help blushing.

When Cousin Mei had finished her prayers, she took leave of the abbot and led us back to the sedan chairs. The abbot saw us as far as the main gate and urged us to visit him again. I was impressed with his genuine goodwill and promised to do so.

However, in the sedan chair my thoughts turned back again to the past, and images of Secunda's every frown and smile passed in an endless cycle through my brain. As a result I began to grasp the principles of Buddhism—that all our destinies are foreordained. What the Buddhists call the "seed" and the "fruit" of an action contained the ultimate truth, and presumably Secunda and I possessed the seed but not the fruit.

Koto's chair was behind mine rather than in front,
ever I thought of Secunda, I wanted to turn and
at Koto. Our two chairs followed one another, their
silk a veil of mist between us. When we came to the
hills, the road took us up and down, and Koto appeared more
charming than ever, but I found it too exhausting to keep
looking back at her.

Fortunately we soon arrived at the temple gate, where
Cousin Mei stood waiting for us. Koto and I walked in hand
in hand. Within the grounds was the Purple Cloud Cave that
Pearlie had mentioned. The Buddha Hall of this temple was
extremely narrow, and it was packed with worshipers, men as
well as women. We followed the covered passageway all around
the temple but found nothing of interest. I tried out a joke.
"Mother came to find a cool spot / Will she strike when the
iron's hot?"

Cousin Mei pointed ahead. "The Purple Cloud Cave, as
it's called, is down there. Wait till I've finished my prayers,
and we'll go together."

Orchid was too impatient and hurried off to see the cave
herself, and Jade went with her. Soon I noticed Orchid beckoning to us, and Koto and I walked over hand in hand, skirting the pond. Numbers of vulgar onlookers trailed along
behind us. Some were of the opinion that we were brother and
sister, while others held that we were husband and wife—a
dreadful embarrassment for Koto. At the mouth of the cave
we felt a cool blast swirling up from beneath our feet. To the
sound of water rushing through jagged rocks, we wound our
way down, the girls' pleated skirts practically torn off by the
wind. Koto hesitated to go any farther, but I took her arm, to
the applause of the onlookers behind us, which only added to
her embarrassment. I could see from her expression how mor-
tified she was, but personally I felt that our love was something worth flaunting in front of others.

Orchid and Jade had taken possession of a stone bench and

were brushing the one next to them for Koto. But when she saw there was only the one bench left, she ignored their offer, no doubt because in front of all those people she didn't want to be seen sitting next to me. And so I didn't sit down, either. Instead I examined the dimensions of the cave—nothing remarkable there; the Peak-That-Flew-Here at Lingyin Temple was far more impressive. The chill, dank air penetrated us to the bone, and our silken fans, which had fluttered so bravely in the sedan chairs, were now as limp and sodden as fallen petals. Koto's dress was as soft as gossamer, and the flowers on her lapels had lost their scent. We decided this was no place to linger in and, emerging from the cave hand in hand, went in search of Cousin Mei.

We found her busy at her devotions and just about to divine her fortune by picking a bamboo slip. I was laughing at her, when Koto, on some sudden impulse, prostrated herself beside her mother on the prayer mat and took the slip container from her hand. When she shook it, however, nothing happened; the wretched slips would not come out. Her agitation and flushed embarrassment would have taxed a painter's art. Only after Cousin Mei had shown her how, did she manage to obtain a slip, which shot out and fell on the ground. I glanced at it as I picked it up: number 31.

The priest handed Koto the corresponding verse. She took one look, then tossed it in the censer, where it burned to ashes. Apparently she wanted to prevent me from reading it, but in my sharp-eyed way I had already done so. It ran:

> *The plainest flowers last forever,*
> *The richest scent will not remain.*
> *The lakes and mountains never change,*
> *The sun and moon will shine again.*

The note said: Middling.

I was greatly affected by the first two lines, which I found depressing. I had once compared Koto to a delicate scent,[27] and if this verse were any sort of omen, it did not bode well for us. As I looked at her more closely, I was filled with an infinite sadness, and had I been anywhere else but in the Buddha Hall, I would have cried aloud. I didn't do so, but foolish tears started from my eyes and had to be wiped away with a handkerchief.

"What's the matter, Shan?" asked Cousin Mei in surprise.

"It's just the incense smoke getting in my eyes."

Koto noticed my reaction and was visibly saddened, so I went over to her. Orchid and Jade were busy passing aesthetic judgments on the various buddha statues, until Cousin Mei accused them of irreverence, at which point they stopped and began giggling instead.

The priest now brought along a tray of food, which he set down in a stone pavilion before inviting Cousin Mei to have lunch. This brought the people standing about in the Buddha Hall down on us like bees and butterflies on lotus blossoms. Whenever Koto took a step anywhere, they hung on her heels, so she refused to eat. I seconded her. It was still early, I said, and we might just as well have drinks at the Pavilion Beyond on the lakeshore. Orchid and Jade agreed with me, and Cousin Mei was outnumbered.

"You can't even take the *occasional* vegetarian meal?" she asked with a smile. "With all this high living of yours, one day your luck's going to run out." After she had paid for the food, we returned to our sedan chairs and headed for the Bai Embankment to have lunch at the Pavilion Beyond.

The view from upstairs was distinctly pleasing. A few weeping willows offered a dense, green shade, and a stretch of crystalline lake reflected the sunlight, vivid as Chengdu brocade. Koto and I leaned on the rail and gazed out over the lake, free from all worldly concerns. The dozen or so bearers, resting beneath the willows, looked up at us, and one could guess what was going through their minds—they were thinking what a picture we made, she and I.

Cousin Mei brought out her vanity case so that Orchid and Jade could freshen up. She called out to Koto to do the same, but she declined. Then suddenly Cousin Mei let out a cry, "That butterfly in your hair—you haven't *lost* it, surely?"

Koto patted her hair. "Oh, dear! I'm afraid I have."

"It must be in the sedan chair," said Cousin Mei. She rushed downstairs and searched the chair herself, but without success. "You must have lost it in Purple Cloud Cave," she said, ordering the bearers to go back and look for it.

"If she lost it in there, someone is bound to have walked off with it by now," said the bearers, evincing a notable lack of enthusiasm. "At noon on a scorching hot day, who's going to go off on a fool's errand like that?"

Koto, who was observing all this from the balcony, called out to Cousin Mei, "It would be such a pity to lose it. If anyone can find it, I'll give him its full value as a reward."

"But in that case you're no better off than if you never got it back!" exclaimed Cousin Mei.

"It's not the cost I'm worried about. I just can't bear to lose the pin."

Cousin Mei said nothing, but several of the bearers got to their feet and said they would go and look for it. Putting down their wine, they raced off, with the others in hot pursuit.

"If all of you go," screamed Cousin Mei, "who's going to look after our things?"

"Don't worry," said the restaurant's owner, emerging at that moment. "We'll keep an eye on them."

Far from reassured, Cousin Mei ordered the clothes boxes and vanity cases brought upstairs. Then she turned to Orchid and began complaining, "Your sister may not be aware of what happens to her things, but how is it *you* didn't notice?"

"What an *extraordinary* thing to say!" said Orchid. "You expect far too much of people, Mother."

"That piece of jewelry is bad luck," Cousin Mei explained to me. "I tried to stop her from buying it. The two pearls at the base of the butterfly's feelers are round and white, but there's precious little else to commend it. The wings are only imitation jade. The pin wasn't worth much, but she fell in love with the design and was willing to pay over a hundred taels for it. If she ever gets it back, it will have cost double that amount—"

Koto didn't wait for her mother to finish. "I take it you think I was wrong to offer a decent reward, but unless you offer something reasonable, you never get anything back," she said with an icy smile.

Personally I had a different interpretation of this incident, one that I couldn't very well mention at the time, so I kept quiet.

Koto must have sensed something of what I had in mind, because she went on, "The point is, whether I get it back or not is my business and mine alone. All I'm concerned about is the loss of something I love. If I get it back, even if it costs several times the price, I'm the one who will be paying it. Mother won't be affected in any way whatsoever."

This answer reduced Cousin Mei to silence, but it led me to take my analysis one step further. I felt that what Koto had said, like Cousin Mei's complaints and the bearers' hectic pursuit of a reward, were all due to the bedevilment of money.

After the hors d'oeuvres had been set out, Koto noticed how gloomy I was and appeared sorry for what she had done. She began cracking melon seeds and making me guess whether they were white or black inside, the penalty for a wrong answer being a cup of wine. Cousin Mei realized how unhappy Koto was, and to cheer her up she, too, encouraged me to drink. Even when I guessed right, Koto would claim I was wrong. I couldn't bring myself to argue with her and simply drank up.

However, it was extremely hot, hotter than I could bear, so I got up and wandered about the restaurant.

On the wall I noticed a poem by someone who signed himself Chishi.[28] It struck me as brilliantly unconventional as well as lyrical, and I committed it to memory.

None of the bearers had returned by the time we finished lunch, and Orchid grew impatient and came up with the idea of hiring a boat and going out to Three Pools. Jade seconded her, and Koto and I, bored with just sitting there, told the waiter to hire us a pleasure boat and leave word for the bearers to go and wait for us at Yongjin Gate. Then, hand in hand, we boarded the boat. Orchid bought some silver melons, white lotus root, and other refreshments, which she piled up on the table in the cabin. Then, asking for a knife, she cut up one of the melons and offered me a slice. Koto protested that melon was unsuitable for someone in my condition and told me not to eat it, but Orchid went on insisting until Cousin Mei shouted at her. The sweep oar splashed, the boat shook, a soft breeze came in, the flowers on Koto's lapel gave off their subtle fragrance, and the glare off the waves beat on our cabin window—a scene worthy of an artist. And yet when I compared this excursion to that earlier one to Guashan, I felt that this one did not measure up. Our boat was narrow, its ceiling was low, and its motion was unsteady. I was ill to begin with, I had drunk a lot of wine, and I soon began to feel queasy. I would have liked to lie down, but with Koto occupying the bunk I could scarcely do so. Instead I leaned over the table and buried my head in my arms. She noticed and, realizing what I wanted, promptly offered me her place on the bunk. But it occurred to me that she was ill, too, and must surely be suffering from the boat's motion just as much as I was. Instead I complained to Orchid about the idea for the trip.

"Well, Shan," she said with a smile, "there's nothing to stop you from going back on your own, you know."

"In my opinion there's nothing particularly attractive about the lake scenery anyway," I replied, "and I do feel awfully dizzy. I really think you had better let me go back." No sooner were these words out of my mouth than I began to retch. Cousin Mei whisked the spittoon over just in time to catch my vomit. Afterward I could hold out no longer and flopped down on the bunk.

As if over a great distance I heard a cry of alarm from Cousin Mei, "He really *is* bringing up blood!"

"You're right," said Koto. "I do think we ought to go back."

Cousin Mei told the boatman to turn around.

"We're already at Little Yingzhou," said the boatman. "Why not go ashore here?"

"Yes, let's!" said Orchid.

"You go ashore if you want to," said Koto icily. "You can wait for the boat to come back and pick you up."

"Don't listen to her," said Cousin Mei. "Turn around at once."

By this time I was too dizzy to say anything. I felt as if the heavens and the earth were wheeling about my head.

The boat made its way back.

I resented the fact that Koto did not come and stroke my brow. If Susu had been there and seen me in this state, I thought, she would certainly have laid my head on her shoulder and run her slender fingers over my chest. It might not have helped me get better, but it would at least have made me feel more at ease. From that point of view, Koto's love for me, unconditional though it was, could not compare with Susu's. This thought made me want to go home as soon as we reached shore, but then I realized the awkward position Koto was in. How could she start openly caressing me in front of her mother and sisters? The caresses she and I had exchanged were not for others to see, so the studied restraint she showed on this occasion was entirely appropriate.

And yet I still felt dissatisfied. Oh, Koto, I have never in all my life been willing to act in a secretive way. If for your sake we are now forced to do so, what a pity it would be! In the past Koto and I had gradually shed our inhibitions, but I now saw in this secretive, guarded manner of hers the reemergence of inhibitions even stronger than before. As to the cause of her inhibitions, could one say that they resulted from fear of her mother or her sisters? Hardly. Only from fear of Mr. Sheng. But he wasn't her legitimate husband, and she had never paid much attention to him, anyway. Moreover, he was now far off and no longer presented a threat. In the last analysis, I decided, she really did place a high value on her own virtue. As a child she had received an education and was familiar with the principle that a woman should be faithful unto death to a single husband. Although born in the mire, she saw herself as a lotus flower growing out of it. I, too, had always placed a high value on morality, fancying myself a second Liuxia Hui. However, by our actions the night before we had plunged into a sea of iniquity. How could I ever face her again? Out of sympathy for me, she had refrained from resisting me outright, and so I had taken advantage of her,[29] which meant I was a sinner in the kingdom of love. If Koto really took that view of me, she would regard me as no better than a wild beast. Oh, what was I thinking of, to do such a thing? I had inflicted on her a stigma that she would bear for the rest of her life. How could I ever redeem myself?

While my mind was preoccupied with these thoughts, Koto assumed I was sound asleep and drew a silken garment over me. I watched as she did so, and was filled with an immense feeling of shame, a feeling that showed in my face.

She was unaware of my reaction. "In your condition, you really must take good care of yourself," she said. "I've worn you out, and I'm ever so sorry."

At first I had no idea what she was sorry for. I thought that her remark must reflect what I had just been thinking and felt ashamed to the point of tears, so I shut my eyes and said nothing. Then I heard her talking to Cousin Mei and taking the blame herself. My illness had been showing signs of improvement, she said, but the outing had made it worse.

"I suppose that means you resent *me*," said Orchid. "But *I* never insisted you two come with us. It's my belief you only came because of a pledge you made to the bodhisattva. You felt you had to climb out of your sickbed and go and thank her for answering your prayers."

I was overcome with embarrassment. I loathed that rapier-like tongue of Orchid's and wondered at the shame and anger Koto must be feeling. Then I heard her give a little laugh.

"I *was* seriously ill and thought I was going to die. But I didn't—and you and the others resented me all the more. The only thing I prayed to the bodhisattva for was a quick death. As for that pledge when I was ill, it was Mother who made it, not me. Why would I go and redeem *her* pledge?"

Orchid laughed in her turn. "Oh, of *course*. But in that case Shan also came here for a quick death."

"Orchid, bite your tongue!" snapped Cousin Mei. "You're only too ready to curse people." She called over to me. "Shan, you should bear in mind the proverb 'For every curse, a thousand years of life.' Those who curse others are apt to take on the ill fortune of their victims."

I made some noncommittal reply. There was something else Orchid wanted to say, but she had no sooner uttered my name than she stopped short, and Jade began to laugh. I looked up and saw that Cousin Mei had covered Orchid's mouth with a handkerchief, making her look both foolish and comical.

By now we had reached the shore, where we were met by a swarm of sedan chairs. Several bearers sprang on board, each trying to be first with the news that the hairpin could not be found. Such was the clamor that one could hardly make out a word they were saying. Koto quickly silenced them. "If it can't be found, that's that," she said. "There's no need for all this commotion. But you did go and look for it, and you deserve a little something for your trouble."

The bearers withdrew, but Cousin Mei kept on clucking her disapproval. Koto paid no attention to her, just removed the garment she had covered me with and helped me sit up. I knew that her concern was for my health and not the hairpin, but I feared that its loss was a sign of bad luck. She helped me on with my jacket, straightened the lapels, and did up the buttons, looking anxiously into my eyes all the while. Her sympathy was really no less than Susu's would have been. Although I had intended to return home at once, I changed my mind and said nothing about it.

Cousin Mei took Koto's place in helping me ashore, and Jade put my hand on her shoulder, as if I were unable to walk on my own. Koto had withdrawn some distance, but her eyes continued to focus on me with loving concern as I got into my sedan chair.

Once I was in the chair, the bearers hoisted it onto their shoulders and set off. I wanted to go back in the same order as we had come, with Koto's chair right in front of mine, but the bearers took absolutely no notice of me. I had to shout at them before they came to a halt, which brought the other chairs to a halt, too. I then told my bearers to urge the others to go on ahead. The first chair was Cousin Mei's. She asked me what the matter was, but I said it was nothing, and she went on. The next one was Jade's, and she gave me a surprised look, but in a moment her chair, too, had passed me by. The third was Orchid's, and she gave me a mocking grin, no doubt realizing what I had in mind.

Koto's was the last chair. She ordered her bearers to stop while she asked me what the trouble was. "The one in front gets the full force of the wind, which gives me goose bumps. I prefer to be in the rear," I said.

"Let me follow you, then."

I shook my head. "The others are way ahead already. Please go on." She told her bearers to set off after the other chairs. From my position behind her I watched the chairs in front as they proceeded in single file, undulating over the ground like a centipede.

It was late when we reached the city. Colored lanterns were on display, and crowds of people jostled each other on their way to the lake. The silk-gowned set with their round, gauze fans were waiting by the side of the road to watch the occupants of the sedan chairs. Our bearers found a new spurt of energy and began chanting in unison. The tassels on the chairs quivered, an evening breeze sprang up, and the scent of pomade grew stronger. I knew that by now the jasmine rosette in Koto's lapel must be completely open. I only wished I could have caught a glimpse of her beauty at night, a thought that put me in mind of some lines in a topical poem:

> *I shall go backward and let you look at me.*
> *To save you turning your head at every step.*

How could I get Koto's chair to go backward?

Soon we arrived at the house. Brightie had heard us coming and opened the gate. Koto and I made straight for her room, leaving Cousin Mei to wrangle with the bearers.

Koto seemed utterly exhausted. Taking off her formal clothes, she chose the couch inside the silk tent, while I lay down on the bed again. A single lamp filled the room with a snowy brightness. I felt a freedom from worldly care such as cannot be put into words. From the couch I heard Koto asking, "Tired, Shan?"

"Yes, rather."

"Why not try to get some sleep? I suppose the mosquitoes are bothering you." She got up and began looking for the swatter. Knowing how tired she was, I tried to stop her.

"It's so stuffy with the net down," I said. "Luckily it's cool, and there aren't any mosquitoes about. The lights have been on for some time, and they've all turned in for the night." She stopped her searching.

"You didn't have much for lunch," she went on. "Are you hungry?"

"I feel so sick at heart I couldn't possibly eat anything. But I expect *you're* famished."

"If I were, I could easily order some food, but I really don't care for anything."

As she spoke, Cousin Mei came in to ask if we wanted any supper. We both declined.

"Oh well, you can always have something when you wake up," she said. "Sleep well."

From a dazed sensation I sank into a deep sleep, but my dreams were violently disturbed, with one terrifying vision following another, until I began crying out in the middle of my nightmare. I wasn't aware of what I was doing until Koto shouted at me to wake up, and I found Cousin Mei and the rest of the family ringing my bed, a row of shapes that wavered so wildly that I could scarcely count them. Brightie, her brother, and then Pearlie called out to me. I tried to answer, but the words stuck in my throat. My eyes were too bleary to see anything properly. I tried raising my hands and feet, but they were as heavy as lead. I'm dying, I thought. My mind went back to my mother and Susu, and I felt an overwhelming pang of grief. The only sound I heard was one of sobbing, but I couldn't be certain who it came from. My soul was some infinitesimal thing, wafting like a gossamer thread—until all of a sudden I lost consciousness. Then I just as suddenly regained my senses, only to be confronted by a vast brightness. I focused my eyes and saw that it was Cousin Mei with a crimson candle that she was shining full in my face. Beside her was someone I didn't recognize who grasped my wrist and inserted a needle that gave me no pain. Koto was lying facedown on the bed beside me, weeping hysterically, while Orchid and Jade stood sobbing in front of me. I couldn't help crying out myself at the sight.

Even with several thousand additional words at my disposal I could not do justice to the confusion that reigned in that room. Since my book is too long as it is, I shall have to limit myself to this brief summary.

My illness was severe enough to bring great distress to Koto, and that night, when everyone else was asleep, she came into my bed. I held her hand and thanked her from the bottom of my heart. "This trivial little complaint of mine has given you so much anxiety," I said. "I'm really upset about it."

"Oh, Shan, I've done you harm, and it's too late to make amends."

"What are you talking about? We all get sick—no one escapes altogether. What does this have to do with you? I was just thinking what a blessing it was that I got sick. Otherwise, I could never have received such loving attention. If I had to, I'd willingly go to my death. If I died today, I'd do so without any regrets."

Her face turned grave. "The reason I respected you was that your love for me was not concerned with physical expression. What I did last night was to demonstrate my love for you, not because I bore you any ill will. You mustn't think of it as a recompense for something *you* had done! Your love for me isn't concerned with such things, and I can't bear the thought that by loving you I have actually done you harm. I have always thought of sexual love as something base and even contemptible. And you, Shan, you were always superior to other men in your moral strength. We were both wrong to let the physical expression of our love come between us, especially when you were ill."

This left me dreadfully ashamed. "Your love for me was so deep, and I'm only flesh and blood, after all, so of course I was affected. At this point I can't find the words to express what I feel." Seizing her hand, I kissed it again and again. She said nothing, merely urged me to get some sleep, but my eyes kept flicking open to look at her, which made her cross.

"Look, I'm right here beside you. If you can't keep your eyes shut, I'll have to leave and get Mother to take my place."

"Don't do that!" I cried. "I'll shut my eyes. Please don't leave!" I shut my eyes tight and didn't say another word.

It must have been late at night. Outside the window the hum of insects filled the air, but inside all was quiet. I kept thinking of Koto sitting beside my bed, and I visualized her graceful pose and wondered how she could endure the boredom. Then, drowsy as I was, my mind began to focus again, and I awoke and stole a glance at her. The silk curtain was down and there was someone on the other side of it, sitting at the table with her head cradled in her arms. Koto must have let my curtain down without awakening me, I thought. On such a chilly night she shouldn't be sitting out there with nothing around her. I opened the curtains and called to her, but although I called for a long time, there was no response. At first I couldn't bear to disturb her sleep and stopped calling, but then I had second thoughts. If she continued to sleep at the table, even if she wasn't affected by the chilly air, those delicate arms of hers would surely be full of aches and pains by morning. I decided to get up.

I was struggling down from the bed when the silver curtain rings jangled, and she awoke with a start. As I looked down to find my slippers, she placed a hand on my shoulder to steady me and asked me what I was doing. Her voice sounded different, so I looked up—and let out a chuckle. It wasn't Koto, but Jade. Koto was not in the silk tent, either, so I asked Jade where she had gone.

"She felt very tired, but she was afraid you might need something to eat or drink during the night, so she told me to look after you. She's gone to sleep in my room."

I could understand Koto's thinking. If she had gone to

sleep in this room, she would have heard me tossing and turning and felt obliged to get up, after which I would have gone
on talking until all hours. Her leaving was really out of con-
sideration for me as well as herself. I began to feel a little eas-
ier in my mind.

I put my hand on Jade's shoulder. "Look, I sympathize with
you for having to stay here. I'm terribly sorry about it, I really
am. But I'm feeling better now and I don't need you with me
anymore. Do go to bed."

She shook her head. "I'm not sleepy. Can I get you something to drink?"

"No, I don't need anything, thanks." I pointed to the silk
tent and told her to go inside and lie down. Again she shook
her head. Acutely sorry for her, I told her to lie down on my
bed and try to get some rest.

She was fifteen at the time but innocent enough to have no
inhibitions about the other sex, and she curled up on the outer
half of the bed and lay down. I cradled her head in the crook
of my arm. Her slight, delicate frame inspired a tender compassion but not a trace of desire. Like her, I, too, relaxed completely and fell into a deep sleep.

The next morning Orchid came into the room and, failing
to find Jade, parted the bed curtains and discovered her pil-
lowed on my arm, sound asleep. I was already awake.

"Uh-oh!" she exclaimed. "Aren't you afraid of being told
off by Mother?"

Jade awoke with a start and sat up, rubbing her eyes. Orchid
put a finger to her cheek. "Aren't you *ashamed?*"

Jade was so abashed she couldn't say anything. One more
word, and she would have started crying. I loathed Orchid for
her spitefulness. "It's only because you judge others by yourself," I said with heavy sarcasm, "that you talk of shame. It's
perfectly normal for family to be together like this. That's all
it is!"

Orchid looked me in the eye and smiled. It seemed that she

was about to say something when she thought better of it. She turned and was about to leave when Jade tugged at her dress and begged, "*Please* don't tell Mother!"

Orchid looked over at me and smiled. "And what do *you* think?" she asked.

"Oh, go and tell her, then!" I said, my voice thick with loathing. "Go and tell her! If people don't believe me, I'll cut my heart open and show them I'm telling the truth!" I said this in a such a savage tone and with such a violent expression on my face that both Cousin Mei and Koto came in to see what was the matter. I was exploding with anger and expressing myself in some very blunt language, including some nasty abuse directed at Orchid, whose smile quickly turned to tears.

"I was only *teasing!*" she protested again and again. "Only *teasing!* But Shan is being so hateful that I shall never say another word to him ever again." She rushed out of the room in tears.

Jade flung herself into Koto's arms, crying so hard that she could barely speak.

"Orchid has far too much to say for herself," pronounced Cousin Mei. "Surely she realizes that Shan was only teasing her? Jade, stop your crying! And Shan, don't upset yourself."

"My conscience is clear," I protested. "For Orchid to insult *me*—that's not important. But I can't bear to hear her insulting Jade. If we took her seriously, it could drive us to our deaths, and then we could *never* clear our names! Oh, what bad luck it was to be born a man! Men are the unluckiest creatures in the world. And now I *am* going to die . . . "

At my mention of the word *die,* Koto hastily shushed me. "Saying these things so early in the morning . . . We all understand how you feel, but you won't succeed, you know. It's never any use protesting. If people trust you, there's no need; and if they don't, your protests won't do any good."

"Quite right," said Cousin Mei, gathering Jade in her arms,

wiping away her tears, and smoothing her hair. She also tried cooling her with a fan.

I was struck by the truth in Koto's advice. But it also carried an implicit reference to herself and to me, dispelling any suspicions Cousin Mei might have. Koto really *was* far cleverer than I. At the same time I began to realize that I had gone too far with Orchid. To be fair to her, she had always been a tease, and what she said was hardly to be taken seriously. Moreover, I was no girl. Even if I were slandered in some way, how would I suffer? Because of the protectiveness I felt for Jade, I had flown into a rage and insulted Orchid in some very harsh language. If I were in her place and had made a teasing remark for which I received such a crushing response, I couldn't have stood it, either. I began to wonder how I could get Orchid to come out so that I could apologize to her. But then it occurred to me that she, too, might already be feeling remorse over her unfortunate remark, and that my apology would make the remorse harder to bear, in which case I would only be adding to her distress. I decided to curb my impatience and wait.

Cousin Mei asked me how I felt. Since I hadn't had any supper the night before, I must be feeling hungry, she thought, sending Jade off to get me something to eat. Koto had already had her breakfast, so she told Jade to keep me company, but with Jade it was a case of once bitten, twice shy, and she adamantly refused. And so for the first time in my experience I ate a meal alone in Koto House, which made me feel that Orchid really was the spoiler of love, and if I had had her there in front of me, I'd have given her a piece of my mind, if only to make Jade feel better.

When I finished, Jade cleared away the dishes and ate her breakfast from them behind the mirror screen. Koto was now ready for her toilette. Cousin Mei called Orchid in, and she was forced to wash and comb her sister's hair, pouting in her characteristic way and saying not a word to anyone. Whenever she passed by me, she averted her eyes as if afraid they might meet mine for an instant, so I didn't dare say anything to her, either. I felt sure she wouldn't respond.

After a while I tried calling to her, without success. "Oh, Orchid," I said, "are you really so angry with me? I feel very guilty about what happened. I oughtn't to have been angry with you. In the dozen or so years that I've known you, I've never once said anything nasty to you. But you did make a hurtful joke, which caused Jade a lot of distress. The protective feeling I have for her is no different from what I have for you. If Jade had said something nasty to you, I'd have stood up for you just as I did for her."

Orchid took no notice, just went on doing Koto's hair. Koto watched both of us in the mirror. When I made as if to get out of bed in the hope that Orchid would reply, Koto looked in the mirror and asked me, "Aren't you tired? Why don't you settle down?"

Then she spoke to Orchid, "Are you really angry with Shan?"

"Oh, Shan's a god! I wouldn't dare offend him. From now on I shan't address a word to the god."

"Since you aren't speaking to me," I said with a smile, "why did you address that last remark to me?"

"I was talking to my sister, not to you," she said.

"Ah, but wasn't *that* addressed to me?"

Realizing she had been tricked, Orchid gave an involuntary chuckle, then swore an oath, "If I ever speak to you again, may my tongue rot off!"

Koto laughed. "But you just did!"

I burst out laughing and stood up. In the center court I could hear Awen talking to Brightie, who was busy denying my presence in the house. I thought Awen's visit distinctly odd and responded at once. From the east door of the anteroom, which opened onto South Court, I called out to Awen and asked him why he had come.

"Her ladyship sent me to Xiangxi to fetch you, sir, but you had left the day before I arrived. The people in the agency told me your family had already sent a boat for you and wondered why I had been sent, too. I guessed you would come here, and I was right. I meant to go straight back and report to her ladyship, but I had a dream about a god who told me, 'Your master is probably visiting Guashan.' When I awoke and thought about it, it rang true. I looked all over Guashan, then happened to see a boat with a passenger in it who looked the image of you, sir. He had a beautiful woman with him and was traveling down river. I ordered my boatman to follow, and after six or seven miles we caught up with them. The gentleman was wearing a white silk gown and he held a hawk's feather fan in his hand. He also had a jasmine rosette in his lapel and a diamond ring on one of his fingers . . ." On and on he went, in full spate.

I interrupted him. "Look, whenever you tell me anything, you always go on and on like this. I simply can't stand it. In short, that wasn't me, I know that. But—*did you report back to her ladyship?*"

"Because of this complication," he went on, "I missed the deadline. I only got to Pingan No. 2 Bridge today. I knocked at the door of our old place, but there was no answer. Then after the longest time there was an answering sound from what I took to be a person, but it turned out to be a young crow from a nest up in the willows, saying all sorts of unlucky things to me. 'No, no,' I cried. I looked up at the house, which was all locked and bolted, clearly telling me that no one was there. I was wandering about, when I saw a young maid carrying water from the well. She was about fourteen, and she stared at me as if she thought I was a thief . . ."

On and on he went like a runaway horse. I was aching for him to get to the point, but he persisted in relating all these trivial details, and I realized there was nothing I could do. If I shouted at him, as I was tempted to do, he would stop for a moment and then go off on another tangent, straying even farther from the point, so I simply put up with him.

He went on to describe in great detail his exchange with the maid, from whom he eventually learned of the family's move. After he had expatiated upon the difficulty of finding his way here, he finally summed up his whole story in one sentence, "I still haven't been home."

Koto and Orchid were listening spellbound as if to a story-teller. Whenever I shouted at him to stop, they objected on the grounds that his tale was so fascinating. I was pleased with his eloquence and praised him for it, which only made him more exuberant than ever. He promptly launched into an account of Susu's apprehension on receiving my letter, of her heartbroken sobs, of her appeals to my mother, and of how my mother had sent him to fetch me home. He was already two days late in getting back, he told us, and couldn't imagine how anxious the family would be. They would certainly assume I was too ill to get out of bed. "And all this time you've been in the best of health and living here safe and sound," he added.

"He was in a critical state as recently as last night," said Cousin Mei. "If he'd been like that on the journey, I shudder to think what might have happened. You only see him now, when he looks as if there's nothing the matter with him. You can tell her ladyship that his stay at our house has done him as much good as a visit to one of those hospitals the Western-ers go to."

Awen laughed and said he would. Then he went on, "But her ladyship is so concerned about the young master that I can't report back without him. The young master may not mind a bit of a scolding, but I know that this tender hide of mine won't stand up to the heavy bamboo."

He put on such a display of trepidation that he had Cousin Mei and Orchid in stitches. Koto tugged at my sleeve and led me over to a corner of the room. "In my opinion," she whispered, "you really ought to go home with him. That way her ladyship will never know that you came back before."

"It doesn't matter if she does know."

"Look, to come back seriously ill and then stop off here, ignoring your own family—that's simply unnatural. People who know the facts may say you did it for love, but all the others will say you showed no respect for your family. Moreover, in your present condition you need plenty of rest in order to recuperate. I'm not well enough myself to nurse you properly, and it's easy to imagine how concerned your wife must be. You really *ought* to go home."

I knew she was right, but I couldn't bear to leave her. She had already sent Pearlie for a sedan chair, which soon arrived, but I still felt a great reluctance to leave and took my time putting on my jacket and doing up the buttons. I picked up a hawk's feather fan and smoothed the feathers until every last one of them was in perfect alignment. All this while she stood fondly by my side.

When I saw we were alone, I asked her for a kiss, and if Jade had not come in, that kiss might have lasted to all eternity. The world possesses no richer or sweeter sensation than a kiss. A strong wine may intoxicate, but its bouquet cannot compare with that of a kiss. Cherries and fresh litchis may resemble a kiss in color and scent, but they cannot transport the soul. If we were to consider every variety of taste in the world in search of something comparable, we should not find anything that could represent a kiss. Nor would we find any writer who has ever successfully described one, even if we examined every book in existence from the ancient past to the present day. As a result my book, too, now finds itself at a loss for words.

Part 3

My mother assumed that I had come back with Awen and she suspected nothing. Nor, since I was ill, did she keep me with her very long or even raise the question of Koto. Only Susu, standing at my mother's side, cast a lingering glance in my direction from time to time, a glance that seemed mocking as well as sympathetic. Once we got to our bedroom, I asked her the reason for the mockery, but she firmly denied it. After telling Ajin to make up the bed and urging me to get some rest, she sat on the edge of the bed and asked me endless questions about my illness. I told her, insisting all the while that I was now completely better, but she continued to worry and asked my mother if a doctor could be called in to examine me. The doctor exaggerated my illness and made it out to be fearfully complicated. Personally, I thought there was nothing the matter with me. I managed to get my food and drink down—with Susu watching over me all the time to see that I didn't overeat. She treated me as if I were a cricket in autumn, and was fully as protective as any cricket fancier.[1]

During my past illnesses Little Tan and Susu had taken turns nursing me, but Little Tan was still away, and it fell to my mother to come and see to my medicine, which made me feel very uncomfortable, partly because I didn't like to put her to such trouble, and partly because she kept Susu and me from showing our affection for each other. Not until late at night when we were safely in bed, did we get a chance to be intimate.

"What made you write that heartbroken letter that frightened us all so much?" she asked me on one such occasion.

"Oh, that was just my delirium talking," I said with a smile. "I really do apologize for giving you such a scare."

"I expect you gave someone else a far worse scare," she said with a wry smile.

"Koto, you mean? But she wouldn't do as I hoped; she turned your proposal down. I felt very bitter and deeply regretted what I had done, and that's what brought on my heart condition."

She laughed. "Evidently you've found a balm for your heart condition."

"Only you, my sweetheart, would be capable of providing that." I went to take her in my arms, but she slipped away.

"Where do you pick up such vulgar expressions?" she said crossly. "I'm certainly not accustomed to *that* sort of language!"

"In the course of your reading, my dear, you must have come across the 'Long Town Ballad' in the 'Life of Liu Yao.'[2] It goes like this:

> *Among the warriors of Long was one Chen An;*
> *His stature was small, but his girth was huge,*
> *And he loved his men like his own sweet heart.*

So as you see, the term *sweetheart* is actually a very refined one."

She laughed. "You're so familiar with the classics you can even fake a locus classicus!"[3]

"Unfair! Tomorrow I'll look it up in the *Jin History* and prove it to you."

"Who's going to discuss the classics with you in bed?"

"Only you, my dear, would be capable of such a thing, and I love you for it and feel proud of you."

"The one thing I've always most disliked is being lied to. And that's what you are constantly doing to me. This sort of flattery is really no better than a lie. Now, let me ask you this: Did you really only get back today?"

"My dearly beloved wife, if I tell you, I beg you not to tell Mother."

I then told her everything that had happened during the last few days. When I came to the lovers' pledge that Koto and I had taken, she rubbed her finger against my cheek.

"Aren't you *ashamed* of yourself? You've told me everything about her, so I suppose at some point you're going to tell her everything about me."

I swore that I would not. "If I do, may I be cast into liars' hell!"[4] She clapped her hand over my mouth to stifle the oath, at which point my love got the better of me. "Some powder has rubbed off on this; I shall have to lick it off," I said, nibbling at her hand.

She pulled her hand away. "Oh, Shan! You seem to have forgotten that you aren't well. I can't bear to make your illness any worse than it is. Why not lay your head on my arm and try to get some sleep?"

I knew this was a jab at Koto and couldn't help feeling embarrassed. For three years now I had been sleeping with Susu, but in the past I was always the one who stretched out my arm to cradle her, so this was a new departure for me. I would have been delighted to lay my head on her arm, but I couldn't bear to, just as I couldn't bear to reject the overture. I sensed a wisp of warm fragrance entering through the crown of my head and spreading down through my limbs, and my body began slowly melting like candy under a hot sun. My rapturous soul and hers were magically transformed into a pair of butterflies flying together into oblivion.

Drowsily I recalled that my head was cradled on her arm and I awoke with a start, pulled out her arm, and let it drop. Pale moonlight flooded through the window, penetrating the bed curtains and shining full on her face. Her cheeks glowed with the sheen of pearls or jade, her eyebrows were a misty black, and the crimson of her lips seemed about to melt. Her beauty in sleep would have taxed the art of the greatest painter. My love for her reached its height, and I could no longer restrain myself—only to find my illness a great deal worse for it the following day.

My mother then issued a decree that henceforth we were to sleep in separate beds. A pair of couches was placed in the room for us, so that when we parted our bed curtains to look at each other, we were like two stars situated on opposite sides of the Milky Way. Oddly enough, the new arrangement proved superior to the old. I once wrote a quartet of "Untitled" poems, which were published in my *New Hint of Rain*.[5]

> *Inside the curtains, green smoke wafting up,*
> *She lets me lie, with no one else in sight.*
> *In silken tent a flower wreathed in mist,*
> *Her stockings bathed in the new moon's light.*
> *I take her chilly hand. "Too rash," she says.*
> *Hindered by hairpins I press cheek to cheek,*
> *When just at that point she changes her mind*
> *And, tugging at her dress, displays her pique.*
>
> *A mere touch on the silver curtain ring;*
> *The marbled mat sets off her sheer white dress.*
> *Her tousled hair upon the pillow spread,*
> *She seeks the quilt to hide her slenderness.*
> *Love-longing comes unbidden to her lips;*
> *Her eyes' allure exceeds the bounds of art.*
> *Unwilling yet to join with me in love,*
> *She allows her love slowly to melt her heart.*

Her beauty fragile as a flower,
She braves the bed's chill in the silent night.
"I feel for your frailty, weak from the wine,
As too shy to face me, you turn to the light."
Without the moon screen, she'd be too afraid,
But nestling against me, tranquil she lies.
When morning comes, she smiles and rubs her brow,
The sleep still there in the corners of her eyes.

She rises late, shadows upon the wall,
Like a sleeping blossom her glowing face,
Then flies to my arms and fingers my belt,
And seeks my hand to pat her hair into place.
"You mocked my innocence, made the girl laugh,
And described how you feel, to my dismay."
Before the looking glass I can't come close,
Lest the parrot see and give us away.

My readers should note that I enjoyed a bountiful love life throughout the course of this illness. In fact my one regret was that my convalescence did not last any longer. After a month I was back to normal.

Then a letter arrived from Xiangxi urging me to return, and because I was worried that the jasmine plants Koto had given me might wither and die, I decided to accept. Unfortunately Awen was responsible for a grave indiscretion. In his eagerness to ingratiate himself with my mother, he gave her a full circumstantial account of my earlier excursion to Guashan and my recent collapse while at Koto's house. My mother then declared Koto a demon of disease so far as I was concerned and, on the assumption that if I went back to Xiangxi I would only repeat my misdeeds, she ordered my wife to write to Mrs. Ling declining the offer. She also confined me to the house and forbade me to stir from her side.

Concerned as I was about Koto, Awen was now firmly under my mother's thumb, and there was no one else to whom I could entrust a letter. My confidant used to be Huanong, but he had been called home by his mother. Since I couldn't think of anyone else to do my bidding, I turned to poetry to express my emotions. I completed the sequence "Koto: One Hundred and Eighty Narrative Poems," which is too long to quote here but is available in a separate volume.

When Susu read it, she exclaimed, "My goodness! I *really* don't understand that Koto. Does she have any love for you, or doesn't she? If she does, why not simply say yes? And if she doesn't, why not give you a definite no?"[6]

"It's solely because she's afraid of Mother's severity."

"Mother may be severe, but she's never gobbled anyone up! Doesn't Koto ever wonder how *I* manage to take life so calmly?"

"Her nature can't be compared to yours. At the slightest irritation with her family, even with her own mother, she flares up without any attempt at self-control. I came to the conclusion that that sort of behavior made her unsuitable as a wife, let alone as a concubine. The truth is, she's suited only to be an intimate friend. She has far too high an opinion of herself, and she's also far too used to being catered to. If she were sharing a house with you, I'd be subjected to all kinds of accusations. Anyone who wants to marry her would need to be a live-in husband if he's to have any peace of mind, but I'm no Cai Bojie from *The Lute*,[7] which is why my enthusiasm has now cooled to the freezing point. The one thing I cannot forget is how deep-rooted our love is, and every so often its shoots burst forth irresistibly. In terms of karmic cause and effect, our relationship may have had a certain *cause,* but it will always lack the *effect* of a happy marriage."

"It occurs to me that you could always set her up in her own apartment—assuming she has any interest in the idea, of course."

"But how could we ever put it to Mother?"

"I daresay we could find a way. What I'm not so sure of is how Koto would react."

"I know exactly how she'd react. She'd point to the house she's in and say it's just as good as any apartment. What's more, I've often thought that if I did insist on her living apart from her family, she would never let me leave her for an instant. If I were single, or if you and I were at loggerheads and thought of each other as the enemy, I could accept that. But I can't stand being away from you for an instant, either. Since I can't be in two places at once, it would only hasten my death to take such a disastrous step! We all have our allotted destinies in this world, and if we try to overreach them, our suffering will be greater than that of the lowliest wretch. Give up, my dear. Don't mention the idea again. It only unsettles me."

She smiled. "Well, what *are* you going to do, then?"

"Mencius once said, 'Fish is one of my favorite dishes; bear's paw is the other. If I can't have both, I'll take the bear's paw and leave the fish.'"[8]

"In that case I'd rather be the fish," she said with a smile.

"If you were the fish, I'd be the water you swam in. If you left me for an instant, we'd have to look for you in the dried-fish shop."[9]

"Oh, Shan! I couldn't leave you even for an instant, which is why I truly wish that all three of us could live together, so that no one would feel frustrated. Now I come to think of it, Xiangxi is a place you know well. Why not ask Mother if you can take me there with you? We could find somewhere to live and then invite Koto to join us. That would really be the best solution."

"But if we left Mother here on her own, who would attend on her?"

"By rights we oughtn't to leave her, but because of my being here, Sister-in-law hasn't had to attend on her a great deal, so it wouldn't be asking too much of her to take over for me. If you agree, why not find some occasion to speak to Mother about it?"

The more I considered the idea, the more promising it seemed, but it was not something I would have dared put to my mother myself. The one person who could do so, it seemed to me, was Little Tan. Susu agreed that she was our only hope, so I suggested to my mother that we write to Little Tan urging her to come back as soon as possible. Because she had been gone such a long time my mother herself was looking forward eagerly to her return, but when Little Tan's reply came, it brought some totally unexpected news.

> *I have been kept by your ladyship for ten years now, and I fully expected to serve you faithfully for the rest of my days, but unfortunately last month my poor husband caught a sudden illness and passed away. You can well imagine my grief as a widow after so tragic a loss. Because I am alone in the world with no children to care for, I have often in my misery wished to follow my husband to the grave. But the matters I have been handling for your ladyship are in such confusion that it will take some time to put them in order. To give up my life now would be a most ungrateful response to your constant affection and regard! For that reason I shall remain alive until such time as I have handed on this responsibility to someone else and then take a graceful exit. However, I have been suffering constant illness myself and for over a month now have been confined to bed. I have just received your instructions, which have caused me even more embarrassment. The reason I did not report the tragic news to you before was that I feared you would only be distressed on my account, but now I have no choice. I only hope your ladyship will consider my request sympathetically and allow me to extend my leave. I shall be deeply thankful, and in life and death be ever mindful of your gracious kindness . . .*

"Poor thing!" said my mother through her tears. "To have to endure such a loss. I can't *imagine* how she is suffering!"

After reading Little Tan's letter, I, too, tried to put myself in her place. Hers really was the greatest trial we have to endure in life. The love she shared with Toad was deep and genuine, but it was bedeviled by a trivial lack of money, which prevented them from living together. Absence had deepened their love, but now they had come to a final parting. As I tried to imagine Little Tan's feelings, I felt sure that she really did want to follow her husband to the grave. And if she had done so, this book of mine would have taken on an extraordinary luster. But because of the need to balance our accounts, she lacked even the freedom to die. Poor Little Tan! The only reason she couldn't die was that she was shackled by money. If she had died, I should have been overcome by grief, so I suppose I should give thanks to money that she didn't die. But in any case, her loyalty to our family was a rare and remarkable thing, so my mother told me to write her a letter of condolence, enclosing a hundred taels toward the funeral expenses. She was to get well as soon as possible and then come and live with us. Little Tan's gratitude is easy to imagine.

After a month or more, she wrote asking permission to bring her sister-in-law and niece with her, these being the only family she had left, and my mother agreed. Three days before the Double Ninth, they arrived. The sister-in-law, Teeny, was a widow in her thirties, while the niece, Aiyun, was only four-teen and, although a village girl, quite attractive and refined. Little Tan herself, in her white mourning garments and with her tear-filled eyes, looked more fetching than ever. And my mother cherished her more than ever—not for her looks but from sympathy with her as a widow. Ever since my father's death thirteen years before, my mother had abstained from meat, and Little Tan now followed her example and also joined in her Buddhist devotions. Gradually she got over her grief, but in her attitude to me she stood on her dignity far more than in the past, so I didn't dare say very much to her—it was out of the question to broach Susu's plan. In any case, by this time Susu and I were inseparable, forever in each other's arms, and I had almost forgotten about Koto.

It was not callousness that had made me forget her, but her persistent discouragement. At first, after I recovered from my illness, my mother kept me under tight control, and I was unable to visit. But later, when Susu suggested moving to Xiangxi, I did manage to put the idea to Koto. To my surprise she was flatly opposed to it. Her reasoning, it seems, went like this: Her lifelong aspiration was to join me in a monogamous marriage. That being impossible, she was not about to settle for anything less. The reason she could not forget me was that after thirteen years of loving me in secret she simply couldn't help it. She felt about me as I felt about her, so what did it matter if both of us were married?

Oh, readers! At first Koto and I were merely close friends. In a dozen years we had never once engaged in the physical act, not until that one careless moment when we plunged together into the snare of iniquity. I fully expected that from that time forth Koto would belong to me and to me alone; I certainly wasn't about to desert her after first seducing her. But to my astonishment she preferred to regard that moment as a recompense for love, almost to the point of giving people the impression that I was her fancy man! Oh, readers! I looked on the love between Koto and me as the purest and noblest of sentiments. One slip, and it was too late for any regrets; I simply had to live with the consequences. I am by no means saying that my virtue was more precious than hers. On the contrary, I looked on hers as incomparably more precious than mine, and I felt ashamed—irredeemably ashamed—with regard to her; that was why I was so full of remorse. If one sexual transgression was too much for me to bear, what would be the effect of a second? With that thought in mind I actually considered it a blessing that we met only rarely, repeating to myself the lines

> *Better not to see her at all;*
> *Of passion 'tis best to have none.*

The old poet's words captured my sentiments exactly.

Oddly enough, she herself did not regard me as disloyal. From time to time I would be invited to a party, at which she would be perfectly agreeable, leaving me with the impression there was no barrier to our continued friendship. In her previous thinking, it was as if she and I had had a debtor-creditor relationship, she being the debtor and I the creditor. But now, it seemed, she felt that her karmic debt had been discharged in full; I was no longer in a position to exercise any rights as a creditor, while she was under no obligation to me as a debtor. As a result our relationship became insipid, and there is nothing for my book to record.

In the eleventh month Susu gave birth to a boy. Because she had dreamed of a jade unicorn just before the delivery, my mother named the child Qi.[10] The pregnancy had lasted twelve months, and Susu was in labor for two whole days, during which her very life was in danger. I wrote a long "Jade Unicorn" lyric in two sequences to record the event:[11]

> *Pound the musk to powder,*
> *Burn the rhinoceros horn.*
> *Sweet-smelling the swaddling clothes,*
> *Tassels aflutter behind the screen.*
> *How pitifully all night she clutches the counterpane!*
> *Faintly I hear her gentle panting.*
> *At dawn I note the anguished frown*
> *And regret the ardor of my passion*
> *That inflicts on her such pain.*

On the mat of prayer I bow,
Suddenly take a momentous vow,
Burn incense, and then kneel down again.

(I had never been a believer in the gods and spirits, but I felt so helpless on this occasion that I made this desperate appeal.)

The hours of night wear on.
Let her choose this lucky day!
At dawn we hear the cock. Light plays on the counterpane.
But whence this clamor of crows and magpies?
I rush to see her without delay.

The pots on the stove their fragrances retain,
And in their silver vase the flowers join.
The children are up too early, I silently complain.

(At the time my second brother's wife had two daughters.)

The simpleminded maid
Pours my water in the silver basin
And wants me to wash again,
While I am beside myself, not knowing where to turn.
If the spirits of my clan are present,
I'll gladly bear her pain.
But who has made this rule
That I may not see my wife?
Like a fly on a red-hot stove, I'm driven near insane.

(In our family it was not the custom to allow the husband to see his wife during the delivery. As I was particularly prone to tears, which would only have distracted everyone, my mother had expressly forbidden me to be present.)

Scented water long aheating,
Then in my ears a sudden din.
"Congratulations!" in a single breath.
Having a son, that's nothing strange.
What pleases me is that she's safe again;
I was truly worried half to death.

These poems give the circumstances in sufficient detail to stand as part of my book, so I shall not repeat the story here.

For the First Month celebration our relatives gathered at the house. My cousin brought along his wife and his concubine, and my second brother and my younger brother also joined us. Ever since the family had split up, my brothers and my cousin had been cool toward one other, but on this occasion they came together in a joyous reunion.

Soon afterward my cousin received an official position and my eldest brother left to fill a vacancy in Suzhou, while my other two brothers returned to the jobs they had. I had been home a long time and felt increasingly at loose ends. As for Susu, she was constantly playing with the baby for my mother's amusement; in Susu's mind, he was distinctly more lovable than her husband. Although she had a wet nurse as well as a nanny solely for the child, she still saw to its most trivial needs herself. She adored that child, idolized it. If the most precious gems had been set before her, or the rarest treasures placed within her reach, she would have spurned them all in favor of this baby. At night she would get the wet nurse to lay him in the bed and then wait until he was sound asleep before carrying him off. In the past I had been the only one occupying her mind and heart, but now, if I showed any resentment toward the baby, she would take his part and even start resenting *me!* I wrote a lyric to the tune "Pacing the Moon Palace" to make fun of her.[12]

Happy or cross, frowning or smiling, he gets his way;
Tirelessly by his side she'll stay.
Who made you such a charmer?
And why pick a quarrel with me?
You pull her back whenever she takes a step away.
Kissing and cuddling, day after day,
She never should have had a baby—
Half her love has been given away!

And that wasn't the only thing. After the child's birth, Susu took warning from the difficult labor she had been through and began treating me rather the way Confucius used to treat the ghosts and spirits.[13] Caring for her as I did, I weighed my pleasure against her pain and saw to it that I did not repeat my previous behavior. From then on she and I lived together like brother and sister.

In the second month of the following year a letter arrived from Xiangxi urging me to go and handle the transition to a new superintendent. Mr. Ling's term was up, and his successor was a certain Mr. Shou, whose son had once studied the zither with me. Mr. Shou knew that I was familiar with the Xiangxi customs agency and was pressing me to join him as his aide. I didn't care for his company and was most reluctant to go, but Susu pointed out that there was nothing for me to do at home, while our daily expenses had increased a good deal. My mother allowed us only fifteen taels a month, out of which we had to pay for a wet nurse, a nanny, and two maids. To those costs my own extravagances had to be added—for wine, flowers, publishing, and travel (invariably by carriage or boat). Where was the money coming from? Susu opened her case and showed me the pawn tickets, all of them for her jewelry. Over the last six months our debts had risen to over two hundred taels.

Confronted with these facts, I lapsed into a gloomy silence.

I thought how my mother's savings were lent out at interest, while my wife supported me by pawning her jewelry; in all fairness, my mother couldn't compare with her. But then it occurred to me that every man has a duty to provide for his parents, his wife, and his children. Was it not irresponsible of me to depend on my parents and my wife? If my father had not left us a legacy, if my mother had not saved up her money, if my wife had not possessed a modest reserve, surely I wouldn't have let myself starve to death? Surely I wouldn't have let my mother and my wife starve along with me? My whole life I had been ignoring the obvious. If I went on like this, how would I ever become independent? I resolved then and there to try to get ahead, to stand on my own two feet. But I couldn't do it all at once; I needed some way to save face in the meantime. So I packed up and returned to Xiangxi.

Mr. Shou was an exceedingly gross man, unacceptable as a friend, while his son, as pretty as a girl, was the exact opposite. The son was harshly treated by his father—more harshly than I was treated at home—and we felt an immediate rapport. It wasn't long, however, before he was called away by his grandfather in Yunnan. I almost wept as we said good-bye.

Since I didn't get along well with Mr. Shou, I was thinking of leaving my job. This was just at the time when the tea market was due to open. A dealer whom I had visited the year before now found himself short of capital and was inviting bids for his firm. Someone brought this to my attention, estimating the profits at a thousand a year. With the bamboo trade included, the profits would be double (tea and bamboo being the main products of the area). At the end of the year the dealers made loans to the hill people, each family receiving anywhere from ten to several score taels, and the following year the produce could be sold only to the dealer responsible for the loan. Then there were the traveling merchants, who came at set times and transported the produce elsewhere. And so the dealers were heavily dependent on their firms' credit. Large sums were not required, three thousand being an adequate amount of investment capital.

I had no business experience whatsoever, nor the slightest interest in making a profit, but because Susu had pawned her jewelry for my sake, I kept hoping for some way to redeem it and reproaching myself that I had found none. When I first heard of this opportunity, my interest was piqued, but as I thought it over, I couldn't imagine how I could raise the three thousand. When my informant, a man named Yang Yuanxiang, brought it up a second time, I told him the problem, but he continued trying to persuade me. "At the end of last year the firm actually lent out fifteen hundred. Even with a thousand you could set yourself up in business." He could provide half the amount himself, he said, but we would have to rely on pawnshops for the investment capital. (There were no banks in Xiangxi, so only pawnshops could provide the necessary backing.) If the pawnshops approved our application, we would have enough cash on hand.

The manager of the pawnshop was acquainted with my family, and when Yuanxiang approached him in my name, he promptly approved a thousand-tael loan. I then drew up an agreement with Yuanxiang providing for joint ownership and, after resigning my position with Mr. Shou, moved into the firm's quarters, which were in quiet and beautiful surroundings. There was a stone bridge near the gate, past which a stream gurgled its way, and tall trees provided a dense shade outside the upstairs windows. The window frames had been redone in emerald green, with "Yu Tai" (the name of the firm, which we retained) emblazoned on the uprights in large characters.

Once the arrangements had been made, I made a quick trip back to Hangzhou to raise the necessary capital. I told no one but Susu, leaving my mother with the impression that I was still employed by Mr. Shou. Susu worried that because of my inexperience I would end up being cheated. I detailed all the precautions I had taken; even if we lost money, my liability would be limited to the five hundred taels of my investment. Still not convinced, she consulted her brother, who recommended the project as a small-scale venture that should give me some experience of the world. Then in her brother's name she asked my mother for a loan of five hundred taels, which she passed along to me.

Taking Huanong with me, I returned to Xiangxi very much the owner of a firm. On the first day of the fourth month the tea market opened, and at our shop, which had been completely redecorated for the occasion, business was surprisingly brisk. The girl tea pickers all seemed to know about the incident with Alian of the year before, and they stared at me as if moved by the feeling I had shown for her. To my eyes, however, none of them was remotely comparable to Alian.

One day, flooded with painful memories, I happened to ask where her grave was. When I learned it was on Mount Tao, I longed to pay a sentimental visit there, but I put the idea aside lest the resulting gossip sully her reputation.

One day Huanong returned from a trip visibly upset, and I asked him why.

"Oh, I've just been up Mount Tao with our buyers."

At mention of Mount Tao, my heart skipped a beat. "Why should you be upset over a visit to Mount Tao? What's it like up there?"

"Not at all bad at the summit. Dense forest with plenty of fine bamboo. The hill people haul the bamboo up there, and our buyers price it according to size. The hill people don't question the price. In an effort to make myself useful, I asked the buyers if I could act for them. They handed me a yardstick and a knife, and told me to give an estimate on each log and certify it by cutting the amount into the log. After that I was to give the logs back to the hill people, who would take them down to the foot of the hill. Our men had set up a table near the ferry crossing, where they checked the logs and took delivery, paying out the price as marked. I felt sorry for the hill people, who looked so pathetic with their meager offerings, and so in marking up the logs I always added something to the price. In their gratitude they addressed me as the owner, but the buyers said I wasn't doing my job properly. I gave them my reasons, which they flatly rejected, insisting I was wrong."

"Why, what did you say?"

"The largest logs we took in cost no more than fifty, yet when sold by our firm they would certainly fetch over a hundred, which is why I thought it wouldn't hurt to pay a slightly higher price for them. But the buyers simply sneered at me and said I was just trying to act the young lord and master. A good deal of what they said involved you, sir, which made me so angry that I wanted to hit them."

"And did you?"

"I realized I'd be outnumbered, so I held on to my temper."

I laughed. "If you had hit them, you'd certainly have come off worst. Now, if Awen had been there in your place, he'd have returned home bawling his head off. I really congratulate you on being able to keep your temper. You must remember that those who don't know their own weaknesses always end up being humiliated. I used to slap people at the slightest provocation, and once I slapped a bearer. He and his mates swarmed around me, and I came within an ace of being humiliated. Luckily Turtle was there with me and, being just a child at the time, I managed to escape, but thinking it over later, I realized that if he hadn't been there, I'd have taken a good pounding. Even if I had complained to my brothers and the fellows had been arrested, it still wouldn't have wiped out the disgrace. Ever since then I've restrained myself—never dared let myself go. When her ladyship told us boys to stop cutting our nails and actually rewarded us for letting them grow, her idea was to get us to curb our tempers. Perhaps you ought to start growing your nails, too."

He grinned, then added, "There's a new tomb up on Mount Tao that the buyers say you built. Is that true?"

I was elated at the thought. "Did you see it?"

"Yes."

"Now that you know the way, why not take me up there?"

He gladly agreed, but then changed his mind. "In the heat of the day that stone path is really baking. It wouldn't make sense for you to go up there in the height of summer."

I laughed. "We're not even at the Dragon Boat Festival yet! What do you mean, summer?" I told him to get an umbrella and take me up.

After crossing the stone bridge we went east for a hundred yards or so, then followed the stream in a southerly direction until we came to the base of the hill. I looked up at the trees soaring into the heavens, so dark and dense that they formed a solid mass overhead. Birdsong greeted us from time to time. Shaking the dust from our clothes, we folded the umbrella and started to climb the hill. A warm wind sprang up, puffing our sleeves, and I felt a surge of elation. Before we were halfway up, Huanong led me off to the left, to a place where a large number of mounds were dotted about. One of them had a pair of new gravestones in front, and I thought that must be hers, but Huanong said no. A few yards farther on, he pointed to an earthen mound. When I went over and looked at it, it proved to be nothing more than a heap of yellow earth a little over two feet high surrounded by rank grass. It wasn't marked in any way, either by a gravestone or a rock. Even in the midst of all this greenery, it had a desolate look. My heart sank.

Then a light breeze began to stir the grasses, as if Alian's spirit were using them to nod to me over and over again.

"Oh, Alian, what a pity!" I said. "A year ago today I saw

you bringing your baskets to market, hanging your head and knitting your brows as if you were holding back a host of secret sorrows. I pitied you as a girl condemned to a harsh fate, but a girl without equal. I never dreamed that in a single brief moment you would wither like a night orchid and turn into a precious gem buried on a remote hillside. How shall I describe the sorrow I feel? I never exchanged a single word with you in life, and you certainly had no feeling for me, but I wonder what your spirit thinks of me now that I'm grieving for you?"

"That woman buried in the tomb, sir—did she *never* have any relationship with you?" Huanong asked in a surprised tone.

"No, never."

"Then what people are saying about you is even more horrible than I thought. Personally, I felt sure she wasn't your lover. If she had been, her grave would certainly have been marked by a stone pavilion as well as a commemorative stele. And you would never have let it get so neglected."

I was reminded of what Koto had once told me. If this tomb had been built for her, and she and I had come there hand in hand to look at it, I wonder what she would be thinking? I expect I would admire it and want to build a double tomb so that we could lie together in death. Would she let me do that, I wonder? And if she did, how would Susu react? If I arranged with Susu that all three of us share the same tomb, our happiness would exceed that of the blessed immortals themselves.

Then another thought struck me. Suppose this *were* Koto's tomb, and it was she who lay inside, how could I bear to linger here in front of it? I quickly reminded myself that this was Alian's grave and had nothing to do with Koto. But then again, how long does a life last? Eventually we were all bound to die. Supposing I didn't die first, heaven would force me to look on while the one I loved died and was laid to rest in this plot of earth. How would I feel year after year, when I came to see it? Even worse, perhaps not only Koto, but also my beloved Susu, might be dead, and there would be nothing I could do about it, nothing. Tears started into my eyes at the thought.

Realizing I was overcome with emotion, Huanong tried to distract me, urging me to return. At first I couldn't bear to abandon Alian, but then I saw people coming toward us and was afraid they might laugh at me, so I made a genuflection to her in my mind and turned away.

That night I had another dream of her, in a filmy dress and with soft, lustrous hair—like the Alian of old.

"I don't suppose you recognize me, Cousin?" she said with a smile.

I took a closer look—it was Secunda! I grasped her hand. "Cousin! I thought you were Alian. Why have you come here?"

"I've been dead for two years," she said in a sorrowful voice, "and my soul has gained its freedom."

Taken aback, I looked into her face again. Obviously it was Alian!

"Poor Cousin 'Lian!" I exclaimed. "I visited your grave just now and was quite overcome."

She was astonished. "Who's this Cousin 'Lian of yours? I don't understand a word you're saying."

At the sound of her voice, I took another close look—obviously it was Secunda again.

"How extraordinary!" I said. "I must have been blinded by the glare, my eyes are so dim. Was it really you who said you were dead?"

"Yes."

I was aghast. "But why did you die?"

"In death you gain your freedom," she said with a smile. "Moreover, everyone has to die. What's so strange about that?"

Her voice did not sound at all like Secunda's, but when I tried to see her face again, she looked away. I persisted, and suddenly she turned her head—and was transformed into an evil spirit! I awoke with a cry of alarm.

The solitary lamp still flickered. I was in a tiny room, completely deserted, but the spirit's face was still vivid in my mind, and my hair stood on end. I shouted for Huanong, but there was no response. Asleep in the back room, no doubt. I thought of getting up and calling him but I was too afraid. I was reduced to pulling the blanket up over my head and trying to get some sleep, but strange noises continued in the room, and I was unable to block them out.

Then another thought came to me. If this was Alian's spirit, she would never do me any harm. We shared no bond of love, she and I, so how could she bear to harass me? Perhaps the nymphs and sprites had seized on my foolish fantasies and assumed the guise of Alian in order to bedevil me. But if the nymphs and sprites *were* capable of transforming themselves into Alian, her gentleness would still have delighted me. And if she had transformed herself into some terrifying vision, it could only have been to test my love. On the other hand, how could I be sure that she wasn't practicing this deception in order to tease me? In this manner the fear I felt was transformed by my tender feelings for Alian, and I thought only of how lovable she was and ceased to think of her as terrifying.

I pushed the pillow away and sat up, then noticed the lamp glowing without its dull green flame. The paper windowpanes rattled in the wind, creating an eerie effect, and I realized that all my terrors arose from my own apprehensions and gave way to a relieved smile.

But then I thought of how pathetic Alian's death had really been and wrote thirty poems by the light of the lamp, recording my emotions—poems that cannot be included in this book for reasons of space.

The next morning I thought of erecting a stone slab on Alian's grave with these poems engraved upon it, but then it occurred to me that that would be inappropriate, so I decided merely to set up a stone inscribed "Here Lies Alian, Tea Picker." The epitaph was sent to the engraver, and when it was ready I had it erected without contacting her family for permission.

To my mind it was nothing more than an earthly memorial to her, but someone talked her fiancé into making trouble for me. He actually brought suit on the grounds that I had opened her tomb. I was furious and deeply regretted my meddling, but by this time I had already received a court summons. Without the slightest knowledge of lawsuits, I was scared out of my wits, but a mediator offered his services, and the case was settled for fifty taels. As I think about it now, it's good only for a laugh, although the truth of the matter is that I'd been bedeviled by a trivial sum of money.

At the time, however, I was more than a little embarrassed and began to feel that Xiangxi was no place to linger in. Unfortunately, I was tied down by the business.

At the Dragon Boat Festival, when the second crop was brought to market, it was the firm's practice to balance the books for the first. We showed a profit of over six hundred, and our buyers were elated. We bought even more tea from the second crop, and the self-styled buyers for foreign firms flocked to our door. A profit seemed all but certain. But the weather was fiercely hot, and I found the human stench intolerable, so I decided to return home for a while and leave Huanong in charge. Then after I arrived home, Xiangxi was hit by torrential rains. The mountain streams flooded, and the river rose over the bridges, so that the boats that had come in to buy tea couldn't get out again. The traveling merchants took up residence at the firm, while an untold amount of tea that we had bought got soaked in the floods. A letter from Huanong reported that they had moved up to the second floor in order to carry on, and that all you could see from the upstairs windows was a vast expanse of floodwater. The villagers continued to bring in their tea in little boats, and the firm had no choice but to accept it; otherwise, the money we had advanced could never have been recovered. The firm borrowed the merchants' boats to store the tea in, but the ovens for baking the leaves were all under water and couldn't be used. Freshly picked tea has to be baked, so they installed the ovens in the boats and carried on as best they could. Meanwhile the storm raged on, and no sooner was one batch baked than it got soaked again. In the case of a natural disaster like this, there was simply nothing one could do. The losses could not yet be estimated.

I dared not let my mother know about this catastrophe; in fact, I didn't even breathe a word of it to my wife or her brother. Nothing was to be gained by telling other people; it would only make them unhappy on my account.

Not until the beginning of autumn did Huanong report that the mountain floods had receded and the river was navigable again. He urged me to come back and see to the necessary arrangements, which I hastened to do.

On arriving, I found that the former site of the customs agency was one big lake. Mr. Ling's old house and the cottage where I had done my writing stood out like the hulks of wrecked ships. A few weeping willows reared themselves above the flood. When the bearers arrived to fetch me, the water came up to their knees. They lowered the chair in the bow of the boat and urged me to step into it, then waded through the water, the bottom of the chair skimming its surface. As we passed the agency, I noticed Mr. Shou squatting at a table on the platform bed, while a few barefooted servants in shorts sloshed through the floodwater. A comical sight, if ever there was one.

Although all the shops were open for business as usual, most of them had constructed platforms from door leaves, on which their staff capered about like puppets on a stage.

It was the same at our shop. In front of the door was a short ladder, while inside, a platform had been erected about four feet off the ground. When anyone stood on it, his head nearly hit the ceiling. Huanong, Yuanxiang, and the others led the way. I couldn't help laughing when I got up there. If you looked out the door, you felt as if you were in a boat. You saw only the top halves of passers-by, who seemed to be traveling without legs on the surface of the water. I had never in my life seen anything quite so odd. On reflection I thought it a magnificent spectacle.

Huanong gave me a detailed account of what had taken place. "How incredibly stupid of you all!" I snorted. "Why on earth didn't you move up Mount Tao?"

"It had never flooded here before," said Yuanxiang. "At first we thought it was just the river, which at its crest came up only to the steps, but then in the middle of the night the mountain streams burst their banks. All you heard was wind and rushing water—like the thunder of the Bore.[14] By the time we realized what was happening, the water was up to our knees. We rushed to move the stock upstairs, but there was too much of it, and even with twenty or more men on the job we had moved only a few tiers before the water was over our chests, making it difficult to breathe, and we had to scramble upstairs ourselves to escape. By then the water was six to eight feet deep, and we all thought we'd soon be joining the fish. Luckily the storm came to an end before much longer, and the next morning the water began gradually receding. But when the level had fallen to between three and four feet, it stopped and remained stagnant. Then a week or so ago it went down further, to about two feet, which nowadays is regarded as no water at all. The popular explanation for the disaster is that a flood dragon appeared east of Mount Tao. I don't know *how* many peasants have lost their cottages! We've been quite lucky in that we haven't taken too big a loss. By now we've moved all of our stock, but at greatly reduced prices and much of it on credit. However, if the profits we made on the first crop are set against our losses on this one, the net loss won't be too large." I nodded.

After supper we went upstairs together, and I slept beneath the west window overlooking the river. When I opened the window and looked out over the water, the moonlight glistened like silver—an eerie but delightful scene.

Huanong brought in the ledgers for my inspection. I felt that losses were only to be expected after such a disaster. Moreover he had been put in charge, and there was no point in second-guessing him. I merely asked the extent of the loss.

He leafed through one of the ledgers and showed me the figures. "For the first and second crops, the total profit works out at a little over twelve hundred taels, but that includes the value of the goods we have in stock. Although the buying price for the third crop was low and won't result in a loss when set against the selling price, the remaining stock from the second crop will have to be sold at the same price as the third, and what with all the discounts due to water damage, we shall take a net loss of six hundred.

"Of the three thousand in investment capital, you put up only five hundred, which was considered a one-quarter share, hence your liability is limited to a hundred and fifty. However, in Yuanxiang's opinion you should take responsibility for *half* the loss, despite the fact that the contract clearly states that yours was to be a one-quarter share. He's quite wrong on that."

"I thought our losses would be larger than this and wasn't expecting to get *any* of my investment back. Now, according to him, I have two hundred coming to me. I'll be quite satisfied with that."

"I wouldn't take that line if I were you, sir. In my opinion you should fight him on this. You can be quite sure that when we have some profits to divvy up, he'll be awarding himself a three-quarter share!"

"But that's hardly your concern, is it? Let's wait until I've had a talk with him."

Huanong had nothing more to say, and I went to bed. It

might not be a large loss, I reflected, but my original intention in going into this venture was to recover the things Susu had pawned, and all I had succeeded in doing was to increase our debt. How could I face her now? However, the loss wasn't due to any great blunder on our part. But for the trick heaven played on us, success would have been assured. Moreover Yuanxiang was refreshingly honest and straightforward, and if I continued our partnership for another year, provided heaven was not too unkind to us, we ought to be able to more than make up our loss.

I put the idea to him the following day, and he agreed. I then took responsibility for three hundred taels of the loss and, leaving one hundred with him to cement the agreement for next year, took my other hundred back home.

There I pretended that I had made a profit of over two hundred, but because of credit sales, some of our money could not be collected just yet, so I had withdrawn only half of what I was due. My brother-in-law accepted this story readily enough, while Susu, who thought I never told lies, believed me implicitly. Personally, I was sick with remorse. I disliked having to lie, but I was afraid that if I told the truth, Susu would only pawn more of her jewelry in order to make up the loss. My venture would be over before it had begun, and I would probably never be able to try another. And so I kept the loss to myself and didn't breathe a word of it to anyone, not even Koto.

One result was that I received a warm endorsement from Cousin Mei. "Cousin Shan's a scholar who has shown he can succeed in business. He's mastered the art of finance without even studying the subject. That just shows that if you can excel in one thing you can excel in all."

She even held me up as an example to her nephew. "You ought to model yourself on Cousin Shan and give up what you're doing. Why must you always be poring over a book and mumbling away to yourself—such awful pedantry! Yet when it comes to totting up the day's expenses, you scratch your head and hem and haw far worse than when you're trying to write an essay. If I tell you to use the abacus, one would think every bead weighed a ton, but you love to tell us how good you are at doing sums on paper. Just imagine, Cousin Shan. In totting up a simple grocery bill, he uses enough brush strokes to make a pagoda! And when he's finished and you ask him for the total, he looks at you in blank astonishment. Then he goes through it all again and comes up with a figure that doesn't match what I actually spent. Ask him why that is, and you give him fits. He's not as fast or as accurate as I am when I do it in my head."

Her nephew laughed at her.

"Paperwork isn't the right thing for daily expenses," I said, "and if you're checking bills that go back months or even years, it's a colossal waste of time and effort."

Her nephew strongly disagreed with me, so we held a contest. Time after time I had the answer while his brush was still creeping over the paper, less than halfway there. Koto and the others ragged him about it.

Spurred on by this incident, he gave up his studies and joined a bank, where he trained for a business career. Through the bank he came to know my younger brother, who often visited him at home. My brother was about the same age as Orchid, and the two of them fell in love, just as Koto and I had done. I had always held a low opinion of Orchid and was constantly warning my brother not to become involved with her, but he took no notice. Fortunately Orchid was not in the least exclusive in distributing her favors, so their relationship was more in the nature of a casual pairing than a lifelong mating.

At that time, however, Koto and I were in much the same situation. When Sheng departed, he had left her responsible for repaying a three thousand-tael debt. Her first inclination was to pay it off with her own savings, but later, I don't quite know why, she suddenly changed course and paid it off without paying, so to speak. The creditor frequently visited her house and, in front of me at least, behaved with studied restraint. Whenever he was there, however, Koto's manner toward me changed and became more intimate, as if she were using me to flaunt her precious love in front of him. I understood her motives perfectly; it was a technique for attracting money, nothing more. I recalled what Turtle had told me long ago and concluded that Koto really had inherited her nature from Cousin Mei. For a natural beauty to suffer from such a defect—was it not part of her natural endowment, like a rose having thorns or the cherry-apple lacking scent? I said nothing to her, but I couldn't help feeling a profound regret.

Once in jest I made a veiled criticism of this tendency. She drew a deep breath and said, "What do you mean, fond of money? My mother is fond of money, but I have always despised it. But when you think the matter through, unless we receive the necessities of life free of charge, we are never able to keep money at arm's length."

"Exactly," I said. "So long as you have the basic necessities, that should be enough."

"But unless you have assets of some kind, even those basic necessities can't be guaranteed forever. Take my family, for instance. Our expenses for the household, including the servants, come to over fifty taels a month, while the banks pay a monthly interest of only half of 1 percent. So with anything less than ten thousand in savings, we couldn't even provide for ourselves. At first I was determined to maintain my virtue, but later, when I thought about it more deeply, I realized it was a lack of assets that had driven my mother to sacrifice the family's reputation. If the present situation were allowed to continue, there would *never* be an inheritance to provide for future generations. It was my bad luck to be born in the middle of all this. My cousin was still too young—we couldn't expect him to support us. And as for my sisters, poor things, how could I bear to let matters take their course? But my own life was already ruined, so as I saw it my only option was to continue on that course for the rest of my days and never remarry. If I could build up some assets for the family, so that future generations would be able to climb out of the mire and lead secure and comfortable lives, then just how important, in the final calculation, was my own virtue? Shan, you're an intelligent man, surely you understand what I am trying so hard to do? You can't just label me the money demon!"

Her argument made me smile. "By your own account, you're sacrificing yourself to benefit a single family and doing it with a certain ruthlessness, which one has to respect. According to Orchid, though, if you could benefit the whole world by pulling a single hair from your head, you wouldn't do it."

She smiled. "And what am I really like, in your opinion?"

"She's not entirely wrong. What I'm truly grateful for, though, is that you play Yang Zhu with other people but Mo Di with me."[15]

She burst out laughing.

Readers, you should note how my words had struck home. No matter how devious people are, they will always burst into laughter if their secrets are exposed by somebody's remark. However, in all fairness, Koto could not have been more generous to me. But I kept applying my characteristic demand for perfection to her, and naturally I found her wanting because of her love of money. In fact her protestations did come from the heart. As a mere girl, she embraced this ambitious plan to secure her family's happiness and see it extended to later generations. So intense a concern for the future was more than we men, to our shame, could have equaled. Had she been able to change her sex and extend her concern for family to the entire nation, she would have left us men far behind. From this time on I did not presume to look on her as deserving of contempt, but rather of respect and sympathy.

That winter, after my cousin had obtained a post as county magistrate, my eldest brother, envying his success, contributed a great deal of money to the court in hopes of an early appointment. Within a few days he got his wish and set off in high spirits to take up his new office. But he had been in Suzhou no more than three days before we received an urgent telegram informing us that he was critically ill and not expected to live. My sister-in-law set off with her children that same night by chartered steamer, but after another three days we received a telegram from her to say that he had passed away.

My mother was prostrate with grief, and my brothers and I were also deeply affected. We accompanied her to Suzhou for the funeral, where the scene can easily be imagined. My sister-in-law's grief at the calamity that had befallen her is more than my book can do justice to, and I shall not attempt to describe it.

I had often pictured Suzhou in my dreams, and now that I had actually set foot there, I saw every hill and stream as steeped in sentiment. My only regret was that Secunda had gone to Yangzhou and no one from her family was left in the house. But simply by being so close to where she had lived, I inevitably received a certain frisson.

One day I met Hua Chishi, who had attended school with my second brother. He was the one whose poem I had seen on the wall at Pavilion Beyond and committed to memory. He was a native of Hangzhou who, dogged by bad luck in the examinations, had given up his studies for a business career. He had started a shop in Hangzhou and was here on a sales trip. After my brother introduced us, we became friends, and Chishi took me on an outing to Harmony Garden, where I composed sixteen poems and wrote them on the wall.[16]

Chishi declared that my poems reminded him of those of his friend He Pianan[17] and went on to describe Pianan as just as much of a romantic as we were. Following my return from

Suzhou, I was filled with an infinite despair that I found difficult to express, so I composed the opera *Peach-Blossom Dream*[18] as a outlet for my frustration. I showed the script to Chishi, who then boasted about it to his friend. Pianan prided himself on his prose and regular verse, but he had no skill whatever in the lyric or the opera, and most of the corrections he made in my text violated the rules. Highly amused, I made some critical comments to Chishi which, being duly reported to Pianan, sent him into a rage. At that time we were all young and intensely competitive—victims of the same disease—and so we arranged to meet for drinks at Chishi's place and have it out in a verbal duel. But when we actually met and exchanged a few words, we felt an immediate liking and respect for one other and got along like old friends.

This development brought out all the wildness of Chishi's nature. Clapping his hands and laughing, he announced, "I always knew that true men of feeling wouldn't let themselves be restricted to love between the sexes. Provided they're kindred spirits, their sort of friendship also qualifies as love. From now on, when we drink, we'll drink together, and when we go out somewhere, we'll go together."

I had never cared much for male friendship, having absorbed Zhen Baoyu's[19] opinion that all men are filthy creatures, and so I used to keep to myself, as isolated from men as any virgin in her chamber. But with these two I felt a certain rapport, the sole difference between us being that where I was cautious they were wild. However, on comparing myself with them, I felt that their uninhibited behavior had its own natural charm, and little by little I came under its influence. Our discussions would range over the great figures of history, men with whom we were arrogant enough to compare ourselves, and there was scarcely anyone in the world whom we accepted as our equal.

Pianan had been born with an extra finger, and I once described him as a latter-day Tang Yin, while Chishi, with his romantic panache and sly roguery, took after the Zhu Yun-ming of the *Three Smiles* opera.[20] Both men accepted these honorifics without protest, meanwhile likening me to Jia Baoyu.[21] I proceeded to imitate the form of *The Story of the Stone* in writing my novel *Destiny of Tears* in sixty-four chapters. As soon as I finished a section, Susu and Koto, Pianan and Chishi, would compete to be the first to read it.

I derived a great deal of pleasure from writing that novel. If I wanted something done, that book was always ready to oblige. Did I want to create a garden? It was done in a flash. To arrange a marriage? It was done as I wished. The people I loved I kept alive, those I hated I killed off. Not even the Lord of heaven wielded the sort of power that I held in my hand. When I expatiated on the joys of free literary creation to Pianan and Chishi, they urged me to publish my manuscript. The only problem was a lack of money.

Just then a letter arrived from Xiangxi. Yuanxiang had managed to recover less than 60 percent of the credit we had extended the year before and lacked the operating capital to continue. He proposed that we cancel our agreement and was returning my hundred taels. The money wasn't enough to repay my mother's loan, and as I hadn't yet learned the art of the cover-up, I consulted my second brother, who was at home at the time and in a position to put in a word with my mother. It so happened that Chishi wanted to raise money on a piece of property and had requested a loan of two thousand from my mother, who told Little Tan to look into the matter. When my mother learned that Chishi was a good risk, she agreed to the loan. My brother then spoke to Chishi on my behalf and asked him to make me a loan of five hundred, which he was perfectly willing to do. I added another hundred and gave the lot to Susu. The amount tallied with my story of making two hundred taels' profit in the business, so she suspected nothing and merely asked her brother to repay the loan. He did so, thereby establishing himself as a good risk in my mother's eyes. If on a future occasion he was able to borrow too large an amount from her, it was due to the credit he acquired on this transaction.

I still had a hundred taels left, which by rights I should have used to redeem some of Susu's jewelry, but I was seized by a bizarre notion—to go into partnership with Pianan and Chishi and bring out a newspaper that would publish our writings and make our names for us. Chishi thought the newspaper would also make a profit and backed the idea even more strongly. My wife, believing that I had earned the hundred taels by my own efforts, let me do as I liked with it.

There was a certain Mr. Jin who had founded a newspaper that had been closed down by the authorities. He still possessed the lead-type platen press, now long out of use, and after negotiating with him, we arranged to take over the payroll and invite the printers back. We decided to bring out a daily paper, which we named *The Grand View.* The editorial offices would be in my house, and I would be the general editor and Pianan and Chishi the associate editors. We also hired two proofreaders. No limit was placed on the number of freelance correspondents, who would be paid one tael for every ten items printed.

There was no other newspaper in Hangzhou at the time, so when ours came out it was widely popular. We set up a distribution center attached to Chishi's shop. At first we sold only a few hundred copies a day, but gradually the number crept up to over a thousand. My *Peach-Blossom Dream, Destiny of Tears,* and other works all appeared in it. Our orientation was literary, news being of secondary importance. Literary societies were flourishing in Shanghai at the time, and the fashion caught on elsewhere, which accounts for the warm welcome our paper received. Correspondence came in from as far away as Guangzhou and Hankou and led to the formation of many literary friendships, particularly in Suzhou.

One of those Suzhou friends, Mr. Yu Binghe, was in the course of establishing his own newspaper, the *Wenhuibao,* and when he was ready to start, he wrote asking for my help. Chishi and Pianan were reluctant to release me, but I had only to hear the word *Suzhou* to feel that it was my birthplace, my spiritual home. If they refused to let me go, I declared, I would be too distracted to concentrate on my work. In the end they agreed on a seven days' leave, during which Chishi would act as editor.

I took only Huanong with me. On the way I wrote "A Poetic Record of My Journey"[22] to send to Chishi.

> *At the last pavilion I leave my horse;*
> *The sun behind the hills glows fiery red.*
> *No need for me to worry about my bags;*
> *Let someone else see they're carried on board.*

> *Mascaraed hills, a bluish sweep of water.*
> *This thirteenth day the moon is almost round.*
> *No wonder the engine throbs with power;*
> *It's clear our boat remembers the south land.*

(The boat we took was named "Remembering the South Land.")

> *Winding river and hills for a hundred miles.*
> *Stem to stern the boats in a single string.*
> *We're late to our bunks, with no word spoken;*
> *All you hear below decks is loud breathing.*

> *A random cock crows, no light from the moon.*
> *Shadows from the woods into the cabin throng.*
> *A couple of arches, a few pagodas—*
> *The people beside me say we've reached Pingwang.*

There are waves close in; farther out it's calm.
The new hills of Wu the Yue hills entwine.
Between Wu and Yue is a solitary sail.
Somewhere a man chants a fragment of rhyme.

A wasted land as far as eye can see;
A toylike city in the evening haze.[23]
There's beauty all through the land of the south;
So why am I haunted by this one place?

The only bridge with so many arches;[24]
The outstanding talents are in this place.
If your heart were likened to the River Wu,
You'd never part and enter the Great Lake!

Where vacant land once lay beyond the wall,
Now fancy houses cover all the heath.
Don't let the girls quail at life's vicissitudes;
They are all so young, they've never known grief.[25]

In Peach-Blossom Village[26] *a sunset chill.*
Bleak, scattered willows, a heartrending scene.
How terrible! I've found the Tiantai road,
But there's nobody here to feed young Ruan.[27]

The reason for my visit to Suzhou was not so much Binghe's invitation as my failure last year, in all the confusion surrounding my brother's death, to find out any detailed information about Secunda. My underlying motive was to try again. Unfortunately, I had very few friends in Suzhou. We had lost contact with most of our relatives, and it would be awkward to call on them now and ask for news of Secunda. Since I was acquainted with Binghe only through our writings, I didn't confide in him, either. However, my feelings were fully apparent in my poetry and prose, and he already had a general idea of them. He told me he was actually a friend of Secunda's uncle, which delighted me, but when I went on to ask about her, he turned secretive and demanded that I write him a story first. There was nothing else I could do, so I wrote two chapters of my verse novel *Peach-Blossom Shadows*.[28] Then, once they had appeared in the paper, I demanded that he tell me about Secunda, threatening to write no more until he did so.

He was trapped. "If you insist," he said, after pondering the matter for some time. "But I'll have to find the right place to tell you"—a condition that struck me as distinctly odd. "There are a number of beautiful girls in Qingyangdi,"[29] he went on. "Have any of them taken your fancy?"

"No," I replied. "Well, yes, there was one—up to a point."

"Either there was or there wasn't. What do you mean, up to a point?"

"I saw her only once. She doesn't know me, and I don't even know her name."

"Can you describe her?"

"Last winter I happened to be upstairs in a teahouse, the name of which has slipped my mind. All I remember is that it was a handsome three-story building. The snow was coming down heavily, but from upstairs you could still see Tiger Mound Pagoda. My brother and I were drinking tea beside the mirror screen, when two good-looking servants, one carrying a lap robe of arctic-fox fur, the other a hand warmer, came bustling up to the divan and arranged the articles neatly upon it. I hadn't gotten over my surprise when I sensed an exotic perfume and, turning to look, saw a beautiful woman in her twenties wearing a white silk dress. She resembled Secunda about the eyes, but she didn't quite have Secunda's charm, probably because, although undeniably attractive, she also projected a certain haughtiness. However, because of the resemblance to Secunda, I often let my eyes stray in her direction, a fact of which she seemed to be aware. After awhile she got up, straightened her dress, and patted her hair, then walked over to the mirror screen, as if she knew of my admiring glances and was coming closer to let me feast my eyes on her. I loved her for her beauty, but then I reflected that, much as she may have resembled Secunda, her manner was certainly not comparable, and I couldn't help feeling a certain disdain. I gave her a mocking grin, to which she responded with a radiant smile. It was really an extraordinarily beautiful smile, so beautiful that I still can't get it out of my mind. I have often regretted that Secunda stood on her dignity with me and was reluctant to smile. If she had given me a full smile, I wonder how it would have compared with this one? But by now the storm was worse than ever, and this woman, evidently bothered by the draft, frowned and muttered something to her servants, which I was too far away to catch. Then she glided from the room.

"I watched from the window as she stepped into her sedan chair. I noticed a big lantern hanging from the back bearing the character 'Lan' and the words 'Candidate for Intendant, Jiangsu Province.' As the chair moved off, I saw on one side of it the title 'Third Rank by Imperial Appointment.' From someone in the teahouse I learned that her surname was the same as Secunda's and that everyone referred to her as Octavia."

Binghe laughed. "*She*'s not one of the Qingyangdi girls! You can't lump *her* in with them!"

"There was also another one," I went on, "whose looks were rather similar. Our boat was moored under Sweet Pear Bridge while we waited for the steamer to come and take us home. We were too early, and my brothers and I were strolling back and forth along the bank, when a great many carriages came toward us through the snow. In one of them, a carriage with a leather canopy, a woman was riding alone. The snow was petering out by then, and the canopy was down. She sat at one end of the seat, while the other end was piled high with flowers—red and white plum blossoms. Her hands were in a muff that fairly glittered with pearls and diamonds. She had all the dignity of a lady in a painting, except that no lady in a painting was ever so lavishly tricked out. I followed her with my eyes as she went away. Then after a while she returned and passed by again. My clothes set me off from all the other people and tended to draw her attention. Altogether she passed by me three times. When she noticed I hadn't budged, she couldn't resist giving me a smile. Even when she was a long way off, she still turned and looked back at me, and I was able to gaze at her to my heart's content. The only trouble is that I don't know her name."

Binghe smiled. "Why didn't you hire a carriage and go after her?"

"My mother was with me on the boat, and we were due to cast off before long, so there wasn't time. But because I admired her so much, I wrote a few poems for her, including this one:

> *A steed with silver mane, a scented car,*
> *A whirl of petals sprinkling her dark head.*
> *Inside the open car soft cushions lie;*
> *She shares her seat with blossoms white and red."* [30]

Binghe clapped his hands. "That's right! Your poem appeared in the *Su bao*, and everyone thought it referred to Hua Yunxiang. Was it really her?"

"But that's absurd!" I said with a laugh. "Hua Yunxiang was my eldest brother's concubine. She's left the family now, but it definitely wasn't her. Who's responsible for such nonsense?"

"Many courtesans have the same name, but the one known as Hua Yunxiang is unrivaled in these parts. She lives in Tanying Alley, not far from here. Why don't we pay her a visit? If she turns out to be the one, perhaps you'd like to treat me to dinner at her place, and I'll tell you all about Secunda."

I was so eager to learn the truth that I accompanied him to Yunxiang's, only to find that she was out. To pass the time we raced our carriage along Sandy Drive. We meant to revisit her in the evening, but then we came upon her at The Trace of Fragrance, leaning against the balustrade. I pointed her out to Binghe, and it turned out that she was the Yunxiang he had mentioned. Returning to her quarters, we told one of her servants to go and urge her to come home.

She appeared to remember me, and merely asked me when I had arrived.

"You remember *him,* too?" Binghe asked with a smile.

She looked me in the eye and smiled. "Weren't you the one last winter who was wearing a silvery gown and a turquoise jacket that was edged in gold, buttoned from elbow to shoulder, and studded with precious stones, as well as a plain white cap with a single pearl on top?"

"I was," I acknowledged.

"I drove past you three times, and each time you were still standing there in a trance beside Sweet Pear Bridge. By that time your blue silk cap strings were almost white with snow, but you seemed totally oblivious to it. What possessed you?"

I couldn't help blushing. I have always felt that if people know I am peeping at beautiful girls, my covetous glances are something to be ashamed of. I didn't need to hide my peeping from Binghe, but I was sorely embarrassed nonetheless.

He laughed. "It's not so surprising that Master Shan hasn't forgotten you. What's truly remarkable is that you still remember him. Visitors to the pleasure quarter are generally forgotten the moment they leave. But after a single chance meeting a year ago, you remember him down to the last detail. This proves that the fortunes of love are foreordained."

Then he began roaring for wine and badgering me for a

lyric to present to Yunxiang—and also to provide copy for the next day's paper. I, too, was deeply impressed by her remembering me, so to commemorate the event I dashed off four lyrics to the tune "Immortal's Song."[31]

Evening chill
And a sliver of moon in the sky.
Her scented car raced back and forth in a whirl of flowers.
I sought her in the house of joy,
Where silken fans flutter
Like butterflies at play.

Who leans upon the balustrade
In slender silken gown,
With graceful back and lustrous hair,
And the merest glimpse of a penciled brow?
At first I wasn't certain,
But she is indeed the girl I'd seen.
And she consents to meet, the flowerlike fair!
The incense of my heart
Has not been burned in vain.

Beneath the hazy moon
I visit her this crisp, cool night,
Directing the car to her apartment.
On the door I recognize her name.
At the corners of the house twin lamps are lit.
As we arrive, the crystal curtains part.

She wafts inside, but why so late?
On her clothes a wisp of scent.
Tiny slippers through the curtain pit-a-pat,
Then underneath the flowers, suddenly, we meet.
Faintly she smiles and tugs at her dress;
A radiant pearl in which I take delight.

She cannot control her heart,
But yielding to my entreaty, loosens her gown,
And raises the jeweled curtain aloft.

In the springtime of her youth,
Younger still than I,
Her native wit inclined to mockery,
She says that I know nothing
Except to pity her,
Which, unbelieving, she believes a lie.

Our cups brimful of wine,
She treats me lovingly;
A free and easy heart, I know.
I help adjust her pure white gown.
She has no need of silken gauze,
For snowy flesh, I've heard, does not perspire.
Handing someone her guitar,
She clears her throat
And, turning from me, sings to me sweet and low.

Her frown and laughing dimples
Join in appeal to me.
Softly spoken, smiling prettily,
With soul-dissolving grace.
Happily that face
I saw in dreams I see now in reality.

Ours but a single meeting
At which the bond was formed.
(Did I show off too much, I feared.)
But now she notes my nails' length,
And taking up my hand,
Falls head over heels in love.
By thread after thread we're bound;
Between us there's a debt of love unpaid.

Yunxiang spread out the paper and prepared the ink for me as I wrote. She seemed to be enjoying herself, and I assumed that she had received an education, but when I asked her, it turned out that she knew only a handful of characters—quite a disappointment. I thought back to Secunda and felt that no one else in the world could compare with her. Her poems resembled Li He's[32] but surpassed them in their delicate touch and smooth arrangement. Not even Susu could match her in those respects.

Readers, if you will pick up Secunda's *Poems from Little Peach-Blossom Studio,*[33] you will see that my praise is by no means overdone.

I took the opportunity to ask Binghe for news of her. He was about to say something, when he stopped. I pressed him again, and finally he mumbled, "In the second month of last year her uncle was transferred to Yangzhou. He sent his servants to Suzhou to hire a boat and bring his family back with them. He was also planning your cousin's wedding, so her trousseau and valuables came with her. In addition to Secunda and her young brother, there were four servants and maids on board. It was to take six days altogether."

As I listened intently, he stopped for a second time. In answer to repeated questions, he would say only, "That's all there is to tell. I expect they got there safely. You can't put any stock in rumors, you know."

This struck me as an extraordinary thing to say, so I questioned him more closely. He sighed. "If I tell you, I'm afraid you'll be driven out of your mind by the shock. At the same time, I know perfectly well it's only a rumor."

"If it's really only a rumor, there's no harm in telling me."

"Well, according to the rumor, the boat was attacked by pirates."

I was aghast. "Did the passengers escape?"

"They *say,*" he went on gloomily, "that the boat was holed

and sunk. The passengers . . . well, someone would have had to rescue them."

"And *were* they rescued?"

"None of the boatmen came back, so we don't know."

"If the boat sank, I don't suppose Secunda was rescued!" I exclaimed in alarm.

"Heaven *should* come to the aid of the innocent," he said slowly. "It may not be as bad as you fear."

I was in shock, utterly bewildered. "Where did you get this dreadful news?" I asked.

"People said that the captain of the boat they hired was a certain Ni Jinfu, a thoroughly disreputable character. So someone wrote a piece in the paper blaming the uncle for tempting the pirates with a display of wealth: His negligence had contributed to the tragedy. The writer went on to claim that Ni Jinfu was one of those responsible for the crime. Otherwise, if it were merely a holdup, why would it have been necessary to sink the boat?"[34]

I was dreadfully shaken. I knew in my heart that Secunda had gone to a watery grave, that there was not the slightest chance of her surviving. I was in such a nervous state that my old complaint flared up and I began retching violently. I thought it was just the wine I had been drinking, but it turned out to be blood, which threw the people in the room into panic, as if I were in my death throes. It was as if I had no vital organs left inside my body, although I felt nothing that could be called grief. I was beyond tears, beyond speech. I was a soul looking back at the body it had left behind. I was numb, lifeless. It was a long time before I could force a sound from my lips.

Binghe now bitterly regretted telling me. Hearing my cries, the neighbors assumed that some kind of tragic drama was being performed at Yunxiang's, and one after the other they came over to see for themselves. I now wished I had not given way to my emotions. If other people came to know the facts, they would almost certainly treat Secunda the way Alian had been treated. Fortunately Yunxiang did not know the whole story and merely told people my cousin had died, and they showered me with expressions of sympathy.

Readers, just imagine for a moment. Had you been there in my place and received such a violent shock, could you have borne it, do you think? But at the time I held fast to a single thought, that all our lives are bound to end in death. Secunda and I had been apart for a long time and, to be quite frank about it, not the slightest connection remained between us. If my heart broke on hearing this sad news, how would I react if Koto or Susu suffered the same fate? As the saying goes, beautiful women and famous warriors never live to see old age. In that case all these beautiful women would probably die before I did. How could I bear such an incalculable number of blows? Moreover, if Susu were to die first, I expect that I would react so violently as to die with her. And if Koto were to die first, I would go mad and die, too, in which case Susu wouldn't want to live, either, and all three of us would go to our deaths together, that much was certain. Today's blow was more severe than others, and if it occurred over and over, ultimately I couldn't escape death myself, even if I tried. So why not follow Secunda's lead? If I died, Susu would die, too. And if we died now, my mother would still be there to bring up our orphaned son. Moreover, my eldest brother had gone before, so my death wouldn't come as too much of a shock. My second and fourth brothers would be there to attend on her. And a baby in swaddling clothes was scarcely old enough to miss. If Susu followed me, her situation in death would be no different from what it was now. Besides, we lived with my family, where there was precious little enjoyment to be had. If I were able to be together with both Secunda and Susu, death would actually be an improvement on life. Of course Koto might not die now, but if she did, she would find reunion in the other world preferable to separation in this one.

By this point I had reached a state of complete serenity. The people around me assumed that my grief had been assuaged by their expressions of sympathy.

Afterward I was invited to spend the night in Yunxiang's apartment. I was a new acquaintance of hers, and since she prided herself on her good name, I should not, according to her normal practice, have been invited to spend the night with her after merely sharing a few drinks. But she had been touched by the depth of my emotion and believed me a true man of feeling; if I felt about Secunda like this, no doubt I would cherish all women in the same way. But the truth was, my heart was in ashes. Not only did I think of prostitutes as beneath me, I was incapable of *any* feeling. And so although Yunxiang was infinitely accommodating, I was a dry well, devoid of passion. I even regarded her with a certain contempt.

When I returned to the office the next day, Binghe poked a little fun at me, which I ignored. I thought of writing a suicide note to Susu, but decided it was unnecessary. She would certainly follow me in death, so there was no need for any last words.

I told Huanong to pack my bags, then took leave of Binghe, excusing myself on the grounds of a slight illness. On the eve of my departure he held another dinner party at Yunxiang's to speed me on my way. I felt an infinite sadness but managed to keep a firm grip on myself and not betray my feelings; I even forced myself to smile. Afterward he saw me as far as Wumen Bridge.

The sun was setting. Suddenly the whistle blew and the boat made ready to cast off. I saw Binghe ashore, then quickly made my way along the side of the boat from bow to stern. The strip of deck outside the cabin was extremely narrow. As I made my way along it, I saw a boatman coming toward me with a heavy load, and at that very moment the boat lurched to one side. I hadn't intended this to be the scene of my death.

I was going to wait until the middle of the night, then cry out Secunda's name and follow her into the water below Precious Belt Bridge. But now the perfect opportunity had presented itself. If I threw myself in here, people would assume that I had lost my footing—no other possibility would even occur to them. So I seized my chance as the boat lurched, silently calling on Secunda, Why not go back? All I heard was shouting from the boat as I splashed into the water like Green Pearl hurling herself down from the tower.[35]

My readers should note that this was actually the second time I had plunged into the water. The first, which occurred in the spring of *dingyou* (1897), was a truly comical incident in which I certainly wasn't trying to kill myself. Let me tell you about it. It was the time of the Cold Food Festival,[36] and my younger brother and I had gone out on the West Lake and, after tying up at Harvest Moon Vista, had sent our boatman up Lone Hill to pick some plum blossoms. Time passed, and he did not return, so I suggested to my brother that we take the boat over there ourselves. There are two ways of getting to Lone Hill; by land it is a few hundred yards, but by water you have to go under Broken-off Bridge and continue west until you come to Xiaoqing's Tomb. I sat in the stern working the sweep oar, while my brother rowed in the bow.

At first all went smoothly, but when we were a little way offshore, a squall sprang up from the east, the waves held us back, and I wasn't able to steer. I realized I couldn't prevail, so I tried to bring the boat to shore beside the pavilion on Broken-off Bridge, but a head wind whipped up the waves, which beat against the shore and kept us away. Twice I approached, only to be driven back. There was nothing else I could do. Noticing an empty boat tied up beside a weeping willow, I brought our boat alongside.

I was about to clamber onto the empty boat, when a girl

lotus picker came rushing up and told me off in charming tones, "Who's that fooling about with my boat?" On coming closer, she saw that it was my boat, not hers, and began laughing. Then she leaped onto her boat, balanced nimbly on the edge, and favored me with a mocking grin, which shamed me all the more. But I wanted to get ashore, and the only way was over her boat. I let my brother go first, then started to follow. Unfortunately, he failed to hold the side of the boat for me, and I had no sooner set one foot on board her boat, than ours, with no one in charge of it, began drifting away. All I could do was try to pull myself on board by clutching at the girl, but I caught her off guard and so, hand in hand, we went feet first into the waves.

Since we were near the shore, I assumed there would be a tree root or stone footing somewhere for us to stand on, but instead we found ourselves in deep water, with the wind driving the waves on like an army at our backs. I didn't dare let go of her hand, but swam with her in the flood, almost as close as if we were making love. Fortunately my boat had drifted with the current and was now directly in front of us. We swam toward it, then let go of each other and, grabbing at the side, tried to clamber aboard, but we were too weak; it was as if all the strength had been sucked from our limbs. We struggled too hard, and the boat overturned.

I had given up any hope of survival when a pleasure boat emerged slowly from Inner Lake. The girl was the first to stick her head out of the water and hail it, but I quickly followed suit. In this manner we were rescued and brought back to Harvest Moon Vista.

I was limp with exhaustion, but the lotus picker, ignoring her dripping clothes, stood slim and erect in front of me and told me off again and again. I took one look at her—like a drowned hen—and burst out laughing, which only intensified her charming little tantrum. Eventually my brother humbly apologized to her, and she departed, still in a huff. I wasn't the only one who chuckled at the sight.

My clothes were sopping wet, but fortunately the weather was mild, and I changed into my brother's lined jacket and trousers and borrowed a brazier from the watchman to dry my shoes and socks. Then, squatting on the divan, I asked for some wine to help fight the cold. A feeling of exhilaration swept over me, and I called for brush and ink and wrote an old-style poem on the wall. It's still there—never been white-washed over—and whenever I visit that place, I am reminded of the incident and cannot contain myself for laughing.

And so my previous experience had amply prepared me for the incident at Wumen Bridge. I swam down freely, content to die, seeking the depths, aware only of a thunderous roar in my ears. Soon my breathing was cut off, my mind became befuddled, and I lost consciousness. Human shapes flitted endlessly back and forth in front of me, but my senses were so dulled that I couldn't tell if they were real or imaginary. My mind was a blank, empty of thought. I assumed I was dead.

It was not to be. When I came to and opened my eyes, there was Binghe standing in front of me and Huanong weeping at my side, and I realized that I had been rescued, that I had failed in my attempt to die. I heaved a sigh and ascribed my rescue to fate. From that moment on I thought of my life as superfluous and of everything about me as belonging to some other world. I understood things intuitively and was filled with a Zen-like serenity. Only with Susu was it different; for some reason that I couldn't fathom, I felt a deeper love for her than before.

Binghe wanted to drag me in to the office again, but I was still too sick to leave my bed. When I fell into the water, Hua-nong had despaired of my rescue and, realizing that he could never face my mother, had decided to follow my example and drown himself, too, but he was pulled from the water by a ferryboat. Although struck in the midriff by the side of the boat and quite severely injured, he took care of me during my convalescence without even mentioning his injury. When later I learned of it, I began to cherish his love for me; he had a heart of gold.

I had spent some time in Suzhou without any desire to leave when a letter arrived from Chishi urging me to return. Thinking of myself as already dead, I put the idea out of my mind. Binghe was glad to have my help and in the time left over from our work on the paper he took me out to Tiger Mound and the Embankment. We visited almost all the sights of Suzhou, the Liu Garden being my favorite. Once I took my writing materials there and rented Cloud-Cap Studio in order to recuperate from my illness and also gather material for my poetry. I wrote a great many poems, but there is no room to quote any of them here.

Binghe was only too eager to please, and he regularly invited Yunxiang to accompany me on these excursions. I had no designs on her, but it was undeniably pleasant to hold hands among the flowers and open our hearts to each other in the moonlight. Binghe encouraged me to go further. He told me that Yunxiang was thinking of buying herself out, and that her jewelry alone was worth a thousand taels. With another thousand I could set her up in her own apartment. At first I was by no means indifferent to the idea, but there was no way I could lay my hands on a thousand taels. It also occurred to me that courtesans value money above all else. I didn't feel anything for her that could be called love, but even if I'd been in the grip of love, I had already sampled all the misery it had to offer and could not face another such ordeal. I shrugged off his suggestion with a smile.

"Your main regret about your life is that you haven't been able to do as you wished," said Binghe in some surprise. "But now that you have a clear chance to do so, you reject it. How do you explain yourself?"

"I don't know how many women there are in this world who resemble Secunda. Although I can't help extending my love to others, I would never be content to accept anyone in her place, let alone someone who couldn't compare with her. Any number of women are prepared to pretty themselves for someone who appreciates them. Even if they could all be set up in their own apartments, where would one find a mansion with the tens of thousands of rooms needed to accommodate them? Anyway, only a vulgarian aspires to surround himself with a bevy of concubines. Anyone with a shred of self-knowledge would find more misery than joy in such a prospect. I once gave an idyllic ending to a novel of mine, *Destiny of Tears*. I chose the most beautiful women from among those my hero loved and married them off to him as wife and concubine. At the time of the wedding, the flowers were all in bloom, the trees in leaf—it was the perfect height of a perfect season. But when I wanted to continue beyond the idyllic ending and write about their marital pleasures, I found the task too much for a single writing brush. I was in a dreadful quandary, torn between treating one thing and treating another. Now, if a novel that I have created myself and in which I can indulge all my likes and dislikes denies me the freedom I seek, just think what my situation in real life would be! That is why, although I have always shared Gao Rou's [37] obsession with women, I have never felt any desire to monopolize them!"

He laughed. "But you still hanker after Koto and Secunda. How do you account for that?"

"Oh, Binghe! I'm afraid you're just not the sort of person one can discuss love with. Let me offer you an analogy. If you were renting this house and right in front of your window were two glorious flowers, naturally you'd cherish them. But suppose they belonged to someone else and despite your best efforts you could neither appropriate them nor buy them; what if one day the owner moved one of them away?"

He laughed. "I expect I'd sneak off with the other one and plant it in my own garden."

"But what if your garden were less than ten feet wide and already had an old flowering plum in it, so that there wasn't room for anything else? Where would you plant your flower then?"

"Surely I could clear a little plot for it somewhere else?"

"Even if you could, the new place wouldn't be next to the old, and when both of them were in bloom, where would you sit?"

"I'd go back and forth, looking at both. What's so unpleasant about that?"

"But even if you were willing to put up with all the bother, wouldn't you still hanker after the one the owner had moved?"

"Of course."

"What if in some beautiful spot you found another flower that bore a strong resemblance to it?"

"I'd try to get it for my own garden."

"And what if you found still another one like it?"

He laughed. "If I could, I'd try to get that one, too, and fulfill my last desire."

"Ah, but there would always be other flowers in addition to this one. Could you ever get *all* of them? How many could your little plot hold? Your desires would *never* be fulfilled. People with the most extravagant ambitions have the greatest number of unfulfilled desires. Moreover the soft stems and tender leaves of those flowers would not stand up to harsh conditions. A sudden change in the weather, and you'd be hard put to save them. If not properly watered, they'd soon shrivel. While one flourished, another one would wither. They might put on a brilliant show for a while, but eventually their blossoms would fall, and when winter came, the only one still by your side would be the old plum. I once wrote the lines:

And if in the end all the glory is gone,
Why toil in your garden the whole of the spring?

"This is the view of most people who care about flowers. I believe that everything in the world is subject to natural law. Defy nature, strive to overcome it by your own efforts, and you bring yourself nothing but misery. But the desires of people nowadays are seldom fulfilled. What's worse, their desires aren't even fixed once and for all but change with the circumstances. Give them a little, and they'll want a lot. Give them a city, and they'll hanker after a kingdom. They drive themselves frantically all their lives and are never content."

"Are *you* content, then?"

"Yes, I am."

"Then why do you speak of your own unfulfilled desires?"

"Look, the deeper my lack of fulfillment is, the stronger and steadier my contentment becomes. None of us is without unfulfilled desires, but when I know that a particular desire of mine cannot be fulfilled, I take that as my criterion and find unfulfilled desire everywhere: Heaven dips to the southeast, Earth to the northwest; spring flowers don't last; autumn clouds are too sparse; sweet dreams are too few; and the winter sun sets too early. When I compare these phenomena with my own situation, what I thought of as an unfulfilled desire seems insignificant, and I actually feel contentment. Knowing that unfulfilled desire is unavoidable, I feel that 'the past is gone forever; the future is ours to mold.'

"A feeling of being unfulfilled is what those who seek perfect contentment always end up with. Personally, I exercise restraint, as the sage bids me, and so I don't ask for too much.[38] I feel like this with Koto, and even more with Yunxiang. You might as well give up."

Binghe clapped his hands in appreciation. The poem he wrote for me contained the following lines:

Discover the truth in the courts of love, and a buddha
   you'll become;
Repay in full the wages of sin, and immortal-like you'll soar.
All you'll have left is your foolish heart, but that you cannot
   destroy;
For there'll come a time when the world seems dull, and
   you'll yield to love once more.

Which only goes to show how well he knew me.

Weary of my travels, I returned home. Along the way I never
ceased to mourn for Secunda, but my thinking was now much
like that of a religious convert. I believed that everything in
the world was controlled by heaven and that all our experiences, joys as well as sorrows, were as inevitable as life and
death. I thought of myself as a believer in the Lord of heaven.

When I found that none of my family had heard about the
incident at Wumen Bridge, I told no one except Chishi, who
painted me a picture titled "Alone at Wumen" to commemorate it. Many people wrote poems on the subject, but since I
am not writing about poetry here, I shall ignore them.

The Grand View was now quite well established, with a cir-
culation of over two thousand, but our printers were constantly issuing threats, and one day money worked its usual
mischief. Because the printers had demanded a raise and not
received all they wanted, they stopped work—and almost
stopped us from publishing. But I said to myself, if those dolts
can get the paper out, why can't we? So I told my younger
brother and the office staff to give it a try. Pianan was the only
one who absented himself.

I took charge of the typesetting myself, feeling my way,
shuttling back and forth, under constant stress. By the end of
an hour we had managed to turn out a single small plate, but
when we tried printing from it, the proof was unreadable; the

lines all ran the wrong way. We roared with laughter—and grasped the first principle of printing, which is that the text has to be reversed, as in a mirror image. And so we changed our procedure and worked through the night until the job was done. In short order we had picked up a knowledge of the printing trade, after which the printers backed down and returned to work. That was evidently the only trick they knew.

While my brother was trying to cast type, the molten lead spurted out and burned one of his fingers, and Chishi, his face covered in printer's ink, began capering back and forth hilariously, like a clown in the theater.

After the strike, Chishi was still so furious with Pianan for staying away that he dragged me along with him on a punitive expedition. Pianan was not at home, however. We were told at the door that he had gone out the previous evening, saying that there was trouble at the paper and he would not be back.

"Oh, that Pian!" roared Chishi. "I knew he'd end up in the fleshpots. Let's go and catch him!"

Having only recently returned, I knew nothing of Pianan's recent activities, but along the way I asked Chishi, and he gave me an account of them. A woman calling herself Mistress of Spring Shadow Pavilion was apparently preparing to become his concubine. The wedding would take place as soon as an apartment could be found for her.

At Spring Shadow's house Chishi confirmed that Pianan was there, then burst in on him, whooping with laughter. This being my first visit, I didn't care to barge into Spring Shadow's private quarters, so I paced back and forth outside, waiting for Chishi to emerge. I noticed some scrolls on the wall, calligraphy in which Pianan took great pride. One of the couplets ran:

> *Lest I exhaust my blessings in this life,*
> *I shall not regard you as my consort.*

Another ran:

> *He must be well provided for*
> *Who'd keep a dozen concubines.*

I smiled to myself. Then I saw Chishi tiptoeing to the doorway and beckoning to me through a gap in the curtain. "Take a peek at this," he said. I looked in the direction he was pointing, and through a glass window in the room on the left saw the woman Spring Shadow lying in bed. Her hair all unkempt, she was stretched over the pillow and looking down at something on the floor. Curious as to what it was, I followed her gaze to the corner of the room, where I spied a man squatting in front of the vaporizer and fanning the coals with a tattered palm leaf. As I watched, the coals crackled into flame, and the sparks shot up like fireflies and settled all over him. He sprang to his feet trying frantically to brush them off, but his close-cropped hair had already been singed. Chishi was clapping his hands and roaring with laughter, and I let out a chuckle myself.

Then the man came bounding out—it was Pianan! He hadn't realized I was there. After seeing Spring Shadow ill in bed, Chishi had said good-bye and left, and only afterward had he and I peeked in and burst out laughing.

Pianan frowned. "You're always up to some nasty trick, young Chi. We have an invalid here who's a bundle of nerves, yet you insist on playing your practical jokes in order to drive her to her grave. Shan, how could you go along with this?"

I apologized, smiling broadly. Chishi wanted Pianan to come out with us, but he was reluctant to leave, so Chishi began roaring for wine, much to Pianan's indignation. "You always were a wild man, and you always will be. Look, she's ill in bed. Who's going to see to the food? Let's hope she gets better soon and perhaps we can invite you to a dinner party. But if you insist on scaring her and making her worse, you'll have to wait a few *more* days with your tongue hanging out."

Chishi continued to badger him, but I made peace between them and dragged Chishi off to Moonlight Gardens for a drink.

As we drank, he filled me in on the details of Pianan's affair. The only point he wasn't quite clear about was how Pianan had met Spring Shadow in the first place, and I didn't press him on it. What I failed to understand was how Pianan, who had always stressed the deep affection in which he and his wife held each other, could even think of such a thing. What's more, his father ruled him with an iron hand. How could Pianan feel secure in the hideaway he was preparing? According to Chishi he shuttled back and forth, eating here and sleeping there, and the best he could hope for with Spring Shadow was to share in the same dream. I wrote a few short poems to poke fun at him.[39]

> *Her face too drawn, her radiance much dimmed;*
> *She wears her hair in "Falling Rider" style.*[40]
> *Where now the vaporizer puffs its trail,*
> *No incense has burned in a long, long while.*
>
> *Offering the medicine, he takes a sip.*
> *He mustn't let it taste too hot or cold.*
> *"See you add some licorice, too," she says.*
> *If her soft throat is harmed, she's bound to scold.*

(The medicine had been made up from Pianan's own prescription.)

> *Try to relax that impenetrable frown*
> *And comfort and nurse her; it's your duty.*
> *Had she not been ill for such a long time,*
> *Where would you get your sensitivity?*

With tenderness complete, love manifold,
I feel for you myself, in such a state.
In the vaporizer's circle side by side,
Whispering, whispering, until how late?

Tossing, turning, softly I call your name.
But you're in East Garden, working away.
With all connection severed between us,
I burn my incense and to Buddha pray.

Too young was I and easygoing, driven
By Chi into this craziness and more.
Knowing full well her timid, nervous state,
I never should have laughed outside her door.

Eyebrows more charming for being untended,
Ill in her bedroom, she lets him come near.
Slender from her head to the soles of her feet;
A touching sight, even if she weren't so dear.

She's wife to a wandering puppy dog,
Who sleeps here, eats there, while she's powerless.
Can anyone tell me why she's so thin
That one width of silk will make her a dress?

Lonely the lamp and chill the counterpane.
With moonlight flooding half the bed, she moans.
As the spring wind rudely urges him home,
She comforts Master He in loving tones.

Regular as the tides, he goes his way,
But again and again he beckons to me.
I send him off. I cannot let him stay.
The lamp is all I'll have for company.

The next morning I published my poems in the paper, infuriating Pianan, who feared that his father would learn about the affair. I managed to turn his fears to my advantage by insisting that he treat us to a dinner party if he wanted us to keep his secret.

Now that he had Spring Shadow, Pianan was busier than before, and the copy for the editorials, which were his responsibility, often failed to arrive on time. If one went to his house late at night to collect it, he would simply refuse to answer the door, and so I had to take on that responsibility in addition to my own. At about this time the Boxer uprising occurred. In the beginning it was quite successful, and I wrote an editorial titled "An Argument against Heresy" strongly condemning it. The authorities regarded my editorial as giving aid and comfort to the foreigner and intervened, forcing us to close down. But before long the Boxers suffered a major defeat, the allied army entered the capital, the court decamped, and the whole country was thrown into turmoil. Unfortunately, my editorial had proven all too correct. With a renewed sense of self-importance I went on to edit the *Zhejiang News* as a vehicle for my opinions, but within three months I had offended the authorities again and that, too, was closed down.

On paper the two ventures showed a profit, but a large number of debts from consignment sales had to be written off; we couldn't collect on them no matter how hard we tried. Our reserve fund had been limited to three hundred taels to begin with, while our operating capital had been borrowed from the bank on a short-term loan arranged by my younger brother. The debt to the bank now stood at over five hundred taels.

The liability was mine, and I was desperate—as was Chishi. After *The Grand View* shut down, he had packed up all of his belongings and left to take the treasurer's post in Qu County. However, his superior, having recently lost his mother, had applied to be relieved of his position and departed without repaying any of the two thousand taels that Chishi had lent him. Chishi returned to Hangzhou in utter despair, and he and I spent our days commiserating with each other. There was no conceivable solution for either of us.

The year was drawing to a close, and my brother, who was at his wits' end over the loan, told Susu about it. When she asked me, I was too ashamed to tell her the truth and tried to cover up. "Everything we are owed can be recovered at the end of the year, but the bank is pressing for repayment now, and our money will arrive too late to be of any use."

She believed me and, fearing that my attack of nerves might bring on an illness, gave her jewelry to my brother and told him to pawn it and use the proceeds to pay off the loan. Although I was now free of debt, I bore an enormous grudge against Chishi and Pianan. By rights they should have shared in the repayment, but both were in such desperate straits that all I could get out of them was a verbal acknowledgment of liability.

On New Year's Day of *xinchou* (1901) we were about to exchange the usual congratulatory visits with our relatives. Custom dictated that we wear formal dress, but if Susu appeared without her full complement of jewelry, she would certainly have had to face a grilling from my mother. My first thought was to make do with some pieces borrowed from my sister-in-law or Koto, but their styles were quite different from Susu's, and I was plunged into shame and anxiety. Fortunately Susu was able to sense what was troubling me, and she gently soothed away my worries. Feigning illness, she took to her bed and stayed there from New Year's Day until the end of the Lantern Festival. In my distress, I looked on this as the most squalid and miserable episode of our whole married life. I asked myself how we had come to such a state and decided it must be because of that initial two hundred taels from the pawnshop. It was imbued with love, that money, but I now feared that the same paltry sum would lead to the bedevilment of love, and I tried to think how I could redeem the items I had pawned. For two years now I had been toiling away in the midst of money, but in fact I had been bedeviled by it, and now the bedevilment was more acute than ever. Not only had I failed to redeem the first pieces I pawned, I had added to our debts by making false statements involving at least a thousand taels more. How could I save the situation? If one day my mother found out and blamed me alone—that I could bear. But if Susu were dragged into it and received the benefit of the maternal instructions, how could I ever face her again? Well then, what *should* I do? I racked my brains, but no ideas came to me. As I thought back over the last few years, it struck me that my behavior had much in common with Awen's gambling. Since I was now in the same predicament he had been in, perhaps I ought to pin my idle hopes on the Manila lottery. But to me that was gambling, something I had never cared for, and so I changed my mind and dropped the idea.

One day, when Susu was home visiting her parents and I was nearly driven out of my mind by boredom, I chanced to call in at Koto House. Aimee and Alcyon were visiting, and they were all playing a game of Examination Dice.[41] There was a brilliant display of fashionably dressed women on hand, and the room was filled with laughter. As soon as they saw me, they pulled me in to join them. I watched as Koto threw the dice several times and lost each time, then asked if I could take her place. On my first throw I got a "five red," which raised a storm of protest, with the others insisting that my throw didn't count. You had to put up your own share of the stake and play for yourself, they said; substitutions were not allowed. It occurred to me that I might well lose, which was scarcely what I wanted to do, so I withdrew. But in a fit of pique Koto put up my share of the stake and told me to try again. I could hardly disappoint her, so I picked up the dice and was about to throw, when Alcyon called out, "Black!" Aimee echoed her, and Orchid, Jade, Brightie, and the rest broke into loud cheers to add to the excitement. Koto was the only one who called, "Pheasant!"

The dice clattered down and spun around and around like beads before coming to a stop. Astonishingly, they showed a "five pheasant." I clapped my hands in delight, while Jade, giggling helplessly, scooped up the winnings. When the first game was over, I was the sole winner. The second game went the same way. In all I won half a dozen times.

"No wonder you're always so successful in business," said Cousin Mei, laying on the flattery. "This year you ought to expand your operations."

Successful indeed, I thought to myself. The fact is, my success is all talk. I've tried three times and lost each time, and now I'm wiped out. Little do you know!

Once the dice game was over, an agitation set in for mahjongg. I felt that my little windfall was not something I could keep to myself, so I offered to play host, sending off to Jufeng Gardens for a banquet and then inviting everyone to a celebration, that is to say, to what in popular parlance is known as a "session." It was a long time since I had been near a musical instrument, but I gave a solo performance, enjoying myself by playing at various times the koto, the flute, and the panpipe, and also by using the clapper; and the words of appreciation I received from the lips of those beautiful girls were more glorious to my ears than any official citation could ever have been.

After supper I chanced to enter Koto's room. I noticed the coals glowing in the stove, the cakes of incense heating, and the embroidered cushions arranged along each side, although the room itself was deserted. I was about to walk out again, when I heard laughter from the bed. I hadn't noticed anyone there, but now to my surprise I found Aimee lying beside a lamp smoking opium with Koto opposite her. They were laughing at me for not seeing them.

I went up to them but felt too awkward to sit next to Koto. Aimee patted the edge of her bed, and I sat down beside her.

"Why don't you try some, Shan?" she asked.

I declined with a smile. "I'm not so fortunate as to share your exotic tastes."

Koto laughed, but Aimee thought my remark was a gibe at her, and she reached over and pinched me hard on the thigh. I jumped up to escape her, but she was not about to let me off so easily. Luckily Koto came to my rescue and persuaded her to stop.

I was about to say something to Aimee when I heard a burst of wild laughter from the central court that sounded like the cackling of geese, and I knew at once that it was Chishi. Not having seen him in some time, I hurried out and found him standing beside the mirror screen.

"I knew I'd find you here," he said, gripping my arm. "I have some news for you. Have you heard the latest about Pianan? He's had the gall to go and get himself married. What on earth are we going to give him for a wedding present?"

I was cheered by the news. "So Spring Shadow is going to marry him after all. It's the perfect ending—he deserves to be congratulated."

"Wrong! You mustn't even mention Spring Shadow to him anymore. For saying what you just did, I almost got a fist in my mouth!"

I begged him to explain, and he told me the full story of Spring Shadow. She was actually a relative of Pianan's. Born in Hunan, she had attended the Capital School for Girls, but her parents and brothers died one after the other, and she came to depend on Pianan and evidently meant to attach herself to him forever. As the sole surviving heir to two branches of the family, Pianan had the right, according to the old custom, of taking two principal wives. So far he had only one, and to Spring Shadow's way of thinking, if anybody were going to fill the vacancy, it would be she. However, in Pianan's view, a woman ought to distinguish herself by good works rather than by artistic talent. Moreover he belonged to the generation before hers and couldn't properly take her as a wife—a situation similar to mine with regard to Secunda. So when Chishi repeated this canard in front of him, Pianan took it as deliberate slander and bawled him out. And now Pianan, under strict orders from his father, was due to marry a certain Madam Wu in order to continue the family line. As for Spring Shadow, Chishi had given her in marriage to one of his protégés.

I chuckled. "How heartless the man is! Surely that's a betrayal of her love?"

Chishi laughed. "It's something only Pian would be capable of. But you have to admit he's setting a fine moral example."

"*She* can't be any too happy about it."

"The protégé is a good-looking young fellow from Jiaojiang whose talent may not be on a par with Pianan's but who's far better looking. In fact he's genuinely handsome. He and she form a striking couple, as if made for each other. Why on earth *wouldn't* she be happy? Moreover Pian has been quite scrupulous about seeing to the trousseau and the gifts, so her feeling for him has changed from love to gratitude. She even calls him her second father."

I sighed. "Poor thing! To have to switch from love to gratitude—and all because of money. If I were Spring Shadow, I'd take out every single item he bought for my trousseau and smash it to smithereens! Anything that remained would serve only to hurt my feelings. How heartless the man is! I can't imagine what possessed him to buy her that trousseau. He *can't* be so callous!"

Koto doubled up with laughter. "If you were in her place and couldn't marry the man you loved and didn't want to marry the one chosen for you, what would you do?"

"If I were in her position, I'd never marry as long as I lived. Instead I'd carry on a lifelong friendship with the man I loved."

"*Are* there any such people in the world?" asked Aimee with a smile.

"Yes, and she's one of them," I said, pointing at Koto.

Koto gave a wry smile. "How can you deduce other people's feelings from your own? People's feelings differ as much as their faces, and the importance they give to love varies according to the situation they find themselves in. Sometimes they are held back by moral considerations, and sometimes they are driven by force of circumstance and have no choice but to seek out the second best. In fact you could describe that as the normal case. If I were Spring Shadow and couldn't fulfill my desires, I'd give up the man for someone else. That way I'd still qualify as an intelligent human being. The only other course would be to waste away and die, and to die in obscurity at that."

Chishi laughed. "Did you hear what she just said, Shan? If that's what she means, I tremble for you. Are you capable of fulfilling her desires?"

I laughed. "Obviously she doesn't think so, but if she wants to follow in Spring Shadow's footsteps, I'll certainly do as Pian did and provide her with a trousseau."

It was Koto's turn to laugh. "If you did that, I'd *certainly* be able to give you up for someone else."

"In that case, does Shan have a young protégé from Jiaojiang?" asked Aimee. "If not, he must find one as soon as possible."

Roaring with laughter, Chishi bowed low before me. "I wish to enroll as your protégé," he said.

Amid the explosion of laughter that followed, Alcyon came rushing in. "Awen from your house is here," she told me. "He says her ladyship is ill and you're to return home at once." I suspected a hoax, but she fixed me with a stern eye. "If you don't believe me, you can go and ask him yourself."

I left the gathering at once with Chishi at my heels. When I learned from Awen that my mother really was ill, I said good-bye to them all and hurried home.

Our house was a good mile or two from Koto's, and I felt nervous the whole way. The bearers flew along, but to my mind we were still traveling at a snail's pace. Arriving at the gate, I immediately asked Huanong about my mother—only to find that I had fallen for another of Little Tan's hoaxes.

"You've no right to play these nasty tricks on me," I snapped.

My mother laughed. "Actually I was the one who called you back. Your wife goes home to see her parents, and you immediately rush off to be with that other one. If we hadn't sent word that I was ill, I don't suppose you'd have come home at all." I didn't dare say a word.

Little Tan offered me a cup of tea, and as she did so, she smiled; I had no idea why. Then it occurred to me that since her bereavement she had never been seen to smile. Why was she so cheerful today? I couldn't puzzle it out, until I heard my mother sending Cloud to the Buddha Room to fetch a sutra.

"Oh, no!" I cried, as I realized what was in store for me. "You're not going to make me read sutras again? Little Tan reads so beautifully. What do you need me for?"

"Her ladyship says my voice isn't as agreeable as yours," said Little Tan. "Moreover you are very good at dealing with misprints. And there are so many punctuation mistakes, which always hold me up, and that can be very irritating for people listening. I've read only the first volume, and I'm stammering so badly it's affecting my reading. I beg you to take over, for your mother's sake."

As she said this, Ajin and Teeny sidled up and also urged me to read. I laughed. "Is this for my mother's sake or for yours?"

My mother smiled. "Stop the talking and get on with the reading." She opened the sutra herself and spread it out in front of me, while Little Tan brought the censer, Aiyun fetched some tea, and Ajin moved the lamp up closer. Everything was in readiness. In addition my mother offered me her hand warmer. After receiving such special treatment, I was happy enough to oblige. However, the text was full of jawbreaking expressions, and colloquialisms and vulgar rhymes abounded. Worse still, much of the content was wildly implausible. But whenever I offered the slightest criticism, my mother would declare that any blasphemy of the scriptures would surely result in evil karma. Every time I pointed out a mistake, she intoned Buddha's name in propitiation of my sin, which sent me into fits of uncontrollable laughter.

Mercifully, it wasn't a long sutra, and I had soon finished. But Little Tan then turned to the "Pu'an Mantra" in *Daily Devotional Zen Chants* and asked me to explain it. It consisted of one long string of syllables such as *zhi, zhi, zhe, zhe,* and although I was familiar with the tune from the zither manual, I could make neither head nor tail of the text.

Little Tan thought I was only pretending and appealed to my mother, who pressed me to explain it. Embarrassed though I was, I didn't dare invent an explanation, which sent my mother into a tirade. "You should be *ashamed* to call yourself a scholar when you can't even explain a single word! I don't know how you ever got your degree! No wonder you failed the provincials last year! Give up your studies! Give them up, I say! I can't *imagine* what books you've been wasting your time on!"

All this was delivered in a tone of high indignation. The other people in the room, who a moment before had been basking in a warm and friendly atmosphere, now found themselves exposed to the chill blast of winter and gloomily dispersed.

Little Tan was full of apologies. Slipping into my room afterward, she had a long talk with me in which she urged me to put more effort into my studies.

I thanked her for the advice. "No matter how hard I studied, though, I could never explain that mantra. For the most part mantras are translated from the Sanskrit, and when the translation was made, it wasn't the meaning that was transcribed, only the sound, and so now, after a long process of transmission, they're unintelligible. Suppose you were translating something from a European language and you transcribed it into Chinese characters according to the sound. If you then read it aloud to people, not even a European would understand it because of the variety of dialectal pronunciations. Take any sentence I've been saying and transcribe it in the wrong characters. If someone from Hangzhou read it out loud, I ask you, would anyone from Suzhou understand?"

Finally she got the point. "In that case, why don't I go and explain it to her ladyship? She's still in quite a state. Let me clear things up for you." She slipped out of the room, and I dismissed the incident from my mind.

The next morning Huanong brought me an invitation to Pianan's wedding, which was to be held the following day. I had nothing that would do as a present, so I composed a prothalamion in five verses and wrote it out on a gilt card set in a mirror, then sent Huanong over with it.

I had no sooner made these arrangements than Susu returned from visiting her parents. When I told her about Spring Shadow, she smiled. "It does one good to hear of people solving their problems of the heart. You and Koto are the only ones who've never managed to do so. She really is the most unreasonable person in the whole world!"

"She might not be unwilling to marry me, but she'd never be satisfied. She feels one person's heart oughtn't be given to two people. Mine belongs to her, she says, but she has only half of it because you took the other half away from her, when the truth is that she took her half away from you. I know you don't consider her in that light, but she's actually jealous of you. It's a truly hopeless case, I'm afraid."

"In my opinion," said Susu with a smile, "she's really biding her time. She's not prepared to be a concubine, that's quite clear, but nor is she prepared to share a marriage with me. So her ultimate goal is perfectly plain: She's hoping that I'll die an early death and then she'll become your second wife. I only hope that that will fulfill your desires as well as hers."

"Oh, Susu! That shows you know *her* heart, but not mine. My love for you and Koto is a matter of 'five sparrows and six swallows.'[42] There may not be any difference between them in weight, but there certainly is in quantity. Koto and I may share a single heart, but you and I share a single destiny. If you should die before I do, I shall not be able to go on living. As I see it, if Koto *were* capable of doing as Spring Shadow did and leaving me for someone else, both our hearts, hers as well as mine, would find peace. Otherwise there will never be a final resolution as long as I live. Because of all of Koto's money, she has no need to rely on anyone for support, nor need she have any concern about her family. She looks upon money as her lifelong support, so I can think of no better name for her than 'money demon.'"

Susu gave a soft smile.

The next day, when I went over to congratulate Pianan on his marriage, Spring Shadow was there with her handsome husband, a dazzling couple in a match made in heaven. Spring Shadow's beauty and charm were very different from those of the woman I had glimpsed through her sickroom window. And Madam Wu's looks were such as to make her seem like Spring Shadow's twin sister. What heavenly art, I wondered, had it taken to create such women? Pianan's joy goes without saying. He responded with a beatific smile to all the jokes that the wedding guests made at his expense.

Chishi's present was different from all the others. It consisted of a length of multicolored silk for use as a valance above the marriage bed. Embroidered on it were the words, "Where Chill Rain Meets the River." At first I didn't get the point, but then it dawned on me that it was a riddle,[43] the bride's surname being Wu, and I doubled up with laughter. Pianan, however, thought Chishi was merely being nasty and, holding his nose in contempt, ordered him to down a huge cup of wine as a penalty. Chishi fled.

I returned home very drunk and that night found myself dreaming. In the distance I could hear drums and pipes coming nearer and nearer. I screwed up my eyes and saw that I was in the south court of Koto's house. The lanterns along the eaves glowed brilliantly, as if strung together. A crimson carpet was spread out on the ground, and tall candles burned high above it. Gilt curtains reflected the glow of the lamps, and the characters of the inscription shone with a rare brilliance. I realized that this was Koto's wedding. She's not marrying me, I said to myself, so who *is* she marrying? As I puzzled over this question, loud music struck up, a line of bridal chairs arrived in the central court, and a swarm of maids rushed out to escort the bride. Then, gracefully emerging from her sedan chair, stepped a beauty of exquisite bearing dressed in a diaphanous gown and cloudlike mantilla.

Peering at her face, I saw she was none other than Koto. But who could the bridegroom be? As I pondered this question, I heard a sudden burst of laughter from the rear court, and there, following the musicians, came a gaily dressed young man who exchanged bows with Koto. I was astonished to see that he was the same Sheng who had taken up a loan of three thousand taels to buy this house for Koto. I had still not recovered from my astonishment when someone tapped me on the shoulder and whispered, "Well, Shan, how does it feel?"

I whirled around. It was Alcyon, a triumphant smirk on her face. Leaning on my shoulder, she went on, "Well? I knew all along that she'd betray you. What do you have to say now?"

Before I could reply, someone touched my cheek and asked, "What do you have to say for yourself? I told you there was no such person in the world, but you insisted that she was one. What do you have to say now?"

I saw that the woman was Aimee, and I was about to respond when Orchid, Jade, Brightie, her brother, and others crowded around me and started laughing. Then Cousin Mei also came up, and I grasped her by the lapel. "Aunt, why is she taking this sudden step? Because you ordered her to, I suppose?"

She laughed. "What makes you think *I* have any such power over her? No, I haven't the faintest idea why she's doing it. Why don't you ask *her?*"

As she said this, I sensed Koto standing at my side. "Tell me, why are you really doing this?" I asked, clutching at her hand.

She laughed. "If I did anything less, I'd never be able to kill your desire for me. And if your desire remained alive, I would be driven out of my mind, driven to my death. Oh, Shan! With that pathetic little love of yours, you would bedevil me for the rest of my days. As long as body and spirit remained alive, there'd *never* be an end to it!"

"No! No! I cried bitterly. "How could love possibly bedevil you for the rest of your days? To my mind, that man you're marrying is nothing more than the money demon, the money demon!"

No sooner had I uttered these words than my ears began ringing with a chorus of echoes: Money demon! Money demon! I awoke with a start and for the first moment or two couldn't tell whether I had been dreaming or not.

I was in a vile mood at that time—unspeakably vile—and to this day, whenever I think back on that dream, I am thrown into confusion and despair; I scarcely know why. And so at this point I find myself compelled to lay down my writing brush, at least for the time being.

One of my readers rises to demand an explanation: "*The*

Money Demon is presumably the love story of Koto and Shan, but their partings and reunions have dragged on now for seventeen years and taken over one hundred thousand words to tell. How can you leave their story up in the air? It's simply not in accord with human nature!"

"There are many things in this world that aren't," I reply. "My narrative runs from *yiyou* (1885) to *xinchou* (1901) and is exclusively concerned with human nature. Then because I had this dream, which departed from human nature altogether, my creative flow was blocked. From *xinchou* to *guichou* (1913), the year in which this book was written, twelve years have elapsed, during which more events than this one have departed from human nature, and without another one hundred thousand words at my disposal, I could not give you an account of them. And even if I had another one hundred thousand words, I still could not provide my book with an *ending*. For to this day Koto and Shan are together one moment and apart the next, without ever finding a definite resolution. Money will continue to bedevil them for the rest of their days, and since my book is not some wish-fulfilling fantasy, I cannot bring their story to a premature conclusion; it *has* to be left up in the air. Should my readers fail to understand this, they will just have to wait for a sequel.[44]

Appendix

The Koto Story ("Zhenglouji")

"Koto" is Nine Fragrances. She used to be a neighbor of ours, and as children we were very fond of each other. In *bingxu* (1886), when I was seven and she ten, she attended classes with my cousin. My mother was much taken with her brightness and rather favored her as a wife for me, although she never did broach the subject.

In *wuzi* (1888) Koto moved away; I was not sure where to. I was too young at the time to leave the compound, so I had no way of finding her.

That same year my mother arranged my engagement to Miss Lanyun.

Not until *jiawu* (1894), when Koto was seventeen and had a small measure of personal freedom herself, did she return, moving into the house opposite ours. In those days I was attending classes at a neighbor's, leaving home in the morning and returning in the evening, and one day I happened to catch sight of her in a sedan chair. I had a glimpse of her stepping out of the chair, but her face was half hidden and I didn't recognize her. Later on I found out that it was indeed Koto, but we were both too bashful to acknowledge each other. Every day at sunset I would walk past her gate carrying my books, and she would always be leaning out of her upstairs window looking for me. Our eyes would linger on each other, and our hearts would respond. This went on for months, after which I managed to get on bantering terms with her younger sister and entrusted her with a letter to deliver to Koto in her private chamber. All the letter said was that I missed her, nothing more. In return I received a silk handkerchief that was embroidered with a Buddhist cross and folded like a billet-doux. I responded with another silk handkerchief on which I had written four lyrics, but I still didn't dare visit her house and ask to see her.

In *bingshen* (1896), five days after the Dragon Boat Festival, she moved away to Pingan No. 2 Bridge and invited me to a party there. It happened to be her nineteenth birthday. On that occasion, as we ate and drank together, we were too shy to say anything, but in my heart I felt wonderfully happy. Noticing that the house had no name tablet, I chose the name "Nine Fragrances" for it. (My reasoning was that both her and her sister's personal names fitted between the characters for "nine" and "fragrance.")

From this point on I visited her every day, but she was restrained and dignified by nature, and I was never able to treat her as anything more than a sister. Nor did I dare indulge in any frivolous banter.

In *dingyou* (1897) my mother arranged for my wedding to take place. Koto had nothing to say; she simply took to her bed with some ailment or other. I did not presume to try and console her. She never would articulate the things that concerned her most deeply.

The following year I received an invitation from Commissioner Ling to take up a post in Xiangxi. As I was leaving, Koto saw me as far as the river, and from then on, whenever I left for my post or returned from it, she would join me. At that time the port had just been opened to foreign trade, and we would take a pleasure boat together until we had to part, when we would change to sedan chairs and go our separate ways. This became our normal practice.

That summer I obtained my licentiate degree. I spent a lot of time at home and felt depressed and out of sorts. My wife was looking through my poetry file when she came upon a dozen photographs of Koto and realized that we were lovers. She hung the photographs up in the bedroom. She felt sorry for me, but she adored Koto, and she spoke to my mother about my marrying her. I was delighted at the idea, but I could scarcely ask Koto myself, so I engaged her sister's help in gently broaching the subject. When Koto heard of it, however, she had absolutely no response.

My spirits crushed, I left once more for Xiangxi, where I developed consumption. In the height of that summer my condition worsened, and I fully expected to die. I wrote Koto a letter of over ten thousand words, attached 180 poems to it, and then went back to my bed and awaited the end.

However, she sent someone especially to Xiangxi to help me come back, and on the seventeenth of the sixth month we arrived at her house. She kept me there to recuperate, seeing to my medicines herself. Finally, after knowing her for thirteen years, I was at last able to spend a night with her and take my pleasure with her on her soft bed and embroidered pillow. (Remarkably enough, we have practically never repeated that experience, chiefly because whenever we meet, we are in floods of tears and numb to all human desire, so that we feel indifferent to any such notion. Is there anyone else on earth who would have behaved the way we did? Regrettable perhaps— but admirable, too.)

The next day, despite my illness, I accompanied her to Purple Cloud Cave to pay our respects to the bodhisattva. While we were out on the lake, I had a dizzy spell and began vomiting, so we called a halt to the excursion and came home together. That night my illness took a serious turn, and she and her whole family kept watch by my bed.

On the nineteenth, hoping to lift my spirits, she brought her musical instruments to my bedside and sang some charming songs for my pleasure. I am passionately fond of music, and the songs helped take my mind off my illness. (Since that day she has never sung for me again, because when we meet we are too busy whispering endearments to each other. That was the one joyous occasion on which I heard her singing voice. Now only her sobbing and sighing reach my ears.)

My family found out that I had come back and was an invalid at her house and, fearing the worst, sent a sedan chair for me. I had no choice but to return home.

I spent over a month on my sickbed before recovering. My mother laid the blame on Koto and forbade me to stir from her side, after which someone gossiped about how strict my mother was and warned Koto it would be no easy matter being her daughter-in-law. And so Koto proposed that I set her up in an apartment outside the household, but although my wife was agreeable, my mother would not permit it. I myself thought of building a place in Xiangxi and living there with Koto, but she objected to it as merely a short-term solution, so I dropped the idea. However, my mother did promise that if I succeeded in the next year's provincial examinations, she would allow me to do as I had proposed. Koto urged me to concentrate on my studies and forbade me to come near her lest I be distracted. I followed her advice and sequestered myself.

I did not succeed in the examinations, which made my mother even stricter in her supervision, and as a result I was no longer able to see Koto at all. I had long cherished the idea of killing myself in order to cancel out my karmic debt, but I also shared Gao Rou's obsession,[1] and because my marriage was an exceptionally happy one, I couldn't bear to desert my wife. Moreover, Koto believed that as long as we remained alive we would eventually be united, and since suicide would do no good, why even consider it?

In *jihai* (1899) my cousin took a post in Zhenghe and my eldest brother obtained one in Suzhou. I asked my mother if I could go to the capital and wait for an opening in the Department of Sacrificial Worship. But just when I had worked out this long-range plan, my brother died in Suzhou, and my mother was so distraught that she refused to let me undertake such a long journey and continued to hold me prisoner at home. In *xinchou* (1901), in an effort to liberate myself, I set up the Cui Li Company. From then on Koto, in her stylish sedan chair with its gaily decorated lantern lighting up the night, would visit me in my little rooms overlooking the city center. She also parted with some of her jewelry and gave me a loan of two thousand taels to expand our operations.

In *renyin* (1902) I set up a lithographic press in Hangzhou, but I was swindled by a dishonest businessman and lost more than two thousand taels. Someone told Koto that the press was about to fail and that I would have to default on my loan to her, but I begged the sum from my mother and paid Koto off in full. She was more than ever impressed by my integrity, and our friendship grew even deeper. When I wished to give up business and return to my studies, she was alone in opposing the idea.

In *guimao* (1903) I placed third in the requalifying examination. Both Koto and my wife strongly urged me to take the provincials. By this time my mother had grown very fond of Koto and was only waiting for the results to be posted before welcoming her into the family. Unfortunately, while the examinations were still underway, Koto was duped by someone, and the ensuing trouble almost led to her family's ruin. Even worse, her enemy proved relentless in his pursuit of her. She withdrew somewhere else, and then another person came between us, so that I wasn't able to see her again.

In the tenth month she packed up and fled to the ends of

the earth, declaring that she didn't know if she would even survive. Before leaving, she called me to her in the middle of the night, and we sat together weeping until dawn. I have no memory of what was said. Then at dawn the whole family departed. I painted the picture "Parting from Koto in Tears" to record the incident.

However, I did blame her for bringing all this trouble on herself, and my reproaches were reflected in what I wrote. After our parting, all news of her was cut off for several months, but eventually I heard that she was renting a house in Wusong under an assumed name. I called on her but was stopped by the gatekeeper, who strenuously denied she was living there. I had no way of settling the issue. After returning from Wusong, I wrote her dozens of letters but received no reply, and I concluded that our friendship was over.

Then on the tenth of the fourth month of the year *yisi* (1905) she suddenly returned like a homing phoenix and summoned me to her under cover of darkness. I found the flowers and trees outside Nine Fragrances just as they had been, except that a dark green moss now carpeted the ground and the place was deserted. It was a good three years since I had set foot there.

When we met, our joy was mingled with sadness. We spent half the night exchanging confidences, from which I learned that she was unaware of my attempt to see her in Wusong. I also found out that there was a reason beyond her control for her failure to reply to my letters. She spoke from the heart and swore that what she said was true, and all the misunderstandings between us melted away. I painted "My Reunion with Koto" to express the joy that I felt.

Notes

Introduction

1. The main sources for Chen Diexian's life are the following: *Xuyuan conggao,* containing his collected verse and prose, published by his own Jiating gongyeshe in Shanghai in 1928 together with a list of his works compiled by Zhou Zhisheng; a special commemorative supplement by the *Zixiu zhoukan* (Self-cultivation weekly), published soon after Chen's death on 24 March 1940, containing a chronological account of his life by his son Chen Qu (alternative names Chen Xiaodie, Chen Dingshan); and the son's own memoir, published in his *Chunshen jiuwen xuji* (More reminiscences of Shanghai) (Taipei: Chenguang yuekan chubanshe, 1955), and reprinted in several collections of modern biographies.

2. See the list in *Sanjia qu* (Songs by three poets), the preface of which is dated 1900, containing art songs by Chen, He Pianan, and Hua Chishi; a copy is preserved in the Fudan University Library.

3. See Leo Ou-fan Lee, *The Romantic Generation of Modern Chinese Writers* (Cambridge, Mass.: Harvard University Press, 1973).

4. *Suiqinlou* was published in *Dongfang zazhi* (Eastern miscellany) in 1910 and *Yu li hun* in *Minquanbao* (People's rights) in 1912. On the latter novel, see Perry Link, *Mandarin Ducks and Butterflies: Popular Fiction in Early Twentieth-Century Chinese Cities* (Berkeley and Los Angeles: University of California Press, 1981), pp. 41–78, and C. T. Hsia, "Hsü Chen-ya's *Yü-li hun:* An Essay in Literary History and Criticism," *Renditions* 17 and 18 (spring and autumn 1982).

Part 1

1. Instead of the first-person "I" at this point, the text uses his pen-name, Tian Xu Wo Sheng, "Heaven Bore Me in Vain."

2. This is the original form of the opening as published in the *Shen bao*. When the novel was published as a book, an extra passage was added; see the introduction to this translation.

3. According to myth, the Old Man Beneath the Moon tied together with red thread the feet of those who were to be married.

4. *Jie* means an elder sister (or female cousin). Secunda's father belonged to the same generation of the family as the narrator, and relatives of different generations were not permitted to marry.

5. He was a little older than his cousin, hence she called him *xiong*, meaning elder brother or male cousin.

6. By tradition, it was a day for viewing the lotus blossom, generally the twenty-fourth day of the sixth month.

7. According to legend the Prince of Huainan ascended to heaven accompanied by his domestic animals (who had drunk some of the elixir of immortality he had prepared for himself).

8. The only son of the author's uncle (his father's younger brother).

9. A quotation from the commentary to the *Daxue* (Great learning).

10. This is Dai, the concubine who was his birth mother. Maternal references from this point on are to his birth mother unless otherwise specified.

11. *Xiu . . . fenjia,* literally, "to sniff the powdered cheek."

12. The turtle *(gui)* symbolized a cuckold.

13. If it is not an exaggeration, the author's sharing a bed with Little Tan at this age is a sign of exceptional immaturity on his part as well as of extraordinary cosseting by his mother.

14. Liuxia Hui (seventh to sixth century B.C.) was the symbol of virtuous self-restraint. (He remained unmoved with a woman sitting in his lap.)

15. Chen Diexian did indeed let the nails on his little fingers grow. The practice, which was quite common, often symbolized a resolution or pledge.

16. Both naiad and tears refer to Lin Daiyu, heroine of *The Story of the Stone*.

17. The reference is to Zhang Zai's "Ni Si chou shi," a poem preserved in the *Wen xuan* 30.

18. In popular legend the Five Genies brought treasure to deserving recipients.

19. At this festival small objects were strung together on a colored silk thread, which was then tied on the back of a small child. See Derk Bodde, trans., *Annual Customs and Festivals in Peking*, rev. ed. (Hong Kong: Henri Vetch, 1965), pp. 44–45.

20. Artemisia (mugwort) was a traditional feature of the same festival. See Bodde, pp. 44–45.

21. I.e., Wukang.

22. The Man of Qi, like Chicken Little, was always prophesying that the heavens were about to fall.

23. Lord Mengchang was the archetype of the magnanimous feudal patron. See *Shi ji* 75.

24. The archetypal mediator. See *Shi ji* 83.

25. Xu Wei (1521–1593) was a dramatist, artist, and eccentric, who gave rise to a whole category of jokes.

26. The maid Jade Flute received a promise from Wei Gao that he would return and marry her. When he did not return, she starved herself to death, was reincarnated, and eventually became his concubine.

Part 2

1. The new Japanese concession, on the Grand Canal northwest of Wulin Gate in Hangzhou, quickly became a pleasure quarter. Its official name was Gongchen Bridge, but Chen and other writers refer to it as Guashan, after the name of a nearby hill.

2. A cliché derived from a celebrated anecdote about Li Jing, emperor of the Southern Tang, who was jealous of the poet Feng Yansi. After Feng's execution, Li Jing quoted Feng's famous line about the spring breeze making ripples on the pond of spring water and followed it with the taunt: "But what has that to do with you?"

3. A traditional occasion for a dinner party.

4. A romance between a student and a girl and her maid that is found in many types of local opera. The situation offers many opportunities for erotic byplay.

5. When someone asked Weisheng Gao for a little vinegar, he went and borrowed some from a neighbor. See *Analects* 5.24.

6. Zhang Chang of the Tang dynasty, the archetype of a loving husband, used to help his wife paint her eyebrows.

7. The tomb of Su Xiaoxiao, the famous sixth-century courtesan, is beside Xiling Bridge, which leads onto Lone Hill (an island in the West Lake).

8. Synecdoche for a sexual encounter.

9. Orchid chooses to take this expression in its derived meaning, as the experience of orgasm.

10. The famous Shanghai lottery.

11. The golden age of the past.

12. The abortive Reform Movement of 1898 led by Kang Youwei, Liang Qichao, and others.

13. See *Xuyuan conggao,* vol. 4, 12a.

14. Ibid., vol. 5, 37a.

15. The image is from *Mencius* 7B.26.

16. The Qing artist (1632–1717).

17. A *mu* is about a sixth of an acre.

18. From a song in the first scene of the opera. It is sung by Zhang on first setting eyes on Yingying.

19. Flying Swallow, Zhao Feiyan, was a consort of a Han emperor. She represents the sylphlike ideal of feminine beauty.

20. Sung by Zhang in the first scene of the fourth act.

21. A reference to the poems attributed to Yuan Zhen in the famous Tang tale "Yingying zhuan." The eight poems by Chen were written to supplement 180 poems he had previously written about this incident. Both sets are reprinted in his *Xuyuan conggao.*

22. The mirror in chapter 12 of *The Story of the Stone* showed a skull on one side and a seductive beauty on the other.

23. The maid Hongniang in *The West Chamber.* She furthers the romance between Zhang and her mistress, Yingying.

24. I.e., Guanyin.

25. The Dragon King's daughters, exactly alike, flanked Guanyin's throne.

26. The statue of Sudhana, the indefatigable seeker after truth of the *Huayan sutra,* stands beside Guanyin's in Buddhist temples.

27. In *Destiny of Tears,* Chen's first novel, one of the heroines, representing Koto, is named Wanxiang, "delicate scent."

28. Hua Chishi, a Hangzhou poet who became a close friend of the author's.

29. The immediate source of two allusions used here (but not reflected in my translation) is the "Yingying zhuan."

Part 3

1. On the custom of keeping crickets for singing or fighting, see Derk Bodde, *Annual Customs and Festivals in Peking,* pp. 81–82.

2. The "Liu Yao zaiji" in the *Jin History,* 103. Liu was a general who fought Chen An in Long (in Gansu). When Chen died in the fighting, the local people made up this song about him.

3. There is a pun on the *du* of Du Fu the poet and the *du* of *duzhuan,* to fabricate.

4. The Niraya hell, in which people who have lied or slandered have their tongues cut out.

5. *Xin Yiyuji,* published in Hangzhou, probably in 1906. The poems are reprinted in *Xuyuan conggao,* vol. 3, 7a.

6. The text contains references to Wen Jiao and Xie Kun of the Jin dynasty, symbolizing acceptance and refusal, respectively.

7. Cai is the errant hero of the fourteenth-century play *Pipaji* (The lute). Newly successful in the examinations, he marries a second wife in the capital while his first wife is still in the provinces looking after his parents. He ends up with both women.

8. See *Mencius,* 6A.10.1.

9. From *Zhuang Zi,* 26 ("Wai wu"). A perch protests that if it doesn't get any water to swim in, "you might as well look for me in the dried-fish shop."

10. *Qi,* meaning jade, is a homonym of the first syllable of *qilin,* unicorn. The author's use of the tune is another pun.

11. The poems appear in *Xuyuan conggao,* vol. 4, 41b–42a. The normal pregnancy is described as ten months, calculated from the last menstruation.

12. See *Xuyuan conggao,* vol. 4, 13a.

13. See *Analects,* 6.22. Confucius defines wisdom as, among other things, keeping a respectful distance from gods and spirits.

14. The famous tidal bore of the Qiantang River at Hangzhou.

15. Yang Zhu was noted for his philosophy of egotism and Mo Di for his "universal love."

16. I have omitted the descriptive poems that follow. They are reprinted in *Xuyuan conggao,* vol. 2, 19b–20b. The poems also appear in Chen's novel *Destiny of Tears* (chapter 27), where they are attributed to Gu Yinglian. The Harmony Garden, last of the great Suzhou gardens, was created by Gu Wenbin, to whom Yinglian was evidently related.

17. A fellow Hangzhou poet. He Pianan, Hua Chishi, and Chen published their art songs *(sanqu)* together in a volume titled *Sanjia qu,* the preface of which is dated 1900.

18. It has the same subject matter as the slightly later *Destiny of Tears.*

19. In *The Story of the Stone.*

20. Tang Yin (1470–1524) and Zhu Yunming (1461–1527) were poets, artists, friends, and celebrated romantics. They appear together in the well-known *tanci* or verse novel *Sanxiao yinyuan* (Three smiles) as well as in opera. Actually it was Zhu who had the extra finger, not Tang.

21. Hero of *The Story of the Stone.*

22. See *Xuyuan conggao,* vol. 2, 19ab. The poems also appear in *Destiny of Tears,* chapters 26–27, where Baozhu and Wanxiang provide them with a commentary. In the novel they are attributed to Sheng Quxian, one of the author's personae. Some changes have been made in the poems here to fit them to the situation. The first two have been newly composed, and there is a slight change of order among the others.

23. According to the commentary in *Destiny of Tears,* this line refers to the city of Wujiang as seen from a distance.

24. This is Precious Belt Bridge, with its fifty-three arches.

According to the commentary, the conceit in the last two lines is taken from a poem by the fourteenth-century writer Yang Weizhen.

25. According to the commentary, the girls are the prostitutes in the pleasure quarter that sprang up in the new Japanese concession known as Qingyangdi.

26. Taohuawu, a part of Suzhou in which the Gu house and garden were situated.

27. The reference is to the story of two youths, Liu and Ruan, who went to the Tiantai mountains to gather herbs and there met two girls who offered them food. See *Taiping guangji*, 61.

28. It survives in revised form under the title of *Xiaoxiang ying*.

29. The Japanese concession, which became a center of nightlife.

30. See *Xuyuan conggao*, vol. 3, 1a. ("You Longhua suo jian"). The incident is described as occurring in Shanghai, not Suzhou.

31. For these poems, see *Xuyuan conggao*, vol. 4, 10b–11a. They have been somewhat adapted in the novel. Hua Yunxiang was the real name of a courtesan with whom Chen dallied in Suzhou.

32. The Tang poet (791–817).

33. To the best of my knowledge, the collection is no longer extant.

34. This incident is told with much the same detail in both *Peach-Blossom Dream* (see the commentary in *juan* 3, 18a) and *Destiny of Tears* (chapter 27).

35. Green Pearl was the concubine of the third-century magnate Shi Chong. When he was executed because of his failure to surrender her, she threw herself to her death from the top of a tower.

36. I.e., the Qingming festival in the second month.

37. A Three Kingdoms figure who stands as a symbol of conjugal love.

38. A reference to the Song dynasty philosopher Zhu Xi's commentary on the *Analects*. See his *Sishu jizhu, juan* 10 (on *Analects* 10.8.6).

39. See *Xuyuan conggao,* vol. 2, 18ab.

40. A Tang dynasty hairstyle, here used sarcastically.

41. The game is played with five dice of different colors that are carved with various symbols.

42. A cliché derived from a problem (concerning the weight of swallows and sparrows) that is contained in the early mathematical treatise *Jiuzhang suanshu.*

43. The kind of riddle that drops the final element from an expression *(xiehouyu).* The quotation is from the poem "Furonglou song Xin Jian zhi" by the Tang poet Wang Changling. The second (dropped) half of the line is *ye ru Wu,* "tonight I enter Wu." In the poem "Wu" refers to the city of Suzhou.

44. Needless to say, no sequel was ever contemplated. Note that the last two paragraphs use a number of expressions that pun on the words *liao* and *liaoliao* ("complete, end, ending, understand").

Appendix: The Koto Story

1. See p. 257, n. 37.

A Note on the Translation

I have based my translation on the 1914 edition reproduced in the *Zhongguo jindai xiaoshuo shiliao huibian* (Materials on modern Chinese fiction) series published by the Guangwen Shuju in Taipei in 1980 as well as on the *Shen bao* serialization. "The Koto Story" is translated from the *Xin Yiyuji* (New hint of rain), which was published by the Cui Li Company of Hangzhou, probably in 1906. The Harvard-Yenching Library has a copy of the first edition, which is reprinted in Chen's collected prose and verse, *Xuyuan conggao.* The frontispiece photograph of Chen Diexian is taken from the University of Michigan copy of *Xuyuan changheji,* a volume of congratulatory verses published on Chen's fortieth *(sui)* birthday in 1918.

In translating names, I plead guilty to certain inconsistencies. When there is a clear semantic point to a name, I have usually translated it. "Koto" is a translation of "Zhenglou," the heroine's studio name, which is derived from the musical instrument she plays. Since the *zheng,* although it originated in China, is known in English by its Japanese name, koto, I have chosen to call her Koto. The wife's name is given as Suqing, except in its first occurrence, where it is Susu; I have taken the liberty of calling her Susu throughout. The maid Xiao Tan I have chosen to call Little Tan, keeping the "little" because she is the only character in the novel with that prefix. "Tan" means night orchid, which withers almost as soon as it blooms, but it does not seem to have any semantic value here, and so I have kept the Chinese word. *"Huangjin sui,"* repeated almost as a refrain in the novel, usually means the bedevilment caused by money, but it is also sometimes personified as "money demon," and I have chosen the latter meaning for the title.

Acknowledgments

I am indebted to Professor Shang Wei of Columbia University for advice on certain textual matters; to Ms. Lin Hua of Harvard for bringing a valuable source to my attention; to Professor Wang Jiquan of Fudan University, Mr. Wei Shaochang of the Chinese Writers' Association, Shanghai branch, and Dr. Catherine V. Yeh of Heidelberg University for their general guidance; and to Mr. Eugene W. Wu and the staff of the Harvard-Yenching Library, Professors Liu Haiping and Zhang Ziqing of Nanjing University, and Dr. Andrew West of the School of Oriental and African Studies Library for their help in obtaining rare materials. I am also indebted, as ever, to Anneliese Hanan.

Also available in the series

The Three-Inch Golden Lotus
BY FENG JICAI
Translated by David Wakefield

The Remote Country of Women
BY BAI HUA
Translated by Qingyun Wu and Thomas O. Beebee

Chaos and All That
BY LIU SOLA
Translated by Richard King

Family Catastrophe
BY WANG WEN-HSING
Translated by Susan Wan Dolling

Imperfect Paradise
BY SHEN CONGWEN
Edited by Jeffrey Kinkley

Virgin Widows
BY GU HUA
Translated by Howard Goldblatt

The Past and the Punishments
BY YU HUA
Translated by Andrew F. Jones

Shanghai Express
BY ZHANG HENSHUI
Translated by William A. Lyell

Snake's Pillow and Other Stories
BY ZHU LIN
Translated by Richard King